CHARITY TRICKETT IS NOT SO GLAMOROUS

A NOVEL

Christine Stringer

SWP

SHE WRITES PRESS

Published by SparkPress, a BookSparks imprint,
A division of SparkPoint Studio, LLC
Phoenix, Arizona, USA, 85007
www.gosparkpress.com

Published 2025
Printed in the United States of America
Print ISBN: 978-1-68463-316-6
E-ISBN: 978-1-68463-317-3
Library of Congress Control Number: 2025901783

Formatting by Kiran Spees

Copyright credits on page 311.

For the dream chasers and the trailblazers

1997

When movie stars were the epitome of celebrity and our infatuation with them was insatiable . . .

CHAPTER 1
CLUELESS

"That's a wrap, everybody," announces the first assistant director. I grab a call sheet from him, eager to see if my little plan will work. *CALL TIME: 11:00.* Perfect. I have a solid twelve hours before I need to be at work again. A tingle rushes through my spine—I'm that excited. I shove the call sheet and my walkie-talkie into my JanSport backpack and bolt from set. If I hurry, I can make it to Duke's place in the city and back in time for work tomorrow. It will be a lot of driving for a short visit, but it will be worth it.

With that salacious thought, I notice Blake Anthony's impressive six-pack. The megastar is holding up his shirt while a sound tech peels an almost invisible microphone from his chest. His lips spread into his signature killer smile, and I ache. Not for Blake Anthony. Sure, he's *People Magazine*'s Sexiest Man Alive, but he's not *my* man.

My man smells of the ocean and has an intoxicating touch. I haven't seen him in three weeks, and while I wouldn't call myself a vixen or anything, I'm feeling the kind of frisky that comes from boozy liquid courage or a sexy beach vacation. I don't care that it's almost midnight and the cast and crew are supposed to go back to the motel right now. I'm going to sneak into my boyfriend's apartment, take off all my clothes, and wake him up with my body.

"Yuck. Wipe that filthy smile off your face, Charity," says Pup, yanking me back to the present. "You're not seriously driving all the way back to Vancouver for one night, are you?" I quicken my pace, and she keeps stride with me.

"One night with Duke," I clarify, pushing open a heavy set of double doors and stepping into the crisp night air. Pup tugs on my arm, forcing me to stop and look at her.

"Charity, we're in the home stretch of an eighty-hour work week. Tomorrow is a really big day. You can't show up tired," she says, her perfect eyebrows arched in concern. I love Pup, but I have to say, the girl worries. A lot.

"Pup, in the last five years that we've been assisting every big-shot producer or director who comes to town, have I ever let anyone down?"

"No." She sighs. "You're annoyingly good at your job."

"Exactly. There's nothing wrong with getting some quick booty." I practically skip toward crew park, filled with sexual energy. "See you tomorrow!"

"But we're back in Vancouver in just three days," Pup calls to me.

"That's why it's going to be such a great surprise!" I holler over my shoulder.

The top is down on my 1988 Volkswagen Cabriolet as I wind along the highway with only the moon for light. My ponytail blows in the wind, and I slide a CD into the faceplate and press Play. Music pours from the speakers as Cyndi Lauper's sultry voice fills my body with bold romance.

I drove all night to get to you.
Is that alright?
I drove all night.
Crept in your room.
Woke you from your sleep
To make love to you.

I sing along and drive fast.

★ ★ ★

I flip over the corner of Duke's doormat and find the key to his apartment. My body practically vibrates with excitement as I sneak inside with undetectable sound. Moonbeams stream through the vertical blinds, cutting through the darkness. It's perfectly romantic. In the hallway, I slip off my Vans and hang my flannel on the nose of Duke's surfboard. I walk further into the apartment and slide out of my Guess jeans, channeling Claudia Schiffer as I toss them onto the couch with sexy abandon. I effortlessly tug my hair elastic, releasing my ponytail and sending a cascade of blonde hair down my shoulders. I'm only five feet, three inches tall, but I envision myself as a supermodel striding down the runway. I pull off my T-shirt and drop it onto the floor as I turn the corner, and there is Duke's bedroom bathed in darkness.

I stop in the doorway of his room and squint into the pitch black. His breathing is slow and steady. In my imagination, he's shirtless, half covered by sheets. In reality, I can't see a thing. I lean seductively against the doorframe with the moon backlighting my silhouette, confident that Duke will be awoken by my potent sexual energy. He'll see my almost-naked body standing at the edge of his bed, and he will think he's dreaming. That's when I'll crawl on top of him and deliver the kind of fantasy he never knew he wanted. I pull my shoulders back to accentuate my breasts, which sit perky in my new push-up bra. I wait. I change my seductive pose to an even more seductive pose. God, he's really sleeping. I know—I'll light our sexy mood-lighting candle. I enter the bedroom with my hands stretched out in front of me and make my way to the chest of drawers. I feel around its surface and easily find the candle. Wait a second . . . it's warm. I drop the candle and gasp in shock when it lands on my foot.

"Hello?" Not Duke's voice.

The bedside lamp turns on. Not Duke's bedside lamp—*my* bedside lamp. A wave of brown hair bounces like in a Pantene commercial as a woman jumps out of my boyfriend's bed. "What the fuck!" she screams.

Duke shoots up. "Oh, fuck," he says.

The world has stopped spinning. The universe is off kilter; I can feel it. My boyfriend stands in front of me, his glorious, naked chest heaving while a woman in lace panties and a tight white tank top stands on my side of the bed staring at me. Wait. Is she in a thong? Who sleeps in a lacy thong? That's not comfortable! And those breasts! They would be too big if this woman wasn't so tall, but they're just right on her. And goddamn, her nipples are perfectly aligned. Who wakes up with perfectly aligned nipples?

As I stand here in my substantially padded bra and plain cotton, full-bottomed underwear, my confidence takes a nosedive, making that sound that every plane in a World War II movie makes just before the pilot dies in a ball of flames. This girl who just got out of my boyfriend's bed is not only gorgeous, she's as opposite of me as it gets. If she's Sophia Loren, I'm Smurfette. This woman looks like she plays soccer at an intermediate level a few times a week. I bet she hikes up mountains to ski down when she could have easily taken a chairlift, like the rest of us normal people. I would turn and run, but the thought of this perfect woman seeing the cellulite on my ass is too crushing. The thought of Duke comparing me to his new girlfriend is debilitating.

"Charity," Duke says, taking a tentative step toward me. I look at him and the sexy V at the bottom of his six-pack, and I suddenly get it. Of course, these two are together. Duke and I are as mismatched as it gets. He's a foot taller than me. He spends his time surfing and mountain biking, throwing his ripped body into one adventure after another. For me, a perfect day in the outdoors involves a lounge chair and fruity cocktails. Sophia Loren and Duke don't just belong together—they belong together in a Calvin Klein ad. "What are you doing here, Charity?" Duke says.

They're looking at me. They want me to say something, but I can't find my voice. My heart is simultaneously pounding and breaking in half. I back out of the room and step on my T-shirt. I pick it up and pull it on with a small morsel of relief.

"Charity." Duke strides toward me. Sophia Loren moves to the bedroom door to take in the scene. I must get out of this apartment, but I still need pants.

"I thought you said it was over with you two," Sophia Loren says.

"It is," Duke says to her. At this, I stop. Fury hits me so hard that my voice practically explodes from my body.

"Oh, it is? It's over? *I* didn't know that. If I knew we broke up, I wouldn't be here right now." I cringe at the sound of my hysteria.

"Hey," Duke says softly. His voice sounds compassionate, but his face shows not an ounce of guilt. "You knew it was over," he says.

I didn't know it was over! When I was driving here and Cyndi Lauper sang, *No one can move me the way that you do. Nothing erases the feeling between me and you*, I believed that she was singing about me and Duke specifically.

"I thought we were happy," I say.

"Happy? Charity, you're never around," Duke says. His voice is sweet, yet his words are tinged with blame. "You're always working." I look into my cheating boyfriend's eyes in search of an apology. Instead, Duke looks wounded, like he is the victim in this scenario. "What was I supposed to do?" he asks. Is Duke actually telling me it's my fault that he can't keep his dick in his pants?

"I'm not always working. I take a ton of time off," I say.

"Yeah, but you're writing in your time off. You're never fully present. It's hard having a part-time girlfriend."

"Well, this is a conversation we should have had before you entered into a new relationship," I say.

"I tried, Charity—believe me. But there was never the right time. You're either at work, tired from work, or tired from going out with your work friends," he says with infuriating calmness.

"'Never the right time'? How about three weeks ago when we spent the entire weekend together?" Duke turns to Sophia Loren. I reach up and cup his chin, bringing his face back to me, willing him to pay attention to the last conversation of our two-year relationship. "How long has this been going on?"

Duke is silent, caught in his deceit.

"Four months," Sophia Loren calls from the doorway. My stomach flips. Tears well up in my eyes. I don't want to cry in front of the perfect Calvin Klein couple, and I can feel them looking at me.

"Can you two give me some privacy while I get dressed, please?" I manage to say. Duke walks past me. He takes Sophia Loren by the hand to lead her into his bedroom. She pulls away from him before he shuts the door.

Alone, I look around Duke's apartment through my tears. Where are the pictures of us? Where's my paperback book that I keep on the coffee table? This is over, right? It is. Oh my God. This is done.

CHAPTER 2
MY SO-CALLED LIFE

"Don't drop it, don't drop it, don't drop it," I quietly chant as I carry an unreasonable number of take-out coffees. The soundstage in this small town is actually a warehouse dressed up to depict an elaborate casino/nightclub. It's packed with stuntmen, a special-effects team, two hundred extras, and our already large cast and crew. Today is a complex shoot, and I feel like ass. My entire body is heavy from a night of crying and driving, and the watered-down catering coffee isn't cutting it.

I needed my grande triple-shot Americano soy misto from Starbucks so I could function. But the closest Starbucks is a ten-minute drive away, and assistants can't saunter off set on a whim. So I asked my boss, Steve, if he wanted a Starbucks coffee. Fortunately, he did. Unfortunately, the associate producer, Saffron, overheard our conversation. She asked if I could also get her a coffee. Of course, I said yes. Then Saffron asked every single person at video village if they wanted a coffee from Starbucks. Nobody ever says no to Starbucks, so now I'm double-fisting stacked carrying trays and praying my arms won't give out on me. Why don't I lift weights? If I lifted weights, I could carry these coffees without my arms burning.

My toe jams into an electrical cable that's as thick as a python and capable of carrying 1400 watts of power. My body flies forward. Miraculously, I manage to get my legs back under me without a tidal wave of coffee landing on the set pieces that surround me: roulette wheels, craps tables, one-armed bandits. If I spilled coffee on anything, it would be disastrous. I lean against a poker table, waiting for my heart to stop racing.

Wait a second. There's a go-go dancer on a small platform right where video village used to be. I scan the hundreds of people who surround me and can't find it. Video village is the set's epicenter. It's where the most important and powerful people (directors, producers, heads of departments) cluster around television monitors to ensure that every frame of their blockbuster film is picture-perfect. It should be easy to spot. Instead it's hiding from me, which makes me suspect that the universe wants my arms to be ripped from my body just like my heart was last night.

"Coming through," I hear. Two grips carrying armloads of forty-inch metal C-stands are heading my way. The long tubes of metal clang against each other, rattling my already sore head. "Hey, Charity! Coffee for us?" one calls out cheerfully.

"I wish, guys. These are for video village. Do you know where they are?" I ask.

"No. Sorry. Last I saw they were on the move."

The grips leave me in a sea of activity. Extras, dressed like casino workers and partygoers, are being placed. Set decorators fix stripper poles to various poker tables. Actors and stunt performers are blocking a shootout scene. Soon the first assistant director will yell, "Rolling!" from video village (that I can't find), and somehow this choreographed chaos will come together to create a scene in Canopy Studios' biggest movie of 1997, *Diffuser*, an action comedy that is described as *James Bond* meets *Men at Work*. It reads like this:

```
INT. THE WRANGLER — NIGHT
Music thumps through the casino like a hot
Vegas nightclub. Strippers perform acrobatics
```

on platforms that hover over drinking gamblers. It's always a party in here, but
tonight it's off the hook.

The bell rings on a one-armed bandit, signal-
ing a big winner.

Billy's pickup truck smashes through the floor-
to-ceiling window next to the front entrance.
Gamblers jump out of the way. Miraculously,
the truck lands without harming a soul.

Security guards, manned with automatic weap-
ons, flood the room. The truck stands motionless, engine vibrating. Both doors open, and
out flies Billy from the driver's side and Jack
from the passenger's—they come out firing . . .

Not only is this the biggest movie I've ever worked on, but my boss is
the most successful person I've ever assisted for. He has a Golden Globe.
What was I thinking, driving into the city last night? I'm a twenty-six-
year-old assistant who should be making smart decisions and moving
up the ladder, not letting romantic fantasies get in the way of my career.

*Alright, Trickett. You are going to pull yourself together and show
these Hollywood heavyweights why you have the reputation of being
the best assistant in Vancouver. Someone in this room could read one of
your scripts and you'll be discovered. This could be your ticket to being
a Hollywood screenwriter. Don't fuck it up!*

I look down at the precariously stacked coffees and will my arms
to be stronger as I set off in the direction where I think video village
may be. Then I see Saffron's runway-model frame walking toward me.
Thank God. "Saffron," I call out to her.

"Charity, you've been gone forever. What took so long?" she asks.

"Takes a while to make this many coffees," I say, motioning toward my load.

"Mmmm. One of them must be mine," she purrs. I scan the coffees for Saffron's, but I can't see all the names on the cups. "Here—let me help you." Saffron lifts the top tray of coffees from my left arm, and I'm instantly relieved.

"Thank you." I sigh. Just when I think that Saffron is going to take the top tray of coffees from my other arm and help me carry them, she surprises me. She plucks her breve cappuccino from the carrying tray and carefully replaces the tray on my arm. I'm shocked. Sure, Saffron is an associate producer, but can't she see that I'm struggling here? And doesn't she remember that she is the one who instigated this enormous coffee run in the first place?

Saffron raises the coffee to her lips, then stops suddenly, staring me down over the plastic lid. "You put in the vanilla and chocolate powder, right?" she probes.

"And a dash of cinnamon," I say in the most pleasant voice I can muster, when really, I want to yell, *Help me!*

"Thanks, hon," she says. Saffron relaxes when she takes her first sip, and I salivate with jealousy.

"Where's video village?" I ask.

"Don't know. They moved it." With that, she walks away.

I finally find video village and hand my boss his coffee. "What a treat," Steve says. Then he sees the trays of coffee that I've placed on the table beside me. "Charity Trickett, are you everyone's assistant today?"

"Do you mind?" I ask.

"Not if you're okay with it," he says.

"It's fine," I lie. "You have your call with *The Hollywood Reporter* in about five minutes."

"Right. What do they want again?" he asks casually, as if being interviewed by *The Hollywood Reporter* is no big deal. It is a big deal.

"Super quick. They want a short statement from Canopy Studios about them making Blake Anthony the highest-paid actor ever," I say.

"Right," he says, leaning back in his director's chair.

"Why don't you give me your cell phone? I'll put the number in there for you, and you can step outside for the call." Steve hands me his phone, and I punch the number in. "The journalist's name is Sarah," I say, passing the phone back to him.

With Steve taken care of, I just need to distribute the rest of these coffees before diving into my triple-shot misto and being transported to the highest level of productivity. Next, I grab the coffee Saul ordered. Through Saul, the most experienced executive producer I've ever worked with, I see glimpses of what Old Hollywood may have been like. He jokes that he missed working with Charlie Chaplin by a hair, but he's not really that old. Saul is old enough, however, to take his drip coffee black. He also sits in the front seat with his driver, and he's old enough to call women "sweetheart" and "darling" without being inappropriate.

I have a soft spot for Saul, so I hand him his coffee next. "Thank you, sweetheart," he says. "Back to the city this weekend. You kids must have something fun planned after being cooped up in this small town for so long."

"There's a big nightclub opening on Saturday. It's going to be pretty swanky," I say.

"A nightclub with Blake?"

"Yeah. You should come. We have extra security, car service, and the club promised to have us well protected in the VIP."

"Too hectic for this old guy. You want to do a screening on Sunday?"

"I'd love that," I say, overjoyed at the invitation. Every so often, Saul and I will screen a classic film in the library of his five-star hotel. He pauses the VHS at various times to explain a shot or tell an anecdote about an actor. After the movie, Saul gives me the kind of education that UCLA students go into debt for, spending hours deconstructing and analyzing the movie scene by scene.

Saul turns to Casper, our very hip director, who will be at the club on Saturday. As they talk camera positions, I can tell Casper is salivating over Saul's coffee, so I hand Casper his latte, and he takes it with a smile. I hand out coffee after coffee, and I'm just about to dive into mine when I hear my best friend's panicked voice behind me. "Charity!"

I turn and see Pup's perfect face twisted with anxiety. I first saw that look in fifth grade when she tore a hole in her pants so big that her entire bottom was exposed, along with her *My Little Pony* underwear.

"What's wrong?" I ask. She pulls me away from video village so we won't be overheard.

"The Canopy Studios publicist is in the bathroom puking her guts out, and *Entertainment Tonight* has been waiting so long for their interview with Blake that they're ready to leave without shooting a thing." Oh shit. If *Diffuser*, Canopy Studios' biggest blockbuster of the year starring the world's most famous actor, doesn't get a segment on *Entertainment Tonight*, the studio will be furious. That means my boss will be furious with me. *Think, Charity, think.*

"Tell *ET* to set up in the office set. That should be out of the way. I'll grab Blake. Oh, here—give the producer and the interviewer these." I hold up two coffees.

"But these are our coffees," she whines. "We *need* these coffees. You got back to our motel room at four this morning, and you pretty much cried until we got to work at eleven."

"I'm done crying. I'm working," I say, not without a little pride.

"Good," she says. "But the point is we are exhausted. We still have so much work to do. Come on, Charity, we *need* these. Please."

"If I have to choose between coffee and *Entertainment Tonight*, I pick the interview and the career advancement that goes along with it.

We need to be more than impressive on this one." I thrust the coffees at Pup.

"Says the girl who chose sex instead of sleep last night," Pup says.

"Look where that got me."

Casper enters our little tête-à-tête. "What's going on with *Entertainment Tonight?*" Pup and I look at each other, not knowing how we should answer. As the director, Casper has more important things to worry about than press. "You were just whispering about *Entertainment Tonight.* What's up?" he probes.

"We were just wondering where we should set them up. How about the office set?" I say.

"Sure. We're not using it today." Then he leans closer to Pup and me. "Listen, are they seriously just interviewing Blake? My manager is trying to call the publicist but can't get ahold of her." Hmmm. Do I tell Casper that the publicist is sick and stress him out? Or can I handle this myself?

"Do you have time right now for a quick interview? I'm sure they'd love it," I say.

"Really?" Casper says, looking pleased. "The special-effects guys are going to be installing the breakable windows for a while. I can sneak away."

"Perfect. Pup can take you over. She was going to deliver these coffees to them."

"Sweet," Casper says. "Hey, think you can get makeup sent over for me?"

"Sure thing," I say.

"This way, Casper," Pup says. I have every confidence that with Pup in charge and Casper in tow, *ET* will be happy. Pup's a smooth operator who can make almost anyone smile, and I'm her biggest fan. She covered for me when I crashed my mom's car in high school. We lived together at college and took care of each other when we drank too much. We've shared gynecologists and groceries and gotten each other jobs and boyfriends. Together, we are a force. All I have to do is shuttle the biggest star in Hollywood to an *Entertainment Tonight* interview and Tah-Dah! Pup and I are Hollywood publicists.

I step up to Blake's trailer and knock on the door. "It's Charity," I holler.

"Come on in," Blake's assistant, Daniel, says in his dreamy Southern twang. I open the door and step inside to see Blake and Daniel at a table playing our favorite card game.

"Charity Trickett!" Blake says. "How's my favorite assistant?"

"How rude," Daniel says.

"Great," I say. "Who's winning?"

"Who do you think?" Daniel says smugly. This is his game, taught to us out of boredom. Over half of the *Diffuser* shooting days have been spent on location in small towns around British Columbia. Cheap locations that are beautiful settings for the film but boring at the end of the day. What started off as a few assistants playing in a motel room at night has grown to include various crew members as well as Casper; our female lead, Erica; and Blake Anthony. But the most competitive out of the bunch are me, Pup, Daniel, and Blake. This silly card game has made us quite the tight-knit group. Even back in the city, Blake will arrange dinners for us at the best restaurants and VIP parties at the coolest clubs, yet somehow we end every night with this game.

"So, *ET* is eager to get your interview done," I say.

"*ET* is eager?" Daniel says, still focused on the game. "Girl, Blake got called in early for this and we've been waiting all day." Daniel has his back to me, and I can clearly see that he is holding a winning hand. Because Blake is the nicest movie star in the world, and because I love fucking with Daniel, I'm going to help Blake win this game. Besides, the quicker the game ends, the quicker I can get Blake to *ET*.

"Oh. I'm sorry," I say. "The publicist from Canopy Studios is very sick. I just found out." I hold up my hands to Blake, indicating that Daniel is holding an eight, nine, and ten of hearts. Blake looks at his hand and discards a three of clubs with an almost undetectable smirk on his handsome face.

"So, we haven't been waiting on *ET*. We've been waiting on Canopy Studios." Daniel picks up another card, and I motion to Blake that it's a six of hearts, a card that could really add points to Daniel's hand.

"You have. Sorry. If it makes you feel any better, *ET* is pissed, too. They're threatening to leave without the interview," I say. Blake picks a card from the pile and practically jumps out of his seat.

"Ace of spades, motherfucker. I get to take one of your cards," Blake says.

"Shit," Daniel says. "Charity, you really think they're going to leave without interviewing Blake?"

"Could be idle threats—you're right," I say. Blake moves to pluck a card from Daniel. I motion with my head for him to move to the right and nod when he reaches the right card. When Blake sees the card he's drawn, he stands, throwing his hand onto the table in victory.

"I win!" Blake yells.

"Come on!" Daniel says, shaking his head. He turns around and glares at me. "You two are fucking cheating, aren't you?" I laugh. Daniel gets to his feet and grabs me, tossing me over his shoulder. "Alright, Trickett. You win. Let's go to fucking *Entertainment Tonight*." Blake opens the door for us, and Daniel plods down the stairs still holding me, my ass in the air and my ribs digging into my lungs.

"Put me down, Daniel," I say in an angry whisper. He places me back on my feet. "God! Be professional." I look around, hoping nobody saw our shenanigans.

"You be professional," he says, shoving me.

"You're a sore loser," I say.

"You two are fun," Blake says, laughing, as we head toward the warehouse.

"Blake Anthony!" From the comfort of his *Entertainment Tonight* director's chair, Casper warmly greets his star.

"Hello, *Entertainment Tonight*," Blake says. He's all smiles as he nestles into the director's chair beside Casper's. Blake clips a microphone to his T-shirt and greets the interviewer. "Hi, Rebecca. Nice seeing you again."

"Always nice to see you, Blake. Casper here has been filling us in on the shoot. Lots of action on this one. But also lots of comedy?"

"That's right. It's nice to exercise my comedy muscles. You know, I don't get to do that too much these days."

Casper and Blake banter as the interview goes on, sharing on-set anecdotes. They have an easy rapport and touch on all the bases of a typical *ET* interview. You can almost see where the *Diffuser* movie clip will be spliced in. Daniel leans into me and Pup and whispers, "When do you think Casper will leave already and let Blake get his interview?"

"Don't worry," Pup says. "Plenty of time."

"It's just that Blake's manager isn't here," Daniel says. "Should I say something?"

"I think it's fine," I say. "Casper will make sure Blake has his solo interview." No sooner are the words out of my mouth than we hear the first assistant director over the walkie-talkies saying that they're ready for Casper and Blake on set.

"Well. Thanks for your time," Rebecca says, standing to shake Blake's and Casper's hands.

"Oh! Are we done?" Blake asks, seemingly taken off guard. Oh, shit. Is *ET* really going to leave without giving Blake the solo interview they came to do?

"We'll hang around for a bit and get some B-roll," Rebecca says. "But don't worry. We won't be in your hair too long. We have to get to Vancouver for a nine p.m. flight back to LA." When I feel Daniel tense up beside me, I head over to Rebecca.

"I can show you to set, Rebecca," I say.

"Um, Rebecca . . ." Daniel trots over to us. "Daniel, Blake's assistant. When there are little breaks on set, feel free to pull Blake aside and get some one-on-one footage."

"Thanks, Daniel. But have you cleared this with Casper? A lot of directors don't like us distracting the shoot like that. We try to be as noninvasive as possible." Daniel looks over to Casper, who is walking quickly to set.

"Got it," Daniel says.

CHAPTER 3
PUMP UP THE VOLUME

There is electricity within our little group. Maybe it's the excitement of partying in the city after being isolated in a small town for so long, or maybe we're just buzzed off the cocktails we enjoyed in Blake's hotel suite. Whatever it is, I have to say, we are a particularly dazzling crew tonight. Not as good-looking as Blake Anthony, of course, with his designer clothes and multimillion-dollar smile. But as we emerge from the stretch limousine and gather under the neon lights of Granville Street, we look like a real Hollywood entourage.

Casper puffs on a cigarette and looks perfectly curated in ripped jeans and a crisp gray shirt, an outfit that probably cost more than my weekly salary. Beside him, Saffron's impossibly skinny body is draped in a gold satin dress, her long hair almost brushing the hemline that sits just below her perfect bum. She is just as glamorous as the actresses in our group, who huddle together, passing a tube of MAC Lipglass between them. Daniel is so Hollywood, impressively unimpressed, as if a ritzy nightclub opening with a group of gorgeous women is just another ordinary night. Meanwhile, Pup and I are a little nervous. We took next-level care getting ready. Our look: laidback Hollywood, carefully curated from the pages of *In Style* and *Cosmo*. This is the most exclusive nightclub in Vancouver, and because of Blake Anthony, we are at the opening party.

My pager vibrates, and I open my clutch to pull it out. It's Duke.

Ugh. He chooses now to call me for the first time since I discovered him in bed with another woman? It's been three days! I swallow, trying to push the tightening sensation in my throat deep down inside me. I am not going to let this idiot make me cry tonight.

I shove my pager back into my purse, and Pup nudges me gently. "You okay?" she asks.

"I'm great!" I say, punching my words unconvincingly. When I turn away from my best friend to avoid a sad conversation, I spot the insanely long line outside of the club. It stretches around the corner, and the people in line look anxious. Pup and I know that feeling all too well. It's the *When will I get in? Will I get in? I hope I get in!* anxiety of the nightclub line.

"We would normally be in that line, Pup," I say. "Now look at us. We're going to waltz in with a security detail." We do our best not to do a dorky happy dance right here on the sidewalk and instead exude nonchalance like our new filmmaking friends do naturally.

Blake's security team emerges from a black SUV and moves to flank the limo's back door, waiting for the actor to come out. The people in line for the club crane their necks and nudge each other, wondering who the high roller with the hired muscle could be. Blake steps out, head down, and in one smooth movement, security ushers him toward the falafel cart that marks the secret VIP entrance.

As Daniel knocks on an unmarked door, we hear, "Oh my God. It's Blake Anthony!" We all turn and see a crowd of eager partiers looking straight at Blake. People gasp. They cover their mouths and squeal. Some walk toward us, eager to get a better look at the star spotting of their lives. Blake waves and the crowd erupts in cheers.

Suddenly, the partygoers pick up speed, jockeying for position to get to Blake. Blake, being an expert at evading mobs, moves further into the protection of his security team. Daniel pounds on the night-club's secret door again, this time aggressively. It opens. Blake rushes in, and I feel the push of the growing crowd behind me. I try to reach for Pup, but she's too far ahead with Daniel ushering her into the red-lit stairwell.

"Come on!" Daniel yells. Casper and Saffron are a blur in front of me, disappearing along with Pup and Blake. I feel a large hand on my back pushing me toward the open door, and I realize it's one of the security guards. I cross the threshold and am bathed in red light, crammed into a narrow stairwell with my friends. The door slams behind me. Gone is the sound of the rushing crowd. All I hear is the club's muffled music and our collective panting as the adrenaline rush dissipates. I've seen fans approach Blake before—it happens all the time. But the frenzy on the street was gnarly.

"Never gets old, does it?" Blake hollers to us all.

Daniel squeezes my arm. "You pumped, Trickett?" he says.

The VIP section is packed with almost every big celebrity who is in town filming.

The strong American dollar, along with Canadian tax incentives for US films, has turned Vancouver into a mini Hollywood. Blake Anthony is the biggest star in the club, if not the world, but he certainly isn't the only celebrity here. Blake and Daniel introduce us to their actor friends, and Pup and I listen as they trade stories from their film sets, making us feel like we are part of the Hollywood "it" crowd. I watch Vancouver heavyweights, who paid their way into this elite crowd, flaunt their money for the gorgeous actresses who were in the limo with us. There's even a peppering of NHL hockey players in the VIP. This is Canada, after all. Some well-known British DJ is spinning, and from the raised position of our roped-off section, we can see people on the packed dance floor pulsing to the music.

I sit between Blake and Daniel, my two new favorite friends, but I'm obsessing about Duke and his stupid phone call. Should I call the pager service to see if he left a message? What could he possibly say? Do I care? I should ignore it, right?

"Girl, you look so sad I want to scoop you up and feed you happy pills," Daniel says. He delicately places his head on my shoulder.

"I'm not sad," I say, plastering a smile on my face.

"Could have fooled me," Blake says. He looks at me with a sincerity that draws me in completely. "You know what Hollywood has taught me?" Blake asks rhetorically. "Once a cheat, always a cheat. In relationships and business."

I'm going to kill Pup. How could she tell everyone that I got dumped? I've barely had time to process it, and she goes sharing my business? I try throwing daggers at her with my eyes, but of course she's devoting her full attention to some hunky actor who is refilling her champagne flute with the communal Veuve Clicquot.

"Hey, don't be mad at Pup," Blake says. "She's a concerned friend, and so am I. I would like for you to be able to look back at this relationship and learn from it. Charity, if you're going to make it in this industry, you need to spot the assholes before they do damage to you. If I were you, I'd think back on your time with this Duke guy and I'd look for the clues that should have been warning signs about his character. You should also think about why you chose to ignore those red flags."

"Oh, God. Life lessons by Blake Anthony," Daniel moans. "You're an actor, not a guru."

"I knew he was an asshole," Blake says to me.

"You did?"

"Hell yes," Blake yells.

I look to Daniel for confirmation.

"Sorry," Daniel says. "He was sort of . . . not nice to you." Daniel and Blake only met Duke a couple of times, so how could they have seen this coming when I didn't?

"Hey, don't beat yourself up," Blake says. "Learn from it. Oh, and I think someone's trying to get ahold of you. Your purse keeps vibrating against my leg." I grab my purse and dig for my pager. It's Duke. He's paged five times.

I descend three stairs, leaving the VIP section, and find myself in a sea of women who have gathered around in hopes of being discovered by Blake Anthony. They crane their necks in my direction, no doubt wondering who I am and, more importantly, if I'm connected to the megastar. I make my way through them, dodging hair flips and cleavage until the crowd thins out.

The pay phone is by the bathrooms in the club basement, far enough away to muffle the pounding music above. I punch in my pager number and ID code, and the messages play.

"Charity," Duke says, sounding like he's holding back tears. "I don't know what I was thinking. You are an amazing person, and you deserve better than what I've been giving you. I want you to have the best Duke there is. If you'll have me back."

I have to remind my heart not to ache as I wait for his second message to play.

"Hey. Duke again. I understand you taking time to think about this. I do. I'm here waiting . . . so . . . I may go to the island tomorrow for a surf, but . . . I'm here tonight. Thinking about how much I hurt you, and it, like . . . hurts me, too, you know." *Beep.*

The third message starts. "Okay, Charity. You're too busy to call me back? You out with your Hollywood friends at some fancy restaurant or something? Are you partying with famous people? You know, this superficial life you're living isn't important. You'll grow out of it. And when you do, I'll be here. But if I don't hear from you in, like, the next ten minutes, I'm gonna go play paintball with the boys. We'll have to talk when I get home from surfing on Sunday night. Unless you want to come over later. Okay. Bye." *Beep.* End of messages.

Superficial? I slam the phone into the cradle. I'm superficial? This coming from a boy/man who's smart enough to do anything with his life but spends his time chasing hot chicks, surfing, and playing paintball. I pick up the phone and slam it down on the cradle three more times. I need to collect myself.

In the bathroom, I steady myself against the counter and look in the mirror. *Don't cry*, I will my reflection. My attention is drawn to two girls who emerge from a stall together. They join me at the sinks, and I pretend not to notice as they lift their chins to the mirror, inspecting their nostrils for traces of their bathroom festivities. When they glance over at me, I realize my hands, as well as my pager, are resting in a puddle of water.

"You alright?" one girl says as she hands me a paper towel. I recognize her expression. It's a mix of concern and apprehension. We've all been there, needing to make sure the girl crying in the bathroom is alright while not wanting our big night out sabotaged by a hysterical stranger. Well, I'm not that girl. I'm not going to hold up the party to cry about my cheating boyfriend on the shoulder of some lady in the bathroom. I can hold it together . . . I think.

"I'm fine," I say, convincing the kind stranger but not myself. The problem with heartbreak is that it's unpredictable. You never know when you're going to cry. I know Duke is a cheater who doesn't deserve my tears, but heartbreak isn't rational. Heartbreak only remembers the good times, the intimacy, the dreams you shared of your oh-so-bright future together. The worst thing about heartbreak is that it believes in true love. The only way to get over Duke is to accept that his love wasn't real. It was all a lie.

Another page arrives from Duke. Once a cheat, always a cheat. I know that. I don't need *People Magazine*'s Sexiest Man Alive to tell me that. I beeline for the pay phone, plop in a quarter, and call the message service. I press *0* for the operator.

"Yes, that number that keeps calling me. Yes. That last one. I'd like to block his calls. He's stalking me."

So long, Duke.

"Fuck him!" Pup hollers over the thumping music. "Let's get you some champagne."

"I don't think champagne is going to do it." I sigh.

"Right." Pup grabs me by my hand and pulls me into the dense crowd surrounding the bar. She politely weaves between people and lands us directly in front of her new bartender friend. Pup is very good at making friends. "Two tequilas," she tells him. The bartender reaches for the closest bottle. "No, no, no," Pup sings to him. She motions to an elaborately decorated bottle on the top shelf. "We're celebrating!"

"What are you celebrating?" the bartender asks as he pours three shots, two for us and one for himself.

"Charity's single!" Pup drapes an affectionate arm over me.

"Congratulations," he says, raising his shot glass to me with a wink. We toss back the silky-smooth booze, and when the bartender catches my eye, I lick my lips in hopes of finding more. He takes the shot glass from me, grazing my fingers with his. A sultry smirk peeks through his dark stubble. I smile despite myself, but not because of the bartender—as if I'm going to hook up with some random guy right after breaking up with my boyfriend of two years. I smile because Pup is the best. I fucking love her.

This is how the night is going to play out. We are going to order another tequila but this time on the rocks. We're going to sip that tequila at the bar while shit-talking Duke and congratulating each other for being awesome. Then we'll move to vodka soda for hydration. We'll drink them on the dance floor, where we dance with *each other*. Sure, we'll flirt with a couple of boys, but mostly we party together until the club closes. Then we'll devour some street meat and cab our drunk asses home. The next day, we'll grab coffee and take her dog to the beach, where she'll let me feel sorry for myself. But tonight we party.

With a devilish twinkle in her eye, Pup throws me for a loop. "Open your mouth and close your eyes," she says.

I do as I'm told and taste the bitterness of a pill.

"It's just a half," she says. "I took the other half."

"What is it?" I ask, dry swallowing. The pill's hard edge scrapes against the inside of my throat.

"Ecstasy. Super pure. Daniel gave it to us."

"Ah. He said he wanted to feed me happy pills. I didn't know he had actual pills."

I look toward the VIP section, which hovers slightly above the crowd of fans, in search of Blake Anthony. I can just make out Blake, Daniel, Casper, Saffron, and some other LA funsters. Everyone is smiling, and they're being a little bit touchy-feely with each other. Most are drinking from plastic water bottles. They're probably a little bit high. Pup grabs me and leads me to the dance floor.

Gradually, the lights perk up and dance with us. I feel lighter. The cavity in my chest bounces with the bass of the music, and I am struck with certainty that this is the best song I have ever heard in my entire life. I close my eyes and dance. I open them and enjoy the lights spinning around me. Eventually, thirst overcomes me and I feel a desperate need to be back at the VIP, sipping water and cozying up to Daniel. Not in a sexy way. In a I'm-a-little-high-and-a-friendly-cuddle-would-be-lovely way.

I look around, expecting Pup to be at my side, but she's not. She's a few feet away on the packed dance floor, playfully grinding with some dude-bro in a puka shell necklace. She could be distracted for hours or minutes—hard to tell.

Getting back into the VIP room on my own is challenging. Ladies have been circling the private area for hours in hopes of catching the eye of the biggest star in Hollywood. "Excuse me," I say as I squeeze through the Lycra and perfume. Someone jabs me in the ribs, someone else steps on my foot, and I'm attacked by death stares from all sides. I manage to position myself within three rows of the VIP entrance, but now I'm stuck. The ladies in front of me are locked in their positions.

I try to get the bouncers' attention. I yell and wave my hands in the air, but I'm not the tallest or biggest person, and I'm not even sure the bouncers will remember me. So now I'm stuck in this desperate mob a little bit high, thirsty, and alone.

It had been so nice in the VIP room. We had lovely servers and there were seats covered in velvet. I'd love to sit on that velvet seat with my friends. But I'm out here with these ladies who hate me. I turn to the gal beside me and say, "If you knew me, I bet we'd be friends." She rolls her eyes. I turn my attention back to the VIP. There's Casper! "Casper!" I yell. "Casper. Hey!"

"Calm down, girl," the eye-rolling lady tells me. "You'll never get in acting like that."

She's right. I'm not getting in. Nobody in the VIP room is paying attention to anyone outside the VIP room. The bouncers don't know who I am. I'm deflated. I'm neglected. I'm all alone.

Then, out of nowhere, Blake Anthony stands at the VIP entrance. The women I'm clustered with shriek. Blake's lips spread into his mov-ie-star smile, and he waves to the crowd. The women get even louder. Some jump up and down. What is Blake doing? He's going to start a stampede. Something pushes me hard from behind, and I'm thrown off-balance. I grab onto the eye-rolling lady, who looks at me in shock. "What the hell!" she yells. Instead of saving me, she tries to pull away, but I'm pulling her down with me.

I grab the woman on my other side, sure that she will rescue us. She cries out. It's a domino effect, and a small group of us go down hard. Splayed on the floor, we are a pile of hair, boobs, and heels strug-gling to get back on our feet. The pandemonium around us dies down, and the ones left standing stare at us in shock. I get to my feet, look toward the VIP, and lock eyes with an angel. Blake Anthony.

It could be the X, but I feel as if my joy could float me over the heads of these ladies and plop me right next to my friend Blake, my heart is that full. He points me out to his security guy. The ape of a man asks the ladies to make way as he descends the three stairs from the VIP to get me. He arrives at a couple of ladies in miniskirts who are trying to get to their feet without flashing the club. He extends them each a hand and pulls them up gingerly. When he gets to me, he puts his hand behind my back and guides me toward the VIP.

I sheepishly look back to the other ladies. "Sorry," I say.

"Fuck you!" says the eye-rolling lady. With this, the women once again whip into a frenzy. This time, though, it's a frenzy of anger toward me. The security guard hustles me up the stairs and into the arms of my pal Blake. I nestle into the safety of his large chest, and it's so much cozier than where I came from.

"Hi," I say, closing my eyes and taking in Blake's musky smell.

"Hi," he says with a chuckle. His voice resonates through my head, making a pleasant feeling in my cheeks.

"This is a nice hug, isn't it," I say.

"It is. Are you okay?" he asks.

I pull back from Blake and look him in the eye. "Now I see why you want to stay home all the time," I say. "That was crazy!"

"Aw. Poor baby!"

"That was totally my fault, too," I confess.

"The lady pileup?" Blake says, looking at me as if he's impressed.

"I took them all down."

From behind me, I hear, "Where have you been all night?" I turn, and it's Casper.

"Dancing. Want a drink? I'm parched." I grab a bottle of water from a silver ice bucket as Casper pulls me aside.

"I want to talk to you about something serious," he says. What? No. No serious talk. Is this about work?

"Casper, I really can't talk about work or serious things right now. I've had a shit few days. It's so wonderful in here. Let's not change that," I tell him honestly.

"Why? What's up?"

"Duke broke up with me. Total asshole. Was cheating. I found them. Whole nine yards."

"Good," Casper says.

"Good?"

"Yeah. Now you can move to LA and work for me without missing some lame boyfriend you left at home."

I laugh. It's comically selfish of him. It's also the perfect thing to say.

"Hey," he says. "I know everyone's partying and stuff tonight, but I'm serious. I want you to move to LA and be my assistant."

"You do?"

"Yeah. Come finish the movie with me in LA. See it through post. I got things lined up after this, too. You should be my assistant. But you've got to be there in two weeks."

"Okay," I say in disbelief. We give each other a little hug to seal the deal. I turn around, and Pup is holding a bottle of champagne.

"Congratulations, my babe!" She fills my glass, bubbles dripping to the floor. I sip, feeling the bubbles pop pleasantly in my mouth.

"Congratulations," Saffron purrs into my ear. I turn around, and there she is, champagne in hand, a dull smile on her lips.

"Thank you." I lift my champagne to hers and we clink glasses.

"Cheers," she says. "You know, Charity, I've been working with Casper for seven years. He runs everything through me." This doesn't sound good. It sounds super serious. Did Saffron take a different drug than I did?

"Seven years," I repeat.

"Yes. You know, there's lots of personal stuff Casper has his assistants do," Saffron says.

"Casper knows I'm not moving to LA to pick up his dry cleaning. I'm not a personal assistant," I say with as much lightness as possible. And given the circumstances, I think I sound pretty light.

"Right. I'm just saying that I'm there every day. I've seen a lot of assistants come and go," Saffron says. Oh, wow. This is a very uncomfortable conversation. *I've seen a lot of assistants come and go.* Who talks like that? Saffron's eyes dart around the room as she sips from her glass. I sense that she's not comfortable, either, but she's intent on delivering her message. "But Casper really likes you, Charity. We have a good feeling about you." I have to get out of this conversation.

"I have to pee," I say clumsily.

As I cruise through the VIP with no intention of actually going to the bathroom, I decide to ignore my entire conversation with Saffron and focus on the positive. I'm moving to LA to assist the director of Canopy Studios' biggest film of the year. This could take me places. Serious places. I am going to live in LA, where I will have the chance to give my scripts to the biggest decision-makers in the film industry, the ones who choose the scripts and put together the teams that win Oscars. I am going to be a famous screenwriter. Duke couldn't have made me single at a better time.

When I duck into a dark corner of the VIP to hide from Saffron, I find Casper and Blake deep in conversation.

"What's going on?" I ask Daniel who, a little high, bumps to the music, clearly enjoying his own company.

"Don't go over there." Daniel points to Casper and Blake with his chin.

"Why?" I ask.

"Blake's letting Casper have it for hijacking his *ET* interview."

"Oh, shit. He's mad, huh?"

"He's the biggest goddamn star in the world, and he had to share *Entertainment Tonight* with . . . Casper." I give Daniel a disappointed look. He can be such a star snob. "What? It's not like he's Spielberg," Daniel says, his eyes sparkling in the club lights.

"Daniel. I'm newly single. I'm moving to LA. I'm going to work at Canopy Studios. Dance with me." He looks me in the eyes and smiles wickedly, then takes my hand in his and leads me to the dance floor.

CHAPTER 4
WELCOME TO THE JUNGLE

Pup and I are dorks. We know that. We are super cliché. We understand. But if you were embarking on the first day of your Hollywood dream, you would also crank your favorite song as loud as your car speakers could handle and cruise down Sunset Boulevard with the top down on your Volkswagen Cabriolet, just like us. I guarantee that you would have a big stupid grin on your face, because we do. And you would be driving at an annoyingly slow speed while envisioning your dreams coming true, just like we are.

I fling my arm out the open window to ride the breeze and let a man in a Lamborghini pass us on the left. He lifts his Oakley Frogskins from his eyes and gives us a cocky wink. Pup and I kill ourselves laughing. Billboards line the sky, telling us what we should watch, listen to, and wear, casting shadows over clubs and bars that I have dreamed of going to. The Viper Room, Laugh Factory, Troubadour, Whiskey a Go Go, the House of Blues—places that make superstars.

"There it is," Pup says. My eyes follow her pointed finger to the hills that skirt Sunset. There, perched just in front of us on a steep and narrow side street, slightly obscured by treetops, stands the legendary Chateau Marmont.

"One drink," Pup says.

"But we're disgusting. We've been driving for two days straight," I say.

"Come on. How can you resist? It's right there."

"I don't know. My entire life is packed in this car." I glance in the rearview mirror at my IBM computer that I have buckled into the back seat, like a precious baby. "My computer," I say.

"Nobody is going to steal your computer," Pup says.

"That IBM holds everything I've written. Five film scripts, a TV pilot, and outlines for three seasons. Plus, all those scenes that don't have a home yet but could be genius," I say.

"We'll valet," Pup says convincingly. How can I say no? Pup has one week off between wrapping *Diffuser* and starting her next film, and she's spending that time with me, driving over thirteen hundred miles to LA and helping me find the perfect Hollywood apartment.

The valet opens the car door, and I feel a little embarrassed. My Volkswagen is filthy, packed to the gills and practically dragging under the weight of all my worldly possessions.

"Afternoon, ladies." The valet plucks the keys from my hand. His smile is so bright it has me reaching for my sunglasses. This is irresponsible, isn't it? One does not valet one's entire life with a dude who looks like he should be in a gum commercial. But when I see the awe in Pup's face as she looks up at the Chateau Marmont, I don't have the heart to be responsible.

"Sorry about the mess," I say to the valet.

"We've all been there," he says, climbing into the driver's seat.

I place a hand on the door, keeping him from closing it, and bend down to confide in him. "This is everything I own," I say.

"How about I keep it up here for you?" the valet says, pointing to the line of Mercedes and BMWs at the side of the breezeway.

"I don't think the hotel would want you to put my car there." I mean, I don't want to get the guy in trouble.

"Sure they would. What's your name?" He pulls out a pad of valet tickets and rips off my half.

"Charity."

"Welcome to Chateau Marmont, Charity," he says, handing me the ticket. "And hey. Welcome to Hollywood."

Inside, the Chateau is chicly mismatched with perfectly distressed antique furniture. A scattering of velvet couches and brocade chairs, grouped together strategically to create privacy—or the illusion thereof—sit atop terra-cotta tiles or Afghan rugs. Beaded chandeliers and bronze lamps barely light the room; instead, the ambience relies on the sunlight pouring through the heavy lancet windows, accentuating the shadows in the corners. It's the perfect place for the who's who to be seen or not be seen.

We step outside to the patio bar and snag a pedestal table just beyond the pool and lounging guests. From behind our menus, we covertly assess the people around us, trying to decipher if somebody is really somebody. "This can't be right," I say to Pup, looking at the menu. Twenty dollars for a margarita? Pup laughs, and I'm shocked that she isn't as blown away as I am.

"I wonder how much a room is here?" she says.

"It would be astronomical," I say.

"We should do it."

"You're kidding," I say.

"One night."

"Pup. There's no way. Do you know how much the Canadian dollar is worth compared to the American dollar?"

"Is it bad?"

"A twenty-dollar margarita is almost thirty dollars Canadian."

"Well, this is one of the best hotels in LA," she says.

"Yeah, but LA is an expensive city. Look at how much a studio apartment is." I rummage through my bag and pull out the *LA Times* housing section where I've circled a bunch of available rental apartments.

Pup's face goes from excited to confused to appalled. "Charity. These areas are bad. Like, *bars on the windows* bad."

"*Bars on the windows* bad?"

Pup has spent serious time in LA. I have spent none. If you can believe it, it's my first time here. If I was nervous before, I'm double nervous now. "I'm exaggerating," she says. But as she scans the newspaper, I sense that she's not.

Back at the hotel breezeway, I feel a little foolish watching the valet jog over to my car, which sits only a few yards away. A silver Porsche 911 Carrera pulls in front of us, and in swoops another valet to open the passenger door. An elegant leg extends from the cream leather seat and places a black stiletto onto the ground. A man, whose hair is perfectly grunge, appears from around the other side of the car. He tosses his cigarette onto the ground and then slides his arm around the lady's waist, thanking the young valet with a folded bill. She looks up at him, her sunglasses gazing into his sunglasses, and they smile at each other in effortless glamour. Pup and I let the world fall away as we watch them float into the Chateau.

The Porsche pulls forward with a purr, and in chugs my little car with the valet barely visible among my life's possessions. A whirring noise that I have never heard before emanates from under the hood. Pup is visibly concerned. Whether it's because she's worried about my car or being seen in my car is debatable.

It's worse than I thought. Two days of searching for an apartment and we haven't seen anything I could live in without attracting bed bugs or petty crime. I'm not overly discouraged, though, as I'm living the old romantic tale of how people come to Hollywood with five bucks in their pockets and hearts full of dreams. So here we are in the outskirts of LA in the least crappy studio apartment we've seen all day. Sure, the oven is avocado colored and probably as old as I am. Doesn't matter.

I don't cook. The curtains are falling off the track. I can fix that. I can live with the peculiar laminate flooring; at least it's not old carpet. This terrible apartment is the perfect first step in my Hollywood story.

"You're messing with me, right?" Pup says. "Why don't you call your parents and explain how expensive rent is here? They'll help you out."

"They won't help me out. They would love this," I say, inspecting a squeaky kitchen cupboard.

"I think if they saw this place, they'd be afraid for you."

"Picture it. Years from now, when Oprah interviews me, she'll say something like, 'It was lean times for you in the beginning.' And I'll laugh and say something like, 'Oh, Oprah! My first apartment was pitiful. When I moved in, it hadn't been painted in so long that the walls actually retired from being a color three tenants before me.' We laugh at my witty way with words, and Oprah and I become best friends."

Pup eyes me warily. "Great story." She turns on the shower and screeches when a giant spider emerges from the drain. "Step on it! Step on it!" she screams.

I jump into the tub, avoiding the water spraying down as best I can. I stomp on the spider and cringe as I feel it pop under my foot. Gross? Yes. Deal-breaker? No. I reach around the falling water and turn the shower off.

"Okay. I'll go tell the landlord to get the contract ready. Let's unpack!" I hop out of the shower filled with energy. I'm in LA! This is my first non-roommate apartment. I'm a single, self-reliant woman on the cusp of great success.

CHAPTER 5
MEET-CUTE

My right thigh bounces rapid-fire off the Barcelona chair in the Canopy Studios lobby, my nervous jitters finding a way out of me whether I like it or not. Above the receptionist hangs a large oil painting of Richard Canopy, the Hollywood icon who started the studio in the 1920s, beside the likes of other notable film studios like Paramount and Disney. Richard went by Dick, but his friends called him Dickey. His story is famous—Dick leveraged every penny he had to purchase a modest piece of land in Beverly Hills, close enough to home so his wife could bring him a homecooked lunch every day and, during those early years when work was never-ending, a homecooked dinner. The studio lot was small with a large gate. On the water tower, high above Beverly Hills, Dickey had scenic artists hand paint the studio's logo, a leopard lying serenely under the canopy of a tree. The big cat could be seen from miles around, lording over Los Angeles and the film industry. It's been years since that water tower was torn down—the studio lot changing locations and structures with the growing company.

When Casper offered me the job as his assistant at Canopy, I envisioned a studio lot with soundstages and movie stars being chauffeured around in golf carts. In reality, Canopy Studios is a dominating glass high-rise, with the iconic leopard insignia prominently displayed at the very top—still, as ever, a beacon of Hollywood. Canopy takes up a quarter of the building and has its own lobby on the ground floor with elevators dedicated to the studio. Sitting in this lobby is like being in a fish tank of corporate activity.

Through the glass wall, I can see a larger lobby where security guards stand behind and beside marble desks greeting people in business suits and high heels. Eight elevators ding constantly, taking people to entertainment law firms, production companies, publicity firms, and the biggest talent agency in America. I pick up a copy of *Variety* magazine that sits on the coffee table in front of me and flip through it, hoping to look as professional as everyone around me. But it's hard to contain my excitement—I am at the epicenter of Hollywood, surrounded by dealmakers in power suits, reading about Canopy Studios' weekend box office revenue in *Variety* magazine while sitting in the Canopy lobby. I have leapt into a completely other level in my career. This isn't filmmaking, this is show business.

A buzz of activity catches my attention, and through the glass door comes a small entourage. At its epicenter is Jennifer Black, the star of television's most popular sitcom for five years running. The group breezes by me in a flurry of conversation and steps directly into a waiting elevator. My first star spotting. I can't wait to tell Pup.

"Charity?"

I hear my name, and when I turn, I see Jessica. At least I presume it's Jessica, Steve's assistant here at Canopy Studios. I stand to greet her while taking in her beige knee-length skirt and black blouse. Her thin, dark hair is pulled back into a no-nonsense low ponytail, revealing a perfect set of pearl earrings. Jessica looks every bit the part of an up-and-coming executive while I am conspicuously underdressed in jeans.

"Jessica, hi. It's great to put a face to the voice," I say. When I assisted Steve in Vancouver, Jessica and I chatted almost every day. I handled *Diffuser* production responsibilities and Jessica handled everything Canopy Studios. Her no-nonsense demeanor is no doubt a product of her tight schedule and endless responsibilities.

"Yeah. Follow me." Although she's smiling, Jessica is curt.

We hop inside an elevator, and she pokes the button for the top floor, shooting the elevator up at such a speed that my ears plug. "Do your ears pop on this thing?" I ask.

"Annoying, right? Really, if you think about the amount of time a person can waste over the years riding an elevator to work, it's a wonder why they don't put the executives on the lowest floor and the people who have time to spare on the higher floors." Jessica smiles at me, impressed by her backward ingenuity, and I smile back, silently wondering if I'll be able to see the Hollywood sign from up there.

The elevator door opens, and we step directly into the expansive executive lobby. Light floods in from two stories of floor-to-ceiling windows, casting a golden hue on the marble entry. The rounded walls on either side of us support wrought iron staircases leading to the executive wing. A large marble desk stretches between the staircases, and a receptionist sits precisely at its center. When she greets us, I realize I'm holding my breath.

As we climb the stairs, it becomes clear why the room radiates gold—the walls are glass cabinets that hold Academy Awards. There must be hundreds of them. I slow down to read titles of films ranging from old classics to one that was released just last year. Then I stop dead in my tracks when I see an Oscar for a film that I love deeply. In this moment, midway up the staircase of Canopy's executive lobby, I have never felt in closer proximity to my passion. I could reach out and touch the Oscar if not for the glass that separates us.

"Charity," Jessica calls, her voice bouncing off the marble. I look up and see that she has made it to the top of the stairs while I'm still somewhere around the middle. I quicken my pace.

"Did someone say 'Charity'?" I hear Saul's unmistakable voice. I lift my eyes to the top of the staircase and see the old man's silhouette against the California sky. I squint against the sun, and my foot doesn't quite clear the next step. I teeter backward. Oh shit. I'm going to—*Shiiiii*—

Hands grip my waist, and I fall against a sturdy chest. I turn my head and find myself inches away from a jaw lightly peppered with stubble. The man's smell—it's not cologne. It's him. I tilt my head ever so slightly so that my nose is closer to his neck. God, he smells good.

"Are you alright?" The bass in his voice vibrates against my rib cage.

"Yes." Ugh. I sound breathless, like I'm channeling Marilyn Monroe. How embarrassing.

"You're Charity." He steadies me. I turn to face him and discover that I have fallen into the arms of someone whom I could easily look at for a very long time.

"I'm Charity," I say dumbly.

He extends his hand for me to shake. "Kai. We've spoken on the phone."

"Oh. Wow." *Wow?* What am I, five years old?

"Welcome, Charity," Saul calls. "I have a meeting. Nice catch, Kai." I assume that Saul leaves but can't say for sure because I'm locked on Kai.

"That means I have a meeting, too," Kai says. I don't realize I'm leaning closer to him until I notice that he's backing away from me slightly. *Get it together, Charity.* I switch directions and lean back, reaching for the banister behind me, but I misjudge the distance and my hand slips. Kai lunges and grabs me, pulling me into him. This time our chests press together.

"Are you drunk or something?" he asks, and he's so close that I feel the soft warmth of his breath on my cheek, sending a surge of pleasure up my spine. It takes a moment before his words find their way to my brain. When they finally do, I'm mortified.

"What? No!" I pull myself together enough to stand without relying on Kai's capable hands.

"I'm joking," he says, laughing.

"Ahem." Jessica clears her throat from the top of the stairs.

"Sorry," I call out to her. "Sorry," I say to Kai, too embarrassed to look him in the eye.

"No worries. I'll catch you later," Kai says, bounding up the stairs. A pun. I love a pun. It takes all my willpower to keep my jaw from falling to the floor as I watch Kai take the stairs two at a time with ease. That's Saul's assistant? The guy with the no-nonsense, all-bass voice over the phone? He's hot. He likes to joke around. And he's Saul's assistant, so he's got to be smart. It's like Kai has seen my perfect-man checklist and has made it his mission to lick all my boxes. I mean, tick all my boxes.

When I reach the top of the stairs, Jessica seems annoyed. She leads me down a hall to a large area that is a maze of cubicles. Each cubicle is filled with an eager young professional. The area is abuzz with phones ringing and keyboards clacking. Surrounding the cubicles are thick wooden office doors, each adorned with brass letters: *CEO, CFO, VP,* and so on.

"This is the bullpen," says Jessica as she motions toward the hive of activity. "Every person here is an executive assistant. All the top brass of Canopy are in the surrounding offices. The most important people for you to know are their assistants in the pen." I see Kai. He grabs a script off his desk in the bullpen, then trots down a hallway. There's an empty cubicle next to his, and for a hopeful moment I think, *Is that my desk?*

"Is that my cubicle?" I ask.

Jessica snickers. "No. The bullpen is only for *executive assistants.* Your office is down on the eighth floor." Well, now I really feel silly. Jessica continues at a rapid pace. "That's for Kai's trainee. Saul is retiring this year, so people are moving up in the ranks. One of whom is your Kai. The empty cubicle is for him to train the person taking over his job," she explains.

I feel myself get a little red when she says *your Kai.* Did she pick up on some sort of animal magnetism between him and me? More likely, she's making fun of my gawking at him on the stairs.

Jessica says, "Go to the eighteenth floor, give them this letter, and they'll give you an ID badge." Jessica places a piece of paper in my hand. "Once that's done, take your ID badge to the third floor, and they'll give you a key card to access your office. Canopy Studios needs you to fill out some paperwork since you're technically doing a different job than you did in Vancouver. Here's your start pack." She practically tosses a stack of papers at me. "Fill it out and hand one copy to HR and the other to Accounting. They're on the twenty-second floor. You'll also need a parking pass. Fill this out and give it to security on the second floor." She places more papers on top of the pile in my hands. "Legal has your contract that you need to sign, so go talk to Deborah on the thirty-seventh floor. Here is a contact list for everyone who is involved in *Diffuser*. Don't contact any of the executives on their direct lines or on their cell phones. Always go through the bullpen for all communications. Here is the post-production schedule, delivery dates, et cetera. This is building orientation, maps, and such. This is the Canopy company protocol handbook. Okay. That's all you need."

I'm standing there dumbfounded, trying to process the mountain of information. My arms are full of loose paper that I try to organize into a neat pile.

"Now, I have in my calendar that Casper starts editing on Wednesday?" Jessica asks.

"Yeah. I'm going to use today and tomorrow to set up the offices," I say.

"Charity," Steve's voice booms. "Welcome." I turn to see Steve walking out of his office toward Jessica and me. Relieved to see my old boss, I give him the best hug I can with my arms full of paperwork. "I have to run to this meeting, but if you need anything, Jess here will sort you out. Come over to the house for dinner some night week after next. Talk to Jess and set it up. Gabe has some new action figures to show you."

"Cute. Will do," I say as Steve takes off. I turn to Jessica and say, "Thanks, Jess."

"Jessica," she says unhappily.

"Jessica. Sorry," I correct myself.

CHAPTER 6
GIRL INTERRUPTED

The glass door leading into the Canopy building opens in front of me, and there he is again, holding it just like he did yesterday and the day before. "After you," he says with a smile.

"Thanks," I say.

"I'm Jack."

"Charity."

"You work at Canopy Studios?"

"I do. You?"

"No. I work up there." Jack nods toward the elevators that are separate from Canopy's. His look is popular with LA's stylish young businessmen: tight haircut, flashy watch. I'm guessing he's a junior agent. "What do you do?" he asks.

"I assist a director. We're in post-production," I say.

"Editing?"

"That's right." My pager vibrates, and I reach into my back pocket to grab it. "Sorry," I say, looking at the screen.

"I'll leave you to it," Jack says with an assuredness that makes him surprisingly attractive. As I watch him walk away, I think he's the kind of guy who knows the LA scene and wants to be seen in it. A little too slick for me.

I stand back to admire my work. Over the last two days, I have managed to transform a sterile turnkey workspace that consisted of three desks, three chairs, and three desktop computers into a creative den using abandoned items that I pilfered from empty offices throughout the building. I nabbed a coffee table that was sitting in the supply room and a love seat from down the hall. I dragged in a neglected fig tree I found on another floor and placed it opposite the couch. I got a scented candle with petty cash, and now we have a cozy sitting room that smells like a five-star Hawaiian hotel.

Across from the sitting room, my signed Blake Anthony *Diffuser* poster hangs above my desk. Casper's and Saffron's offices are located right off the sitting room, and I've stocked them with office supplies. In Casper's office, I taped a large calendar to the wall and filled in the post-production schedule so he can easily see when his various cuts are due. There are about a dozen cuts he has to deliver to the studio, each implementing notes from the executives or adding post-production elements like music or visual effects.

On my first day at Canopy Studios, it took all morning to get my security clearance, parking pass, and key card because I couldn't keep Jessica's ultrarapid instructions straight in my head, so I made a welcome packet that clearly outlines her instructions. Following these instructions, Casper and Saffron should accomplish everything in about an hour. Come to think of it, I should give this to Jessica for all her newcomers. That could make her life easier.

There's a knock on the door, and I practically skip across the office to answer it, excited to see who my first guest is. I pull the door open and Saffron breezes in, holding her morning coffee and shouldering not one but two large Kate Spade bags, the straps straining with their load.

"Morning. Morning. Welcome," Saffron sings.

"Can I help—"

"No. No. Just need to put these down." She makes her way directly into Casper's office and drops her bags onto the desk with a thud. "This is nice," she says, looking around the office.

"You like it? I actually put you next door. Same setup in both offices. Just different paperwork on your desks and little stuff." Using the knowledge I acquired from watching *Working Girl*, I assigned Casper this particular office because from where he sits, he can see me at my desk and say things like *Get so-and-so on the phone*.

I follow Saffron as she lugs her bags into her office. She smiles with appreciation at the pot of calla lilies I bought with petty cash, but as she surveys the office, her eyes turn critical. "Where's my post-production calendar?" Saffron asks.

"I printed you off one. It's right here." I riffle through the stack of papers on her desk. "Canopy Studio contacts, map of the building . . . here it is. Post-production schedule." I hand her the piece of paper. "I just taped mine up on the wall behind my desk."

"So much easier seeing it on a big calendar like the one in Casper's office, isn't it?"

Her disappointment can only lead to one response. "I'm happy to make you one," I say.

"Honey, I'd love that. Thank you." She sticks her long, thin arm into one of the Kate Spade bags and pulls out two scripts that are dog-eared and covered in notes.

The office phone rings, and I run to my desk and answer it.

"Hello?" I say.

"Hi. Is this Casper's office?"

"Yes."

"Is this Charity?"

"Yeah."

"Charity, it's Kai from Saul's office."

"Oh, hi. How are you?" Our first and only encounter flashes in my head: Kai's arms around me, leaning against his chest, my lips tantalizingly close to that spot where his jaw meets his neck.

"I'm good, thanks. Have you always worked on set?" Kai asks.

"Yeah."

"First time in an office?"

"Yup."

"Okay. Answer the phone like this: 'Casper's office, Charity speaking.'"

"Got it. Thanks," I say. He must think I am an idiot.

"Now, you see the little screen on your phone? You see how number one-oh-five is on that screen?"

"Yeah."

"That's my extension. You should have a list of extensions there somewhere. If not, you can print one off from the Canopy database. Put it next to your phone. That way when you need to call someone, their extension is at your fingertips. Also, you can check to see who's calling you. Gives you a second to prepare."

"Are you saying that I should prepare myself for you?" *Why, Charity! Why did you say that? It sounds like you're flirting with the guy.* There's a *thunk* on the line and then nothing. "Hello?" I say.

"Hi. Hi. Sorry. I, um . . . I dropped the phone. Look, can you ring me when Casper heads down to the editing suite? Saul wants to say a quick hello before they dive into work."

"Will do," I say with a wicked smile. Did I fluster him?

I hang up the phone and slide into my chair, enjoying the afterglow of Kai. I wonder how often I'll hear his sexy voice on the phone. Will we go to the same meetings? If I could see Kai two times a week, that would be ideal. I want to stare at his handsome face and nothing more. I've slept with a coworker before—it's not smart. Not that Kai would want to sleep with me. He probably has a girlfriend. I don't know. I don't care. I don't care because this isn't an issue. Kai is a coworker, and we don't think about unbuttoning our coworker's oxford shirt.

What is wrong with me? It's not like me to have a brief encounter with some guy and then fantasize about him. I am going to stop thinking about Kai. I will not flirt with him. I will not stand close enough to smell his sweet smell. I will allow myself to enjoy looking at him from afar. I will allow this twice a week, tops. That's settled.

Saffron hollers at me from her office. "Who was that?"

"Kai," I answer.

"Who?"

"Saul's assistant."

"What did he want?"

"He wants me to give him a call when Casper gets in."

"Why?" If Saffron is going to be this inquisitive about every phone conversation I have, this could get tedious.

"Saul wants to pop down to editing to say hi to him."

"Oh. Hey, why is our door locked?" she yells again.

Some people don't mind having conversations through walls. I'm not one of them. I get up from my desk and walk to Saffron's office.

"The door to the hallway locks automatically. You need a key card to unlock it." I pluck the welcome packet from her desk and hand it to her. "Here, I made this for you. It's a step-by-step guide to get you set up at Canopy. The key card is part of it."

Saffron thumbs through the package with malaise. "Ugh. I really should get to work on a couple of time-sensitive things. Can you handle this for me?" Saffron holds the welcome packet out for me to take.

"I can't, actually. They need to take your picture, get your driver's license, your signatures, all that good stuff."

"Fine." Saffron stands in a huff, and I move aside as she brushes past me.

"See ya . . ." I say, but she's already out the door. "Later."

I've always thought Saffron is a bit of a buzzkill. Not that she popped my balloon today or anything. She just put a little hole in it so that I'm slightly deflated. I can turn this around. I'll make Saffron's calendar and hang it in her office by the time she gets back. She'll be fine.

I'm typing away at my computer when the door swings open and a stranger strides into the office pushing a cart filled with envelopes and boxes. He must be from the mailroom, just like Michael J. Fox in *The Secret of My Success*. As I sign for a thick package, I wonder if I should watch more corporate-America films to prepare me for this environment.

The mailroom guy leaves, and I flip over the package, revealing the distinctive blue-and-white William Morris logo. If I were a betting gal, I would say that the package contains scripts Casper's agent has sent for him to consider. I place the package on the corner of my desk, resisting the urge to peek inside. Casper's next film could be in there. This may be where all my hard work pays off—the years of soaking up every bit of knowledge on set, studying screenwriting in my spare time, attending seminars, writing, rewriting, workshopping, rewriting again. I know what makes a good script, and I am confident that I can help Casper find one.

A knock on the door pulls me from my ambitious daydream, and when I open it, Casper walks through, gold-rimmed Ray-Ban aviators and a huge smile on his face. "Charity Trickett in LA. Sup." He pulls a little rolling cart behind him that is filled with art books, vinyl records, CDs, VHS tapes, a turntable, and a boom box. It's an eclectic collection of art and music. Basquiat, De Palma, Prince, Cassavetes, Joe Cocker.

"Hello," I say. "What's all this?"

"Inspiration." We hear a click from the door. Saffron walks in looking miserable, but once she sees Casper, a smile spreads across her face.

"Casper!" she sings.

"Hey, Saffy. Nice setup in here," Casper says.

"It'll work," she says. "Hey, I was talking to Marcia yesterday. She had some interesting thoughts about that project. Wants to chat with you today."

"Cool," Casper says.

"I have a call list going. I can add her, if you give me her contact info," I say, jumping right into my role as assistant.

"Who's on the list?" Casper asks.

"Nothing urgent. Your agent, Richard, and Blair. Do you want to settle into editing? Then maybe you'll have a sense of when you'd like to make those calls," I say.

"Yeah. Good idea," he says.

"And Saul's going to pop down to the editing suite to say hi," Saffron says. Hmm. I was just going to say that.

"Saff, give Charity Marcia's contact info for the call list. And, you know, whatever calls I need to make, just let Charity know."

"Okay," Saffron says. But her tone is strikingly pitched, like she has a problem with me being responsible for the call list. It's just a clerical document that tells Casper who has called him and who he needs to call back. Maybe Saffron is worried that she'll be out of the loop if I handle it. But come on, she's the associate producer—she's not going to be answering the phone. That's what assistants do.

"I should get to editing," Casper says.

"Sure. Leave this stuff and I'll set it up in your office," I say. "Here. Take my key card. It gives you access to almost the whole building. You'll need it for the editing suite. We'll set you up with your own later," I say.

Casper sees the package from William Morris on my desk. "These scripts?" he asks.

"I haven't opened it yet, but I assume so," I say. He rips the package open and takes a quick glance, then hands two scripts to Saffron and two scripts to me.

"Let me know what you think," he says. Casper wants my opinion on what his next film should be! This is amazing!

"But Casper, that's my job," Saffron shrills.

"She can do some," he says with a careless shrug. "I'll be in editing."

Casper manages to leave without noticing how stunned Saffron looks. Her body is beyond tense, hands in fists, arms like pistons at her side. She may even be holding her breath. Without a word or a glance my way, Saffron pivots hard on her heels and strides to her office, slamming the door shut behind her.

An hour later, I knock tentatively on Saffron's office door. "I made that calendar for you," I say.

"Come in." When I open the door, Saffron does not lift her eyes from the script she is reading.

"Would you like me to hang it for you?"

"Yes, please."

"Where would you like it?" God, I sound like a suck-up.

Saffron takes a deep breath and sits back in her chair. She stares me down. Her thin lips are pursed, her arms crossed. It's clear that Saffron is not going to tell me where she wants her calendar, so I decide to put it up across from her desk, just like I did in Casper's office. As I tape the calendar to the wall, I can feel Saffron's eyes burning into my back.

"Straight?" I ask when I finish.

"Yes. Thank you, Charity," she says.

"Can I borrow your key card for about fifteen minutes? I need to pee and run something up to the executive floor," I say.

"Absolutely." She hands me her card. "Oh, and Charity, can you grab me a coffee on your way back? There's a great little café across Century Boulevard."

"Sure. The usual?"

"I love that you know my coffee order." For the first time all day, she smiles.

I enter the bullpen and glance surreptitiously in Kai's direction. He's on the phone with a spreadsheet open on his computer. When I approach Jessica, she looks surprised to see me. "Charity. What are you doing here?" she asks.

I hand her the welcome pack. "You were so helpful yesterday that I typed up your instructions for Casper and Saffron. Thought it could be handy for you to give people in the future. I also saved it on this CD so you can print it off whenever."

Jessica regards the document with what looks to be disgust. "I'm not a welcoming committee," Jessica says.

"Pardon me?"

"I'm not a welcoming committee. I don't generally—wait, I have never greeted someone new at Canopy and shown them the ropes. Furthermore, I have never made dinner plans for another assistant." She drops the welcome packet and CD into the garbage and turns back to her computer.

Oh God. I offended her. "I'm sorry. I didn't mean to put you out."

"You didn't put me out. This just isn't what I do. While I have you here, though, how about Tuesday after next for your dinner at Steve's house with his family?"

"That's fine."

"Consider this confirmed," she says professionally. "I assume you have the address."

"I don't."

"Well, neither do I, as I've never been invited to his home."

Oh. Now I get it. "I'm sure that he's taking pity on me because I just moved here and don't know anyone," I say.

"Over half the bullpen, at one time in our lives, just moved here and didn't know anyone." She looks down at her hands and picks at the cuticle of her thumb.

"Have you ever worked on a movie set?" I ask her.

"Well, I've worked on a ton of movies and gone to watch them shoot."

"But you were never a PA or anything?"

"No."

"When you go to set, who shows you around?" I ask. Jessica leans back in her chair and sighs. I can tell she sees what I'm getting at.

"The assistant," she says, rolling her eyes.

"Yeah, me. You know, two days ago was my first time in an office building." Jessica looks like she doesn't believe me. "I don't know how things work around here. It's completely different than being on set. Sorry Steve made you hang out with me. He kind of dads me sometimes."

"Wait. Steve dads you?" Jessica asks.

"Look, we were shooting in small towns with nothing to do. The *Diffuser* cast and crew spent a weird amount of time hanging out. In Vancouver, when Steve's family came to visit, I even babysat Gabe so he and Julie could go for dinner." I can tell that Jessica's striving businesswoman sensibilities do not approve of this, but she is softening.

"So, he dads you?" Jessica asks with a hint of a smile.

"Yeah. You know what his big advice for me was when he found out I was moving to LA?"

"What?"

"He said that people in LA are notorious for running red lights. So, when the light turns green check before you go."

"That's actually solid advice," Jessica says. I think she's warming up to me.

"I'm back!" I say, coming into the office with Saffron's coffee. When I pass my desk, I notice the scripts that Casper gave me have changed. Gone are the fresh-off-the-press pages with the crisp William Morris logo. These scripts are covered in handwritten notes, the pages are dog-eared and coffee-stained, and they all have *PASS* scrawled across the top in red ink. These must be from Saffron's Kate Spade bags. In exchange for the scripts from William Morris, scripts that have the potential to be Casper's next film, Saffron has given me scripts that Casper has already passed on. I'm furious, but I stop myself from bursting into Saffron's office. Instead, I should think about how to address this properly and choose my words carefully.

You know what? Fuck it. I'm going in.

I take the garbage scripts and Saffron's fucking brevé cappuccino and walk right into her office. She's talking on the phone with all four scripts from William Morris piled in front of her. She's ignoring me. "I know," she says into the phone. "Listen. That's the way it is." I smack her coffee down in front of her. She looks up at me. *Thank you*, she mouths. I hold the passed-on scripts up to her. She sticks her index finger in the air and mouths, *One minute*. One minute is actually more like three.

I remain planted in front of her desk, staring at her, until she finally hangs up. Without pause, she says, "Oh good. You got them."

"What is this?" I hold up the rejected scripts.

"Yeah. I need you to do coverage on those," she says.

"But they've been passed on. It says so right here. This is Casper's writing, too, isn't it?"

"Yeah. But he really values your opinion, Charity, and we wouldn't want to miss anything. What if you read those scripts and find something that we've completely overlooked? You could find a gem," she says, as if she's doing me a favor.

I nod to the crisp new scripts sitting on Saffron's desk. "But Casper gave me those scripts," I say.

"Oh, you'll read these, too, Charity. I'm not taking them from you. Of course you'll read them. But first, there's a whole backlog of scripts that we want your opinion on." She points to the sad bookshelf beside her desk. Stacks of well-worn scripts lie on it, and from what I can tell, they all have *PASS* written on the title pages.

"And are there any scripts on that bookshelf that you have taken particular interest in? Or has Casper passed on all of them?" I ask.

"Casper's busy right now editing the biggest project of his life. Some of these he hasn't had the time to read," Saffron says.

What I can assume from that statement is that some of the scripts are so awful she hasn't bothered Casper with them.

"Casper doesn't have the time to get into the day-to-day process of coverage. That's my job. In the past, we hired assistants who we thought could help with this process, but they were horrible and didn't last long. That's why we have you, Charity, the writer." This is the second time Saffron has referenced past unsuccessful assistants. The threat is loud and clear. She smiles at me and adds, "You know how to do coverage, right?"

Coverage is a one-page document used in the industry to summarize a film or TV project's plot and salability. It's a quick tool that some people use to pitch. When pitching a script, you need to think strategically. A script could be good, but it may not be a good fit at the moment. Has a similar film come to market recently? Does this fit with the trending cultures, pop and otherwise? Who is the audience? Does it fit the budget? Picking the right script is tricky, and I have learned from extremely successful filmmakers how to assess a script's quality and marketability. I mean, just look at my resume:

Charity Trickett

Assistant to:

Steve Lien: Executive Producer, Canopy Studios — *Diffuser*

Ryan Coe: Executive Producer, HBO — *Gold Digger* — Golden Globe–winning miniseries

James Lawson: Executive Producer, Director, NBC — *First Base* — TV series

Lee Simpson: Executive Producer, Miramax — *Is He British?* — Feature film

Lorne Park: Executive Producer, Fox — *White Oaks* — Feature film

Douglas Frehs: Writer, Director, and Executive Producer, Universal — *Bad Tattoo* — Feature film

Brian Markovich: Director and Executive Producer, Paramount —
The Tall Cousin — Feature film
Wes Van: Writer, Director, and Executive Producer, NBC —
Collingwood — TV series

My resume is better than any film degree. I have learned from
people who have won awards for their work and are established in
their careers. They are always looking for the next project. They are
always reading scripts and always pitching. I've read their scripts, I've
done their coverage, I've sat in on their meetings, and I've listened to
how they make their decisions. I am far more qualified than Saffron is
to lend my opinion on which projects Casper should consider.

While shooting *Diffuser*, Pup and I couldn't tell what Saffron's role
as an associate producer consisted of. The duties of a producer, and
certainly an associate producer, are varied and vague. But everyone
plays a part, lending their expertise to the film, whether it be cre-
atively or financially. As far as we could tell, all Saffron did on set was
sit around and read scripts for Casper. We never saw her contribute
to the shoot. So we searched for her on IMDB and were shocked to
learn that Saffron had only one credit. She'd worked as a producer
on Casper's independent film *Flicker* about a million years ago. That's
all there was! Yes, she has a producing credit, but *Flicker* was a small
film and certainly wouldn't have prepared her for the massive task of
producing a huge studio action film.

At the risk of sounding full of myself, I think Saffron is threatened
by me. If I find Casper his next film, then I'm in a position to produce.
Having me read Casper's garbage scripts is Saffron's ploy to waste my
time and keep me from being an integral part of Casper's team, but it's
not going to work. I can do coverage in my sleep.

There's a scene in *Cinderella* where the wicked stepmother tells
Cinderella she can go to the ball. Cinderella is overjoyed. Then the
stepmother lists off a multitude of redundant chores that Cinderella

has to complete before she can go. Cinderella is crestfallen, for she surely won't finish all her work in time for the ball. So what did Cinderella do? She worked her ass off to get that shit done, and she got herself to that party. She even married the prince.

Game on, Saffron. I'll be your Cinderella, but this won't last long.

CHAPTER 7
REALITY BITES

I spend every free moment with my nose in a script. I take scripts home and read them over dinner. I take them to the beach and read until sunset. I fall asleep with scripts in my bed and wake with the sensation of them in my hands. Every single one is bad, and the more I read, the more I worry about my ability to properly assess their quality. It's natural. When you read so many crappy scripts, you're eventually going to read one slightly less crappy and think, *Maybe this one.* That can't happen to me. If I pitch Casper a piece of crap, he won't trust my judgment and will forever see me as just an assistant.

Luckily I have experience with wading through crap. Vintage shopping. Pup and I used to spend entire days scouring vintage stores in search of that one-of-a-kind garment. It had to be unique (the more vintage the better), it had to be cheap, and, of course, we had to look awesome in it. The problem Pup and I found was that when we dedicated an entire day to vintage stores and nothing else, our tastes were compromised and we often bought things that were more gross than Gucci. So, we worked out a simple formula that has proven to be one hundred percent successful. We visit one designer store for every vintage store. This strategy maintains fashion mindfulness as we consistently visit and study our goals.

I am adapting this same strategy to script reading. I read one quality script or watch one awesome movie for every script Saffron gives me. Nora Ephron, Quentin Tarantino, Eric Roth, Callie Khouri. I also go for runs between scripts; it clears my head, and I get to explore LA.

It's been two weeks of my read-run-watch-repeat lifestyle, and I'm becoming disheartened, so I pick Venice for my run this morning, thinking the ocean breeze will make me happy. But it doesn't work. Even after running for seven miles, my mind keeps going to a dark place.

I have been trying to get a Hollywood agent for years with no luck, but I have always kept the faith that I'll find one in the near future, knowing there are countless reasons an agent would say no to taking on a new client, timing and luck being a huge part of it. Now, having seen the quality of the scripts that are submitted to Casper, a successful director, my confidence is rattled. Are these scripts better than mine? All of these writers are represented by William Morris, one of the most prestigious agencies in America, and I can't even get the smallest boutique agency to read more than ten pages of my work. How the hell did these terrible writers get signed by William Morris? They must know somebody at the agency, right? Maybe they're all fraternity brothers or something. I'm better than these writers . . . I mean, I think so . . . I hope so . . .

The scripts I'm reading for Casper are ridiculous. I read about a reclusive sports fan who is so obsessed with a team that he commits murder to secure their championship. Another is about a group of American mercenaries in Afghanistan who get trapped in a cave haunted by the ghost of Genghis Khan. I read comedies that are not funny and thrillers that are not thrilling. Why are these scripts being sent to a Canopy Studios blockbuster director while mine collect dust?

Frustrated, I cut my run short and head to the coffee shop where my car is parked. I stand in front of my open trunk and pull the sweat-soaked tank off my body, tossing it into my gym bag. My bare back catches the soft ocean breeze, and it feels deliciously cool. I quickly sniff myself to make sure I'm not too offensive before pulling on a fresh white T-shirt. I grab a script and slam my trunk closed.

"Charity," calls a man's voice. I turn around and am pleasantly surprised to see Kai. *God, I hope he didn't catch me smelling my armpits*, I pray as he strides toward me, his muscular biceps peeking out of his T-shirt. I hold my breath, trying to suppress a fantasy of being tucked under his arm, running my hand up the inside of his T-shirt.

We meet on the sidewalk in front of a coffee shop. "You heading in here?" Kai asks, nodding toward the door.

"I am. You?" I say.

"Every Sunday." Kai holds the door open for me.

In line, I feel a little self-conscious and stand farther away from Kai than probably seems normal. But his easiness soon makes me forget that my hair is slightly sweaty and my face is probably still flushed from my run. He chuckles when I order a breakfast sandwich. When it's presented to me, I see why—it's enormous and messy. Yolk oozes through a mountainous pile of sprouts and drips onto the plate after sliding down a thick bagel.

"Can I join you for breakfast?" he asks, running his hand through his mess of brown hair. I wonder if he woke up and, like a typical boy, barely looked in the mirror before leaving home. Or is disheveled his curated look?

"If you're trying to share my sandwich, no way. I'm starving," I joke. Then I slice the sandwich in half and push it between us.

Between bites, Kai and I slip into easy conversation. He's a Colorado boy, went to film school at UCLA, and misses the mountains.

When we're finished, he shows me around Venice. We walk, looking through store windows, and Kai shows me his favorite hangout. It's a dive bar, the kind of place I would hang out at after a day of skiing. Sticky tables, classic rock, and fries that come in a red plastic basket lined with waxed paper.

Kai nods to the script that is tucked under my arm. "That Casper's next project?" he asks.

"I hope not," I groan.

"Not good?"

"Awful."

Kai slides the script out from my arm. "Oh. I know this guy," he says.

Oh no. I hope I didn't offend him.

"He's a nice guy," Kai says. "Bad writer, though. Casper can do better."

"Thanks. Yeah, that's what I think, too. Actually, I've been disappointed with a lot of the scripts he's gotten."

"Really?" Kai seems surprised. "Let me see that script." I hand it to Kai, and he thumbs through it. "I remember this one. It made the rounds years ago. I'm surprised his agent is still pitching it."

"Hmm," I say, piecing things together. "When did you read it?"

"Ages ago. I think I'd just started on Saul's desk."

Relief washes over me. This script isn't being pitched to Casper as the director of Canopy Studios' biggest blockbuster of the year. It was pitched to him years ago, probably when he was an indie director struggling for gigs. All the scripts that Saffron has given me were probably dead in Hollywood while I was still in university.

"What kind of project is he looking for?" Kai asks.

"I don't really know."

"Wait. Casper asked you to find his next project, but you don't know what he's looking for?"

"Yeah," I say, feeling foolish. Kai must think that I'm an idiot. And he's right. I *am* an idiot. I've been doing my job blind. Does Casper want another action/comedy? Does he want to do something completely new? He may want to do TV for all I know.

"So, what's your endgame, Trickett?" Kai asks.

"Oh. I'm a writer," I say.

"Any good?"

Rude! He can't even be bothered to hide his skepticism. I stop walking, which makes him stop walking. That's good—I need to take a good look at this guy while I answer his question.

"Yes. I'm a very good writer. That's why I'm pursuing a career in it." That came out more curtly than I had intended.

Kai starts to walk, and I mimic his slow pace. "Sorry," I say. "You caught me in a bit of a mood."

"I can tell," he says with a laugh.

"You have to admit, though—that was a stupid question."

"I asked you what your goals were."

"Yeah. Then when I told you I wanted to be a writer, you asked if I was good at it. That's condescending, Kai."

He pulls the script out from under my arm. "Is the guy who wrote this script a good writer?"

"No."

"See? Plenty of bad writers out there."

I suddenly feel deflated. "How did this guy get an agent at William Morris?" I whine.

Kai softens. "He was a production assistant on a TV series that was canceled after one season. He did good work, so the producers hired him back for the next TV show they did, this time as a script coordinator. That TV show was a big success. After years of this guy collating scripts, making sure production drafts were formatted properly for shooting, taking notes—you know, the grunt work in the writer's room—they gave him a job as a staff writer. He wrote a couple of episodes. They were good, and he got an agent."

"Oh. You really know this guy," I say sheepishly. "I wasn't trying to be mean about him or anything."

"I know. Don't worry about it."

We leave the commercial block and head through a neighborhood, both of us trying to redeem ourselves through pleasant small talk, but it's awkward. There's a hill ahead of us with a palm tree–lined street that cuts straight to the top. Kai says he lives in that direction, and we head our separate ways.

I can't help but feel that Kai was a nice fantasy I'm saying goodbye to.

CHAPTER 8
FIGHT CLUB

I am finished. I've summarized and analyzed every horrible script that Saffron gave me, and it took less than two weeks. An extraordinary pace, given that my days are consumed with my duties on *Diffuser*. I am now attaching my coverage sheets to each script and stacking them on the coffee table in the office, shaking my head at the insurmountable number of bad ideas in front of me.

My office phone rings, and I'm delighted to hear Pup's voice. "Did you finish them all?"

"I did," I say. "But the plan has changed since we last talked."

"Oh. Do tell."

"End of day yesterday, after Saffron had already left the office, I got a call from Casper's manager's assistant. The manager has a cold, and instead of meeting for breakfast in Beverly Hills this morning, he wants to do a phone call."

"Charity Trickett . . . are you plotting?"

"Saffron plotted first. Now, here's the plan: Saffron thinks that Casper is going to be out this morning, so I have laid all the terrible scripts on the coffee table in our office. When Saffy gets to work, we will sit down to go through it all, and Casper will just happen to walk in on us."

"Hmmmm," Pup says. I can tell she's not impressed with me.

"It's perfect! This way, I can casually show Casper that Saffron has had me working on stuff that he already passed on—no, correction, that all of Hollywood passed on years ago—instead of having me do my job and read the scripts he asked me to read."

"Are you sure Casper doesn't know that Saffron is bossing you around? And that maybe he's okay with it?"

"Saffron only asks for progress updates when Casper is out of the office. I don't think he knows."

"Okay. Here's an idea. Why don't you talk to Casper?"

"You don't think that's a bad look? Saffron and Casper seem close. I'm the assistant for five minutes and I'm already causing trouble on the team? Think about it. This scenario is like a gift from the Hollywood heavens. When Casper walks in on Saffron and me this morning, I'm going to behave as if Casper already knew about this project from Saffron. As far as I know, I'm not rocking the boat."

"Oh! They're calling my boss to set. Gotta run," Pup says. She hangs up before I can say goodbye.

The door clicks to unlock, and in walks Saffron, sunglasses atop her perfectly straight hair, Kate Spade dutifully at her side. "I got you a coffee," I say, handing it to her. My intention is to make Saffron think I'm working for her. It's what she wants, after all.

"Oh, you are a doll." She takes the cup, and her eyes move to the coffee table. There it is—the look of surprise. "Honey," she says. "You finished *all* of them?"

I nod. "I don't have much of a social life yet." I plop down on the couch and start talking about running into Kai, hoping she will sit down next to me. It takes a bit of time. First she lifts her sunglasses off her head and slips them into their Prada case. Then she sips her coffee while smiling and enjoying the embarrassing fact that Kai may have caught me smelling my armpits. Eventually, she warms up and sits down next to me.

"So let's chat about these scripts," I start. I praise her notes and turn to dog-eared pages where I point out specific comments that I agree with. "Of course, all the scripts are passes for sure. But this process has been valuable to me. I now understand what your tastes are, and I believe that our tastes are similar. So moving forward, it's great that we think alike. Now just a matter of finding a good script. So, what's Casper looking for?"

Saffron barely has time to respond before the door opens and in comes Casper. "Hey, guys." He stops in front of us with a broad smile. "What's all this?" I look at Saffron, shock all over her pretty face. Casper lifts one script off the coffee table. "This script? Shit. What are you guys doing?" He looks at Saffron, expecting her to answer, but she can't. She is a deer caught in headlights. This confirms it—Casper didn't know about Saffron's plot to waste my time. "Charity, did you do coverage on all of these?"

"I did. It was Saffron's idea." Saffron stiffens even more. No need to salt the wound, though. I've already won this round. "Before I look at those scripts you gave me, Saffron wanted me to have a good understanding of what kind of projects you've passed on."

Casper picks up another script and skims through my work. "Saffy, you kept all of these? Why?"

"I . . . I . . . I . . . you know. I keep them. You never know," she stutters.

Casper shakes his head. Then he asks me, "Charity, when did you do all of this?" He riffles through the scripts on the coffee table.

"In my spare time."

"Your spare time," Casper says. It's hard to interpret his tone.

I look back to Saffron, whose hands are clenched tightly in her lap.

"And what did you think?" he asks. "Any standouts?"

"No. Well, there was one terrible script that stood out," I say lightly.

"Let me guess," he interrupts. "*Rattlesnake Pow*." He plucks a script from the pile and holds it up, exposing the huge letters written in red Sharpie: *PASS*. He laughs, and I can't help but join in.

"Yeah. That's the one! It's the worst."

"Saffy," Casper laughs. "Why the fuck would you keep this script?"

Saffron's face turns red. She struggles to laugh along. Sheepishly, she shrugs and shakes her head. Is she speechless? Gradually, the laughter dies down and Casper looks at Saffron expectingly. She's holding her breath. Oh my God. Say something, Saffron.

"I . . . I . . ." she stutters. "I think there's value for our new employees, you know, seeing what projects have come across your desk." Saffron swallows hard. Wait. Did she say *employees*, plural? These scripts must be part of her standard repertoire with all of Casper's past assistants who she has seen, as she said, *come and go*.

Casper gives Saffron an odd look, like he doesn't know what to make of her. Saffron's nails dig into the sofa as though she's bracing herself for impact. I don't know why I want to throw her a lifeline, but I do. "Saffron's idea for the exercise was for me to get a sense of what you don't like. I get it. We all don't like these. Thank Christ, we're on the same page. So, what kind of projects are you looking for?"

"I want something cool and different than *Diffuser*," Casper says.

"So, no action/comedies," I say.

"Well, unless it's really cool. Then I want to read it," Casper says. "Did you read the scripts I'm considering?"

"Pardon?" I say.

"The scripts I'm thinking about pitching for. Have you read them?"

"I didn't know you have projects that you're interested in. That's exciting," I say.

"Yeah." Casper turns to Saffron and says, "Get her *Snow* and *Break Room*." As he heads into his office, he says to me, "Read those next and write me some coverage."

I smile to Saffron and ask, "Should I put these back in your office?"

"Throw them away," she says, struggling to look civil.

Wildfires blaze up north and the wind has pushed the smoke into Los Angeles, making my morning run about as healthy as smoking a pack of cigarettes. So, I'm treating myself to a step class. Instead of zoning out to the club-thumping music, I am obsessing about work. More precisely, I'm obsessing about Saffron and Casper. I thought the business with those old scripts would have had better results. I thought Saffron would see that she can't boss me around. But maybe she can. Ever since my little stunt, I've been Saffron's bitch. It's like Casper walked out of our meeting (re: garbage scripts/waste of my fucking time) and thought, *This is weird, but if this is what you guys are doing . . . okay, I guess.* Not okay! It's not okay that I have been working unpaid overtime because of an insecure associate producer.

"Grapevine," the perky instructor yells. In one swift motion, all thirty-six people in the room move to the right, crisscrossing our feet to the beat of the music. You would think that being part of this cool LA exercise class with all these cool LA ladies would put me in a stellar mood, but I'm cranky. Saffron is under my skin, and I can't sweat her out. My thoughts persistently drift back to last Tuesday when the whole script thing repeated itself. The exact same thing!

Four more scripts had come into the office from William Morris. I'd called down to editing to tell Casper. He'd said, "Great. You guys read them first. Let me know what you think." While I was on the phone with Casper, I watched Saffron take all the scripts off my desk and bring them into her office. Then she walked back and placed four old, passed-on scripts on my desk. What the hell! When I hung up the phone, I went into Saffron's office as composed as I possibly could be.

"Saff, Casper just asked that we split those up," I said.

"But you haven't read those other ones," she said.

"Oh, come on. They're from a few weeks ago. Casper has already passed on them."

"They'd still be good for you to read."

"But Casper asked me to read those," I said, pointing to the new ones.

Saffron looked at me as though she was concerned for my well-being. "Are you okay, Charity?" she asked.

"Yeah."

"Are you unhappy? Because we love having you here. You're a real asset."

"No, I'm happy. I just thought that Casper—well, he told me to read those scripts."

"Should we sit down with Casper?" Saffron asked, kindness oozing out of her like maple syrup. I was thrown. Was she going to hold the door open for me so that I could tell on her? Or—wait. Was this going to be a meeting where they tell me how it is?

"I don't need a sit-down. It's cool," I said.

I hop on top of the step and do a jumping jack, sweat dripping down my temple. Typically, the endorphins would have kicked in by now and I would be on an exercise high. Instead I'm ruminating. I work as much for Saffron as I do for Casper, and I fucking hate it. It's not just my ego and the fact that I have more experience than her. She's not good at her job. The two scripts that Casper is considering are *Break Room* and *Snow*. Saffy likes *Snow*, which is an okay script. It's like *Basic Instinct* meets *Groundhog Day*. The script isn't attached to a studio, and there aren't any actors who are interested. It's Saffron's find, and she's trying to package it. She's pitching to actors, investors, artistic directors, costume designers, and anyone with a name who, along with Casper, can get the project rolling.

Meanwhile, the script that I like is being ignored. *Break Room* is a beautiful biopic about a leader in the feminist movement. It's different from Casper's previous films, but this is a movie that could pivot him from being a big-time action director to an Academy Award–nominated director. The script is gold. Even better, Canopy Studios owns *Break Room* and has asked Casper to pitch for it. He can roll from one Canopy project straight into another. The only problem is that Casper is too busy to build a pitch on his own because he's editing *Diffuser*.

This would be a perfect project for me to take on, and I would love to do it. I want to find an actress for the lead who is so good that with her attached, Casper would be guaranteed the film. I know this sounds difficult, but this lead role is an actress's dream. It requires a performance so intense that, if done well, it could make the actress very busy come award season. Plus, since Casper just finished working with Blake Anthony, everyone will want to work with him.

If I did this, though, it would put me in direct competition with Saffron. Is it smart to compete with her? She is already overly demanding and impossible to please. She fills my days with mindless tasks that she relentlessly micromanages. She asks a multitude of questions and never seems satisfied with my answers. She says, *Are you sure? Are you sure? Are you sure?* so endlessly that I'm second-guessing myself, double- and triple-checking the simplest things. It's throwing me off and taking up a lot of time. Then, out of the blue, she's kind. She'll invite me to the mall across the street for lunch. She even pays sometimes. She'll tell me intimate details of her dates or her bikini waxes. Sure, she's pinning me to the ground, but she's kissing me on the cheek at the same time. If I step toe-to-toe with Saffron, will the kisses be replaced with more punishment?

After step class, I shower at Canopy, as getting space in front of the mirror to do your makeup at the gym risks personal injury. I'm standing in front of the mirror with a bare face and wet hair when Saffron walks in.

"Is the hot water out in your apartment?" she asks.

"No. I was at a step class down the street."

Saffron hoists a hip and half sits on the counter, letting a long leg dangle. "My parents are coming out next month," she says to my reflection.

"Where are they from?" I ask, applying a light dusting of blush.

"Utah. But they're at their pied-à-terre in Barcelona."

"Very cool," I say. "You spend any time there?" I search my makeup bag and pull out mascara.

"Oh, tons. Great city and good location to hop around Europe, you know?"

"I've never been," I say.

"Oh, you'd love it. Mom and Dad have been living there part-time since I was in college."

"They here for long?"

"A couple nights. They're staying at Shutters."

"Oh. I've run by that place. Looks swanky."

I finish my makeup, and Saffron looks at me with amazement. "Look at that dramatic transformation," she says. "You'll have to teach me how to do makeup one day, Charity. I'm hopeless at it, so I never wear any." She flashes me a smile, then disappears into a bathroom stall.

I look at myself in the mirror, and for a moment, I think about doing Saffy's makeup just like I would Pup's. Then I realize Saffron wasn't bonding with me. She just called my morning routine a *dramatic transformation*. That was a backhanded compliment delivered with subtle expertise. She wasn't shooting the breeze with me while I did my makeup. She was judging me. Every brushstroke of color I applied added to her superiority. Saffron doesn't need makeup. She's naturally tall and thin and so has no need to kill herself at step class. Her hair is long and shines with streaks made by the sun, not bleach, like mine. Some of us aren't blessed with natural beauty—some of us need to work at it a little.

"Hey, want to go to the mall with me for lunch today? I need a big-ass salad," Saffron calls cheerfully from the other side of the bathroom stall.

"Sounds great," I say, matching her cheeriness. Although I'd rather not have lunch with Saffron, I can't exactly claim to have lunch plans. She knows my schedule as well as I do. I pull out my hair dryer to begin the arduous task of making my hair look effortlessly wavy, like I've spent the morning at the beach.

Saffron and I are coming back from lunch when we see Jack in the building lobby. He walks over to us with a big smile. "I was just thinking about you," Jack says. I'm a little surprised.

"You were? Jack, this is Saffron," I say. Jack extends his hand toward Saffron, and I see her take in the gold Rolex that peeks out from under the cuff of his suit jacket.

"Do you want to go to a movie premiere with me on Friday?" Jack asks. Now I'm completely stunned. A date? A movie premiere? A real Hollywood movie premiere?

"Sure. Really? I mean, I'd love to." All thoughts of *This man could be an axe murderer* and *Why is he always lurking in the lobby of this building?* and *I'm not entirely attracted to him* fly out the window. I'm going to a Hollywood premiere! My first Hollywood premiere!

He pulls a business card from the inside pocket of his blazer and hands it to me, telling me to call him tonight to make plans.

In the elevator, Saffron's silence is concerning. Tension emanates from her body, and I know it's because of Jack's date invitation. If history is any indication, I'm sure Saffron will try to stifle my happiness with her thinly veiled insults or make-work projects. I press the button for the fifth floor, deciding to escape captivity with her by visiting Casper in the editing suite.

"You're going to editing?" Saffron asks.

"Yup," I say.

"I'll join you," she says with a smile that doesn't seem very happy.

"Great," I lie.

"So, how do you know that Jack guy?" Saffron asks.

"From here," I say.

"He works at Canopy?"

"No." The elevator doors part and we walk down the hall together.

"Where does he work?" Saffron asks. I look down at Jack's business card, which is still in my hand. There's his name, phone number, and AOL email address. There is no mention of any business on this business card.

"In the building," I say, and now I'm struck with the fact that I've made a date with someone I know absolutely nothing about.

"Yes, but where?"

"I actually don't know," I say.

"You don't know? Will this be a first date?"

"Yes," I say. My pulse races a little. I've never been on a date with someone I truly didn't know. I've never been on a blind date. My boyfriends have always started off as friends. What if Jack is a pervert? He could be a stalker. I've never run into anyone in this building as often as I've run into Jack.

"First date and he's taking you to a premiere?"

"Yep." Oh, shut up, Saffron. I know that judgmental tone.

"Well, Charity, you must have done something to really impress him."

I quicken my pace.

"You know, there are a lot of creeps in LA. Maybe you should call me every so often while you're on your date. You know, just to be safe. You should probably give me his phone number, too. Just in case."

I stop walking and turn to face Saffron. Is this genuine concern, or is she fucking with me?

She reaches out to me and places her hand on my shoulder. "It's fine. I'm sure he's not a creep. You're Charity Trickett. Things always go your way. Your decapitated head is not going to end up in the trunk of his car."

CHAPTER 9
IMPULSIVE

I have no idea what to wear to a movie premiere. I try on everything in my closet, and nothing works. So, I call for backup and have the two coolest people in Hollywood styling me via telephone.

"What movie is it?" Blake asks. He and Daniel are shooting an action film in Japan, which is a bummer. It's getting lonely in LA, and I wish they were here.

"I don't know," I say.

"Where is it?" Daniel asks.

"I don't know."

"Ugh, Charity," Daniel says with a hint of exasperation. "The kind of movie and the location of the premiere dictate the outfit. A premiere at Sundance is casual. Cannes is black tie. A kid's movie, casual. Big studio drama that could win an Oscar, dressy."

"Okay. Okay. I get it. I should have asked. But he's going to be here any minute."

"Do you have a kimono?" Blake asks.

"A kimono?" I ask. Did I hear him right?

"Dude," Daniel says. "Not helping."

"If she wears it open? With leather pants?" Blake says.

"Oh. Shwing!" Daniel says, impersonating *Wayne's World*.

Blake laughs, "Shwing!"

"You guys, focus. What about a black halter dress?"

"How dressy is it? You don't want to look like a try-hard," Blake says.

"It's just a plain black cotton Lycra dress," I say. "I can do a jean jacket over top."

"Perfect," Blake says.

"And wear the heels with the straps that you say are uncomfortable. They're sexy as hell," Daniel says.

"You guys are the best. Thanks!" I say.

"Have fun!" they say in unison.

"I'll send you a kimono. Email me your address," Blake says. And with that, they're gone.

I'm tying up my strappy heels when there's a knock on the door. As I survey my apartment, panic hits me. It's a disaster. On my kitchen table, aka the desk where I've been writing, are a heap of papers, a couple of dirty teacups, and a half-eaten sandwich. Clothes are scattered on my unmade bed and floor—the remnants of tonight's fashion crisis—and if you peek into my bathroom, which you can from the front door, you will easily see my hair dryer and makeup scattered all over the counter and my wet towel on the floor. Jack can't see this mess. He's a meticulous kind of guy; I have seen him perfectly match the color of his tie to his socks.

I grab my clutch and open the door a crack. "Hello," I say while squeezing through the opening.

"Hi. This is your apartment," Jack says, craning his neck for a peek inside.

"Watch out. I'm looking after a friend's cat. He's a runner," I lie, locking the door behind me.

We approach Jack's seemingly just-off-the-lot BMW, and I can't help but notice how out of place it looks parked under a broken streetlight in front of my decrepit apartment building. My spidey senses kick in. Jack, as a package, is the kind of perfect that borders on psychotic. His casual look, much like his work look, is pieced together with *GQ* precision. His T-shirt looks ironed, and its hem grazes the waistline of his jeans at just the right spot so that the brass *H* of his Hermès belt buckle plays peekaboo. His hair is slick and his nails look manicured. I take note of his car's large trunk, big enough for a body or two.

Jack places a hand lightly on my back, guiding me toward the passenger-side door that he opens for me. *He opened the car door for me! Relax, Charity. When was the last time you had a guy open a car door for you? Duke certainly never did. Your anxiety is Saffron infiltrating your thoughts.*

I nestle into the smell of new BMW leather and focus on the positive. I am on a date with a guy who is nice and well put together, and he's taking me to my first movie premiere. I can't help but smile.

Jack slides into the driver's seat and turns to me. "Excited?" he asks.

"Very," I say.

"I am, too," he says, giving my leg a light squeeze. He's cute. Jack starts the engine, and my foot hits something on the floor. I bend over to see what it is. "Oh, you can toss that in the back," Jack says. I pick it up. It's a photo album or scrapbook. On the front cover, in gold marker, it reads, *Jack 1994/95.* "Or you can take a look at it if you want," he says casually as he pulls onto the road.

I open the scrapbook, and there's a picture of Jack with Samuel L. Jackson. On the next page, there's a picture of Jack with Bruce Willis.

"Bruce is a cool guy," Jack says.

"That's nice." Oh my God. I'm holding a fan book. Each page is filled with pictures of Jack next to various celebrities. In some, there are other people in the picture with Jack and the celebrity. But the consistent element is Jack smiling enthusiastically while the celebrity smiles politely, literally grinning and bearing it.

My internal alarm goes off. Jack's not a serial killer—he's a superfan. I continue flipping through. There is a picture of Christian Slater eating dinner in a restaurant with Jack standing over him, smiling. There's a picture of Jack smiling like a child as Drew Barrymore pushes a grocery cart at Bristol Farms. What have I gotten myself into?

"So, Jack, you never told me what you do for a living," I say, hopeful that he's a talent manager and his clients put together this odd scrapbook for him.

"I'm an accountant," he says.

"Oh. Are these your clients?"

"What? No. I wish."

Ring the alarm. I know the kind of fan Jack is. I have seen it before. He's the kind of person who doesn't respect social norms when it comes to celebrities. He will interrupt their dinners for a photo op. He will approach them while they are on their cell phones, interrupting their conversation. He takes liberties with celebrities that he would never take with a typical stranger just to get a photograph with them.

I can't go to a film premiere with a superfan. This is a networking opportunity. What if he embarrasses me in front of someone I want to work with? Should I fake sick? Maybe I can use that imaginary cat in my apartment somehow.

I'm wracking my brain about possible ways to get out of this date, but Jack and his incredible stories about various celebrities are distracting me. He describes meeting Tom Hanks at a roadside taco shack. They spent a half hour eating tacos and talking about film. He somehow ended up bowling with Lars from Metallica and won, which Lars didn't like. His anecdotes fill the car with entertainment. He's a phenomenal fan—in a good way, with a true appreciation for Hollywood. He tells me about all the movie premieres he's been to and which ones were the best. He goes to so many that he must legitimately be in the industry. Maybe his accounting firm specializes in film financing or something. So of course, the stars aren't his clients— the producers are. I'm sure this is fine. Right?

Jack and I ride the elevator from the underground parking lot to the movie theater. He pulls a camera out of his pocket, and I panic.

"Would it be okay with you if we don't take any pictures tonight? As an assistant, it's kind of frowned upon," I say.

"Really? Okay. I already have a pic of me with Vivy Parker anyway," he says. Vivy Parker? He doesn't mean . . . he can't mean . . .

The elevator doors open and we are hit with the sound of an amped-up crowd whose decibel level hovers just under the thumping music. When we step off the elevator, I crane my neck skyward toward a larger-than-life poster of the stunning Vivy Parker, leaning against a giant weeping willow. I know that poster. I know that poster because I saw mock-ups in the Canopy marketing department weeks ago. This is a Canopy Studios movie premiere! Is this a good thing or a bad thing?

We approach the crowd, and each person tries to move closer to the barricade that separates them from the red carpet. Photographers are yelling, their cameras clicking and flashing like mad. The night sky is cut by two perfect beams rhythmically crisscrossing each other. This is quintessential Hollywood. It's a dream. The elevator doors close behind us, and all my trepidations about attending this premiere with this man are left in that metal box.

Jack drapes a lanyard around my neck. "Follow my lead," he says, looking into my eyes with a glimmer of excitement. He takes my hand and leads me into the crowd, moving people aside to make a path for us in a way that's both impressive and rude. We reach a queue tape at the end of the red carpet, beside the theater entrance. Jack unhooks the queue tape, leading me through the barricade like he owns the place, his arm curved around my waist. I look behind us, toward the red carpet. I know it's not my place to walk it, but I'd be a liar if I said I wasn't disappointed that I didn't set one foot on it.

We walk toward a small line of people waiting to be inspected by security. Jack expertly drives us past them. "Shit. I was supposed to meet Bill ten minutes ago. Hope I didn't miss him," he says gruffly.

What is he talking about? Who is Bill?

"Sir. Ma'am." A security guard stops us.

"Hey, man," Jack says, quickly flashing his lanyard while trying to move past the him. An oversized arm blocks our way.

"It's backward," says the security guard.

"Thanks, man," Jack says.

"Sir. I need to see the front of your ticket."

Jack looks down and sees his mistake. "My bad." He turns the lanyard around.

"That's not for this movie." The security guard does not look pleased.

I look down. Yes, it's a Canopy Studios lanyard, but it's from a premiere that happened last year.

"What? Charity," Jack says, pissed off. Is he bringing me into this? "I'm ten minutes late meeting Bill because you got caught up at work, and now you fuck up the tickets? What's everyone going to say if you don't show up to your own movie premiere?" Oh, God. He is bringing me deep into this. Jack is getting louder, and I'm afraid that the little scene he's making will soon become substantial. "Don't you have your Canopy ID card on you or anything?"

I watch, disbelieving as Jack grabs my clutch and opens it. I snatch it back and dig out my ID card. I show it to the security guard, who regards my credentials with expertise.

"I hope this is good enough, man. We don't have time to go all the way back to Century City," Jack says, shaking his head in frustration.

"Go on, guys," the security guard says. I'm shocked when he wishes us a good night.

We walk quickly toward the crowd of people standing around the entrance to one of the theaters. "Good job," Jack whispers into my ear.

I circle my fingers around his wrist and draw him closer to me. "Just to clarify, we snuck in?" I ask.

A smile stretches across his face. "Yes," Jack answers, impressed with himself.

But then he stops walking, almost stunned into motionless. I follow his gaze and see Vivy Parker and her heartthrob boyfriend, Alexander, posing for the paparazzi. Vivy says "Thank you" and smiles politely as she moves away from the cameras. Once in the privacy of the crowd, Alexander takes his hand off the small of Vivy's back. She floats away from him and he from her.

"This way," Jack says. I follow him into the movie theater because although I probably shouldn't be here, this is the most interesting date I have ever been on.

The after-party is in a giant tent that sits in a parking lot across the street from the movie theater. Stepping inside, you could forget that the structure is temporary. There is carpet underfoot and bars are set up throughout. People cluster around pedestal tables or lounge on the colorful modular sofas scattered about. A stage with a purple velvet curtain waits to come alive and crystal chandeliers shine from above, making the party picture-perfect for invited paparazzi and magazine photographers.

I hear my name, and I'm only slightly surprised to see Kai. Earlier, in the darkness of the movie theater, I'd spotted him sitting a few rows in front of me and slightly to the right. Even when I was focused on the movie screen, Kai's silhouette was in my periphery. I would catch myself daydreaming about our morning together in Venice. What had we looked like to the strangers around us? Me with a messy bun and him with a wrinkled T-shirt, sharing breakfast. We could have looked like a couple who strolled over to the coffee shop from our beach bungalow after having slept in late. We could have looked like we'd shared a hundred breakfasts. In the darkness of the theater, I watched Kai and fantasized. What I would have given to be next to him in that theater—to have our knees inches from each other's, to play with the short hairs at the nape of his neck.

I was sure that once the credits crawled and the lights came on, Kai would feel my eyes on him. I was certain he would turn in my direction. But he didn't. He streamed out of the theater with everyone else, and my heart sank a little.

"What are you doing here?" Kai asks me now. What am I doing here? Of course, people from Canopy are going to wonder why the new assistant is attending a premiere for a movie she didn't work on. I had the duration of the film, ample time, to create a logical answer to this logical question. But instead I'd been daydreaming about Kai. Now here he is in front of me and I'm stammering like an idiot.

"I . . . I . . . I . . ." I don't know what to say. He smiles at me. He looks happy to see me. I'll keep my explanation short and sweet. "I'm somebody's guest," I say.

"Really. Who?"

With a lump in my throat, I search the room and see Jack edging dangerously close to Vivy Parker. He meets my eyes, and I wave, prompting him to elbow his way through the crowd toward me. "See that guy pushing people out of his way? That's my date." I look at Kai. He's trying to hide a smile, with little success.

When Jack arrives, he's a ball of excitement. "Hey, babe," he says. I will ignore Jack calling me *babe*.

"Jack, this is Kai. We work together."

"Hey, man. So, is it true that Boyz II Men are playing tonight?" Jack asks. I look to Kai.

"I don't think so," Kai says. "They're not attached to the picture."

"Aw. Too bad. That would have been rad," says Jack.

"You like Boyz II Men?" Kai asks.

"The most beautiful lyricists ever," Jack says. Then he looks at me with smoldering eyes and sings, "Girl relax, let's go slow."

What the fuck? Is he serenading me?

"I ain't got nowhere to go."

I glance at Kai, who smiles so enthusiastically that I kind of want to smack him. I look back at Jack, whose eyes burrow into mine.

"I'm gonna concentrate on you / Girl are you ready? / It's gonna be a long night."

Jack has now drawn the attention of a small crowd. I want to find a hole and bury myself in it.

"Throw your clothes / On the floor."

"Wow, Jack." I cut him off.

He beams, confident that he has just swept me off my feet. "I took voice lessons. Want a drink?" Jack asks.

"Yes, please. Some bubbles?" I say.

"Sure thing. Kai?"

"I'll take a beer," Kai says.

Jack lightly slaps my ass before he sets off for the drinks. I jump a little at this unexpected spanking, a reaction that Jack is oblivious to as he's already pushing his way through the crowd to get to the bar. I look up at Kai. His eyes are wrinkled at the corners, pushed up by his wide smile.

"A singer and a spanker," Kai says.

"It's hard to find that combination in a man," I say.

"Really?"

"Yeah, I lucked out."

"Is Jack from Vancouver?"

"No, I met him here."

"And already smacking ass."

"As I said, I'm super lucky."

"What did he do on the movie?" For a millisecond, I think about lying. But I'm pretty sure Kai knows everyone on the movie because he actually worked on it. I have to come clean.

"I don't believe Jack had anything to do with making the movie. We snuck in."

"You snuck in?"

"I did. I never thought my first movie premiere would be something that I would sneak into, but Jack wanted to make our first date special. So . . ."

"Are you serious?"

"I am. This might be another example of my poor judgment when it comes to men." Kai lets out a laugh that delights me, so I continue joking around. "He might not be *the* one. But I'm torn because I'm a sucker for Boyz II Men."

"He could be the next Bobby Brown," Kai says, and we laugh a proper laugh. When it dissipates, we lock eyes. In that instant, I am certain that I could love this man. I'm also certain this is not what Kai is thinking right now. No logical person has a handful of encounters with another person and thinks they're in love. Not that I'm *in* love. I simply have a feeling that I could fall in love with Kai and spend the rest of my life with him. In the silence of our post-laughter, this realization shrouds me in insecurity. I'm insecure about my feelings, about being here, about my candidness. "I should leave before I get busted," I say.

"Busted? Are you kidding? You can't leave. Saul's going to love this." Kai grabs my hand and pulls me into the crowd in search of Saul.

When we find him, his wife, Elaine, is in the middle of telling a story. She's a natural. It makes me wonder if she was an actress back in her day. "You see? It's a fake," Elaine says, handing me one of her rings.

"No way!" I say, holding the diamonds up to the light.

"No, the jewels are real. It's not a real Cartier. A gift from this guy for our tenth wedding anniversary." She wags her finger at Saul, who nods his head in an admission of guilt. "Five years after the love of my life placed this ring on my finger, a diamond falls out."

"Uh-oh," I say.

"Uh-oh is right," Elaine says. "I take it into Cartier. The man working there says, 'Sorry, madame, but this is not our piece.' 'Well, it is five years old,' I say, thinking that he may not recognize it. 'I realize, madame, but this piece is not Cartier,' the man says. I was shocked. Then he pulls out the same ring from the jewelry case and shows me.

'You see, madame, this is how the word *Cartier* should appear on the ring.'" Elaine turns the ring over in my hand and points to the word *Cartier* etched into the gold. "This is not the Cartier font." Then she points to another ring on her hand. "This is the Cartier font. See? My husband got me a fake!" She wags her finger at Saul again, and we all laugh. "I spent five years waving that ring in everybody's face. Thinking I was a fancy wife to a hotshot movie producer."

"What the fuck?" I hear loudly behind me. The conversation screeches to a halt. All eyes focus on Jack. He holds three drinks and is fuming. Uh-oh. I thought that Jack's abrupt attitude with the security guard was an act to get in here. Now I'm worried that this is the real Jack, someone who is crass and doesn't care enough not to show it.

"Jack," I say. "There you are. Let me introduce you."

"Where the fuck have you been? I go to get you and your friend drinks, and you disappear," Jack says.

"Sorry, bud. Totally my fault," Kai says. "I dragged her away to meet some people."

"Jack," I say. "This is Saul and his wife, Elaine. Saul was a producer on the film."

"Hey, man," Jack says to Saul. I can tell Saul already dislikes him.

"Hey, man," Saul says, imitating Jack's rudeness.

Jack hands Kai and me our drinks, and I pull him into our little group. Steve comes up to us, and I can tell that he's surprised to see me.

"Charity. I thought that was you," Steve says.

"She snuck in!" Saul says with pride.

"For real?" Steve says.

"In my defense, I didn't know we were sneaking in until we were right in the middle of sneaking in. And I didn't know it was a Canopy Studios premiere. But this is a memorable first date. Thank you, Jack," I say.

"Do you do this often, Jack? Sneak into parties?" Elaine asks, tapping Jack lightly on the arm.

"I do. There's only been one party that I haven't gotten into," Jack says proudly.

"Which one was that?" Elaine asks.

"*Vanity Fair* Oscar party," Jack says.

"You tried to get into *Vanity Fair*? That's ballsy," Kai says.

"Well, I left Elton John's party and was like, if I got in there, I might as well try," Jack says like it's no big deal. Every mouth in our little circle drops, even Saul's.

"You snuck into Elton John's Oscar party?" Kai asks.

"Yeah. But it was a full-on sit-down dinner, so I had to get out of there, or else I'd be busted for sure. Great gift bag, though." The group laughs, and I'm put at ease. Sure, Jack is a little odd, and sure, he was calculated in using me to sneak into this premiere, but he's true to who he is, and once again, he's entertaining.

"You're a breath of fresh air," Elaine says, nodding in approval. Her gray curls bounce enthusiastically. "We have been to hundreds of these things, and I don't think I've ever met a self-confessed party crasher before. Party crashers, sure, but they never confess to it."

When the topic of conversation turns, I take the opportunity to speak with Jack discretely. I lean close to him and quietly say, "Jack, I'm sorry. I didn't think we ventured too far away from where we left you. I see now that it would have been harder than I thought for you to find us." I smile at him, but he doesn't seem completely pacified.

"If someone goes to the bar to get you a drink, you stay put. Anybody knows that," Jack says.

"You're right. Let's have a fun night, okay?" I say, trying to warm him up.

"Totally. Why wouldn't we have a fun night?" He slides his arm around my waist and pulls me toward him. I'm taken off guard. "All we need to do is dump these old guys," Jack says into my ear. I reflexively tilt my head away from his hot breath. I reach down and peel his hand off me, making distance between us while smiling politely.

"I work with these old guys. Give me a couple more minutes with them, then we'll do a lap of the party."

"Two minutes. Deal," Jack says, and when he checks his Rolex, I know he's serious.

I look up to Kai, who is watching me carefully. When our eyes meet, my heart warms. I don't think Kai likes Jack's hands on me any more than I do. Two minutes passes too quickly, and Jack escorts me away from the group.

We make several laps around the party. His eyes compulsively dart around the room, assessing where to stand next. He constantly pulls me into him so he can share his running commentary on everything from the outfits to the canapés. He hates her hair. She looks like a tramp. His suit is overkill. This song is played out. That guy had an affair. She got her boobs done—trust him, he knows. With every dig he makes, he looks at me with wild excitement in his eyes. I'm on guard and stop drinking. Jack touches me more often and more intimately as the night progresses, his hand inching either from my waist to my bottom or from my waist to my breasts. I have to slip out of his embrace time and time again.

The lights dim almost to black and a spotlight appears, illuminating a single microphone on the stage. The crowd becomes quiet as a twentysomething guy with a guitar approaches the light. He closes his eyes and draws in a breath, then sings sweetly in a cappella. He strums his guitar, mesmerizing the audience, but the moment is ruined for me as Jack's hands begin moving up and down my arms, slowly rubbing me. I shrug my shoulders and step away, but people have gathered around us and we are squeezed together more than I'm comfortable with. I feel Jack leaning down to me, and his cheek rubs against mine. The smell of his cologne is too strong.

Then, to my disgust, I feel his lips move against my cheek as he talks. "This guy is going to be fucking big. Trust me."

I move away as much as the crowd will let me. Suddenly the stage lights up, exposing a full band. The drummer and bass guitarist pound out a strong backbeat, and the bodies around us move to the music. From behind, Jack wraps his arm around my stomach, pulling me into him. I can feel him gyrating against me. This is intolerable.

"I have to pee," I yell over the music. "I'll be right back." Jack nods, and I slip through the crowd for my escape.

I come out of my bathroom stall and find *the* Vivy Parker leaning one hand on the counter for support while dabbing the back of her neck with a wet towel. To give her space, I leave a sink between us while I wash my hands. We lock eyes in the mirror, and I smile at her politely, noting that her skin is flushed and her eyes look puffy under her professionally done makeup. This is a big movie, even by Vivy Parker standards, and I wonder if she may be feeling overwhelmed. She runs the cloth under the tap, her hands shaking slightly, and I can't help but ask, "Are you feeling okay?"

"It's hot in here, isn't it?" Vivy says.

"It is a little," I say, just to be agreeable. She wrings the towel out, folds it, and places it on her forehead, letting out a small sigh when the chill hits her.

I reach into my clutch and pull out a little bottle of grapefruit essential oil. I open it and deeply inhale the sweet citrus smell. Vivy looks at me, tilting her head like a puppy trying to figure something out.

"Grapefruit essence," I say. "It's supposed to energize you and clear your head. I have a situation out there with a very handsy gentleman that I need to stay alert for. Want to try?" I hand Vivy the bottle, and she sniffs it tentatively.

"That's nice," she says, bringing the bottle closer to her nose.

"Freshens you up, kind of. Doesn't it?" I say.

"Do you mind if I put some on? Maybe my wrists?" Vivy asks.

"Keep it," I say.

"No. I can't. What about the handsy guy?"

"It's your big night. You need it more than me," I say.

"Thank you," Vivy says.

I look around the party, considering my next move: find Jack on the dance floor or . . . Then I feel a hand on my arm. I cringe, thinking it's Jack, but when I turn, my body instantly relaxes because the hand belongs to the most delicious man in the room. "Hey," Kai says gently.

"Hi," I say.

"Are you okay?" He looks serious.

"Of course, I'm okay."

"Really? Because Jessica is distracting your date over there to give you a break." Kai nods toward the crowd surrounding the stage, and sure enough, Jessica is dancing beside Jack, acting like she's having a good time. She sees me and winks. I mouth, *Thank you.* Jack tries to turn around, presumably to see who Jessica is winking at. She strategically places a hand on his shoulder, and his attention is drawn back to her.

"This is a serious favor. She has no idea how awful he is," I say to Kai.

"Come with me," Kai says. He takes my hand in his and leads me away.

We seclude ourselves at the far end of the bar, at the periphery of the party where there are no more barstools and the lights are low. I take the occasional sip from his whiskey sour, which sits between us while everything around me fades away. My only focus is on Kai's finger sliding down my thigh. The first time he does this, it's so gentle that for a moment, I wonder if it was a mistake. Then it happens again, his voice never straying from casual conversation. If someone were to see us standing at the bar, they would never guess that Kai is seducing me, his hand and my thigh hidden under the counter. It's thrilling.

"How did you like the movie?" he asks.

I smile at him, unable to think of an answer.

"You didn't like it?"

"I was distracted. You were at my two o'clock," I say. A sexy smirk spreads across his face. *I am not going to hook up with a coworker*, I tell myself. *This is just innocent flirting.*

Kai's hand moves toward the bar and I think he's reaching for his cocktail, but instead, his fingers trace the line of my neck and down my shoulder. Goose bumps perk up on my arm as he continues sliding his hand toward my bicep. He talks, but I'm not listening, my mind distracted by delight as his hand drifts toward mine. He plays with my pinkie finger before reaching across the bar for his drink. I watch as the muscles on his forearms flex when he grips his whiskey glass. I move closer to him like it's second nature to share a cocktail, to stand so close. If we are technically at work right now, Kai doesn't seem to care. His hand has found its way under the hem of my skirt, and he's gently tickling the back of my thigh. I give in.

We never discuss leaving the party; we simply walk away from it together. He takes my hand in his, interlacing our fingers. Kai switches direction, and within a few steps, we are pressed together in a dark hallway. I look up at him, and instead of being inches away from his kissable lips, I'm met with his jawline pointing into the darkness. I follow his eyes and see Alexander, Vivy Parker's boyfriend, making out with a young woman I've never seen before. I'm brought back to my encounter with Vivy in the bathroom and am flooded with sympathy for her. It wasn't long ago when I was the heartbroken girl in the bathroom trying to hold it together. I instantly turn and walk back to the light of the party with Kai following.

We are steps away from leaving the premiere when Steve cuts us off. "Charity. Thank God. I need a favor," he says anxiously. When I was Steve's assistant in Vancouver, I never saw him rattled. This seems serious.

"Of course," I say.

"It has to be handled discretely," he says. I'm now shamefully aware that my panties are a little wet and the man who made them that way is standing between me and my former boss. It seems that I'm at work, and I probably should not have let my coworker slide his hand up my skirt.

"What can I do to help?" I ask.

"It's Vivy. She's been . . . well . . . she's been . . ." He looks around the room and lowers his voice. "Vivy's been in and out of the bathroom a lot tonight. We're afraid that she might be . . ."

"She's not doing drugs in the bathroom," I say, and Steve gives me a look that says he's not buying it. Kai draws in a breath to speak, and I pinch the back of his leg to stop him, hoping to keep what we saw in that dark hallway to ourselves. Vivy shouldn't have to discuss her heartache with her employers at Canopy. She's probably hiding in the bathroom until either she can compose herself or the night ends, a tactic I know all too well.

"How do you know?" Steve asks.

"Can you trust me?" I ask.

"Will you go in and get her?" Steve asks.

What?! I was steps away from a super-hot make-out session and now I'm knee-deep in the most awkward task.

"Me? I don't even know her," I say.

Steve's look is grave, and he's more serious than I've ever seen him. "She may not be doing drugs in the bathroom. Fine. I believe you. But that doesn't change the optics. Look at the press."

I turn and see a group of men, maybe about a dozen. They are positioned outside the ladies' room, cameras aimed at the bathroom door. I think back to the fragile young lady shaking in the bathroom and wonder if she's still holding it together. If she isn't—if she's crying in the bathroom and comes out a mess—every style and entertainment magazine will publicize it and profit off her broken heart. I have to help her.

I've been in a bathroom stall for a while, waiting for Vivy Parker to come out of her stall, running possible opening lines in my head. *Excuse me. Can you spare a tampon?* Then what? She gives me a tampon and that's it. *Hey, Vivy, I was sent in here by the Canopy execs because they think you're doing cocaine in the bathroom.* Too crass? Vivy blows her nose, then gulps in air, obviously crying. She's never coming out of the stall. I have to go to her.

I unlock my stall door loudly, hoping to give Vivy some time to compose herself. As I walk toward her stall, she goes silent. "Vivy?" I say. "Vivy?" I tap gently on her stall door.

"Who is it?" she says, trying to hide her sobs.

"I'm Charity. I gave you that grapefruit essence."

"Oh, yeah. Well, I'm in the bathroom right now," Vivy says through her stuffy nose.

"I'm sorry. I'm a fan . . . in a good way. Although two chance meetings in the bathroom in one night may tell a different story. Um, I work for Canopy." Silence. I wait. "Sorry. I shouldn't have said that I work for the studio. That's not the reason I'm interrupting you. I don't know how to start this conversation. You're being very patient with me, by the way. In fact, I think you're handling yourself really well. It wasn't long ago when I was that girl crying in the bathroom because my boyfriend cheated on me. Except I didn't have *Us Weekly* and *People Magazine* waiting outside the bathroom door to take my picture."

"What do you want?" Vivy asks in exhaustion. She must think I'm a crazy nutjob. How do I get her to understand that I'm an ally?

"My boyfriend and I were together for two years. Late one night, I went to his apartment to surprise him. I stripped down to my underwear and practically crawled into bed with them. That's how I found out he was cheating on me. And she's gorgeous. Like, Cindy Crawford gorgeous. And I'm a little short and disproportionate. And Duke, he's so hot and athletic, and she was in a lace thong. I mean, who sleeps in a lace thong? Well, you're Vivy Parker. You might sleep in a lace thong. I'm not making a character judgment based on anyone's sleepwear. What I'm trying to say is that when you get cheated on, it kind of crushes your self-esteem and your heart. It's a real double whammy, isn't it?"

I wait for her to chime in. Nothing, so I go on. "Earlier in the bathroom, you seemed so sad and alone. Then I saw Alexander with that other girl and put two and two together. When it happened to me, I had my best friend to help me through it. And I know I'm a stranger, but I am here if you need anything. Oh, and don't worry, I think I'm the only one who saw Alexander and that girl. They were kind of hiding."

I stop talking, hoping that Vivy will say something. She doesn't.

"I'll leave," I say. "Sorry to bug you. But, you know, this is one of those scenarios where I really didn't know what to do. I mean, if you knew someone was crying in the bathroom, you'd check to see if they're alright, wouldn't you? I don't know. It's like when a bird smashes into a window. You debate, right? Do you try and help the bird? Do you leave the bird? What's more humane?"

I wait. "Well, I hope you feel better," I say.

Even though I've failed Steve, this is so incredibly embarrassing that I'm dying to leave this bathroom. Then it dawns on me that Vivy is probably dying to leave this bathroom. "Hey. Do you want me to help you get out of here? Like out of the premiere? Right now? I think I can help you get out of here."

The stall door opens and there stands Vivy, a wounded bird.

"You're heartbroken," I say, and with those words, Vivy's tears fall hard.

"He . . . he . . ." She can't get the words out. She's really crying.

She's crying like someone just died. She's crying like a two-year-old who just lost a balloon. The bathroom door flies open and three ladies come in laughing. Vivy pulls me into her stall, shutting the door behind me. A panicked finger hovers over her pursed lips, pleading with me to be quiet. I nod and place a finger over my lips, too, willing her to trust me. Her eyes pool with mascara. Her face is blotchy and red, and my heart rate skyrockets at the thought of the paparazzi seeing her like this. Bad for the movie, bad for Vivy, bad, bad, bad.

"Is your makeup artist here?" I whisper.

"Is it really bad?" Vivy pulls a compact out of her purse. Her eyes become wide. "Fuck," she whispers.

"It's not that bad," I whisper to her.

She shoots me an angry look. "I thought you were here to help," she whispers back.

"You're right. It's bad."

The bathroom empties, and Vivy gets to work. "Hold this," she says, handing me the compact. I hold it up so that she can see herself in the mirror. She opens her purse, revealing the kind of kit typical for a professional makeup artist. She rips a makeup removal pad from the packaging and wipes the mascara clean. Then she drips Visine into her eyes with precision. She conceals, colors, and powders all while venting in a manic concoction of furiousness and sadness. "I . . . I . . . He . . . I mean . . . It's unreal. She's at . . . It's my movie premiere. My heart is broken, and now he's—" She looks to me for support. What do I say? It's Vivy Parker. She's young and beautiful, a millionaire, a star. What advice could I possibly give her?

"Don't cry, Vivy," I say.

She points her eyeliner at me, eyes filled with sadness, and says, "He cheats on me, then he brings her to my premiere. I let him pose with me on the red carpet." That's when it dawns on me that it doesn't matter how beautiful, famous, or rich you are; getting cheated on is awful, and Vivy needs the same thing everyone needs in this scenario. So, I'm going to talk shit about her ex.

"He's an asshole," I say.

"Total asshole," Vivy says.

"Why would he even come to this if you're broken up?"

Vivy scoffs and returns to the mirror, lining and smudging her eyes with expertise. "Photo op, contracts, bullshit. You know, as I became more successful, he became more shitty to me." She tosses the pencil into her bag and assesses her work, tilting her face this way and that.

"Insecurity breeds contempt. You look hot, by the way," I tell her.

"You don't think he's going to make a thing of this tonight, do you? Like, steal my press?"

"Would he do that?"

"He's done things to me that I never thought he would do." She falls quiet, and I can tell the wheels in her head are spinning. "Are you really okay with helping me to get out of here?"

"Of course. I'm your girl." With that, Vivy throws her arms around me.

"Thank you," she says. Then she takes my hand and leads me out of the stall, out of the bathroom, and into an onslaught of popping cameras.

Vivy glides in front of the paparazzi and pauses to smile. Her name is being called from every direction, over and over. She angles her body in various poses: smiling and then pouting, one hand on her hip, both hands on hips, giving the photographers plenty to play with.

"Charity," Vivy calls to me with an outstretched arm. I walk over to her and she takes my hand, pulling me into her. She delicately cups the side of my face and leans into me. I'm shocked when I realize we're so close I can feel her breath on my mouth. I'm motionless as her other hand slides down my body to rest on my hip.

The clicking of the cameras overtakes the music, filling the room like cicadas on a summer day. Then Vivy Parker, one of the hottest young stars in Hollywood, kisses me on the lips and I kiss her back, letting her lips linger. When she pulls away, she moves her mouth to my ear and, over the madly clicking cameras, says, "Want to grab some sushi?"

Vivy and I breeze toward the exit in perfect choreography, hand in hand. The paparazzi scrambling to gather their equipment and make haste. We make it to the double doors before they catch up to us, screaming and clicking in a frenzy. We push the doors open and they follow us onto the red carpet. We quicken our pace.

"Who's this, Vivy?" the pap screams.

"Girls, this way!"

"What's your name, darling?"

"How long have you two been together?"

"What's your name, sweetheart?"

Lights flash around us. I can't see where I'm going. Vivy's grip on my hand tightens. Just when I think the mob will close in on us, security guards from the party swoop in, pushing the paparazzi back, allowing us to escape into Vivy's waiting limo. The door slams behind us. I hear the automatic locks click and then cameras bang against the car, flashes blasting through the tinted windows.

"Drive!" Vivy yells to the chauffeur and the car begins to roll, slowly at first as hands hit the hood of the car and the trunk, then faster, leaving the paparazzi behind.

"But wait . . . you guys didn't kiss?" Vivy asks, her face glowing in the light of the outdoor fire. We are cozied up with blankets and pillows on a plush outdoor couch, eating sushi and downing sake. I'm convinced that every meal should be eaten this way, alfresco in front of a fire pit with the scent of the ocean washing over Malibu.

"No. I was saving myself for you," I say.

"I'm sorry," Vivy says.

"You did me a favor," I say. "I can't hook up with Kai. He's the golden boy of Canopy Studios. What would people think?"

Vivy takes a sip of her sake. "Do you really care what people think?"

"Yes. I just moved here. This job is a big opportunity," I say.

Vivy sighs and stares into the fire in contemplation. "People told me about Alexander, you know," she says. "They said I should do something about him, but I didn't care what they thought. I was sure that the affair was just a blip. But then it wasn't showing any signs of ending, so I had to call him out on it."

"How long did you live with him knowing that he was cheating on you?"

"Oh, he hasn't moved out yet. All his shit's still here. He's probably staying at her place and buying new clothes. Meanwhile, I wander around this big house all by myself, and there are memories of him everywhere. I still have pictures of us hanging on the wall." She sits back and looks so small as she pulls her knees to her chest. A shadow of sadness casts over her face when she looks toward her home, glowing softly in the moonlight. "He brought her here. While I was shooting on location. They sat under these stars on this couch that my mom picked out. They cooked in my kitchen together. They slept in my bed. This is my house. Alexander moved in with me."

"Maybe it's time to tell him to get his shit," I say.

"I should throw his shit on the street."

"How about you and I go through this house right now and we throw all of his stuff into bags and your driver can take them over to Alexander tonight."

"He's gone home."

"What about someone from your security team?"

"I don't have a security team," Vivy says, wincing at her stupidity.

"Wait. You live here alone? Without security?" This is worrying. Vivy is the kind of celebrity you would envision having a psycho fan. The kind of fan who would have made a papier-mâché shrine to Vivy

Parker using hundreds of tabloid magazine pictures of her. The kind of fan who would sit outside her house . . . maybe even try to come into her house. "Vivy. You need security," I say.

"I know. With Alexander here, I didn't have it. But I will get security."

"Like, tonight," I say firmly.

"Ugh. You sound like my manager. Who is also Alexander's manager. Who is not letting us announce the breakup until after opening weekend because of a fucking Guess campaign."

"What are you talking about?"

"Zander and I shot a campaign for Guess to be launched at the same time as the film. You know, cross-promotion."

I picture it: the sexy Hollywood couple in acid-washed jeans, photographed in black and white with a backdrop of cacti, probably a vintage sports car thrown in there. "Anyway, our manager doesn't want the breakup to affect Guess or the movie, so we're pretending to be together."

"Oh. So that's why you let him come tonight. Did you know *she* was coming?"

"I knew when I got in the limo and *she* was sitting next to him."

"And where was your manager tonight?"

"He was there," she says sadly.

At that moment, all the glitter and sparkle that I associate with stardom goes gray. Wealth, fame, talent, and beauty don't exempt you from being treated poorly. As I listen to Vivy talk about the awkward limo ride and how she tried not to cry all night until she finally broke down in the bathroom, I am struck by how young and alone she is. So tonight, I will be her friend and support her. I will get drunk with her, I will shit talk Alexander with her, I will make her laugh and feel valued, and I will distract her from heartbreak. Just like Pup did for me not so long ago. Tomorrow we will focus on cleaning up her life. She needs a new manager and probably a new agent. She definitely needs someone she can depend on in times like these. But the security guard thing can't wait.

"What do you think about me calling Blake Anthony and seeing if he has security in LA that we can get in tonight?" I ask Vivy.

"Shut up! You know Blake Anthony?" she says, perking up.

"I do. And he would hate this scenario."

"Call him. Can I say hi?"

CHAPTER 10
SHE'S ALL THAT

As an assistant, I typically arrive at work before my boss does to get a jump on the day with zero distractions. I print out my boss's schedule, update the call list, and address any pressing issues, getting the basics out of the way while most people are still commuting to work. Now that I'm working with Saffron, this tactic is not a bonus like it was in the past—it's a necessity since her mission in life is to waste my time. She sends me on two to three coffee runs a day, keeping her sharp enough to endlessly micromanage me. Multiple times a day, she asks me pointless questions that interrupt my thoughts. She has me proofread her emails and triple-check my work that's already perfect. She sends me all over LA, running errands that bare little to no significance to the production. My productivity is taking a serious hit.

When I bitched to Vivy about Saffron while I was fueled with sake after the premiere, that smart little starlet had some sage advice. She told me I need to put an end to the bitter competition between us and instead harness positive energy. Vivy said positivity is so powerfully contagious that even someone as sour as Saffron will be susceptible to it. So that's my plan on this Monday morning. I am determined to bring positivity to my working relationship with Saffron. I will convince her that if we work together as a team, we can help Casper and advance both our careers.

I take a sip of my chai tea as I log on to the Canopy server to check my email. A shocking number of emails appears in my inbox. What the heck? I have emails from *The National Enquirer, Us Weekly, Entertainment Weekly, Star Magazine, OK Magazine,* and *Life & Style.* There are emails from people I've never heard of and people who I haven't heard from in ages. What is going on?

The office door unlocks and in flies Saffron. She throws a magazine at me, and it lands face up on my desk. I look down at it, and there I am, lips puckered, eyes closed, pressed against one of Hollywood's most prized rising stars on the cover of *Us Weekly.* The caption reads *Pucker Up, Ms. Parker* in hot pink.

"What the fuck, Charity?" Saffron screeches. She stands in front of my desk, red-faced, hands on her hips.

I pick up the magazine and shake my head. I'm on the cover of *Us Weekly,* and I look *hot!* Vivy's hand is under my chin and she's tilting my mouth toward hers. Our lips are slightly open, gently pressing together. Our breasts graze one another's. There's a slight arch in my bare back. My strappy heels are spicy. I have never looked this sexy in my life, and this look is on the cover of the most widely circulated tabloid magazine in North America.

"Charity." Saffron's stern voice brings me back to her. "Why are you making out with Vivy Parker, and why is it on the cover of *Us Weekly*?"

"Well," I croak. "It was just silly, really." How do I explain this? Should I explain this? I mean, isn't this my personal life? Besides, I don't want to betray Vivy's trust. I hear the muffled sound of a ring-tone, and I expect Saffron to dig her cell phone out of her purse to answer it, but unfortunately, she doesn't.

"So, I guess this movie premiere that Jack took you to wasn't some low-budget suck-fest by some UCLA film undergrad," Saffron says, continuing to ignore her phone. "No, of course not. You're Charity Trickett. Charity Trickett moves to LA and goes to Canopy Studio premieres and ends up on the cover of magazines." I have no idea what to say. I just pray that Saffron will answer her phone and let me off the hook. "Where is that ringing coming from?" she yells.

"Um. Your cell phone?" I say quietly, hoping that pointing out the obvious doesn't make her angrier. She pulls her Nokia from her back pocket and holds it up.

"Not me," she says.

"Oh! It's *my* cell phone," I realize. I bend over to get my purse from under my desk.

"You got a cell phone?" Saffron asks, astonished.

"Yeah. Vivy said I was living in the Stone Age not having one, especially in LA. And this way I don't need to get a home phone, so . . ." I pull the ringing phone out of my purse and hold it up to Saffron. "Cool, right?"

"Are you going to answer it?"

"Oh." I flip open the phone. "Hello?"

"Hey, it's Viv." I can't help but smile when I hear her voice.

"Hey. How ya doing?" I ask her.

"Awesome. Did you see the magazines?" Vivy asks.

"I saw *Us Weekly.* There's more?"

"Yeah. You know, if you're on the cover of one, you're typically in them all," she says. "You cool with this?"

"Yeah. Of course." I look up, and Saffron is burning holes in me with her eyes. "Um, can you hold on a sec?"

"Sure," Vivy says. I put my hand over the little speaker and look up at Saffron.

"It's Vivy. Do you mind? I won't be long." If Saffron was a cartoon character, her face would be red and steam would be coming out of her ears. She turns on her heels and stomps into her office.

"Sorry about that," I tell Vivy.

"No worries! I'm just making sure you're alright with this," she says.

I look at the long list of emails on my computer screen and feel my heart beating faster. "I'm fine!" I say a little too enthusiastically.

Am I equipped to deal with this? I never wanted the spotlight. I'm a writer.

"Phew!" Vivy says. "My publicist called this morning, and we talked through everything. She thinks this is good press."

Oh God. Does Vivy want me to do more of this? "That's good," I say. "I think I'm getting interview requests and stuff."

"Really? Who have you heard from?"

"Um. I have emails from, like . . ." I scan the long list in my inbox. "Everybody."

"Oh," Vivy says.

"Is it okay if I ignore them?" I ask.

"Yes! That's the right thing to do. That's why I'm calling. I was hoping that we could just not respond to anything. Let this run its course. It'll fizzle out in a week, I'm sure."

"Perfect," I say, feeling a weight lift.

"Now, can I ask for another favor?"

"Jeez, Vivy," I joke. "Haven't I done enough?"

"You have. Thankyouthankyouthankyou. It's just that I love the security guy you got for me. Can you please tell Blake Anthony thank you for recommending him?"

"Oh, Vivy, that's such good news. Of course I'll tell Blake."

"And maybe, when you talk to him, could you see if he has thoughts on a new team for me?" Vivy asks somewhat sheepishly.

"Like, new management?" I ask.

"And agent," she says.

I'm so happy she's taking control of her life that I fist pump the air. "Do you want me to get him to call you? He's super nice, and I know he'd love to help."

"Um, career advice from the biggest star in Hollywood? Charity Trickett, you are the best. Want to come over tonight? I'll cook you dinner."

"Aw! That sounds nice. I'll be at your place around seven. Got to run." I hang up the phone and take a deep breath, steadying myself as I head into Saffron's office.

"Hey," I say, taking a seat across the desk from her.

"That was Vivy Parker?" Saffron asks.

"Well. Yeah," I say.

Saffron makes a face like she smells rotting fish. "Charity," she says, but before she can say anything else, the office phone rings again. She motions toward the phone sitting on her desk, allowing me to answer it. I lean over and pick up the receiver.

"Casper Murray's office," I say. It's Jessica. Saffron is staring at me, and I don't want this to seem like a personal call, especially since my call with Vivy seemed to upset her, so I keep it short and sweet. "Aw, you're welcome. No. Thank you . . . Okay. Bye."

"Who was that?" Saffron asks impatiently.

"Jessica, Steve's assistant."

"What did she want?"

"To thank me."

Saffron rolls her eyes. "Thank you for what?"

"I left a little bouquet of flowers on her desk to thank her for helping me out on Friday night," I say.

"She was at the premiere, too? Were, like, all the assistants there?" I don't know how to answer this question. Is it rhetorical? Is she seriously pissed off at me? "Why are assistants at the Vivy Parker premiere and not the director of Canopy Studios' biggest blockbuster ever?"

Saffron looks at me expectantly. Oh! She does want me to answer. Hmm. What I want to say is that I don't control the guest list for Canopy Studio events. But instead I choose a lamer approach.

"Maybe because the assistants worked on the movie?" I say.

"You didn't work on the movie," Saffron says.

"I was with Jack."

"How the hell did you and Vivy Parker end up kissing, and why is it everywhere?" Saffron's whole attitude is derisive, and I've had enough.

Whatever problem she has with me being on the cover of a magazine is her problem, not mine.

"I'm starting to feel a little interrogated here," I say, standing up from my chair.

"I'm not interrogating," she says, her voice now smooth and calm. "It's girl talk. I mean, I'm sure the premiere was rad. I want to hear about it." A forced smile spreads over her face. It's painful for both of us.

There is no way in hell I'm going to tell Saffron on Friday night I was introduced to Dom Pérignon and made friends with Vivy Parker. I'm not going to share that Vivy and I chatted until two o'clock in the morning and I ended up sleeping in her guest room. I'm certainly not going to tell her that flirting with Kai, the soon-to-be Canopy executive, will inspire sexual fantasies in me for the rest of my life. If she learns anything about my weekend, I'm dead. So I stand here, not knowing what to say, wishing for the phone to ring again.

"Let's chat over lunch," Saffron says. "Want to go to the food court with me?"

"I can't. Thanks, though," I say.

"Already have plans?"

"I'm having lunch with Steve."

Saffron rolls her eyes, and I get the hell out of her office.

Steve is under the shade of a large yellow sun umbrella at the hostess stand when I join him. "I'm trying to get us a table outside, but it doesn't look like they have any," he says.

"Oh, that's too bad," I say.

"Excuse me," he says to the hostess. She raises her head from the reservation book in front of her. "My friend's here now." The hostess looks at me and stalls. Her eyes grow wide as if she recognizes me. Do I know her?

"Would you like inside or out?" she asks.

"Outside. I asked you for outside." Steve sounds annoyed.

"Right this way." She grabs two menus, and we follow her through the restaurant to the patio. I'm sure it's just my imagination, but it seems like I'm drawing attention. Two twentysomething ladies look my way and whisper to each other. A guy at the bar nods in my direction, and his friend follows his eyes until they land on me.

We step outside to a patio that is a garden oasis in Century City. Tops of high-rises are visible through the palm trees that shade the patio and dull the sound of traffic. We slide into our seats, and Steve orders immediately. "I'll have the seafood Cobb and an iced tea," he says. "You know what you want?"

I don't know what I want. I've never been to this restaurant. I can't afford this restaurant.

"I'll do the same," I say, not wanting to waste his time.

"I'll get your server," the hostess says with a smile.

"Or you can tell her our order and save me some time." Is he pissed off?

"Um, sure," the hostess says before she leaves, sounding a little frazzled.

"How did it happen?" Steve asks.

I stare at him blankly. "How did what happen?"

"*Vi-vy*," he enunciates.

"Are you mad?" I ask, surprised.

"I don't know if I should be mad. The press didn't seem to hurt. Opening weekend was great." He shakes his head. "The situation could have been handled more discreetly."

My mouth is wide open in disbelief.

"I mean, it's a stunt, right? To get her out of the premiere in a hurry. Why?"

"She spoke to me in confidence, Steve." He leans back in his chair, staring at me, and it's clear I'm going to have to explain everything. "Look, you're going to be fine with what I'm going to tell you. But it's about Vivy's personal life. She's so hurt and embarrassed. I'd hate for her to think that I would betray her," I say.

"That's fine," he says. "I'll keep it between us."

"She was diverting attention."

"Diverting attention from what?"

"Alexander."

"What about him?" Steve asks.

"Exactly. Why isn't anyone asking about him? All they care about is that Vivy is in love with a woman." I tell him about Vivy's heartbreak. I tell him how Alexander brought his new girlfriend to the premiere. I tell him about the Guess campaign and the advice from Vivy's manager. Steve knows about the campaign because it was a deal that Canopy made with Guess to help promote the film. I keep the personal details to myself but tell him enough to placate him.

"She's brilliant," he says as he pops a prawn into his mouth. "This kiss is everywhere."

"Tell me if I'm being completely self-involved, but I think people recognize me," I say.

"You're turning heads, that's for sure. Live it up. We wouldn't have the best seat on the patio if it wasn't for your newfound fame."

"Oh, please," I say, a little uncomfortable.

"How long are you two going to keep this up?" he asks.

"We're not keeping anything up."

"Keeping silent is the same as keeping up the facade. Did you sign anything?"

"You mean, like a contract or NDA?"

"Yeah."

"No."

"Don't sign anything. How are you handling the press?"

"I'm ignoring it."

"Smart," Steve says. "Good job."

With those words, I can finally relax and enjoy my thirty-dollar salad, which Steve will bill to Canopy Studios.

When I come back from lunch, Casper is in his office and Saffron is in hers. "Charity Trickett!" Casper greets me with his arms stretched wide and a smile on his face. "The coolest assistant in LA. People are calling me to talk about my assistant. Aren't people supposed to be calling my assistant to talk about me?"

"Yeah, right," I say, embarrassed.

"Trickett, you're killing this Hollywood thing. Do you think you could get Vivy Parker to do my next film?" he asks. Saffron emerges from her office and leans against her doorframe.

"Seriously?" I say.

"Seriously," he says.

"To be honest, I already talked to her about *Break Room*, and she's interested."

"That's my girl," he says, sounding proud and intrigued.

"Now, I know that casting this role is serious business—I mean, it's challenging, dramatic material, and the woman she's based on is a leader in the feminist movement."

"Hold on. You're pitching Vivy for the lead?"

"I know. It's completely against her type. But when I told her about the story she pitched herself to me, hard." Casper looks skeptical, so I pitch him, like Vivy pitched me. "She's motivated. Artistically she wants a dramatic role. Career wise, she wants it to be her next project. It's only a matter of time before she ages out of these romantic comedies she's known for. And she wants to produce."

"Produce?" Casper says, his face spreading into a small smile, and I think he's enjoying the curveball I've thrown him.

"She has a long history with Canopy, and she thinks, given the amount of money she's made for them, they'll support her producing one of their movies."

"Vivy Parker starring in *Break Room*," Casper says, trying it on for size.

"She's willing to read for it, too."

Casper looks at me, stunned. "Really?" This is clutch. Actresses of Vivy's status get offered parts. They don't audition. But Vivy understands the risk Casper would be taking, so she's asking to audition.

"It could generate a ton of buzz. People will expect that role to be played by someone who's been nominated for an Academy Award," I say.

"You really like the script, huh?" He smiles at me.

I look Casper dead in the eye, confident about what I'm selling him. "It's outstanding," I say. "How much do you know about the woman it's based on?"

Casper gives me a sheepish look.

"Fair enough," I say without judgment. "I didn't know who she was, either, so I did some research on her. Let me put something together for you so you can see how important she is."

"Okay. Thanks."

"And Vivy?" I ask, holding my breath.

"Send her the script," he says.

"Will do." It takes a serious amount of self-discipline to not leap in the air in celebration. "While I'm at it, I can put a list together of actors that I think would be good for other roles. I could work on packaging it for you."

"Sweet. Do that," he says, walking to the door. "I'm going to editing."

"Wait!" Saffron says, her pitch higher than normal. "What about *Snow*?"

"You work on *Snow*. Charity, you work on *Break Room*. See where we get."

Casper leaves, and I'm sure he doesn't realize that by putting Saffron and me in direct competition, this office could turn into a war zone. I look over to Saffron. She's still in the doorway of her office, arms folded across her body, mouth in a hard line, staring at me. To think, I started off the day with the hopes of having a more harmonious working relationship with her. That's clearly not going to happen.

"I have to pee," I say, using my standard line to get out of awkward situations with Saffron.

I push the bathroom door open while speed-dialing Kai. "Charity Trickett," he says, answering the phone. I feel a pleasant warmth through my body. He already has my phone number memorized! I barely have it memorized.

"Hi," I say.

"How are you?" He's probably sitting at his desk, so why am I picturing him shirtless?

"I'm good. I'm really good," I say.

"Where are you? It sounds like you're in a cave."

"I'm in the bathroom," I say.

"You want me to meet you in the bathroom? What floor are you on?"

I smile. "No, I don't want you to meet me in the bathroom. I just wanted to have a private conversation," I say.

"Are we going to talk dirty? Should I go in a bathroom too?"

"No. Yuck. Kai." I can't help but laugh.

"So, no dirty talk?"

"I have a question," I say.

"The answer is yes," he jumps in.

"Kai!"

"It's not yes? No. My answer is no. No dirty talk. Yes to meeting you in the bathroom."

I can't help it. He's adorable. I catch a glimpse of myself in the mirror, and I am beaming. My cheeks are flushed and my smile is so wide that almost every tooth is exposed.

"Can I please ask you a work-related question?"

"Shoot," Kai says.

"Does Canopy have any actors in mind for *Break Room*?"

"No. Just directors. Casper going to pitch?"

"He's thinking about it. Do they have anything specific that they want for the film?"

"They were thinking about shooting in Georgia for the tax credits, but I don't think they're married to it. It's early days. Casper can have a lot of leeway with his pitch."

The bathroom door swings open, and I'm not surprised that it's Saffron.

"Thanks, Dad. I appreciate it," I say.

"Daddy? Thought you weren't into talking dirty, little girl," Kai says.

"Say hi to Mom for me," I say. I hang up and slide my phone into my back pocket as Saffron goes into a stall.

CHAPTER 11
O.P.P.

I descend four flights of stairs, leaving my car in its designated spot on the roof of the Canopy Studios parking lot, about as far away from the building as one can get, giving me plenty of time to catch up with Pup before work. "The paparazzi were outside her house last night?" Pup asks.

"Vivy says that never happens," I say.

"How long have they been there?"

"There were a handful on Saturday, she said, but I guess that magazine sales have been going through the roof since our picture came out, so last night there were about ten or so."

"Is that a lot? Like *Princess Diana* a lot?"

"I don't know. But she's putting gates up at her house and she's taking off to Montana to be with her parents."

"It's that crazy?" Pup asks.

"I don't know if it's so crazy or maybe she thinks this will die down faster if she gets out of town."

"So, what happened when you went over there? Did the pap see you?"

"Nope. She had someone from her security team pick me up at Zuma Beach, and they smuggled me into the house."

"Oh my God. This is, like, Blake Anthony–level stealth," Pup says.

"Totally. Huge SUV, tinted windows. I ducked down in the back seat. We drove right past the paparazzi and straight into her garage."

I push the door open and step outside into the breezeway leading to the Canopy high-rise. It's my favorite part of the morning. The warm California sun bathes the walkway, planters overflow with the most gorgeous creations, and the Canopy Studios leopard looks down from the top floor of the building, welcoming me to his film studio. "Charity!" a man says, approaching me with a warm smile.

"Yes," I say. He raises a camera and snaps about a dozen pictures of me in quick succession.

"How long have you been sleeping with Vivy Parker?" he asks.

"Pup, I've got to go." I slip my phone into my back pocket and quicken my pace. Then another man appears.

"Charity, Alexander is calling you a homewrecker," he says.

"He what?" I say, stopping. Three more men approach, and now I have four cameras in my face. That's when I remember Vivy's instructions: *They'll say anything to get the kind of reaction that sells magazines. Never engage with the paparazzi.*

"Excuse me," I say, walking toward the building. The questions fly at me from everywhere.

"How long have you ladies been together?" *Click, click, click.*

"Charity, is this love?"

"How do you feel about being a homewrecker?" The men stand in my way, walking slowly backward, allowing me to move only inches at a time. I start to get really nervous as the building is still about a hundred feet away.

"Excuse me," I say more forcefully, trying to push us along. "Have you always been gay?" *Click, click, click.*

"Don't you think you should apologize to Alexander?"

"Think Vivy will ever do another romantic comedy now that she's out of the closet?"

"Gay porn maybe," I hear a gruff voice snarl, and they all laugh. *Click, click, click.* The men tower over me, blocking my path and making it impossible to see how much further I need to go before getting to the building. My heart pounds and my ears ring. My stomach flips and I'm suddenly nauseous.

"That's enough," I hear from an authoritative voice. Then I see Canopy security guards, and the paparazzi make more room for me. "You're on Canopy property, fellas. You know better." Two guards appear at my side and guide me to the building as the paps snap their last pictures. The door opens in front of me, and I'm finally in the safety of the building, the clicking gone.

I bend over and put my hands on my knees, trying to catch my breath. I'm shocked—I almost feel like crying. How can a group of men just attack me like that?

Someone holds a glass of water in front of me. "Here. Have a sip." I look up. A tall man in a Canopy security-guard uniform regards me with kindness in his eyes, and I know I'm safe. "It'll help," he says, extending the glass closer to me. I take it and have a sip. "Drink it all," he says. I tip the glass back, and when the water hits my mouth again, I realize I'm parched and gulp it all down.

"Thank you," I say, handing the glass back to him.

"You're welcome. Now, who are you? And why didn't anyone tell me there was going to be paparazzi at my building this morning?"

"Sorry. I'm Charity Trickett, an assistant at Canopy."

The security guard bursts into laughter. "An assistant? Well, I've never seen so much attention for an assistant."

"They think I'm Vivy Parker's girlfriend," I say.

"Ah. Well, you need a new parking spot, Charity Trickett, assistant at Canopy Studios," he says. "From now on, you will park directly below this building and you will ride that elevator right up to the lobby with all the other celebrities." He points to the set of eight elevators in the building's main lobby. "No more paparazzi. Now, give me your keys. I'll have your car moved."

I dig out my keys and hand them over. "I'm so sorry. I had no idea this would happen," I say.

"Aw. We're used to it," he says with a smile.

"Alright. Thank you," I say, walking away.

"Oh, and Charity," he calls after me. I turn. "I know you're not planning on leaving this building without letting me know."

I nod to him, knowing that I will eat lunch at my desk today.

Kai and I sit thigh-brushingly close on a banquette. We're surrounded by bullpen people who have become so boisterous with cocktails that we are drawing attention from the rest of the bar. "So, Charity, what you're saying is that you are not in a romantic relationship with Vivy Parker?" Kai says, pointing his whiskey sour at me.

"I am not," I answer with a smile.

"Then why don't you tell the press?" Jessica asks, and I don't know what to say without getting serious and dampening the mood.

"It sounds like the audience wants to hear from Vivy's new lover," another assistant says.

"I think it's time for a commercial break," I say. This is met with moans of disappointment.

"A gift from the house," a waiter says to me. I look up. He's holding champagne flutes and a bottle of Moët & Chandon.

"A gift?" I ask.

"Yes," he says, flashing me a movie-star smile. "Shall I open it?"

"Open it!" Jessica says. The waiter works the cork, and I mentally add this moment to the list of positive things that have occurred since the kiss. Free coffee at my normal coffee shop, lunches with people from the bullpen, a lecture from Blake about navigating fame, Casper's fancy Hollywood friends shooting the breeze with me when they call the office. Once I even got asked for my autograph.

I raise my champagne flute in the air. "To my girlfriend," I say.

"To Vivy," the bullpen chimes in. Kai slides his hand behind me and leans in as we clink glasses.

The night goes on, and the more time I spend with Kai, the more I find myself swimming against the current of my natural instincts. Instinctively, I want to wrap my arm around his broad shoulders and bury my nose in his neck. I want to nibble on that appealing ear and graze my thumb over the fine stubble along his jawline. When I see him at the bar with his back to me, I envision myself sliding my hand up the back of his T-shirt to feel his warm skin. It's a natural instinct that, under any other circumstance, I would follow. But I'm the new girl here and I don't want to be misbranded. One minute I'm making out with one of Hollywood's biggest starlets, landing me press that most people in Hollywood would pay a fortune for, and then I'm getting it on with Canopy Studios' golden boy. Nobody wants to be perceived as the girl who sleeps her way to the top.

I think Kai is being a little careful, too. Neither of us have told anyone that before coming here, we had a glass of wine on my fire escape. In the ambience of the alley, we exchanged stories from our days as on-set production assistants. As a PA, Kai once shot a music video in the desert for twenty straight hours, which left him sun-stroked and blistered. That same year, I was a PA on the side of a ski mountain, soaked and frozen from wet snow, while the crew shot a snowboarding monkey. As PAs, we changed garbage cans and directed traffic. We sat in parking lots all day babysitting cars and trailers. We yelled, *Rolling!* about ten thousand times.

"When I got the job with Saul, I thought that I was made," Kai said. "The man's a legend, right? I work on the films with the biggest budgets. I learned a ton. I'm still learning. But there's something special about a little indie film. It's intimate. Small crew, two people having a real conversation that just happens to get caught on tape. You know?"

"No explosions. No car chases," I said.

"No squibs." He chuckled.

"Yeah. I haven't worked on one of those in a while, either." I sighed.

When our wine glasses emptied, we made our way through the apartment, where Kai stopped at the corkboard that rests on my dining table. It's where I've outlined a film I'm writing.

"A comedy?" he asked.

"Not really."

"Don't see any car crashes or explosions."

"Not one." My phone rang and I checked the number. "Oh, it's my friend Daniel, Blake Anthony's assistant. I think he just got back into town."

"Daniel? Never met him, but I've heard the reviews. Invite him out tonight. You'll make girls from the bullpen happy," Kai said. Then I enjoyed the view of Kai's behind while he made his way to the bathroom. When he closed the bathroom door, I answered my phone.

"Are you home?" I asked, not bothering with *Hello*.

"I'm finally home. What are you doing?" Daniel said.

"I'm just about to walk out the door." I tiptoed farther away from the bathroom and whispered, "With a really cute guy, actually."

"Oh girl, do tell," Daniel teased.

"It's nothing—or it can't be anything. I work with him."

"Well, thanks for the riveting story, Trickett."

"We're going to the Opium Den with a bunch of Canopy assistants tonight. Wanna come?"

"The bullpen girls? Fuck yeah."

Kai appeared at my side as I hung up the phone, standing a little closer than he normally does. He looked down at me and smiled softly, sending a flutter in my tummy. As we left the apartment, he took my hand in his, and a small part of me glowed as I imagined that he was already mine, even though he shouldn't be.

Now, in the bar with this group, Kai and I are colleagues who are getting playfully flirtatious over drinks. He leans into me and says something, but all I can focus on is his breath tickling that tender spot on my neck. Just then, I hear a voice.

"Am I interrupting?"

I glance over and see Daniel looking at me with a filthy smirk.

"I missed you," I say as I snuggle into his hug. We turn to Kai, and Daniel drapes a protective arm over my shoulder.

"And you are?" Daniel asks pointedly. Kai stands up with a pleasant smile and extends a hand toward Daniel.

"Hey, man. I'm Kai. Saul's assistant." Daniel keeps one arm wrapped around me while he shakes Kai's hand. I glance sideways, feeling eyes on me. Sure enough, a couple of girls from the bullpen are drooling over Daniel.

"Pleasure to meet you, man. Hope you're taking good care of my girl here," Daniel says. I slap Daniel on the stomach and shrug his arm off me.

"Take your macho act someplace else, please, Daniel. It's not welcome here," I say.

"Aw, now, kitten. Don't get so feisty," Daniel says, knowing he's annoying me.

"Why don't you make yourself useful and go get me a drink," I say to him.

We hear a boisterous game of Ping-Pong in the adjoining room, and we are instantly drawn to it. Jessica and Beth, the assistant to Canopy's CEO, stand together at one end of the Ping-Pong table. They throw their arms into the air and groan in disappointment. At the other end of the table, a leggy brunette claps her paddle against the palm of her hand, applauding herself and smiling. Jessica says something, and the leggy brunette tosses back her head in laughter, shaking her hips in a little dance.

"Who the fuck is that?" Daniel asks, jaw on the floor.

"That's Albana. You'll like her," Kai says.

"Hot girls having fun," Daniel says, pulling me by the sleeve. I toss Kai an apologetic smile, but he seems perfectly at ease. I get the feeling that not much ruffles Kai's feathers.

We move to the Ping-Pong table, and the girls' competitive banter becomes audible. Jessica is searching the floor for the ball. "I can't find it," she says.

"Maybe you have bad eyes? Maybe that's why you keep missing the ball," Albana teases.

"Well, when I find it, it's coming straight for your head," Jessica threatens.

"My head is a small target for someone with your skills." Albana smirks.

Kai moves to the corner and picks up the missing ball. "Whose serve?" he asks.

"Me," Albana says.

"Two against one? This hardly seems fair," he says, tossing her the ball.

"It's not fair—you're right. I should recruit someone to join me. Someone who is bad at this game so we can even things out," Albana says playfully. Daniel and I move simultaneously to volunteer, but I manage to speak over him.

"I'm horrible at Ping-Pong. Can I be on your team?" I ask, pushing Daniel back and away from Albana.

"Perfect," Albana says.

I fumble and hit the ball into the net. Albana bows her head toward Jessica and Beth and says, "Looks like the teams are even."

An hour later, Daniel and I are collapsed on the couch together. Across from us, Jessica and Beth share slugs from a bottle of water while Albana wipes a hint of beer foam off her lips with her pinkie finger. Daniel licks his lips in a subconscious reaction, falling under Albana's spell.

"Earth to Daniel," I say, pinching his arm lightly.

"What?" he says, still staring at Albana.

"Feel like paying me any attention tonight?" I say.

"Sorry," he says, turning to me. "Oh, hey, I can't believe you fucking wrote that!"

"What?"

"That script. That fucking script! *This Family Thing.*"

"Oh. I forgot I gave that to you," I say.

"Oh, you forgot," Daniel says, mocking me.

"It was a long time ago."

"Yeah. Sorry I didn't read it sooner. Everyone and their dog wants to give me their fucking script."

"You didn't have to read it."

"Like I'm not going to read your script, Trickett."

"Thank you. And I want your notes," I say.

"Here's my biggest note: That script is fucking gold."

"Really?"

"Not gold like it's gonna break box-office records or anything. Gold like—even though the chances of this film making real money are slim, it should still be made because it's awesome." I laugh at Daniel's refreshing honesty.

Daniel leans forward, engaging Beth, Albana, and Jessica. "So, how do y'all know each other?" he asks.

"Well, they are the little piggies in the pigpen," Albana says, pointing to Beth and Jessica.

"It's the bullpen. We are bulls," Jessica corrects her.

"You little piggies are so particular. 'No, Albana, we're bulls. We're not pigs.'"

"Wait. Are you Albana Rugova?" Daniel asks.

"I am." She seems genuinely happy to be recognized.

"I'm a fan," Daniel says.

"I love fans!" she beams, clapping her hands in delight.

"Sorry. What am I missing? Why do you have fans?" I ask.

"I made a movie about a little girl who is all alone and makes friends with a hawk. They have a beautiful bond," she says.

"Wait. I know this movie. It's . . . um . . . it's . . . um, it's . . . the little girl's name. *Penny*. You made *Penny*?"

"Yes. I directed that movie."

"Shut up. I love that movie!" I say.

"Thank you," Albana says.

Daniel moves to sit closer to Albana. His demeanor changes from relaxed and flirtatious to serious and engaged as he draws her into conversation. My phone vibrates. I pull it out from my clutch and look at the screen. Kai's calling me. I look up and find him standing in the warm hue of the bar with his back to his friends—a crooked smile on that gorgeous face and a phone pressed against his ear.

"Hello," I say, answering my phone, looking right at him.

"Should we call it a night?" Kai asks.

I look at him and smile, shaking my head but wanting to say yes.

"Okay. One more drink, then we go back to my place."

"I can't."

"I have an extra toothbrush."

"Oh, no girl wants to hear that you stock up on toothbrushes," I tease.

"It's not for girls. I was just at the dentist. No cavities. We should celebrate."

"Charity," Daniel says, reaching out to me with his strong arm.

"One sec," I say to Daniel, and I turn away from him slightly for a little privacy. It's not that I don't want to go home with Kai. The thought is thrilling. But after my kiss with Vivy, I feel like I'm walking a thin line at Canopy with my professionalism.

"It's just that with everyone here, I don't think it's a good idea," I say. From across the bar, I see Kai's shoulders slump.

"I get it," he says. I'm relieved that he does, but I'm also completely bummed that I'm not tucked under his arm. I watch as Kai says good-bye to his friends and walks into the shadows toward the exit.

I turn back to the group. Jessica and Beth are putting on their jackets. "We're going home," Jessica says.

"I have one more in me," Albana says, drawing Daniel and me in.

"I'll join," I say.

"I'm down," Daniel says.

Somewhere between tequila and vodka, Daniel has Albana Rugova, a Sundance Film Festival darling, thinking I'm the next up-and-coming writer, and she agrees to read *This Family Thing*. This is huge! But wait. There are some changes I want to make to the script before I give it to her. I don't know if it's ready for someone of this caliber.

Then Albana looks at me and winks. "If your writing is like your Ping-Pong, I will be very amused."

Daniel and I slide into a cab, feeling that end-of-night mixture of exhaustion and exhilaration. "I'm your manager, Trickett. It's perfect. You'll produce your first movie and I'll have my first client. We'll pop each other's professional cherries."

"You really think my script is good enough for Albana?" I ask.

"Fuck yeah, I do. And hey, I discovered you. I am going to manage the shit out of your career."

"Hell yes," I say, high-fiving him.

"We are transitioning, Trickett. You and me together. Goodbye, assisting."

CHAPTER 12
CRUEL INTENTIONS

More times than often, sitting at my desk is like sitting in a drizzle of bone-chilling rain. Then, out of nowhere, a hurricane comes through and blasts me. I'm always ill-prepared for the storm, and the damage takes time to repair. This is the erratic ecosystem of Saffron. With Casper around, Saffron is lovely and the sun shines. When Casper leaves for editing or a meeting, the cold rain returns. She's like the sister who is nice to you in front of Mom and Dad but pins your head under the water when they're not looking during bath time. Not to drown you, just to show you who's boss.

And a boss she is, one who is ruthless and underhanded. She stands uncomfortably close as she assesses my work at a nitpick level, and she has no shame in taking up obscene amounts of my time. I did the math. Her coffee runs alone take up nine to thirteen percent of my day, depending on the number of times she sends me out. Saffron even has me doing her work on *Snow*. I photocopy countless scripts and hand deliver them to various agents and managers around Los Angeles. On top of that, she sends me on meaningless errands at any moment, throwing a wrench in my day. Yesterday, for instance, I wasted three hours because Saffron had me drive a cut of a scene to the composer, who lives in Laguna. When I arrived at his house, he was surprised to see me; he'd told Saffron not to deliver it since he would be at the studio tomorrow. Lesson learned: Call ahead.

I thought that once the buzz of my kiss with Vivy died down, Saffron's jealousy would fade and she would ease up, but it's been over three weeks since my picture has appeared in any magazine and she's still riding me so hard that I have to work on *Break Room* in my spare time. Lucky for me, I have an amazing new partner—Vivy Parker. Together we are working on a pitch for Casper that will prove to him, and hopefully Canopy Studios, that Vivy can take on a serious acting role with award-winning potential while also producing, leading the film both on-screen and off. If I bring Vivy onto the movie and she attracts more talent, then we are both in excellent positions to be Canopy producers, she executive, me associate.

Last night we cozied up on her overstuffed couch, popped popcorn, and watched back-to-back episodes of an Australian TV show that I discovered at an indie video store in Westlake. On the cover of the dusty DVD box set was a picture of the show's star, Cameron Steed. There was something about his face that drew me in, so I brought it over to Vivy's and we watched the entire first season.

Cameron is a captivating actor and the kind of discovery that every producer dreams of. He's skilled, having proven himself in Australia, where he's a star, and he's unknown in North America. Most English-speaking foreign actors who want to break into Hollywood will some-times accept a good role in the US that's below their paygrade in the hopes of establishing a Hollywood career. This is why we are stoked to pitch Cameron to Casper. The role we want him for is smallish but significant. That's a tough hire. Good actors are expensive and want big roles. If we can cast Cameron, not only would we get a skilled and seasoned actor at a good price, but we could generate some serious buzz for *Break Room* by introducing him to the American public. I have to say, he'd look good on the cover of magazines.

Vivy's positivity is infectious, and for the first time in weeks, I sit at my desk and don't feel like I'm trapped under a cloud. I feel like a boss. Last night, after Vivy and I devoured the entire first season of

Cameron's Australian drama, we chatted excitedly about *Break Room* until I was too tired to drive. She put me up in her guest room, where I slept on a bed worthy of a five-star luxury hotel. This morning, Vivy laid yoga mats on her lawn, and we stretched our bodies while overlooking the Pacific Ocean. Instead of going home to change, she styled me in her designer clothes, then sent me off to work with an organic soy latte and a smoothie she made with ingredients from her garden. Now I'm a buzz of productivity. I just got off the phone with Nicole Kidman's American agent, who offered to compile a list of Australian agencies so I can start the hunt for Cameron Steed.

Watch out, Hollywood. I'm a badass boss today.

Saffron breezes in, barely looking at me. "Casper here yet?" she asks.

"Not yet," I say, watching her walk into her office. The phone rings and I have a quick chat with Dave, the editor.

"Who was that?" Saffron calls out, and I'm glad there's a wall between us so that she can't see my significant eye roll.

"Dave," I say, my badass-boss attitude seeping out of me like a tire slowly deflating. Who was I kidding? It doesn't matter what I'm wearing, how I feel, or who I'm friends with, Saffron's the real boss. A boss whose managerial style is directly influenced by her erratic mood. If she's in a good mood, her micromanaging is tolerable. If her mood is bad, she will interrogate me for a ridiculous amount of time to learn the smallest piece of information that bears no significance to her working day. The process sucks the life out of me, so I've developed a strategy to preemptively give Saffron every piece of information I have. It takes some time, but not nearly as much time as her interrogations.

"What did Dave want?" Saffron calls to me.

"He has to leave a little early today," I say.

"Why?" There it is. Saffron shouldn't care why Dave has to leave early. She's not his boss. She's in a bad mood and is on the path to interrogate me, so I walk directly into her office and launch my pre-emptive strike.

"Dave wants me to tell Casper he'll be leaving the office at four thirty today but can work earlier or later tomorrow if need be. He has to pick up his daughter at day care because his wife is stuck at work. Did you know that she's a lawyer? I'll call Casper and let him know. He's at the physiotherapist's getting his shoulder looked at and is due in editing at ten. Do you need Casper in the office this afternoon, or should I tell him that his schedule is clear?"

Saffron squints at me. I've never seen her squint like this. Oh dear.

"Why don't you write him a memo?" she asks.

"A memo?"

"Yeah. You're so good at writing memos. Aren't you?"

Oh God. A memo. She must be mad about a memo I sent out. I can't for the life of me recollect an out-of-the-ordinary memo.

"The system upgrade," she says, crossing her thin arms.

What? She was cc'd on that memo like everyone else at Canopy.

"The system upgrade for next Thursday. You got the memo I sent," I say. Ugh. I think I sound like a suck-up.

"Pretty important information, Charity."

"Yes. There will be no editing on Thursday after three in the afternoon because they're updating the software. But things should be back to normal first thing Friday," I say. What is she mad about?

"So I read in your memo. The point is that you cc'd all the executives on that memo. You can't just send a memo to all the executives at the studio from this office without me knowing about it," she fumes.

"Understood," I say.

"From now on, if you need to send a memo to anyone above the line, I need to proofread it. Now call Casper and tell him about Dave."

"Sure thing," I say, turning to leave.

"Wait a sec!" Saffron says. "Is that a Prada blouse? This season?"

I smile with my back to Saffron, knowing my answer will annoy the shit out of her. I turn to face her, pretending to be sheepish. "It's not mine. It's Vivy's. I crashed at her place last night, and she loaned me clothes for today."

Saffron's expression could be described in so many ways that bring me joy: *bitter, resentful, jealous.*

Just then, there's a knock on the office door. When I open it, I'm surprised to see Casper's fiancée, Charlotte.

"Charity," she says, walking into the office. "How's LA treating you?"

"Good. Hey, sorry, but Casper's not here." I'm just about to explain why when Saffron emerges from her office, Kate Spade on her shoulder, sunglasses on her head, wide smile spread across her face.

"Here comes the bride," she sings.

"I'm so excited," Charlotte says, embracing Saffron like a sister.

"I can't wait to see what you've picked out for me," Saffron says.

I stand back and hope that my smile looks sincere because inside, alarms are going off as if my brain is a supersystem of computers controlling a nuclear power plant that's about to explode. What am I looking at?! Saffron and Casper's fiancée are friends? And not just friends. This is the kind of hug you give a really good friend on a special occasion.

Saffron locks eyes with me while embracing Charlotte. She can tell that I'm shocked—although there's a smile on her face, there's also a malevolent look in her eyes that says, *I win.*

When they break apart, Saffron hooks her arm through Charlotte's. "Did I tell you, Charity, that I'm Charlotte's maid of honor?"

"That's lovely," I manage to choke out.

"Anyway, we're off to look at dresses. Gone for the rest of the day," Saffron says, leading Charlotte to the door.

"Bye, Charity," Charlotte says. And they're gone. Fuck.

Jessica, Beth, and I sit in the open-air food court at the mall in Century City. Beth dishes about her boss between bites of salad. I have heard that the CEO can be tough, and by Beth's account, the gossip is true. Bellotti has a temper. He yells at her. He swears. He can be vulgar. This morning, he had Beth make a hotel reservation for him and his girlfriend. He also had Beth make a four-hour spa appointment for his wife across town that coincides with his hotel reservation. I'm shocked. Jessica, apparently used to this kind of behavior, simply rolls her eyes.

"It's just another day in the life of Bellotti." Beth sighs. She goes on to explain his many character flaws and indulgences. He chooses work dinners over his little girl's dance performances. A tailor comes to his office to fit him for custom shirts. He bailed on taking his son to sit courtside at a Lakers game in favor of taking a young actress he was trying to sign for a movie. His cars are collectively worth over a million dollars. He's type A. When his last assistant resigned, Bellotti offered to double her salary if she stayed, but she still quit. The job she had lined up next fell through, and she hasn't found another job in film or television since. It's rumored that Bellotti ruined her career.

"Hey, ladies." We look up and see Jack standing above us, holding a tray from the food court. "Can I join you hotties?"

"Jack, what did we discuss at the premiere? You cannot call us hotties." Jessica laughs while scooting over for him.

"But you *are* a bunch of hotties," Jack says, lightly nudging her with his shoulder. Beth looks annoyed, and Jack picks up on it. "I'm fucking with you," he says. "Jessica gave me the full rundown on how I'm sexually inappropriate with women, and I'm trying not to be . . . what did you call me, Jess?"

"A slimeball," Jessica reminds him.

"That's right," Jack says, nodding his head seriously. "Charity, nice to see you again. How are you this fine day?"

"I'm great, Jack. You?"

"Well, I'm having lunch with a group of intellectual ladies, and it's a beautiful day. Life's pretty rad," he says.

I can't help but laugh a little. This is a new Jack.

"Oh my God. You're the guy who snuck in at the last premiere," Beth says.

"I am *the* guy who sneaks in to *all* the premieres. You are Beth, the assistant to the bigwig."

"Good memory." Beth's phone rings, and she looks anxious when she answers. "Hello? Yes. Oh no. Can you fax me over other options? Thank you." She hangs up the phone and lets out a frustrated growl.

"What is it?" Jessica asks.

"It's the company in Cannes that owns the yacht that Bellotti likes. It's not available for the festival. Fuck."

"He takes a yacht to the festival?" I ask.

"No. He stays on a yacht during the festival because he doesn't want to be stuck in a hotel where people bug him all the time," Beth says. "He always hires the same yacht for the festival week. Costs Canopy Studios four hundred thousand dollars and it never even lifts anchor."

"Baller!" Jack says.

"It has a Michelin-star chef and staff of ten," Beth says.

Jack smacks the table, and our trays rattle. "That's fucking pimp!" he says.

"He's going to kill me," Beth says.

"Aren't there other yachts?" Jessica asks.

"Of course there are, but he's still going to be pissed. Not everyone has a Steve for a boss," Beth says.

"I miss having Steve as my boss," I say.

"You don't like your boss, either?" Beth asks.

"Well, it's stupid to complain, especially after hearing about your boss," I say.

"Come on. Spill," Beth says.

"Most days, it's small things that are inconsequential, but when you put all these small things together over time, it's a lot to handle."

"Like what?" Beth asks.

"I get blamed for everything, even stuff that I have no control over.

I'm micromanaged and questioned so much that I feel useless and insecure. The backhanded compliments are almost daily. And she wastes my time. She has me running all over LA doing errands for the movie that either aren't necessary or seem silly. Saffron is—"

"Wait," Beth interrupts. "Saffron? Who's Saffron? I thought you were assistant to the director of *Diffuser*. Casper, right?"

"I am. Saffron's the associate producer. She's been working with Casper for years. When Casper isn't around, she steps in and acts like my boss," I say.

"Oh, her. I heard she doesn't even get paid," Beth says.

"What? Is that legal?" Jessica asks.

I am dumbfounded. Not only do I have more experience than Saffron, but I'm also making more money than her. I can't wait to tell Pup.

"So, your boss basically has, like, two assistants," Jack says. "Hollywood's the fucking bomb."

"Not for assistants," Beth says. "Anyway, sounds like Saffron is a classic narcissist."

"That sucks. Sorry, Trickett," Jessica says. I don't quite know what a narcissist is, so I just try to match my expression to their grave faces.

"And next time she asks you to run an errand, call a courier," Beth says.

"I can do that?" I ask.

"Absolutely. I'll email you the courier's information." A little help from a fellow assistant just made my life a little easier and Saffron's a little more frustrating.

As I sit at my desk after lunch, the word *narcissist* runs over and over in my mind. What *is* a narcissist? I reach for my dictionary and flip through the pages. Webster's defines *narcissist* as "an extremely self-centered person who has an exaggerated sense of self-impor-tance." Hmm. Sounds like Saffron. She's in editing with Casper right now, so maybe I'll poke around the World Wide Web and see if I can find anything else.

I click on the AltaVista icon and type *narcissist* in the search box. My computer starts making that annoying dial-up noise, a mix of crackling and shrieks. I wait for the longest time, watching the door and praying that Saffron doesn't come in and bust me psychoanalyzing her.

A list of articles pops up on the screen. I click on one that was published by the American Psychological Association titled "Narcissistic Personality Disorder." There's a list of diagnostic features, including a grandiose sense of importance and inserting oneself into positions of power, even when that power isn't earned. Narcissists also lack empathy. They are typically passive-aggressive. They have little self-awareness and excel at being the victim. My jaw is on the floor. This is Saffron.

The article suggests that if you have a narcissist in your life, you should establish strong boundaries and distance yourself from the person since having a healthy relationship with them is impossible. Now, how do I distance myself from someone who works fifteen feet away from me and has inserted herself into the position of being my boss? The article suggests quitting your job if you have a narcissistic boss. If you can't quit, it suggests some coping mechanisms. I should keep my head down and not engage with the narcissist. I should also limit the narcissist's emotional impact on me by realizing that the narcissist will never change, no matter what. Seriously? My best option is to just deal with it?

The scariest thing I learn is that when threatened, the narcissist will apparently stop at nothing to ensure their own success, even if they must ruin the lives of their competition. I am screwed.

I am in the elevator holding six DVDs, each of which contains the editor's cut of *Diffuser*. It's a raw piecing together of the movie before sound is mixed in, music is laid over, color is touched up, and visual effects are added. It's the first cut of the film that Canopy executives will see—the first of many—and Casper is nervous. I asked him to deliver the cut with me, and he emphatically declined, which is silly. He has nothing to be nervous about; the film, even at this early stage, looks fantastic.

I'm eager to hear what the execs have to say—almost as eager as I am to see Kai. The anticipation of seeing him is delicious. Since that night at the bar, we've been keeping our distance, and I miss our flirty chats. When I think back to watching him leave that night, part of me regrets not going home with him, but logically I know I made the right decision. I think, *Charity, remember your original plan when it came to Kai. You will admire him from afar. That is all you are allowed to do.*

I enter the bullpen and distribute the DVDs to the assistants. I look for Kai but don't see him. That's when I spot a man in blue coveralls carrying a cappuccino machine out of the executive kitchen. I run over to him. "Hello, sir. Can I ask what you're doing there? Is the cappuccino machine broken?"

"I don't think so," he says. "They got some fancier one I got to install."

"And what are you doing with that one?" I ask.

"Garbage."

"Can I have it?"

"I guess." He plunks the machine into my arms, and I am hit, once again, with the realization that I need to lift weights to handle my coffee-delivering needs.

With my arms wrapped awkwardly around the cappuccino machine, I manage to make it down the golden executive staircase and to the elevator. The doors part and a crowd of people scurry around me, leaving the elevator before I can get in. Then I feel the weight of the cappuccino machine leave my arms and there he is: the perfect man.

"Thank you," I say.

"No problem," Kai says, backing into the elevator he just exited. The doors shut in front of us, and we are alone. I turn to him. His shirt sleeves are rolled up and his hair is a wavy mess. In short, he's stunning. He looks at the numbers above the door instead of looking at me, and my heart sinks. Did I completely blow it with him? I wanted to cool it down a little between us, sure, but if I'm honest, I still want to flirt.

"Haven't seen you in a while. How are you?" I ask.

"Good," he says, still not looking at me. I take a deep breath and catch a blissful whiff of Kai. He has a different smell than usual. I lean closer to him. It's the ocean.

"You smell like the ocean," I say, innocently breathing him in. He glances at me, and I notice a smile creep onto his face. He fights to contain it.

"I went for a swim this morning," he says. "I hope I'm not an accessory to a crime here, Trickett." There he is, Mr. Playful. *You can't be mad at me, Kai.*

"You'd be a bystander at best," I say, nudging him. He stiffens. The elevator doors open, and we walk toward my office in silence.

In my office, I clear a spot on a table so Kai can set down the cappuccino machine. "Hey, Kai," Casper says, emerging from his office with Saffron in tow. "What's up?"

"Hey, man. Just helping Charity steal this from the executive floor," Kai says, slapping hands with Casper. How does he do this? How is he so casual yet professional at the same time?

"Awesome," Casper says. "Check it out. A fancy cappuccino maker. Saffy, you're going to get a lot of use out of this thing."

"Yeah. Awesome," she says, eyeing me with venom.

"Well, I should get back to it," Kai says.

I follow Kai out of the office, struggling for something to say. His attitude toward me is so blah. Should I apologize for that night at the bar? Should I ask him if he's mad at me? "I want to—I mean—thanks. Thank you for helping me," I say.

"Sure." Kai walks away without a smile, his shoulders slumped. I feel like I made a horrible mistake.

"Kai!" I call after him, suddenly realizing something. I run down the hall. "I forgot to give this to you." He turns, and I get one more chance to see that gorgeous face. "It's the editor's cut for Saul."

His look of disappointment is crushing as he takes the DVD from me.

I wander through Steve's house picking up toys and throwing them in the wicker basket under my arm. Gabe is asleep after reading five books. I would have gone for six, but he was pretty tired. I love being in Steve and Julie's house—it's a real home with family pictures on the mantle and leftovers in the fridge. Being here makes me a little less homesick.

The front door opens, and Steve and Julie come in. She heads straight to the couch while Steve heads into the kitchen.

"Steve, can you open a bottle of red for me and Charity?" Julie hollers.

"Way ahead of you. I don't know why they can't serve better wine at those school fundraisers." Steve comes in with a bottle and three glasses, and we get cozy. Julie talks about the TV series she's producing for NBC. This could be her year at the Emmys.

"So, how's Canopy Studios, Charity?" she asks.

"Great. Casper has me working more in development, like finding his next project, so that's exciting."

"That's great," Steve says.

"I'm having trouble with one thing, though. Mind if I bounce it off you?"

"Sure," they say in unison.

"Saffron. I'm having a hard time working with her."

"Well, she's crazy," Steve says.

"You think?"

"Oh, yeah. And she's stubborn and entitled," he says.

"Wow. Tell us how you really feel, Steve," Julie says.

"I was under the impression that development was Saffron's gig with Casper," Steve says.

"You see my problem," I say.

"Well, if it means anything, I trust your opinion over Saffron's all day."

"Really?"

"Charity, you have far more experience than she does. Saffron was part of Casper's contract. He wanted to give her an AP credit. Canopy agreed, but it was understood that this is a learning opportunity for her. She's not producing anything."

"So, when she's not invited to meetings . . . ?"

"Studio doesn't want her there."

I think Steve is done talking, but I suspect there's a story here, so I keep quiet.

"Look," he says. "You've really got to know your stuff to go toe-to-toe with a Canopy exec. Saffron came into preproduction thinking she was just as valuable as a producer with decades of experience. One day she had a particularly bad idea. I mean, she had a few bad ideas, but this one was a doozy. We shut her down, but she kept pushing and pushing. She was belligerent. So, Saul let her have it. Basically told her to sit down and shut up for the rest of production."

"So that explains the giant chip on her shoulder," I say. "If Casper gets another movie with Canopy, what's the likelihood that Saffron will be welcomed back as a producer?" I ask.

"Zero to none," Steve says.

"Okay. All I need to do is make it through *Diffuser*, hope that

Casper gets another Canopy film—which he's pitching for, and hang in there."

"Cheers to that," Steve says, and we raise our glasses. As the wine hits my lips, I realize I need to up my game because Saffron is fighting for survival.

CHAPTER 13
POETIC JUSTICE

I am watering the fig tree in the office when the door swings open and Saffron breezes in, all smiles, like she's in a tampon commercial. What is she on?

"Voilà!" she says as an older couple follows her in. "This is my office! And this is my assistant, Charity. Charity, these are my parents, Jan and Bill." Uh, did Saffron just introduce me as her assistant? Bold! Really bold!

"Nice to meet you," I say pleasantly. Jan glances at me before looking over my head at the *Diffuser* poster.

"Oh. That's Blake Anthony," Jan says.

"Mom. You know who Blake Anthony is. Like, everyone knows who he is," Saffron says.

"You know me. I prefer a good book," Jan says.

"This is my office here," Saffron says. "And this one's Casper's."

"When are we having lunch, pumpkin?" Bill asks.

"We can go," Saffron says, and I see her deflate. Here she is trying to make her parents proud, and they seem less than impressed. "Any messages for me, Charity?" With this question, the sympathy I felt a second ago vanishes.

"No," I say.

"Anything going on I should know about?" she asks.

"No. In fact, you're not needed at all. You can have a long, leisurely lunch with your parents. Enjoy your visit."

Saffron studies me for a moment. *You heard me right, Saffron. Two can play passive-aggressive.*

With Saffron out with her parents and Casper consumed with editing, I have been working on *Break Room* all day without interruption, and I'm in a good mood. This is what I am currently typing into the office calendar: *Casper, Vivy Parker, Charity mtg re: Break Room.*

"Okay, it's in the calendar," I say to Vivy over the phone.

"Cool," she says.

"Now for even more exciting news," I say.

"I don't know how much more I can handle."

"Well, hold on to your hat because I found Australia's own Cameron Steed."

"Aaaaand?" Vivy says.

"And . . . he's not exactly thrilled at the prospect of working with you."

"Shut up!"

"He's insanely excited."

"He's interested?"

"His name is officially on the list for the role of Bryce."

"Yes!" Vivy screams.

The office door flies open, and Saffron strides in looking like a woman on a mission. "I've got to go," I say to Vivy. Just as I hang up the phone, Saffron slaps a Post-it note on my desk containing a list of about a dozen agents. *Oh, Saffron, you think you're going to waste my time?* I smile at her, waiting for my instructions, knowing that my day just got better.

"I need you to photocopy *Snow* scripts and hand deliver them to these agents today."

"No problem. I'll take care of it," I say, reaching for the phone.

"What are you doing?" Saffron says. "Charity, I need you to stop what you're doing and deliver the scripts now." Saffron is pissed. I hang up the phone, stand, and pull a Bankers Box out from under my desk. It's filled with *Snow* scripts that are already in envelopes. I place the box on my desk.

"Don't worry, Saffron. I already have them printed and in envelopes. I just need to call a courier to have them delivered. Canopy will cover the cost," I say.

She shakes her head like she's frazzled. "This isn't for *Diffuser*. You'll have to go."

"It's for Casper. Don't worry—Bellotti's assistant told me that I should be using a courier for this kind of thing." I reach for the phone and dial the number for the courier as Saffron stares me down. It's not until I begin listing the addresses for delivery that she goes to her office, leaving me with a task that will take me about ten minutes instead of four hours. The day keeps getting better.

The courier has come and gone, and Saffron has been bossing me around while keeping her switch firmly in place at Super Bitch mode. The *Variety* magazine on the coffee table was last week's issue and the printer paper was in danger of running out. Not out, but in danger of running out. She required a green highlighter and had me search office supply rooms throughout the building until I found one. There was, of course, the ever-important afternoon coffee, which has morphed into me becoming her personal barista with the cappuccino machine I pilfered from the execs. And because of behavior typically reserved for children, Saffron's huge calendar was ripped almost in half, so I had to make her a new one.

I am cleaning up Casper's call list, my final task before leaving today, when I feel Saffron walk toward my desk. I don't look up for fear of engaging with her, and she throws a pile of receipts in front of me. "I need you to submit these for petty cash," she says. One receipt falls to the ground. "Be careful, will you? I'm not going to be out of pocket for a Canopy expense."

My head is under my desk in search of the fallen receipt when Saffron starts at me again. "I need you to schedule a conference call tomorrow for Casper, Mary, and the Pozner team. Charity, you should write this down."

I retrieve the receipt and place it with the others. I reach for my pen, knocking over my water bottle, but my quick reflexes catch it before water douses my keyboard.

"Charity! Be careful. Two o'clock for the phone call," Saffron says.

It's the end of the day and I'm at the end of my rope. "Saffron," I say calmly. "Can you please slow down?"

"If you can't keep up—"

"I can keep up just fine. It's the way you're talking to me. Are you cool with me?" I ask.

"Of course, Charity. You're an asset to the team. Casper loves you," she says with a hint of disdain.

"Okay. I'll reach out to Mary and the Pozner team."

"Thank you," she says, and although her tone is more tolerable, I know she's not done. "I notice that we are dangerously low on sunflower seeds and blueberries. Charity, you know I'm a vegetarian and I need my sunflower seeds for the iron. And blueberries are a must-have in this office for the antioxidants. Run to the grocery store, will you?"

"Sure," I say.

"Write it down, Charity. We wouldn't want you to forget," she says, rolling her eyes. Saffron lifts her Kate Spade off my desk and leaves.

I cannot work with this woman on another film. It will surely end in homicide, and I don't know if I'm smart enough to get away with murder.

★ ★ ★

The editing suite has been in a focused frenzy all week. Meetings were changed, messages taken, and emails put off for another day, all in the hopes of giving Dave and Casper enough space to finish the next cut of *Diffuser* on schedule. Even with this wide berth, it's still not ready for tomorrow. At eight o'clock in the evening, I poke my head into the editing suite to find Casper and Dave looking exhausted in the glow of the monitor lights, a scattering of junk food wrappers around them. I call the Mexican place on Pico Boulevard and put an order in for three tortilla soups. If they're not going to come out of that room to clear their brains, then maybe a little spice will stimulate something.

"Tortilla soup," I say, opening the door.

"That smells so good," Dave says, tapping Pause on his computer with relief. He takes a bowl out of my hands. I set another one in front of Casper, who looks truly dejected.

"Are you okay?" I ask him.

"It's this fucking scene," he says, shaking his head. I look at the screen and see the casino/strip club/nightclub with Blake's face frozen mid-sentence. "We've cut it so many ways. It just sucks." Casper sighs.

I click Play on Dave's keyboard and watch the action unfold. The scene is shot well, but Blake's and Erica's performances are awkward. I have to watch the scene two more times to take it all in. Then I hit Pause, realizing it doesn't matter how it's cut—the problem is the screenwriting.

"It's terrible," I say. "And you can't cut it out entirely. You need that information for the story."

"We've been at this forever," says Casper.

"I think the dialogue is the problem," I say.

"You're right," Dave says.

"Why don't we rewrite the scene?" I suggest.

Casper throws his hands in the air as if vindicated.

"Thank you!" he says. "I asked them to re-write the scene in pre-production and everyone thought I was crazy."

"Maybe we can rewrite it so that we can still use this scene with it. Have Blake and Erica do voice-overs for the whole thing. Will that look goofy?" I ask.

"It's done," Dave says. "It's not ideal. What you get is a whole scene of reaction shots or watching the actor's back while they talk. People see through it, but it's done."

"What if we rewrite the scene and you use it to talk Canopy into a reshoot?" I say. "Casper, you and I can do the voice-overs for Blake and Erica. You show them both versions—this one because it's already shot and the one we write."

"Rewrite the scene how?" Casper asks.

"Give me a few minutes," I say, grabbing a pad of paper off the desk. I take a seat on the couch and start scribbling dialogue while Casper and Dave eat their soup.

I put my head down and write, reworking the scene and talking through the changes with Casper. Eventually, I come up with something that works. We record the dialogue, him as Blake and me as Erica, and it's actually good.

Casper and I sink deep into the couch, watching Dave masterfully cut and splice, finding pieces of film that work with the new dialogue to show the value and intention of the changes we've made.

While Dave cuts, I switch gears with Casper. "Want to talk *Break Room* while we wait for Dave?" I say.

"Sure," Casper says.

"Here's the latest submission spreadsheet." I hand him a piece of paper with a list of actors who we have reached out to for the film. "The response so far has been positive."

Casper smiles and shakes his head. "Your friend Vivy sure knows a lot of good actors," he says.

"People want to work with her. She'll make a good producer, too. She's been researching like mad, diving really deep."

"Cool," Casper says. "This could be a stellar cast."

"Yeah, it's an impressive list," I agree.

"Hey, you think they got any beer in the executive kitchen?" Casper asks.

"Now you're talking," Dave says.

"I'll go on a mission," I say.

When I get to the executive floor, there is one desk light still on in the bullpen. Kai. He looks tired. Handsome and tired. He looks up when he hears my footsteps.

"It's late," I say, perching myself on the edge of his desk.

"Ugh." He runs a hand through his mess of brown hair. "Numbers. Going over numbers."

"That sucks. I hate numbers. I'm more of a letters girl," I say. He nods, and I get the feeling that he wants me to leave. I need to fix this. I can't have this stud mad at me.

"We haven't chatted in a while. All good?" I ask.

"Yeah. I'm good," Kai says.

"Good. Are we good?" I ask, feeling supremely awkward.

Kai leans back in his chair and looks at me as if he's trying to figure me out.

"I was just thinking about us," I say.

"*Us?*"

"Not like an *us* kind of us."

"What kind of *us* are you talking about?"

"Not that kind of us."

"Okay. Just so I'm clear, we're talking about us. Not *us*," he says, trying to suppress a smile.

"I feel like since the bar there's been less us," I say.

"I guess at the bar, I thought that maybe you were interested in being in a different *us*."

"What?"

"Daniel?" Kai says.

"Daniel? Gross. No! I didn't leave with you because we work together. And you're, like, this rising star here, and I don't want people thinking that I'm sleeping my way to the top. Especially because of the Vivy kiss and . . . This is a big opportunity for me. I have to be smart."

"So, we *are* talking about *us*." Kai's smirk says it all. He's adorably smug. He rolls his chair in front of me and his head hovers just above my knees. He gently places his hands on top of my legs. What is he doing? I just told him that I can't be involved with him, and now he's touching me. He's looking up at me from my legs, and I melt. "You don't need to worry about what anybody thinks, Charity." He stands up and spreads my legs apart, making space for himself to slide between them. I want to give in to him.

"*You* don't need to worry about what anybody thinks," I say. "I haven't proven myself yet."

He takes his time, searching my eyes. Then he nods and lightly taps my nose with his finger, like I'm a child. "Okay," he says. "Now, what are you doing up here so late?"

"Oh." I almost forgot that I'm on a mission. "Do you guys have any beer?"

"You have to stop stealing our shit, Charity." He pulls me up by my hands and leads me to the kitchen.

I walk down the hall with Casper's and Saffron's salads from Bristol Farms in hand and a knot in my stomach. I'm nervous. Casper, Dave, Saffron, and all the Canopy executives have been in the screening room for two hours and thirty-six minutes, and the movie is only ninety minutes long. They must be debating the merits of a reshoot. The sets are still in storage in Vancouver, a protocol for every studio if they indeed do need a reshoot or add scenes. Yes, it's a cost to reshoot, but it's not unheard of.

As soon as I enter the office, I hear Saffron's voice from behind

Casper's closed office door: "I think the scene was written well. It's the performances that lacked."

"The performances lacked because the dialogue is shit," Casper says. "Remember, Saffy, when I first read the script, I told you I hated that scene and you said it was good."

"Really? I don't remember that."

"You don't? We had the conversation a few times before shooting," he says.

"Really?" Saffron says.

I should leave. If Saffron knew I could hear them right now, she would be pissed. I should wait in the hallway, but this is far too captivating.

"Just because they're Canopy Studios doesn't mean that everything they put out is good. On the next one, I've got to follow my gut."

"The next one. With them?" Saffron asks. "You're going to pitch for *Break Room*?"

"Yeah," Casper says.

"What about *Snow*?"

"No. I don't think so, Saffy."

"When did you decide this?"

"Late last night when we were finishing up the cut," Casper says. Oh shit!

The front door to the office opens, and Dave bursts in cheerfully. "Hey!" he yells when he sees me. Casper's and Saffron's muffled voices go silent. "Great work last night, Charity Trickett. It worked," he says, clapping my shoulder.

"Shhhhh." I grab Dave, hoping to drag him out of the office before we're caught, but I'm not quick enough. Casper comes out of his office with Saffron in tow.

"Hey, man," Casper says as they slap hands.

"That went better than I thought it would," Dave says.

"Yeah." Then Casper turns to me. "So Charity, why don't you

get the writer on the phone for me. And can you put the changes into the shooting script? We should email him the original scene and the scene that you wrote. That way he can see the changes easily. And Dave, if the writer wants to come in and see the scene for himself . . . ?"

"No problem, man," Dave says. "I'll work on the fight in the woods while you get this ironed out."

"Cool," Casper says.

The boys disperse to work. I sit at my desk and pull the writer's phone number up on my computer.

"You ready, Casper?" I call out to him.

"Yup. Put him through."

As I dial the phone Saffron looks at me suspiciously, crossing her lanky arms over her flat stomach. I get the writer on the phone and patch him through to Casper. Saffron is still staring at me while I pull up the script on my computer to cut and paste my words into it.

"I didn't know you were an actress, Charity," she purrs.

"Huh?" I say.

"That was your voice with Casper's on the cut, wasn't it?"

"Oh, yeah. Embarrassing." I type away, trying to look busy, but it doesn't work.

Saffron sits on the edge of my desk. "You were very convincing. Quite the performance," she says.

"Thanks."

"Were you also acting when you told me how much you liked *Snow*?"

I take a deep breath, remove my hands from my keyboard, and look up at her. "No," I say.

"So, Casper changed his mind on his own about it."

"I don't know what Casper thought about *Snow* or what he thinks now."

"You didn't discuss *Snow* last night, while you were working late?"

"Only *Break Room*," I say.

"And your friend, Vivy Parker, does she like *Break Room*?"

Casper comes out of his office full of enthusiasm. "The writer's cool with the changes. Charity, call down to Dave and let him know. And Trickett, you cool with going back to Vancouver for the reshoot?" he says.

"Absolutely!" I say.

"Great. Start checking availabilities. Start with Blake. Call the production manager from Vancouver and see if we can get the same crew but a lot smaller. Like, a skeleton crew is all we need."

Casper directs all the instructions to me while Saffron looks on dumbfounded. Organizing a reshoot would typically be an associate producer's domain, but it looks like Casper is putting me in charge. While he talks about possible dates that work for the schedule, Saffron drills me with her eyeballs. It's not until Casper heads for the door to leave the office that she truly reacts.

"Casper!" Saffron screeches. Casper turns, perfectly framed in the open doorway, waiting for her to speak. "If you don't do *Snow*, I'll do it without you," she says, and I can tell her statement was impulsive because underneath her bold words, she looks scared.

"That's good, Saffy. You should do that," Casper says. He closes the door behind him, leaving Saffron alone with me and her failed tactic. Is this Casper's way of telling Saffron he doesn't need her anymore? From what I can tell, her only job here was to work on *Snow*, so now what?

I type away at my computer, pressing random keys in a clumsy attempt at creating the illusion of work. Saffron is motionless, staring at the door that Casper just walked out of. Her anger is palpable. Pink face, fists in balls, jaw clenched. Did I just replace Saffron?

CHAPTER 14

BRAVO

Nestled among Venice's canals and weeping willows is Albana Rugova's bungalow, the picturesque home with a picket fence where she lives and works. A grand piano takes up a large portion of the small living room. On top of it, my script pages lie in neat piles, decorated with colored Post-it notes and Albana's illegible handwriting. This woman is not only a stellar Ping-Pong player, charismatic charmer, and talented independent film maker, she is also an amazing script collaborator. What I thought would be an hour-long meeting this morning has stretched well into the afternoon.

I sit on the floor, legs crisscrossed, drinking bitter black tea from a ceramic mug that Albana made, ignoring the throb in my right hand as I write down every precious word she says. I watch her red-painted toes skip across Afghan rugs as she weaves her ideas into my script. She acts out scenes, and I jump in, improvising new dialogue, bringing my characters to life, and shaping my story with the kind of insight that comes from her years of directing.

"I don't know how to thank you, Albana," I say, standing at her front door before leaving.

"I had so much fun!" she says. "I can't wait for the revisions."

"Oh. You don't have to read another draft. You've already given me so much of your time."

"Charity, I want to. It is always interesting to see how a writer works with feedback."

"It's going to be so much better."

"It was already a beautiful script. Now it will be more . . . in focus," she says. To both of our surprise, I hug her. Not a polite, soft little pat on the back. I throw myself at her. And when she hugs me back, it's a bona fide hug.

★ ★ ★

Tomorrow Vivy and I will sit down with Casper to show him our pitch package, so I came into the office early this morning to put it all together. There's a lot to accomplish today, but with my early start, I'm confident I'll get everything done without feeling much pressure . . . if I can just get Daniel out of my office.

"That's got to mean that she's interested," he says, lying on the couch, tossing a basketball into the air.

"Daniel, you have to really listen to me this time—Albana never said that she was interested in directing *This Family Thing.*" I flip through a stack of headshots, cross-referencing them with the *Break Room* casting spreadsheet, making sure I'm not missing any.

"Send her flowers," Daniel says.

"Nice idea. I'll do that right now. Or should I deliver them myself when I give her the new draft?"

"Charity!" Daniel stops tossing the ball, gets up, and walks over to my desk. "She wants to read the revisions? I've been here for twenty fucking minutes, and you're just telling me this now. I don't care about how many Afghan rugs she has in one room."

"It's a beautiful look," I say.

"I care that you spent the whole day with her working on the movie and that she asked to read the next draft."

"I just told you!"

"You should have led with that!" he says, exasperated.

"Sorry. Jeez."

"You should talk to Vivy about playing Allison," Daniel says seriously. "We should send her the next draft."

"I can't pitch my movie to Vivy."

"Why?"

"She and I are pitching Casper tomorrow on a project for Canopy. Me pitching her something else is too much," I say.

"Charity, people are always pitching. It's nonstop in this town."

"Wouldn't it be nice to just be someone's friend, without making it about work and personal ambition?" I say.

"You lost me," Daniel says.

"Daniel, leave. You're annoying, and I don't want you here when Saffron gets here."

"Why? Are you afraid I'll be mean to her because she's mean to you?"

"I don't need you to defend me, Daniel. I definitely give her the gears," I say.

"No, you don't. You're Saffron's bitch," he says, pointing the ball at me.

"Am not. I lay down the law with her—trust me."

"You know who else 'gives the gears' and 'lays down the law'? My mom."

"What do you want me to do? She's in Casper's wedding party, for Christ's sake. They're close."

When Casper and Saffron come into the office carrying their morning coffee, I give Daniel a pointed look.

"Hey, Daniel," Casper says. "Come to shoot hoops?"

"Nah. I had to pick this ball up for Blake from Charles Barkley's manager. He's in the building. You didn't hear it from me, but Barkley's coming to the Lakers. This is a signed ball." He tosses the ball to Casper, then crosses the room and goes directly for Saffron. I stiffen. "Saffron, how are you?" he asks, giving her a small peck on the cheek. Gross.

"I'm great. What a nice surprise," Saffron gushes.

"Almost forgot." Daniel moves to the couch and picks up a parcel. "This is for you, Trickett. From Blake," he says.

"A present?" I say, tearing through the paper to reveal the most beautiful, intricately embroidered piece of silk I've ever seen. I lift it out and stand to let it unfold. "What is this?"

"A kimono!" Daniel says, happy as a clam.

"Why would Blake get you a kimono?" Saffron asks.

"Inside joke," Daniel says.

"It would look good with leather pants," I say, slipping it on.

"Looks good with jeans, too," Daniel says, nodding in appreciation.

"Blake Anthony, stylist," I say.

"Glad you like it. I should run," Daniel says, opening his hands for Casper to pass the ball back, which he does. "Nice seeing y'all."

"Later," I say as Daniel leaves.

Casper drops two concert tickets onto my desk. "Another gift. You like those guys, right?" he asks.

"Oh my God. The Chemical Brothers. I love them," I say.

"Yeah, I remember you playing them a lot in Vancouver. Have fun."

"Really?"

"Yeah. I've got to go to The Beverly Hills Hotel tonight," Casper says with a bashful smile. Saffron, on the other hand, looks a touch more than smug.

"No way!" I say. I'm thrilled for him. Tonight's party at The Beverly Hills Hotel is an A-list event. Everyone in Hollywood wants to go.

"I should get a haircut probably," he says.

"Are you wearing a suit?"

"Yeah. I've got to pick it up at Saks."

"Don't get a haircut," I say. Casper looks at Saffron for confirmation.

"Classy grunge," Saffron says. "It's a thing."

"Casper, when are you going to get to Saks? You're jammed all day," I say, handing him a printout of the schedule.

"Damn," he says.

"I can go," I say.

"I've got to try it on because they made some adjustments," he says, patting his little pot belly.

"I'll go right now and bring it back here. If it needs more work, I'll rejig your schedule and you can go back to Saks later," I say.

"Okay, cool. Thanks," Casper says.

"Can you pick my dress up, too?" Saffron asks.

I'm thrown for a beat, surprised that Saffron would be invited to such an elite Hollywood event. "Absolutely," I say, recovering quickly.

"Charlotte's out of town," Casper says. "Saffy's my plus-one." Now, that makes sense.

I'm on my cell phone with Jessica as I hold Saffron's Armani dress high above my head so it doesn't drag on the ground. The sales associate at Saks is in the back locating Casper's suit, and I can't help but feel like I am a pimple on a newly facialed face. Some of these clothes cost more than my car is worth. They hang preciously on velvet hangers as perfectly manicured hands belonging to women who don't need jobs sift through silk, suede, and cashmere.

"I love the Chemical Brothers," Jessica says. "How much are the tickets?"

"Don't worry about it. They're a gift from Casper," I say. "He's going to The Beverly Hills Hotel party tonight."

"Casper is getting big-time. Shit's going to get crazy for you," she says. I brace myself, knowing that Jessica is right.

Another call dings and I tell Jessica that we'll talk later.

"Charity." It's the production manager from Vancouver who's doing the reshoot. "I've been needing to talk to Casper since yesterday," she says curtly.

"I thought you two connected," I say.

"No," she says.

"I'm sorry. Must be a clerical error on my part. I'll get him to call you immediately." I hang up and call Casper, who immediately calls the production manager. I could have sworn the call sheet said Casper had returned her call. This has happened a few times now. Come to think of it, the phone calls that have been missed all had to do with the reshoot. It would be easy for Saffron to mess with the call sheet as it's constantly emailed between her, me, and Casper, but would she go to the extreme length of sabotaging the reshoot to make me look bad?

Then it dawns on me that maybe I'm a casualty of war. Maybe it's Canopy Studios who Saffron is after. If Casper's next film is at another studio, Saffron is more likely to remain his producing partner, but if he stays at Canopy she's out. I feel a little neurotic thinking this, but would Saffron sabotage the reshoot so Canopy won't hire Casper again? Is Saffron so selfish that she's willing to risk Casper's career to save her own?

I walk up to the Canopy Studios building with clear resolve and thousands of dollars of couture slung over my shoulders. It's Saffron or me. Do or die. I crane my neck toward the massive leopard that sits at the top of the Canopy high-rise, a symbol of what this studio represents—power and triumph. It feeds my determination. I know it's cheesy, but I give the big guy a wink. Me and him, we've got this.

"Who are you winking at?" I hear Kai's unmistakable baritone voice, and I know I'm blushing with embarrassment.

"Nobody," I say. I breeze by the world's most desirable man as he holds the door open for me.

"Really? I could have sworn that you were winking at the leopard."

"I don't know what you're talking about."

"Weird. It was a real strong wink. Like, I expected you to pull out your finger pistol." Kai makes a gun with his hand and clicking sounds with his tongue.

"I have something in my eye." I blink dramatically a few times, and Kai takes my arm, pulling me into him.

"Let me help you," he says. He cups my face with both of his hands, lifting my chin gently so that I look up to him. I am inches away from the most perfect man on earth, and the hustle and bustle of the Canopy Studios lobby becomes a blur.

"The right eye?" he asks.

"Yes," I say, enjoying the lie. He holds me there, looking me in the eyes, but not in a medical way. I feel the light stroke of his thumb against my cheek. Tingles surge through my body as if every molecule is delighted by Kai's touch.

"Sometimes I talk to the leopard," he whispers.

"That's very disturbing behavior," I whisper back.

"No more than winking." His phone rings and he pulls it out of his pocket. "Your eyes look perfect," he says before walking away to answer his phone.

I load myself into the elevator with the rest of the Canopy commuters, disappointed that Kai isn't brushed up against me and also aware that yet again, this man has managed to wet my panties. I'm going to have to start bringing an extra pair to work because of him.

Casper and Saffron are in their respective offices, trying on their formalwear. Saffron comes out first. I'm gobsmacked. She's stunning in her Armani dress. Her thin silhouette is embraced by chocolate-brown silk, her long hair drapes like a waterfall down her exposed back, and a lean leg peeks out from the side slit that ends just before becoming too provocative.

"Saffron, you look gorgeous," I say.

"Really?" she says, faking self-consciousness.

"Seriously beautiful," I say, admiring her.

"I think I'll do my hair in a slick low pony," she says.

"Perfect."

Casper comes out of his office looking stylish in his suit. He whistles at Saffron. "Hot dress, Saffy," he says. She looks positively impressed with herself.

"Suit looks good," I say to Casper.

"Yeah. Feels good," he says while doing a quick squat to test the pants.

"Hey, I don't know what's going on with the call sheet, whether it's me or something technical, but it's kind of messed up," I say. "So, I printed you both a paper call sheet. I'll hold off emailing you guys copies until I have this sorted. Make your adjustments on paper for now, and I'll update it throughout the day," I say, handing them each a paper version of the call sheet.

"Sure thing," Casper says, taking the paper from me. Then he goes into his office. Saffron simply stands there, eyeing me with suspicion. I extend the call sheet toward her, and she waits a moment before slowly taking it from me, her eyes never leaving mine. Why is Saffron so fucking freaky? Finally, she turns and saunters back to her office.

I haven't taken a seat yet when Saffron emerges from her office once again and places a DVD on my desk. "I need you to run this to the VFX guys in Studio City," she says. What? I've already wasted hours getting the outfits from Saks. I've barely made a dent in my to-do list for tomorrow's meeting with Vivy and Casper, and this errand could take the rest of the day.

"I'll call a courier," I say.

"No. Can't do that. It's a big scene. We don't want it to get into the wrong hands and get leaked," she says. "You'll need to take it yourself."

Oh, sigh! Saffron and Casper are probably sipping champagne at The Beverly Hills Hotel right now, I think as I take a sip from my steaming cup of chai tea. Bravo, Saffron—another battle won. I gave both concert tickets to Jessica when I finally returned from Studio City, knowing my night would be spent working on *Break Room*. But whatever. As I settle in front of my computer at six o'clock, my excitement about tomorrow's pitch outweighs my disappointment about missing a concert. What Vivy and I have put together is impressive, and I am certain Casper will agree.

I move my cursor around my computer screen toward the *Break Room* folder. Wait a second, it's not here. Where is the little blue folder icon labeled *Break Room*? *Don't panic.* I open my desk drawer and pull out the floppy disk where I store a backup of my work. I insert it into the disk drive and click on the little orange floppy disk icon. It's empty. What on earth? I pull up folder after folder on my desktop and sift through all my documents. I can't find the *Break Room* file anywhere. All my research is gone. The files with the resumes of every single actor Vivy and I have reached out to for every single role—gone. All my notes and research—gone. There is no *Break Room* folder. Did I put it in the trash by mistake? I open my trash folder, and it's empty.

I sit back in my chair and take a deep breath. I empty my trash once a month, and it isn't due to be emptied until the end of this month. There is no way that my trash should be empty. Oh, Saffron, you are a ruthless opponent. But I have a superstar in my back pocket named Vivy Parker. I call her.

"Hey," she says, answering her phone.

"You'll never guess what Saffron has done now," I say.

"What?"

"I'm pretty sure she erased all the *Break Room* files off my computer."

"No!"

"They're gone," I say.

"Oh, she's out for blood," Vivy says, cackling. "What do you need? I'll email it to you."

"Well, I want to print off all the headshots and resumes of all the actors."

"Good idea."

"I'll lay them out, just like a casting session, and Casper can give his yay or nay."

"I love being on this side of the table," Vivy says. "What else?"

"Can you send the research? I'm going to condense it and make a CliffsNotes version for Casper."

"This is a lot for you to do tonight. How about I come and help?" Vivy says.

"Really?"

"It'll take forever to upload all the headshots and email them to you. Plus, it'll be fun."

"Okay," I say, feeling a weight leave my body.

"Awesome. I'll pick up dinner."

An hour later, Vivy shows up at Canopy Studios with a hideous vegan meal and an enormous smile. She sits on the floor stapling headshots to resumes while I go through the research. We cue VHS tapes to specific performances we want Casper to watch, and then we rehearse our pitch late into the night. I don't know who's more excited: Vivy or me.

I have laid the headshots and resumes on the office coffee table. Casper sits on the couch with Vivy, and I'm in an armchair across from them. They do that thing people do when they meet someone new and talk about possible mutual friends until Vivy expertly steers Casper into focus. "So, you have to know—wait a second. She's here somewhere," she says, riffling through the headshots on the coffee table until she finds the actress she's looking for.

"Matilda. Yeah," Casper says.

"She's keen for the role of Olive," Vivy says.

"Really. You talked to her?"

"She's in if I am." And . . . meeting started.

The door opens and Saffron walks in with an apologetic smile. "Sorry I'm late, everyone," she says, pulling up a chair.

Nononononononononono! "Vivy. So good to finally meet you. We are so excited that you're here." Saffron extends a hand across the coffee table to Vivy.

"And you are?" Vivy says.

Nice one! No, they haven't met, but Vivy knows damn well that this is Saffron.

"Saffron."

"Affron. Nice to meet you," Vivy says. I love how juvenile she is.

"Saffron. With an *S*," Saffron says, maintaining her warm smile. She leans back and tells us to *please go on*.

As we continue to talk casting, Casper lifts a headshot and exposes the photograph of our favorite actor, the unassuming Australian. I reach for his headshot to make the introduction, but Saffron gasps and lunges for it, catching me off guard.

"Him!" she says, holding up the headshot. "This one, Casper, I'm so excited about." What? I'm sure Saffron is only excited about Cameron Steed because she read how excited I am about him in the files she stole from me.

"Who is he?" Casper asks. Saffron and I both start at the same time, but it's clear she isn't going to be quiet, so I let her have the floor.

"Casper, you are going to love him. He's Australian," she says.

That's when Vivy steps in. She politely steers the meeting away from Saffron and focuses on the work that she and I did. She fills the role of executive producer with natural expertise, and I can tell that Casper likes her. Which means that Saffron likes her.

In fact, Saffron likes everything Casper likes, and about forty-five minutes into the meeting, their dynamic comes into focus for me. Saffron is Casper's yes-girl. Who doesn't love a yes-girl? Everyone wants to be perceived as smart, maybe even brilliant. And this is what Saffron does for Casper. She agrees vehemently with everything Casper says. *Everything* is fabulous, extraordinary, so interesting. The ass-kissing adjectives go on and on as she tries to weasel her way onto the film.

Saffron is taking two hundred years to give us her two cents on the actress whose headshot she holds in her hands when Vivy catches my eye and gives me a look that is unmistakable. She's had enough of Saffron. I give her a little look of apology. What am I supposed to do? Then I see that Casper has taken notice of our exchange. He looks at Saffron, who is talking without realizing she has lost the room, and I can tell he's a little embarrassed.

Casper clears his throat. "Do you have any tape on this girl, Saffy?" he asks her.

"I can get something together for you by the end of the day," Saffron says with an air of accomplishment.

"We have tape," Vivy says. "Casper, Charity found some real diamonds in the rough here—talented actors who are under the radar and ready to take off. With that in mind, we knew that you may be unfamiliar with some of them, like I was. So Charity spent I don't know how many hours going through everyone's work and pulling clips to help you visualize the actors in their roles."

"Really?" Casper says, nodding at me with appreciation.

"We have clips of every single actor on this table," I say. "Whoever you want to see, I can run it for you now or I can send you home with the VHSs and you can watch at your leisure. Vivy's cleared her day for you—"

"Oh my God, Charity. Don't guilt the guy into spending the day with me!" Vivy says bashfully.

"Shit," Casper says. "I would love to spend the day with you." He eyes the clock, and I see that Vivy has also noticed this. Caper has about a half hour until he's supposed to be in editing, and he should get some lunch first. Vivy knows this. We've already prepared for her exit.

Vivy adjusts her posture. She gets a little taller, more composed, and more sophisticated. She's not the bashful actress pining for the director's appreciation; she's a producer and she's stepping into it.

"Casper," she says. "I hope I'm not coming on too strong. I'm excited. Take your time. Give our pitch a think. If you're interested in moving forward, we'll chat." She gets up and shoulders her purse.

"Vivy, we will be in contact," Saffron says, extending her hand.

"Saffron. Thank you so much for your cheerleading today," Vivy says as she shakes Saffron's hand. "It's always nice to get positive support from the sidelines. Later, guys."

When the door closes after Vivy leaves, Casper turns to me and says, "Trickett, you're killing it."

CHAPTER 15
TRUE ROMANCE

A soundstage. A proper movie set where films are made, not sold. Coming home to Vancouver settles me —the freshness of the cool air, the familiar feeling of my bed in my parents' house, hanging out with Pup and my old friends. I drive without looking at maps, and there's always someone to go for a drink with. But the best thing about being back in Vancouver is being back on a movie set. A movie set is playing make-believe on a grand scale. It's tree forts and blanket tents. It's dress-up in the adult world.

Daniel and I are hunched in the corner, sipping green tea and waiting for the next setup. I'm trying to talk to him about *This Family Thing*. But right now, instead of acting like my manager, he's being a complete goof. "How's Vivy Parker?" Daniel asks with a smirk. He joined Vivy and me on a hike the other day, and he's completely smitten. Vivy is not at all what one would imagine a Hollywood starlet to be. She doesn't shop on Rodeo Drive or lunch on Beverly Hills patios. Her hiking boots are worn and her makeup is sparse. She owns a paddleboard and a skateboard and actually knows how to use them. She has a vegetable garden that she tends with care.

"She's not interested in you," I say.

"She will be," he insists. "No woman can resist me."

"Umm. I did."

"You flatter yourself. I am way out of your league. Better you stick with that nerd."

"Kai is not a nerd," I say.

"Yes, he is."

From behind me, I hear Saffron's voice in the distance. "Pup, I simply can't believe it," she says. She's using the tone that makes me drop everything and focus primarily on her. She's upset, and an upset Saffron can lead to a multitude of bad things: a miserable Charity, a ruined reshoot, another failed assistant in Saffron's wake. I practically run to the commotion.

"I just don't believe it, Pup," Saffron says, crossing her arms the way she does when she's serious.

"You think I'm lying to you? Call them yourself, then," Pup says. Okay. Pup's losing her patience.

"Sorry, Saffy. What's going on?" I ask.

"It's that hotel you put us in, Charity. What kind of hotel only has synthetic pillows?" Saffron looks at me as though I should be as appalled as she is. But I'm confused. I have never had anyone complain about that hotel, ever. It's the best. Saffron's standard room is five hundred dollars a night. "I'm allergic to synthetic pillows." Saffron looks surprised that I don't know this.

"They are hypoallergenic pillows, Saffron," Pup cuts in. "People are allergic to down pillows."

Pup needs to leave this conversation before she makes Saffron more upset.

"I have very sensitive skin. I only sleep on down pillows." It's final. Saffron has made up her mind. She is definitely not going to sleep on a synthetic pillow. She needs a down pillow, and she needs me to get it. That's my make-work task of the day.

"I'll get you a down pillow. Do you like it firm or soft?" I say.

"I'm just not sure about the hotel, Charity. I mean, what kind of hotel doesn't have down pillows? I want to move."

"Move hotels? Everyone is in that hotel. It's the best in the city," I say.

"You're kidding, surely," Saffron says.

"Look, how about I go out and get you two or three pillows to choose from. Okay? They'll be in your hotel room by the time we wrap," I say.

"Okay. But I need options," Saffron says, unfolding her arms, a sign that she is coming around.

"Got it," I say.

I pull Pup away from Saffron and lead her toward the set of double doors that exit the soundstage. "What the hell?" Pup says.

"It's easier this way. Trust me," I say as we step outside.

"You are a suck. A suck fest. You're a complete kiss ass. And to Saffron? Charity, I hate to say this, but ever since you guys got here, I've watched you pander to her. It's really gross."

"Hey," I say.

But Pup doesn't stop. "She's not even a real associate producer. She shouldn't be using you as her personal assistant."

"It's a complicated dynamic in the office," I say as Pup follows me into the AD trailer. I find the petty cash and hand her some money. "Can you please go get Saffron some pillows?"

"Me? I'm not her assistant! And you shouldn't do it, either. You give that kind of girl an inch and she'll take a mile," Pup says.

"Pup, this is bigger than pillows."

"What does that mean?"

"Saffron doesn't care about the pillows. She wants me off set. She's going to fuck up this reshoot. But if I don't get her the pillows, she'll find another way to punish me."

"Okay. She's making you paranoid."

"I'm not paranoid. This is the Saffron game. Help me win it!"

Pup looks at me and sighs. "Okay. What do you want me to do?"

"We can't let Saffron out of our sights. We must keep her calm. We must act like we like her, especially when there are other people around. Got it? Got to make her feel like she's important. And we've got to get her some pillows."

Pup's mouth is open. She's not blinking. She doesn't say a thing.

"What do you think, slugger—you in?" I say.

Pup shakes her head like she's disappointed in me. "All the shit you complain about with Saffron. You're making it worse. You're letting her treat you like this. Christ, Charity, don't you see? She's making you her personal assistant, and she doesn't even have a fucking job. Bitch doesn't even get paid."

"Pup. Can you please just help me get through this reshoot?"

"Fine," Pup says. "I will acquire the pillows of varying firmness. But know this: You are digging your own grave."

I watch Pup walk off, and I understand her disappointment in me. There is a distinguishable line between personal assistant and professional or executive assistant. The assistants who want film or television careers on a creative or business level strive to remain on the professional side of that line. Once you cross the line from personal to professional assistant, you rarely go back to being a personal assistant unless you want to. For girls like Pup and me, being a personal assistant was a means to an end, and we've surpassed that part of our career. I get why Pup is so upset. I have gone from being the assistant to the director of Canopy Studios' most highly anticipated film of the year to being the personal assistant of a fake associate producer.

My plane lands at LAX, and I'm struck by how much I missed Kai while I was away. At work, we've been emailing less and calling each other more. We always pepper in a little flirting while we schedule meetings or attend to some other business.

He was on my mind so much in Vancouver that on my last night, I brought a group of my oldest girlfriends together to debate the age-old topic of whether you should date your coworker. We sat around

my parents' living room with bottles of wine and a charcuterie plat-
ter in front of us while we discussed ethics and romance. We quoted
from the women's studies classes we took in college and analyzed the
possible perceptions that coworkers might have toward the romantic
couple—or, more accurately, the women.

As bottles were consumed and more were opened, the conversation
turned to how hard it is to meet someone. We shared stories about
the awful reality of dating. The countless awkward and disappointing
first dates. The wasted time, the wasted effort, the wasted money. And
what about getting your hopes up? Every date is filled with the hope
that this guy is the one, and yet most dates end in disappointment.
My girlfriends were exhausted from the endless stream of hopeful
encounters. And here I am with Kai.

I told them about how Kai's confidence is sexy and how his humor
keeps me on my toes, how smart he is and, ugh, how broad his shoulders are. When I told my girlfriends about our near kiss at the Vivy
Parker premiere, we cackled over how sexy it is to sneak around and
how if we work well together in the office, we'd work well together . . .
in bed. The consensus was that I should sleep with him immediately.

As the plane taxis to the gate, I call Kai.

"Welcome home," he says when he answers the phone.

I am caught off guard by this sentiment. Is LA now my home? I
always knew I couldn't achieve my dreams by living in Vancouver;
maybe it's time to grow up and stop living in LA like it's temporary.
My career is taking off at Canopy. I could buy a proper bedframe,
paint the walls in my apartment, and get a gym membership. It would
be prudent to put a California license plate on my car and get medical
insurance. And I should definitely work on building relationships. So
when Kai suggests we go for dinner, I say yes.

Groups of stylish people share tapas and drink sangria among the
hanging plants and crystal chandeliers of the Spanish restaurant Kai

booked. When the hostess sat us, Kai slid in close to me on the banquette, leaving an empty chair across from us. The floor-to-ceiling windows are open, and from our red velvet booth, West Hollywood seems to be at our feet. He tells me to order for us, but I don't know what he likes. He tells me he likes what I like, so I assume that means he'll eat anything.

He stays next to me all night as we share little plates of delicious food and sip on cocktails made with as many ingredients as the dishes in front of us. He slides his hand down my leg just as a motorcycle blasts by. I jump, feeling the engine's rumble in my belly.

Kai pulls me closer to him and says softly, his lips brushing against my cheek, "It's just a motorcycle, Charity." I look into his eyes, and for a moment I think that he's going to kiss me.

"I'm still thinking about this," I say, suddenly panicked.

"Charity, I'm serious here," he says.

"I know you are. But I have to be careful. Canopy is a boys' club. There are no women in upper-level positions. Now, I'm not saying I want to be a studio executive, believe me. But, you know . . . optics."

He pulls away from me. It's just an inch, but I'm instantly disappointed.

"We're not going to be working together forever," Kai says with a smile.

"Right. So maybe we should wait until my contract with the studio is over."

"Maybe." He takes my hand in his and kisses my fingers. "Do you want to wait, Charity?"

"We should hold off for a little while," I say. But I don't mean a word of it. If Canopy Studios didn't exist, and if I didn't care what people thought about me, I would straddle this man right now and make out with him in this restaurant. I wouldn't give a shit.

"Okay. Let's compromise," he says. "We'll start your plan tomorrow. Tonight you're coming home with me. We'll go for coffee in the morning—or, better yet, I'll bring you coffee in bed. Then I'll take you home and we can put your plan into action." He pulls me closer to him, and when I feel the heat from his body, I know it will be difficult to keep my pants on until my contract with *Diffuser* is over.

"Kai." I slap him on the leg, laughing.

"Okay. You want to be colleagues. Fine. How was the reshoot?" he asks.

I get instantly excited and turn to face him on the banquette. "It was so cool to hear Blake Anthony deliver my dialogue. He made the scene better than I imagined it could be when I wrote it."

"You wrote the reshoot?"

I nod and smile with pride.

"I didn't know that." Kai pulls away from me, a wrinkle forming on his brow that makes him look serious. "You know, I was in the screening when Casper pitched to reshoot. I got the impression that he wrote the scene." I'm disappointed for a moment, but if I'm real with myself, I'm not surprised.

"Well, I get it," I say. "What would studio executives take more seriously—something written by an established director or something written by me, an assistant who's been working in Hollywood for two minutes?"

"Yeah," Kai says. "It can be perceived as shady, though."

"True. But I don't think it is. It'll all come out in the wash, whether it's Canopy discovering after the fact that I wrote it or Casper promoting me on his next film. I'm fine with it," I say.

I can tell that Kai isn't so sure, but he drops the subject, pulls me into him, and says, "Now, about this compromise . . ." He's relentless.

CHAPTER 16

JUST A GIRL

I just got off the phone with Vivy, and she was in a state. Casper called her this morning and said his pitch to the studio went well, but they are going to take some time before making their final decision. I wonder if Canopy is waiting to see how *Diffuser* performs at the box office before deciding whether to hire Casper. In any case, Casper told Vivy that the studio loved all the casting options—including her for the lead—but they didn't want Vivy as an executive producer. Vivy told Casper she wouldn't act in the film unless she also produced it. He said he was disappointed, and that was it.

I'm shocked. Vivy's out? She did so much work on Casper's pitch. You'd think he'd fight for her a little. I mean, he convinced Canopy to give Saffron an associate producer credit, so I'm sure he can convince them to give a superstar an executive producer credit. It's just a matter of selling it to them. So yes, it's Saturday, but I'm going to Casper's house to see if I can fix this.

I take a left onto Lookout Mountain Avenue, paying more attention to my car's temperature gauge than the road ahead. It's not a hot day, but my old car is in danger of overheating again. This has been happening a lot lately, and as I watch the dial move toward the red line at a millimeter a minute, I fear the worst. Then I hear a *clunk*. What was that? I know nothing about cars except that they are expensive to fix, and if this old girl dies, I'm in serious financial trouble. Plumes of hot steam billow from under the hood, and I feel a knot form in my stomach, knowing this is bad. But the only thing I can do is wait for her to cool down, so I pop the hood, grab my purse, lock the car, and climb the steep street toward Casper's Hollywood Hills home.

When I arrive, Casper takes me to the back deck of his 1960s bungalow. He has a view of the canyon, and on a clear day, you can see the Hollywood sign. It's peaceful here, and that's good because I'm a little on edge.

"So, no Vivy?" I ask.

"She's not *really* going to pass on this role," Casper says.

"Casper, she's out."

"Really?" Casper looks skeptical.

"Yeah. I talked to her this morning. If Canopy Studios doesn't give her this, she's never going to work for them again."

"But the role. They're giving Vivy Parker, a romantic-comedy star, a serious role in a huge movie. She's not going to walk away from that," Casper says with confidence.

I'm a little disappointed that he doesn't take Vivy more seriously. "Okay, look," I say. "I'm not pushing you either way. I'm just relaying a message in case you *are* seriously interested in Vivy. She's firm that she will be the executive producer of the next film she stars in."

Casper looks at me doubtfully. "So she says to you."

I take a deep breath. Why doesn't he trust me on this? Does he think Vivy would use me to bluff?

Casper continues, "Canopy made Vivy famous. Now they're offering to make her a serious actress. She's not walking away from them."

"A couple of hours ago, I read a draft memo from Vivy's agent to Canopy. It said something like, 'Vivy has made Canopy Studios hundreds of millions of dollars. If they won't promote her, she's moving on to fulfill her ambitions elsewhere.'"

Casper looks stunned.

I say, "Vivy knows her longevity in this industry depends on her producing her own projects. She's looking to be the boss, and if Canopy doesn't give that to her now, she doesn't think they ever will. She's walking."

Casper pushes his palms against the railing and steps back into a lunge, letting his head fall between his arms. "They haven't offered me the film yet," he says. "Even if they did hire me, I don't have any pull with the studio over this."

Silence falls between us, and I'm not sure if I should address this, but I want to know. "Because of Saffron?" I ask. Casper looks up to the sky. I wonder if he's considering whether to fill me in on the Saffron saga.

"I pushed the studio to hire her, and she fucked up. Made me look bad, too. So, I can't fight them on who to hire. They won't listen."

Casper is probably right. We fall into silence and turn our attention to the view. As we watch two birds fly across the canyon, a nagging question tugs at me. "Can I ask . . . why did you bring on Saffron as AP?"

Casper takes a deep breath. "This stays between us." I nod in agreement. "Saffy is a close friend of Charlotte's. They were roommates when we went to UCLA. After grad, Saffy went traveling while the rest of us started working. She's got family money. After a few years, I think Saffy's parents got on her ass to do something with her life. She came back to LA, and I had this film I wanted to make independently. Saffy helped pay for it. She helped pay for a lot of it. Because of that film, I got my first big break as a studio director."

"I get it," I say. "Vivy aside, though, I've been thinking about this. Canopy needs a female producer on this movie." Casper turns to face me, so I continue. "You know, they've never had a female executive producer. There isn't one female board member. Never has been. Their average producer is a fifty-year-old white man. These men have purchased a feminist film. Meanwhile, they've never had a woman in any significant role in the company. They should consider putting a woman in a serious position of power on this film."

"If I point that out to them, wouldn't I also be saying that the film would be better if it was directed by a woman?"

At least he gets it, I think.

"On the bright side," Casper says cheerfully, "Lionel Reid is still in, even without Vivy."

My heart sinks. Vivy loves Lionel. They met years ago when she first moved to LA, and now they're close friends. If he accepts this role, Vivy will be hurt.

"That's great," I manage to say.

A friend once told me, *Everyone is looking out for number one, Trickett, and you're not it.* At the time, I thought it was cynical. But as I get older, I realize she was warning me.

That afternoon, I feed my poor little car some fresh engine oil and let her rest. Daniel picks me up, and we meet Vivy at an exclusive rooftop restaurant in Santa Monica so Vivy and I can lick our wounds. I don't know how long we've been cozied into these rattan chairs or how many hibiscus cocktails we've consumed, but I have noticed that the sun umbrellas have come down, candles have been placed on the tables, and a DJ has appeared out of thin air. Stylish people now surround us, swaying to the music, some taking note of Vivy and others hoping to be taken note of. Even though the atmosphere has gone from cool to chic, we're bummed, a little buzzed, and talking shit.

"Down with the patriarchy!" Vivy says, raising her glass for a toast.

Daniel squirms.

"Come on. I'm not saying, 'Down with Daniel.' You, too, can contribute to the cause." Vivy tilts her glass toward his and clinks them together.

"Daniel," I say. "You love women! You want to see more women working in film."

"A hundred percent!" Daniel says. "I like working with women. I like working with you, Charity."

"Aw," I say.

Daniel checks out a woman who floats by in a plunging neckline. He smiles in appreciation of her. "I like going out for drinks with women on rooftop bars where there are more women," he says. We laugh.

Then Vivy gets contemplative. "I think I should start my own production company," she says.

Daniel's eyes light up. "I might have your first movie." He looks at me sideways for approval. I discretely nudge him with my foot to hold him back. This is not the right time to pitch Vivy my project. I just seriously disappointed her.

Vivy laughs. "I think a Blake Anthony movie may be a little too big for my first producing gig. I'm going to the ladies.'"

Vivy stands, and I stand with her. "Want me to go with?" I ask, not wanting her to go alone in case a fan gets too fansy.

"I'm cool. I brought Roger." Vivy motions to a nearby corner where the security guy Blake recommended is posted up.

"I didn't even notice," I say, waving to him.

"I was talking to him for, like, fifteen minutes when we got here," Daniel informs me.

"You were?"

When Vivy leaves, Daniel gives me a disappointed look. "Charity Trickett," he grunts.

"The timing isn't right."

"Vivy should read your script. Does she even know that you write?" he asks.

"Of course she does. Just give it rest for now. She had her heart set on *Break Room*. She's upset. Plus, the script isn't done yet. I don't want to do anything premature."

"You're frustrating," Daniel says in defeat.

"And your support means the world to me," I say, reaching for his hand.

"No touching," he says, pulling away. "I've been distant flirting with this girl."

When I turn to look, Daniel kicks me. "Don't ruin it for me!" he says.

"That was hard!" I say, rubbing my leg.

"You kicked me first," he says.

"That was barely anything." I look around in search of Daniel's flirty birdie. He puts his sunglasses on and leans back in his chair, trying to be nonchalant. "Is it the girl who just walked by?" I ask.

"No."

I look in the direction where I think he's looking, and I spot her. Long brown hair, legs for days. He has a type. "Her? Since when?"

"Since we got here." He says it like he hasn't a care in his very cool world.

CHAPTER 17
STILL NOT A PLAYER

Rough cut, director's cut, producer's cut, studio cut—they're all done, and then some. The music has been arranged and the orchestration recorded. Visual effects have been designed and laid into the picture. We sat in a dark theater while engineers worked a giant mixing board to perfectly balance every sound imaginable, from car crashes to birds chirping. Colors were amplified and atmospheres dimmed, making each frame of film picture-perfect. *Diffuser* is close to being finished, and Canopy Studios has high expectations for the film's success. They've increased the marketing budget, expanded distribution, and even cut a soundtrack that will be released a week after the film premieres in the US. There is hype in Hollywood, and it's for Blake Anthony and *Diffuser*.

Saffron walks into the office and gives me an awkward smile. She's in a good mood. It's been like this for weeks, and I think I know why. Since Vivy split from *Break Room*, progress on my pitch has slowed considerably. Most of the actors who were interested have backed out in solidarity with their friend Vivy Parker, and rebuilding the cast list without a high-profile celebrity attached is challenging. Maybe Saffron doesn't consider me a threat anymore. Or maybe *Break Room* has shed light on the boys' club that we find ourselves not a part of, and this is her act of sister camaraderie. Whatever it is, we are about as friendly with each other as we can get, but I still don't trust her. That's why if I'm going to get out of work early today, I need to lie.

"How's your tooth?" Saffron asks, standing in front of my desk.

I immediately tense up. "Awful. I have a dentist appointment at one o'clock. Hope that's okay." God, I hate lying.

"Of course. Tooth pain is the worst," she says.

There's no tooth pain and no dentist appointment. I'm doing something a little more fun this afternoon. Blake Anthony has arranged for his helicopter to take me and Daniel to his estate in Ojai to celebrate his birthday with his closest friends and family for the entire weekend.

If Saffron knew this, I'm certain that she would find a way to keep me from going. So, for days I've been making a big show of complaining and rattling a container of painkillers before fake popping them. Today I've even made an ice pack that I hold preciously to my cheek.

By noon, when I leave for my "dentist appointment," Saffron seems genuinely sympathetic. "Seriously," she says. "If you need anything, call me."

At one o'clock on the dot, Daniel and I arrive at a log cabin–like structure that sits between agricultural land and a runway, making this small airport look more like a high-end fishing lodge than an airfield. We are greeted with warm hand towels, scented with eucalyptus. There are no crowded lines where your heels are threatened by luggage carts and no crying children threatening your sanity. Gentle music plays from hidden speakers, and a fireplace made of river rock crackles with a real fire. Here, checking in for our flight involves two minutes of pleasantries with a woman named Marsha, who knows our names without ever being introduced to us. We trade our eucalyptus towels for crystal champagne flutes sparkling with Napa Valley bubbles. Our bags are taken from us and are loaded onto a bellhop's trolley, like something in a luxury hotel, and taken to the airstrip, and I think: *Yes, a conveyor belt for the luggage would ruin the look in here.*

In the sitting area, Daniel introduces me to Blake's cousin and his wife, along with a couple of Blake's high school friends. We sip our sparkling wine while melting into plush leather seats, warmed by the sun streaming through floor-to-ceiling windows. There are aviation and yachting magazines beneath our sweating champagne bucket. I sit back and enjoy the easy conversation, feeling as though my vacation has already begun. In my real life, the airport is a challenge that needs to be overcome before I can enjoy my vacation. This private-flying thing is as enjoyable as that first poolside cocktail.

Our pilot, Captain Shay, comes to fetch our party of six from the lounge, looking like a pool boy in his khaki shorts, crisp white sneakers, and polo shirt. He guides us to the helicopter, its blades cutting through the air with a *chck chck chck*. The thunderous slapping makes us all duck even though our common sense knows it's not necessary.

Shay's "bird," as he likes to call it, flies us over the shoreline—not because it is the most direct route but because it is the most scenic. Every so often, we lean over each other, sharing the armrests to see a pod of dolphins or a particularly spectacular oceanfront home. We tilt right and head inland while I happily listen to the old friends' banter through my headphones. When we touch down in the belly of a valley, the tall grass shimmers and then flattens with our arrival. Blake comes running to the helicopter, greeting us warmly and eager to help with bags.

It had always been Blake's dream to live on a farm, but his estate isn't a farm in the traditional sense. It's a brand-new home, designed by Blake and some German architect whose name I can't pronounce, built to resemble an old barn, long and rectangular with a gambrel roof. There is a swing on the porch and muddy boots at the front door. Inside, the exposed beams and cedar walls remind me of a farmhouse, but the twenty-thousand-dollar couch and designer rugs are ideal for the pages of *Architectural Digest*.

Daniel plops himself on the couch with the latest draft of *This*

Family Thing in one hand and a lemonade in the other. "Come on, Trickett. We have work to do," he orders. Across from the open-concept living room, on the other side of the gigantic kitchen island, I'm poking around, looking for a snack. I open the fridge, but all I see are drinks and hot dogs—lots of dogs.

"What's with all the hot dogs?" I say, taking an iced tea.

"Blake's favorite. We're going to make a bonfire tonight and roast them. It's fun. The caterers are coming tomorrow for the big dinner."

"I'm peckish. Anything I can munch on?" I ask.

"Check the other fridge," Daniel says.

"Two fridges!" I pull the other one open. It is the most organized fridge I have ever seen, filled with cheese platters, cut vegetables, dips, and sliced fruit. "Bingo!" I say, pulling out veggies and hummus. "Want some?"

"Bring it over," Daniel says. I place the snacks on the coffee table and sit next to him with my script.

"It's better, isn't it?" I ask, plopping a carrot loaded with hummus into my mouth.

"It is. There were holes in the story that I didn't pick up on until Albana's notes. This is tight, Charity," he says.

"Thanks."

"I do think the older brother is a little diluted in this draft. I'd like to give him more," he says, looking at his notes.

"Okay."

"What do you think of Guy Taylor?"

"The actor from *Bunny Ears*?" I ask.

"Yeah. I think he'd be good for it."

"Good call. I'll give him more to work with," I say, scribbling notes on my script, ideas already percolating.

"Cool. But don't push it. Just flesh out the character a little more and write with him in mind," Daniel says. He flips through the script as seriously as I've seen him flip through Blake's contracts, and I feel as though I'm in good hands with him. Daniel has been with Blake for over seven years, and during that time, they've become so close that Daniel is now exposed to every aspect of Blake's career. Blake knows that Daniel is ready to start his next Hollywood chapter, and he's made sure that his assistant and friend is perfectly positioned to start a management company or produce movies. I just can't believe that Daniel is starting with me. "I think you took Albana's notes and ran with them in a good way," he goes on. "I have a couple other things, but they're small. You should be able to give Albana the new draft pretty soon."

"Hey," I say, nudging him with my shoulder. "You're a good producer."

"Thank you." He looks down at the script, clearing his throat. A touch of pink fills his cheeks.

"Are you blushing?"

"No!" he says.

"You are. You're blushing. Oh, Daniel. My producer. My manager." I lean over to give him a hug.

"Shut up!" he says, pulling away from me.

I laugh and force my hug on him.

"Get off!" he says, but I hold on to him because I know he loves me. "Ugh. You smell like hummus," he whines.

Late that afternoon, with the sun sinking in the distance, Daniel, Blake, and I are perched on a fence that borders the horse pasture. "Aren't they beautiful?" Blake says in a lazy voice, looking at the horses dotting the pasture.

"How long have you been riding?" I ask.

"Oh, I don't ride," Blake says.

"Get ready for this." Daniel smirks.

Blake ignores him. "These aren't riding horses."

"Oh," I say.

"Now, I ask you, Charity, who has horses they don't ride?" Daniel says.

"I'm sure it's done," I say, uncertain.

"Have you ever heard of someone owning horses but never riding them?" Daniel asks, as if he's a lawyer in an over-the-top crime drama.

"They're free!" Blake says with pride.

"They're in captivity! We are literally sitting on the fence that keeps them here," Daniel shrieks. "You have more money than sense, Blake. Really."

"How did you like the scenic route in that chopper?" Blake asks Daniel.

"Alright." Daniel backs down.

"Burning jet fuel for you, buddy."

"That's true. Thank you, Blake," Daniel says.

Blake smacks Daniel on the inside of his leg, playfully hard.

"Ouch! I'm sorry. I like that you have no common sense," Daniel says, rubbing his leg.

Then Blake smacks his other leg.

"Ouch! Motherfucker," Daniel says, hopping down from the fence and running away from Blake, into the pasture.

"I'm not going to chase him," Blake says through his laughter. "That's a minefield of poop that boy's running through right there."

I reach into the pocket of my oversized jacket and pull out the package I've been cradling all afternoon. "Happy birthday," I say, handing it to Blake.

"You shouldn't have gotten me a gift," he says, surprised. I watch him untie the string that bounds the brown paper, and when he opens it, I'm thrilled to see a smile stretch across his face. "Cookies! You know, I love cookies."

"It's our one true bond."

"What kind?" he asks.

"What do you think? Chocolate-chip walnut."

"Because a cookie without chocolate chips . . ." he says, waiting for me to help him finish his sentence.

"Is bullshit," I say.

"Mmm." Blake takes a cookie in his big paw and takes a healthy bite. "Mmm. You baked this?"

"Of course."

Blake plops the rest of the cookie into his mouth. "Damn that's good."

"Blake," I say, looking up at him. "Thank you."

"Aw. Happy to have you here," he says, brushing me off.

"This is really nice. It's not just your generosity. I'm . . . well, I'm homesick. So being here with your friends and family is helping a lot." There's a lump in my throat when Blake looks me in my eyes. He drapes his meaty arm around me and pulls me into him, kissing the top of my head lightly, like an uncle would. I lean into him, letting all the tension melt away from my body.

"I'm glad you're here," he says. "And I like your script." I pull back from Blake a touch. Wait . . . Blake Anthony read my script?!

"You read my script?"

"Daniel gave it to me to read on the plane ride from Shanghai to London. Or was it Madrid to Toronto? I can't remember. Important thing is that you and Daniel could really do something with it," he says. "Keep me updated, okay?"

"Did Daniel tell you about Albana Rugova?"

"Sure did. Congratulations."

My heart dances. Blake Anthony likes my script!

That night, we gather around a campfire, resting against overstuffed pillows and bales of hay. Blake plays the guitar, and we sing along. We roast hot dogs and marshmallows, drink beer, and pass joints while old friends reconnect and new friendships form.

The next day, we play California kickball with the sound of Blake's helicopter coming and going in the background, shuttling caterers and decorators in for tonight's birthday celebration. After a lazy afternoon, the guests disperse to change for dinner. I emerge from my little guest house at nightfall and notice that someone has placed little paper bags with lit candles inside to line the walkways around the estate. As I walk down the path toward the party, I worry that my dress, the one I wore to my cousin's wedding, isn't fancy enough for tonight. Sure, everything up until now has been casual and relaxed, but I overheard some of the other ladies talking about their outfits earlier, and it was very Gucci this and Valentino that.

"Hey, pretty lady," I hear Daniel say, and when I turn and see him, I gasp. Daniel is handsome, there's no doubt about it. He has a roster of women who would say the same. But man, with this guy in a tux, even I may have a hard time resisting him tonight.

"Not fair!" I whine.

"What?" he says.

"You're, like, insanely hot," I say.

"Trickett, I am insanely hot. I believe I've told you this before."

"Oh, there it is. It's the mouth. When things come out of it, your hot level goes down."

"No, it doesn't," he says, walking toward me with a sexy smirk on his face. I know he's playing up his sex appeal as a joke, but it's making me uncomfortable.

"Don't look at me like that," I say.

"Like what?" he says, giving me a smoldering sexy look. When he gets to me, he takes my arm and loops it through his so we can walk to the party arm in arm.

"I don't think I want to touch you in case I get turned on," I say, pulling away from him.

"Girl, you are teetering in those heels. Take my arm," he says.

"Rather fall," I say, walking in front of him.

"Trickett, don't be stupid. The best thing about our friendship is that you are so not sexually attractive."

At this I stop and turn to face him. "To you. I'm not sexually attractive to you," I say.

"Okay. If that's how you want to put it," he says, offering me his arm.

"I could say the same thing, you know. You're not attractive to me," I say, shoving my arm through his to prove my point.

"Right," he scoffs. "You just called me hot."

"You're annoying," I say.

We turn a corner, and there under a huge oak tree is a long table, set for thirty people. The tree sparkles with twinkle lights, and arrangements of fresh flowers hang from the branches with long ribbons. Baccarat crystal glasses sparkle next to Hermès plates, complete with horses painted on the china. Candelabras drip with wax, lighting the calligraphy on the place cards as stylish people take their seats.

That night I try caviar and Krug for the first time. We dip lobster in drawn butter and eat pepper-crusted steak. Toasts and roasts are given in honor of Hollywood's brightest star. I sit back in my chair and watch in awe as two servers carry a three-tiered cake while a Grammy Award–winning singer sings "Happy Birthday." I already know this night is going to end too soon for my liking.

CHAPTER 18
I LEFT MY WALLET IN EL SEGUNDO

It's first thing in the morning and I'm still on cloud nine from my over-the-top, insanely cool weekend celebrating Blake's birthday. Saffron arrives and places a paper cup of delicious-smelling tea on my desk. "How's the tooth?" she asks. Oh! Right. The tooth.

"Root canal," I say, remembering the lie I prepared last week.

"Brutal," she says. "Are you okay?"

"It feels better now, though," I say. "Thanks for the tea." God, she's being so nice, I almost feel bad.

Casper comes in all smiles and excitement. "Hey, guys. Big day," he says.

"Sure is." Saffron smiles at him. This evening, we are test screening *Diffuser*. For the first time an audience full of regular people will see the film in a regular theater and we will get their opinions on it. It's basically the last big step before the film is released.

"I'm not here for long," Casper says. "I have a meeting downtown. Charity, will you ask Dave to make me a DVD copy of the movie? I'll grab it from you at the test screening."

"They need a DVD for the test screening? I thought it would be on a film reel like in a regular movie in the theater."

"It's not for the screening. It's for me. I'm going to work tonight right after the test screening while the audience feedback is fresh in my mind. I need a copy of the film to take home."

"Oh. Okay," I say.

"So, we'll meet you at the screening?" Saffron says.

"Yeah," Casper says. "Hey, Trickett, how was Blake's birthday weekend?"

"Blake's birthday weekend?" Saffron says, surprised. *Fuuuuuuuuuuuuck!*

"It was . . . lovely," I say, shitting my pants. This is why I hate lying. I very rarely get away with it.

"Lovely? Sounded pimp," Casper says. "Blake helicoptered everyone into Ojai on Friday and put them up for a weekend of partying," he says to Saffron. "How did you snag an invite, Trickett?"

"Oh, Daniel, I'm sure. They're taking pity on me because I just moved here and my social life is pathetic," I say.

"Pathetic social life? Come on," Casper says. "Friends with Vivy Parker, weekends at Blake Anthony's Ojai estate."

"How did your tooth feel on the helicopter ride?" Saffron asks with venom in words.

"You know, I was so highly medicated and there was champagne on the helicopter. I didn't feel a thing."

"Champagne on a private helicopter. Wow." Saffron crosses her arms and pierces me with her eyes. I am unbearably uncomfortable.

"I called Blake on Saturday to wish him happy birthday," Casper says. "He said he'd send the chopper for me, but I had to do all this wedding planning stuff with Charlotte, and she would've killed me if I bailed. Who all was there?"

"It wasn't, like, a Hollywood party or anything. It was mostly his family and friends."

"Hold on. Didn't Chaka Khan sing him 'Happy Birthday'?" Casper asks, sending Saffron's jaw to the floor.

"She did," I say, trying to sound casual when all I want to do is run from Saffron. "I should go ask Dave to burn that DVD for you. See you at the screening," I say, backing out of the office, cursing myself for lying to Saffron. Things were going so well. How on earth is she going to do to punish me now?

The door to the editing suite is open, and I find Dave sitting in front of three screens, all showing different images of the film as he eats a bowl of cereal.

"Am I interrupting?" I ask.

"No. Just tweaking." He smiles. "What's up?"

"Can you please make a copy of the film and put it on a DVD for Casper?"

"Umm. Why?" Dave says, taken aback.

"I'm going to take it to the test screening tonight."

"Hell no!"

"Why not?"

"You can't just walk off the lot with a copy of the film tucked under your arm, Charity," he says seriously.

"Why do people call this place a 'lot'? It's a high-rise, not a studio lot."

"Whatever. You can't have a copy of the movie," Dave says, taking a bite of his cereal.

"Copies of the movie get taken off the lot all the time," I say.

"Yeah, by executive producers delivering a pretty raw cut to a sound mixer or something. Charity, we are one step away from this being a locked picture. I'm not giving a copy of the film to an assistant to take to a test screening in El Segundo. You realize that test screenings are the number one way that films get leaked before they're released, right?"

"Casper wants to watch the movie right after the Q and A while the audience feedback is fresh in his mind. He wants to make sure the changes are good."

"You know who finds their way into test screenings? People who pirate movies. That's why the security is so tight at these things," Dave says.

"I'm not asking, Casper is. Maybe the two of you could come back here after the screening and you can play it for him off the editing bay," I say. Dave rubs his face vigorously. There's no way that he wants to come back to work after the screening and continue working until midnight. He has a young kid and is tired enough as it is.

"Casper has to know this isn't allowed," Dave says, and I can tell that he's close to caving.

"I don't know. Do you want me to get him on the phone? You can talk to him."

"No." Dave pushes his cereal bowl away from him and leans back in his chair.

"Look. I'm just doing my job. If you can't do it, you can't do it. I'll just ring Casper really quick so you can tell him why." I look at Dave as he contemplates the scenario.

In film, people rarely say no. Well, producers say no all the time and directors say no, but everyone else is there to say yes. It is our job to make sure the director has everything they need to make their movie a success. If we can't support their vision, we won't get hired.

I once sat in on a production meeting where the production designer was adamant that the director was asking for something impossible. *I can't do it. It can't be done*, he kept repeating. The director brainstormed for a while to come up with a solution, but the production designer set up roadblock after roadblock. The conversation ended with the production designer putting his foot down and saying, *It's just not possible*. The director simply turned to the producer and said that he needed someone who could make this possible. The production designer was fired on the spot. It's *yes* or die if you work below the line. So, there is no way I'm telling Casper he can't have this. Dave is going to have to tell him.

"Come back after lunch and I'll have it ready for you," Dave says, not looking at me.

"Thank you."

"Yeah. Yeah. And Charity, you didn't get it from me."

"Of course not," I say. But what I think is *Who else would I get a DVD copy of the film from?*

The AMC movie theater in El Segundo is exactly like all the other AMC theaters across America, except for two distinguishing features. The first is the small group of impressive people who gather in the lobby: Bellotti (Canopy Studios' CEO), Steve, Saul, and three other executive producers all stand out in their well-tailored suits and loafers, along with Casper, Saffron, Dave, and me. The other distinguishing feature of the El Segundo AMC movie theater is the security. Dave wasn't kidding—it's tight and a sure indicator of *Diffuser*'s value. Canopy put $270 million into making it. They hope to make $700 million. To get into the theater, we had to go through security that was as thorough as what you'd find at an international airport. Moviegoers went through metal detectors overseen by beefy security guards who carried metal-detecting wands and searched for video cameras. The guards also checked bags and patted people down—no studio wants to hear about a cheap, pirated in-theater recording of their film. It doesn't matter that someone's silhouette blocks part of the screen or you can't hear the actors' dialogue because the audience is munching on popcorn—any leak hurts ticket sales.

After the screening, Saffron and I stand side by side listening to Dave, Casper, and the Canopy Studios executives chat about the question-and-answer period that followed the screening. This is what a test screening is all about—picking the average Joe's brain. What made them laugh or cry? What didn't they like? The live Q and A lets the filmmaker have real conversations with film fans. That, along with written questionnaires, helps to make the film better. It also helps the marketing department target specific demographics. I place a protective hand over the DVD copy of *Diffuser* that's tucked under my left arm. It's bundled with a stack of questionnaires that the audience filled out after the screening. I'm ready to hand everything to Casper as soon as he asks for it.

"I'm going to go through those questionnaires as soon as I get home. I can't wait," Casper says, motioning toward the papers under my arm. The line of people who are exiting the building curves closer to us, and we shuffle aside, making room for a somewhat private conversation.

"Well, all in all, the audience's reaction tonight was positive," Bellotti says.

"I still think the pace is a little slow before the restaurant scene," Steve says.

"Easy fix," says Dave.

They chat until the theater empties out and Casper and I are finally alone with the cleaning crew. He turns to me and says, "Okay. You got a copy of the movie for me?" I look down at my left hand. There are the questionnaires, but no DVD. I feel tiny prickles scatter around my forehead in panic. I lock eyes with Casper. He's searching my face in disbelief. I can't say a thing. I look at the floor, but there's no DVD. I leaf through the questionnaires. No DVD. *Where the fuck is the DVD?!* I look up at Casper in shock. I had hundreds of millions of dollars tucked under my arm, and I lost it.

"It's not here," I barely manage to say.

"Where is it?" Casper looks petrified.

"It was right here," I say, pointing to the questionnaires. "I was holding it right here, under my arm, like this. It was on top of the questionnaires."

"You sure? What about your purse?"

I remember pulling the DVD out of my purse after the Q and A so I'd have it in my hand when Casper asked for it. But there's always a chance that I could be wrong. I rummage through my purse but don't see it. Then I dump my purse out onto the floor. I get down on my hands and knees and shuffle through the entire contents of my twenty-six-year-old life with Casper looking over me. Phone, lipstick, lip moisturizer, tissues, Discman, script pages, book, mechanical pencil, blue pen, black pen, tampon, wallet, sunscreen, pressed powder, dental floss, toothbrush, Visine, perfume, car keys, sunglasses, bikini, and gum. No DVD.

"Maybe I left it in my car," I say. I pick up the scattered items and toss them back into my purse.

Running toward my car, I pray that it's in there. If it is in my car, that means that I didn't drop it somewhere and it didn't end up in the hands of someone who has the potential to pirate thousands of copies, costing Canopy Studios hundreds of millions of dollars. Even though I'm 99.9 percent positive I did not leave it in the car, I will check. I rummage through the front console, the garbage in the back seat, under the seats, in the trunk, and through my gym bag. It's not in the car.

I'm in full-on panic mode. I burst through the glass door of the movie theater entrance and don't stop when I see Casper. "I'm checking the theater," I yell to him. In the theater, there is a four-member cleaning crew. "Did any of you find a DVD?" They shake their heads.

I run up to where I was sitting. I sigh with relief when I see my bag of popcorn still sitting on the floor. My area hasn't been cleaned yet. I crouch down and pick my popcorn bag off the floor, but I don't see the DVD. I lower myself onto my hands and knees, my cheek within an inch of the sticky floor, to look under the seats. Ugh. There are bits of candy covered with dust, pools of dried soda, and no DVD. My stomach churns. I look under every seat in my row, shuffling through candy wrappers and sodas, crunching popcorn under my Converse. No DVD. I look in the rows in front of and behind my seat. I search under every seat in the theater. No DVD.

I burst out the theater door and shake my head at Casper, silently telling him that I can't find it. "You're sure you had it?" Casper asks. It's just him and me in the lobby. The concession stand lights turn off. I don't know what else to say to Casper. I lost his movie. "Find it," Casper says. He walks away from me, heavy steps pounding toward the glowing orange of the parking garage.

The cleaning crew emerges from the theater rolling large trash bins. "Wait!" I shout, running over to them, my hands waving in the air. I grasp the side of a trash bin. "Can I look in these?" The lady on the other side of the trash looks confused. "Please. I . . . I . . . lost something. It's . . . it's important," I stammer, holding on to the trash bins as if my life depends on them.

The lady pulls the bins away from me. "Our shift is over, and they don't give us no overtime. We got to put this trash in the dumpster and go," she says.

"I'll pay you. This will only take a minute, but I will pay your overtime." I make my way to the nearby ATM. "See? I can get you all cash right now. How much do you want?"

"Can I help you?" a voice calls from behind. I look up, and it's the theater manager.

"Yes. I would like to search these trash bins, please," I say.

"You lost something?" the manager asks.

"Yes."

"What did you lose?"

"A DVD. I really need to find it."

He nods to the cleaning staff. "You guys can go home. I'll finish up here." The manager turns to me and says, "Let me know when you're done."

Not one trash bin in that whole theater contains the DVD. The manager is fed up with waiting for me and says he has to close. I follow him to his office to give him my phone number in case the DVD shows up. As he takes down my name and number, I spot two small television screens sitting side by side, high above his desk.

"Are those security cameras?" I ask.

"Yes," he answers.

"Can we watch the footage from tonight?"

"No."

"You mean I can't watch them or they don't physically work?"

"*You* can't watch them," he says.

"Please. Please will you let me? Look, this is serious."

The manager studies me for a moment. "Was the DVD you lost a copy of *Diffuser*?"

"Yes," I say.

Pity fills the manager's face. "Okay," he says.

We watch the fuzzy security footage. I don't know how this is going to help me. I can barely make out what's happening on-screen. The picture quality is terrible and the camera is positioned really far away from the action so the people are tiny. The manager points to a dark patch on the screen. "I think that's you," he says.

I wouldn't be able to tell that spec on the screen was me if I hadn't lived it. I see the group of execs standing in the lobby after the film. There's me standing next to Saffron. There we are moving away from the encroaching crowd. There we are saying goodbye. There I am sprinting out of the theater. But really, we are all blurry specks moving on-screen. What I need to see is whether the DVD was tucked under my arm, like I remember it was. If I can figure out where I dropped it, maybe I can find it.

"Can I watch it again?" I ask the manager.

"I really have to close up. Now I'm going to have to call the MPA and file a report. I'm going to be here for a while."

"File a report? What? What's the MPA?"

"Motion Picture Association. If a film from a movie theater goes missing, I have to call the MPA in case someone stole it. It's a piracy thing." My dry mouth suddenly fills with saliva, a true sign that I could vomit.

"You don't have to call the MPA. This wasn't one of your films. It's not even the final cut. It's not released yet."

"Yeah." His tone implies that the scenario I just described is one the MPA would be very interested in.

"Please. Please don't call." I don't know what I'm saying. I'm just pleading with this gentleman to help me out.

I don't know why he takes pity on me, but finally he says, "I won't call."

Back in the parking garage orange light soaks me and everything in my little car. My hand moves over the buttons of my phone to call Casper, but I'm shaking, which makes me aware that I need to calm down first. I try to take a breath, but I can't get the air deep enough into my lungs. I sit up straight and expand my ribs. I can't breathe. I try again. Seven hundred million dollars. Canopy Studios was projected to make seven hundred million dollars. I just lost a seven-hundred-million-dollar commodity. I can't breathe. If the DVD gets into the wrong hands . . . I roll down my window for some fresh air, but the dry ethanol in the warmth of the parking garage makes me gag. I take smaller breaths, trying to get as much oxygen as my lungs will allow.

I'm startled when my phone rings. It's Casper.

"Hey," I say as I answer.

"Any luck?"

"No."

"Don't tell anyone. Got it?"

CHAPTER 19
SCREAM

Today can play out in so many ways. It all depends on the location of the lost DVD. It has been eight tense hours since I lost the movie, and in those hours, I have played out every scenario I can think of, from good to career-on-fire bad.

Best-case scenario: The DVD is sitting in a dumpster outside the movie theater, waiting to be taken to the landfill. Best best-case scenario: It's already in the landfill, buried deep in waste and ruined forever.

Bad-case scenario: I did have the good sense not to put a label on the DVD. Some teenager could have picked it up off the movie theater floor, took it home, and now it's in his cluttered bedroom, sitting in a pile of junk where it will be forgotten.

Worst-case scenario: The teenager who picked the DVD up off the ground takes it home and plays it. He is shocked to find a pristine copy of Blake Anthony's yet-to-be-released film and plans on using it to stoke his social status at school. Luckily word about the film spreads like molasses because he and his friends are a little nerdy. It's not until the film is released that a few less desirable young ladies get lured into the nerd's home to watch the movie and dodge sloppy attempts at groping. Word spreads. By the second week after *Diffuser's* theatrical release, one of the nerds burns several copies of the film in the school computer lab and starts selling them. Copies of the DVD spread like a virus. By *Diffuser's* third week in theaters, bootlegged copies are being sold on Canal Street in New York, in LA's Garment District, and anywhere else such fakeries are sold. Box office numbers take a hit, but by now the film has broken even. Worried that the bootlegged DVDs will reach international markets, Canopy releases *Diffuser* overseas before the intended date. Unfortunately, they're too late. The international box office numbers are a huge disappointment, and *Diffuser* profits are a fraction of the predictions.

Worst worst-case scenario: The DVD was found by a film pirate mastermind who has already made thousands of DVDs and has told his contacts all over the United States to be ready to sell bootlegged copies of the biggest-budget film of all time by this afternoon. *Diffuser* goes down in history as the most widely distributed pirated movie ever, crushing any chance of Canopy making a profit since the entire world saw the blockbuster film in their living rooms before its theatrical release.

So, yeah, I didn't sleep much last night.

Outside the Canopy Studios building, a mist hovers over the grass. It will burn off by the time most employees arrive at work. I came in early hoping to strategize my day, but sitting in the quiet office was stifling so I went outside. I'm stretching my stiff back, bent at the waist, hanging my head between my legs and taking deep breaths.

"Charity Trickett," calls a familiar voice. Still hunched, I look through my legs and see Saul. I pop up and try to act normal.

"What are you doing here so early?" I ask, walking toward him.

"I'm old. I go to bed early. That means I'm up with the birds. Elaine doesn't like me banging around the house, so I come to work. You?"

"I felt like getting some writing done before the day started and was sick of my apartment, so here I am," I lie.

"Oh, the life of a writer," Saul says. We walk toward the building together. "You got anything for me?"

What's he talking about? Like, do I have a confession for him? "Um . . . pardon me?" I stammer.

"Any scripts? Come now, Charity. I would catch you, you know. On set scribbling notes on the back pages of your sides. I want to read one," he says.

"You want to read one of my scripts?" I heave the door open and let Saul enter the building first. He tips his imaginary hat to me, and I warm inside. Pantomime first thing in the morning—another reason to love Saul.

"I want to read your best script. Don't think about what Canopy Studios wants. Just give me your best." I'm shocked, thrilled, and relieved in equal measure.

"I'll print it off right now and bring it up to you," I say.

"Thank you," he says.

"Thank you, Saul."

As we ride the elevator in comfortable silence, I smile. Despite my anxiety, and despite my fear, I smile. Saul, one of Hollywood's most respected producers, wants to read one of my scripts. I'll give him *This Family Thing*.

Wait a minute. Saul is retiring. *Diffuser* is his last picture. My smile hits the floor when the realization hits me. I look over to the kind old man beside me, a man who has mentored me and invested his time in me. Little does he know that I may have tainted his entire career. I can see the *Variety* article now:

Saul Rubenstein Held on Too Long

Saul Rubenstein, iconic Hollywood producer, should have retired years ago. After over half a century of working in Hollywood, Saul Rubenstein's career ended tragically when, under his watch, a copy of the film Diffuser, Canopy Studios' biggest-budget film to date, was taken off the lot by an assistant and lost. Before the film was released, it landed in the hands of the world's biggest pirating ring and audiences were able to watch the blockbuster for a fraction of what it would have cost them to see it in movie theaters. Saul Rubenstein's retirement picture is the first in Canopy Studios' history to net negative dollars.

The unmistakable click of the office door unlocking fills me with dread. Facing Casper this morning is going to be rough. "Morning," Saffron says, striding into the office.

"Morning," I say. Does she know?

"Any word on when Casper is coming in?"

"No."

"I wonder how late he stayed up working with the questionnaires." Saffron looks at me expectantly. A million synapses fire inside my skull, trying to piece together the expression on her skinny face. She didn't . . . she wouldn't . . . did she steal the DVD from me? She was standing right beside me at the theater last night. She could have reached one of her lanky arms behind me and slid her stick fingers over the stack of questionnaires that were tucked under my arm. She could have lifted the DVD without me ever noticing.

Now, like a true sociopath, she stands in front of me with no sign of shame or guilt, cool as a cucumber after stealing a multimillion-dollar commodity from Canopy Studios in a plan to ruin my career. Would she do that, though? It's risky. If she was discovered, her career would be ruined. Her relationship with Casper and Charlotte would be ruined. How crazy is Saffron?

"Are you okay?" she asks.

"Don't talk to me," I say.

"Charity. What's wrong?" she says. Is that shock on her face? Or is she pretending to be shocked?

"I can't talk right now," I say.

"Fine," Saffron says, and she goes to her office.

At 9:22, there is a knock at the door. I answer it. "Are you Charity Trickett?" asks the petite sixty-year-old woman in front of me.

"Yes," I say. She crosses the threshold of the office and heads directly to the couch, where she sits herself down. Her hair is a perfect brown bob, her lipstick is red, her conservative heels are polished, and there isn't a speck of lint on her navy suit. She is a real professional, the type of person with whom I have very little experience. She opens a briefcase and pulls out a legal pad and pen.

"Join me, Charity," she says. I sit with her on the couch. Saffron peeks her head out of her office.

"And you are?" the woman with the red lips asks Saffron.

"Saffron."

"The associate producer?"

"Yes."

"You can have a seat, too." Saffron sits in the chair opposite me and the woman with the red lips. I can feel Saffy's eyes on me, but I'm too focused on the legal pad resting in this woman's lap to care. Her hand-writing is small and messy, making it illegible from where I'm sitting.

"Charity, I'm Judith. I'm a lawyer here at Canopy Studios. Why didn't you tell us that you lost a copy of *Diffuser*?"

I . . . I . . . I can't talk.

Judith continues. "I received a call from the MPA this morning at nine sharp. They received a call from the manager of the—" She looks down at her notes. "The AMC theater in El Segundo at 11:17 last night. The manager reported that someone named Charity Trickett from Canopy Studios lost a copy of *Diffuser* at the theater after a test screening. Is that correct?"

"Yes," I say.

"What format was the film in?"

"DVD."

"Why did you have a copy of the film?"

"To give to Casper."

"Did you ask the manager of the AMC theater in El Segundo to not call the MPA?"

"I did."

"Why?"

"I was scared of getting into trouble," I say, looking at the floor.

"Good thing he didn't listen to you. Hopefully we can get ahead of this thing." Judith packs up her briefcase while she finishes off the meeting. "The FBI has been notified, and a full investigation has already begun. We will be in touch." She rises, and I open the door for her as she leaves.

I go directly to my desk, ignoring whatever Saffron is saying, her voice sounding like a distant rumble. I pick up the phone and dial quickly. Casper answers.

"They know," I say.

Saffron, Casper, and I stand on the back deck of Casper's Hollywood Hills home. We look out at the gully that lies lush and green in front of us. The Hollywood sign in the distance cuts through the mid-morning haze. As soon as I told Casper that Canopy knows about the lost movie, he said Saffron and I should pack up our stuff and come to his house.

I turn my back from the view to take in Casper's house. I wonder how long it will be until his home office is turned into a nursery. Not too long after his wedding, I'd guess. Then I'm hit with a realization so awful that I want to shrivel up. It's not like Casper is a twenty-six-year-old assistant, like me. He has been building his career for almost two decades. This film is supposed to catapult him to a level of distinction that most directors dream of. Now Canopy may never hire him again, and if other studios hear about this, he may never work again. I may have fucked Casper's entire future. He looks over his astonishing Hollywood view. His jaw is clenched, his body is hunched over, and his hands grip the railing like he's holding on for dear life. I want to vomit.

"You were both there, talking to the lawyer?" Casper asks.

"Yeah," I say.

"What was said?" he asks, looking directly at Saffron.

"She basically asked why Charity had a copy of the film," Saffron says. "Charity said that it was for you."

Casper nods. I stand there looking back and forth between the two of them, talking as if I'm not there. Casper's phone rings. When he looks at the screen, his jaw clenches. Then he walks into the house for privacy.

Saffron makes small talk, but my focus is drawn toward Casper's muffled voice from within the house. Saffron is talking about her nephew. How can she talk about her nephew at a time like this? Shut up. I'm pretty sure her insignificant banter is meant to prevent me from hearing Casper's conversation. I can't take it anymore. "I asked you not to talk to me," I say.

"I'm just . . . I don't know. I'm trying to take your mind off things," Saffron stutters.

"I'm sure," I say.

"Charity, I'm trying to help," Saffron says.

"As if. I'm sure you're enjoying every minute of this," I say. I turn my back to her, and we stand in silence, looking at the view.

"Charity," Casper says as he walks out to the deck. "It's Bellotti."

Bellotti? The CEO? Last night at the screening was the first time I met him, and he looked just as intimidating as his assistant had described him. His slick red hair was pristine, and the veins pulsating from his neck implied that there was an imposing body under his custom-made suit. If there is a God, I'm thanking her right now that I'm not standing in front of Bellotti in person, but I'm also cursing her for introducing me to him last night.

Casper puts his cell on speakerphone and says, "Okay. I have Charity here."

"Fucking Charity Trickett. Are you there?" Bellotti's voice is so angry that it freezes me to my core.

"Yes," I manage to say.

"You fucking cunt. I would fire your fucking ass right now if legal wasn't so uptight. You took my fucking movie, you fucking cunt. To a test screening! You dumb bitch! You dumb fucking whore!"

I look up to Casper. He locks eyes with me and mouths, *Are you okay?* I nod and look at the phone as the nastiest, most vile words are flung at me by one of the most powerful men in Hollywood.

"You steal from me, you fucking bitch, I will ruin you. You are done. You'll be lucky to get a job as a Hollywood stripper by the time I'm through with you." Bellotti goes on and on. Eventually, my mind and body grow numb from the verbal abuse. I don't cry. I don't say anything. I just take it.

Saffron sends me to the office to pick up a script that she left there. I think she and Casper need a breather from me, and in truth, I'm happy to get into my car, but Canopy is the last place I want to go. I pull up to the security guard who checks IDs at the parking garage entrance. He scans my ID, and I hold my breath, wondering if I'm going to be let in. Has word gotten out that I'm a thief, a slut, a dirty whore who Canopy Studios hates, a stupid bitch who Bellotti is going to ruin?

The gate in front of me opens, but I'm not relieved—I'm terrified that I'm going to walk into the most prestigious film studio in the world and everyone there is going to know that I don't belong. When I walk along the breezeway from the parking garage, I don't look up to the leopard that sits at the top of the building or crane my neck in hopes of a celebrity spotting. Instead I keep my eyes on the ground and speed walk. I wish I were invisible.

The elevator opens on my floor, and I peek out the doors to make sure the hallway is empty before getting off. Once I'm in my office, I sit at my desk and pick up the phone. I'm dying to call my parents. My dad will have advice on how to handle this kind of thing. When I hear his voice say hello on the other end of the line, something in me comes undone and I cry. I can't get words out. I just cry.

"Are you alright? Charity, what happened?" my dad asks, but I can't talk. "Charity, are you okay? What happened?" He sounds helpless.

I have to calm down. *You're not dying, Charity,* I tell myself. *You're just in trouble. Calm down.* Eventually I manage to tell him the story. When I finish giving him every awful detail of the last seventeen hours, there is silence on the other end of the phone.

"Dad?" I say.

"Why don't you come home this weekend? It's Friday. I can book you on the last flight home tonight or the first one in the morning. We'll talk things out. You can rest."

"Really?"

"Absolutely. I'll call you back in ten minutes with your flight information."

"Oh, Dad. Thank you so much." I hang up the phone, thankful for having a supportive family.

I go to Saffron's office and grab the script off her desk. When I come out, there is a knock on the door. Oh God. Who is it? The lawyer? Bellotti? Maybe it's Saul or Steve. Does Kai know? I swallow hard. The thought of their disappointment is crushing.

I open the door, and it's Beth. She's panting like she ran here. "Beth!" I say with as much enthusiasm as I can muster. She walks into the office, letting the door close behind her. "Hey, so, message from Bellotti. He says that he knows that you're Canadian and you're not allowed to leave the state."

My mouth drops to the floor.

She says, "Is there anything I can do to help? Why can't you leave the state? Are you okay?"

"It's . . . I have to make a phone call. I'll see you later." I shuffle Beth toward the door and open it for her.

"Okay. Keep me updated," Beth says as the door closes on her.

I can't leave the state? Is Bellotti telling me this? Canopy Studios legal? Oh, shit. That lawyer said that the FBI had been notified. About me? Am I under FBI investigation? Do they think I stole the movie? How do I tell my parents that their daughter is under FBI investigation? What a proud moment for them. This will rank highly on the list of disappointments. Crashing the car, getting kicked out of sleepover camp because I snuck into the boys' tent, smoking weed, failing math, getting caught masturbating. This FBI investigation might be enough to end parental support altogether.

My dad answers the phone, and I explain my latest predicament. There is silence on the other end of the phone. "They just told you that? I'm on the other line with the travel agent right now," he says.

My heart is pounding so hard. "Dad. I'm under criminal investigation."

"Charity, it's okay," he says.

"Like, the FBI."

"Really, honey." He cuts me off. "Let's talk later." My computer dings, notifying me of an incoming email. It's from my dad. *Coincidence that Canopy told you this so shortly after our convo. Do you think they bugged your office phone?*

Like a deer in headlights, I become abruptly and perfectly still. The timing of Beth's arrival is too coincidental not to be suspicious.

"Okay. I'll call you later," I say and hang up the phone.

I quickly delete the email from my dad. I sit for a while looking at my office phone. *Is there a bug in there?* I pick it up and look underneath. *How do I get this thing open?* Even if I figured it out, I don't know what a bug looks like. Or maybe there's a camera hidden in my office. Maybe Canopy built this place with cameras in all the offices, and they turn them on when they suspect something.

I walk slowly around the office in search of a camera. I balance on a chair and peer into the ceiling vent. Nothing. I examine a lamp and a bookcase. I stand in the middle of the office, alone and surrounded by silence, thinking, *Are they watching me?*

CHAPTER 20
"YOUR SPY CAR IS A MINI?"

Tonight has been an exercise in distraction. I've tried everything I can think of to take my mind off the fact that my world is crumbling around me. I drank wine and tried working on Albana's notes for my script. Didn't work. I put on calming music and flipped through *People Magazine* while drinking more wine. Didn't work. Then I put on TLC. I sang, I danced, my heart pumped new energy throughout my body, and for about six minutes I forgot my troubles. Then my neighbor banged on the door, yelling at me to shut up, so I took my bottle of wine to bed where I put on my favorite movie. Guess what? The first thing to appear on the screen was an FBI warning, and for the first time I paid attention to it. Piracy is a felony with a maximum penalty of five years in prison and/or a two-hundred-fifty-thousand-dollar fine. The reality of my situation crashed down on me hard. Prison? There is no way I will survive prison. When Pup and I backpacked around Europe, I barely survived youth hostels. I turned the movie off, drank the last of the wine from the bottle, and ran a luxuriously hot bath, complete with bubbles, because who knows how many nights of freedom I have left.

Now I stand naked in front of the bathroom mirror, every inch of me pink and steaming. Is that a zit? I lean closer to the mirror and work at popping it. Then I go for the blackheads, letting myself air-dry instead of covering my naked body with a towel. Next, I reach for a bottle of coconut oil and pour a generous amount into my hand. I lift my foot onto the counter and massage the oil onto my naked body, really working it into my skin, massaging the cellulite and moving my flesh in unflattering ways. *Don't look in the mirror*, I think. *The last thing I need is low self-esteem to go along with the stress.*

There's a loud crash in the alley, which startles me. I grab a towel and wrap it around myself before going to the bathroom window to investigate. From my fourth-floor apartment, I look down to the alley and see a white cube van parked close to the two-story warehouse across the street. There is a man lying on the van's roof, curled in the fetal position as if he's in pain. Could he have fallen from the warehouse roof onto the van? Was he climbing the lamppost?

The man rolls to the edge of the roof and drops down to the pavement just as the van's back door opens and out rushes another man. They are dressed in identical coveralls and seem concerned as they look up toward the telephone pole that sits directly across from my window. Then they look directly at me, and for a split second we see each other, and in that split second they are just as shocked as I am to be seen. I hit the floor and clutch my towel. I hear truck doors slam and an engine ignite. I crawl to the light switch that's on the opposite side of the bathroom and turn off the lights. I spring to my feet and get back to the window in time to see the van's taillights speeding off in the distance.

I'm high enough in the building that, unless I'm standing directly in front of the window, nobody from the street can see me. I can brush my teeth at the sink and get out of the shower in complete privacy, while enjoying the blue California sky through my little bathroom window. I've never bothered closing the blinds. Why would I? But now, as I look at the lamppost directly across from my apartment glowing in the night sky, I feel like I'm being watched. The wine may be making me paranoid and they may not be the FBI, but for the first time since moving in, I close my bathroom blinds.

Movie clips play in my mind, all with various villains, spies, and investigators looking through binoculars to spy on their targets: *Rear Window, The Conversation, Stakeout, Another Stakeout.* People get spied on—it happens. And I'm apparently under FBI investigation, so . . . Did some dude in a cube van just watch me pop zits and rub coconut oil all over my body, and not in a cute way? Ugh! Did he record me? Did he put a camera on the lamppost? Now what? Are a bunch of government workers going to sit around some office watching me pop pimples and moisturize?! Is my cellulite going to be entered into evidence?

The last thing I want to do right now is party. I'm emotionally drained, possibly paranoid, and a touch hungover from last night. But it's Jessica's birthday and she has been so nice to me since I moved here that I want to celebrate her. I'm sure I can put a smile on my face for a couple of drinks at a bar. I called Kai earlier to see if he wanted to come over for a glass of wine before heading out, but he didn't get back to me until an hour before we were supposed to be at the party. He was biking all day and didn't have cell reception. He still needs to shower and eat, so he's meeting me there. Is he avoiding me because he knows?

I arrive at the bar and move through the crowd to find Jessica with a group of people, some are familiar faces from the bullpen. When Jessica sees me, her eyes grow wide and she quickly walks my way. "I'm so glad that you decided to come," she says, her face full of sympathy. "Are you okay?"

"I'm fine," I say, plastering on what I hope is a natural-looking smile. Behind Jessica, a few others from the bullpen look our way.

"Good. Everyone's going to be relieved to hear that. Come on. Let's get you a drink."

While following Jessica through the bar, I register what she just said. *Everyone* will be relieved to hear that I'm fine. Does everyone in the bullpen know that I'm under FBI investigation? Fuck me! I order a glass of prosecco and sip delicately, wary of where the night might take me. Jessica and I join a small group of assistants who are gossiping about which stars have been considered for which projects, a conversation that happens regularly with the bullpen crew. Knowing who is attached to a picture is a good indication of how much financial backing a film has.

My boss on such-and-such movie reached out to so-and-so for the lead.

Yeah, well, my boss on such-and-such movie signed papers today for so-and-so to direct.

This kind of information offers insight into your next year of work. Are you working on the next huge blockbuster? Are you working on a smaller film that might be a sleeper hit and launch careers? Or are you working on that film where your audience gets stoned before watching it? The level of prestige attached to a project establishes a hierarchy in the bullpen.

I feel a hand on my back and instantly relax, knowing that it's Kai. I turn to him and manage a weak smile. "How are you?" he asks. His face is intense, and I can't tell if he's concerned or angry.

"I'm okay," I say.

"Do you need a drink?" He's so serious.

"No." I raise my champagne flute. "But I'll join you at the bar." I follow Kai, feeling that something between us isn't right. He doesn't pull me by my hand like he normally does or look back at me with his killer smile. I keep my eyes on his broad shoulders and the muscles moving under the light cotton of his navy T-shirt, suppressing the urge to press my lips to the patch of skin below his hairline.

Kai finds plenty of room for us at the bar, and I'm silently disappointed that we won't be pressed together by the force of a crowd. He orders his whiskey sour. "This is serious," he says.

I must look confused.

"Your situation. It's serious, Charity. What are you going to do?"

"You know what happened?"

"I know. I don't think they know the details." He motions to Jessica and the others from the bullpen. "They do know that you're being investigated by the FBI, but they don't know that it's for piracy of *Diffuser*."

"Am I really under FBI investigation?"

"Yes," he says.

"You should have heard Bellotti screaming at me yesterday."

"He's a rough character."

"It was awful," I say. "What should I do?"

Kai takes my hand and holds it gently in his. "I don't know. I've been thinking about this since I found out yesterday, and I don't see a way out of it." A look of guilt crosses his face. "I should have called," he says.

"You don't want to get messed up in this," I say. Then I lean in and whisper, "I think my phone's tapped."

"Hmm," he says. His intensity brings legitimacy to my paranoia.

"Should I quit?"

"You'll still be under investigation."

"Investigate me. They'll see that I have certainly not been groomed for a life of criminal activity. I have a degree in fine arts. I studied mime and voice because I wanted a well-rounded education. I was a nanny. I volunteer at animal shelters. I've never been fired from a job. Do you know how many people have trusted me with their house keys and credit card numbers?"

Kai smiles. It's his first smile tonight, and the knot in my stomach loosens a bit. "I don't think you should quit," he says. "Let's see how things play out."

A voice rings out from behind me. "Okay, Charity. What the fuck happened?" I pivot and see Beth with a girl from the bullpen whose name I can't remember. "Come on. Everyone is talking about how you're under FBI investigation. What the fuck did you do?"

I stammer and stall. She motions to Kai, who stands behind me. "You know, don't you? Saul tells you everything," Beth says.

"You talking about that rumor?" Kai says with a relaxed smile.

"Kai, get serious. When Bellotti yelled 'you fucking cunt' from behind closed doors yesterday, guess who put the call through?"

I can't take this conversation anymore. I look around the room, hoping for a friendly face to escape to, but all I see is that everyone from the bullpen is staring at us. It's like Beth had announced to the group that she would find out what Charity did, and now everyone is watching for the answer, even Jessica.

I set my drink on the bar, preparing to run away, but Beth places her well-manicured hand on top of mine. She says, "He wanted to talk to you, Charity. So I called down to your office, and there was no answer. I tried your cell. Then I tried Casper. So who was Bellotti calling a cunt, a bitch, and a whore? Casper or you?"

I remove my hand from under Beth's and stand my ground. "I'm sure that as Bellotti's assistant, he would have told you the details of that phone call if he wanted you to know. Good night." I turn my back to her and face Kai. He hands me my glass of prosecco, and we sip casually.

"Oh, come on, Charity. It's not like I'm wearing a wire or anything."

I'm struck with panic. Why would Beth think that this would be a wire-wearing scenario? Is someone here wearing a wire?

Kai bursts out in a short laugh and a drop of whiskey sour falls from his mouth onto his T-shirt. He shakes his head, trying to suppress his laughter so he can swallow the remaining alcohol. I hand him a napkin, and when I do, I see Kai's game. He's looking at Beth as though he finds her deeply funny and stupid. I follow his lead, realizing that I need to be far more slick if I'm going to survive Hollywood. I look at Beth as though she's dim-witted.

"I think that you're confusing the movies with real life," I say. With that, she and her friend leave us to join the onlookers at the other side of the room.

If I thought I was falling in love with Kai before, I am now 110 percent sure of it. There is no denying that I have been stifling my feelings for this man since the day I fell into his arms. Everyone in the bullpen has given me a wide berth tonight, not wanting to be associated with me, but this man doesn't give a shit. He is his own man, so self-assured that I wonder if it's possible for him to be any girl's man because I want him to be mine.

Alone at the bar once more, we ignore the eyes glancing our way. I sip my warm prosecco slowly, knowing that when I'm done, I will go home alone. As we talk, he gently presses his knee against my thigh. He tries to distract me with a little humor and small talk, but I can't perk up.

"Kai, I thought I was just doing my job," I say.

"You were," he says. Relief hits me. "You're always doing your job." He rubs the side of my waist that's hidden under the bar. "If you weren't hell-bent about us being professional, we could leave here right now. I could take you home," he says, leaning toward me.

I can't look at him. "You don't want to get involved with me right now, Kai. I mean, I realize that you standing here with me right now is getting involved, and I appreciate it. I know what you're doing. Thank you."

"What am I doing?"

"You're acting like it's no big deal so that everyone else thinks that it's no big deal."

"You're wrong. I'm being supportive and caring so that you let me into your bed." Under his joke lies sympathy and soft eyes.

"I should go," I say.

"Really?" Kai looks crestfallen. I would love nothing more than to tuck myself under his arm and let him take me home, but that's not fair to him.

"Kai, you're moving on to really great things in the most iconic film studio in the world. A studio that I'm in a lot of trouble with. You should not be involved with me. You should be over there with the rest of the bullpen, avoiding me."

"Charity, they're idiots."

I smile at Kai because we both know that's not true. "I'm sure that everything will be cleared up soon. I'll see you later," I say. I walk away, leaving my warm prosecco on the bar and hoping that what I just said is true. Hoping that I haven't lost Kai forever.

CHAPTER 21
MISERY

I t's been a week and a day since I lost *Diffuser*, and strangely it's business as usual at Canopy Studios. Casper has been editing based on the notes from the test screening, Saffron is only mildly irritating, and I still have access to the entire building. There has been no mention of my losing a copy of the year's biggest blockbuster, and I have heard nothing from the FBI. One would think that no news is good news, but in fact, it's nerve-wracking. I have spent the week jumping every time the phone rings, worried that it's Bellotti calling to yell at me again or Judith from legal telling me I'm fired. It's finally Friday and you would think I would be relieved that the week is almost over, but this is the day that I have been dreading the most.

Today I'm tasked with setting up a screening for Blake Anthony in the Canopy Studios executive theater, a VIP event that will involve Dave, Casper, all the Canopy executives, and board members. It's supposed to be a celebration between the biggest star in the world and the most iconic studio ever. Instead I've tainted it. We have all been instructed to tell Blake nothing about the lost film, so the screening will be a masquerade and my involvement in it will be torture. In a matter of minutes, I am going to be trapped in a room full of men who are suited up and ready for business. They talk about money in the millions. They know every person in Hollywood, including influential politicians and leaders of industry. They consider actors to be commodities and networks to be purchased. Suddenly I am on their radar as the girl who potentially cost them hundreds of millions of dollars. If I said I was nervous, it would be an understatement.

I am halfway down the hall, making my way toward the bullpen, when I realize a wheel on my rolling cart is wonky, causing the coffee cups to clang together loudly. I shuffle the coffee, tea, snacks, and mugs so they don't bang together, but there's only so much room on the cart. Feeling defeated by a simple task, I continue on with my head down and cups clanging away, trying to be discrete. The bullpen comes into view and I look up, hoping Kai's friendly face will put me at ease, but his cubicle is empty. I smile awkwardly at a few of the assistants, and I'm met with less than enthusiastic bulls. Jessica sees me and waves before answering the phone, and I can't help but wonder if there really is someone calling her.

Once I arrive at Canopy Studios' state-of-the-art, forty-seat executive theater, I lay the refreshments on the marble table. I walk through the five rows of plush leather recliners, placing bottles of chilled water in each cup holder. On each seat, I place a monogramed Canopy Studios notepad adorned with a matching pen and clip-on reading light for taking notes in the dark. Everything is perfect for Blake's screening.

I've just taken a seat in the front row to review my to-do list when the door opens and in walks Steve. I haven't seen him since I lost the film, and I've been dreading this moment for days. I don't know why, but I instinctively pull my legs to my chest like I'm a scared child.

"Charity," Steve says, placing a tender hand on my knee. "I hope this is the hardest thing you'll have to endure in your career." I know Steve is trying to be supportive, but he's terrifying me. It's the word *endure*. *Endure* suggests that I have no control over what is happening. Steve is saying that all I can do is live through this.

"Thank you, Steve." I need some fresh air. How can I get out of this room? "I should go down and get Blake," I say as I stand up to leave.

I am almost outside the building when Jack stops me. "Charity," he says while happily jogging my way.

"Hi, Jack," I say, managing a smile.

"Hey, want to grab lunch today?"

"Um. No. Sorry. I can't," I say, unable to come up with an excuse.

"Are you sweating? You feeling okay?"

I touch my forehead, and I am indeed sweating. "I'm fine. Just running behind today and rushing," I say. Then I hear the unmistakable bravado of the biggest star in Hollywood, and Jack hears it, too.

"There she is," Blake says, emerging from the elevator with Daniel.

Jack's jaw drops. "Oh my God," he says. Blake and Daniel walk our way, Blake's arms outstretched for a hug. "Oh my God. He's coming right to us," Jack says, patting the pockets of his suit jacket in search of his small camera. Blake folds me into his arms.

"I'm excited for you to see the movie," I tell Blake, my pitch a little too high, my volume a little too loud. For some reason, I high-five Daniel, which he doesn't seem to like.

"Jack, this is Daniel and Blake," I say with too much enthusiasm.

"Huge fan!" Jack says. "Huge! Can I get a picture? Charity? Can you?" Jack says, handing me his camera. Blake stands next to Jack and makes a peace sign while Jack looks like he just won the lottery. I try to hold the camera steady, but my hands are shaking. Do they notice?

We leave Jack and get into one of the Canopy elevators. Daniel is beside me with Blake across from us, and suddenly the elevator feels like it's closing in on me. The word *endure* swims around my head. I need to endure the next few moments of my work. Endure being in the same room as Bellotti. Endure being called a bitch and a cunt. Endure being a pariah at Canopy Studios. Endure an FBI investigation. I have no control. Just like being in this elevator. There's an illusion of control when I press the button, but I have no control in this box that's flying up and down so fast the air pressure changes. I'm hot.

God, it's hot in here. Do I have armpit stains? Is this claustrophobia? Is this a panic attack?

The elevator doors open, and we step into the opulent executive lobby. I struggle up the Oscar-lined staircase as Blake and Daniel joke around. Their words are fuzzy and distant. We pass Oscar after Oscar. Goodbye, opportunity; goodbye, Canopy Studios; goodbye, career; goodbye, Los Angeles; goodbye, future.

"What's wrong with you?" Blake says.

I stop climbing. Does he know? "What do you mean?" I ask.

"Are you feeling okay?" Blake asks.

"Jesus, Blake. You look great, Charity," Daniel says.

"No, she doesn't. She's pale. No—she's green. Are you sick?" Blake asks.

"I'm fine," I say.

I continue up the stairs and hear Daniel smack Blake. Thank you, Daniel. What's Blake's problem? Alright, I probably look like shit; I haven't been sleeping and I feel nauseous. In fact, I think these stairs are giving me vertigo. I keep my eyes focused on my feet, willing myself to make it to the top.

The elevator dings behind us, and we hear, "Hey, guys." It's Casper and Dave. They meet us on the stairs, and Casper introduces Dave to Blake and Daniel. Oh shit. What about Dave? Where does Canopy and the FBI think I got the DVD? Poor Dave. He just started a family, and this is the biggest film he has ever edited. The same can be said for Casper. This could change the whole trajectory of their lives. What if they never get another film again?

As I continue trudging up the stairs, my mind spirals. Casper and Dave will suffer before making the decision to give up on the film industry. They'll wait for offers that never come. Eventually they'll force themselves into meetings where they passionately pitch in vain. It will be the first time in years that they won't have a steady paycheck and will have no idea when the next influx of cash will come in. Plans to have children will be put on hold. Their marriages will take a hit because of it. Eventually they'll do a commercial—a big one, like Nike. But things will never be the same. The title of Big Time Hollywood Director or Editor will never be attainable for Casper and Dave. This is bigger than a company's bottom line. Bodies are piling up around me.

My chest feels tight. Why are there so many fucking stairs? The boys pass me, and I follow them to the screening room. My hope is that once we're in the theater, Blake's mere presence will distract Bellotti and the other execs from noticing me. A real star grabs hold of people's undivided attention, and when we enter the Canopy Studios executive theater, it is just this way—all eyes are on Blake. While hands are shaken and shoulders slapped, I move inconspicuously to the corner of the room where the remote for the projector sits. I wedge myself as deep into the corner as I can and watch the room full of men swirl around me. I have become that unspeakable thing that hides in the corner. Saul shakes Blake's hand, and I mourn for last week when I would have entered that conversation flawlessly.

"What's up?" Daniel asks when he approaches my corner.

"Nothing," I say a little too defensively.

"What's wrong with you?"

"Shh."

"Why are you hiding in the corner like a weirdo?"

"I'm not hiding." I push myself out of the corner as if I'm trying to prove something, but the lump in my throat and the heat in my cheeks threaten tears.

"You're being weird," Daniel says.

"Shut up."

"Charity, this isn't what you do, is it? You're not that assistant who is here just to assist. Get in there."

"Daniel, please." I can't cry right now, but if Daniel continues to berate me, I just might.

"Are you fucking kidding me? You need to get in this room and get known. You're a writer ready to take off. These people should know you," Daniel says.

I look around the room and count the number of powerful decision-makers. I think, *Oh, they know who I am.* That's when I spot him: Bellotti, his slick hair, flattened against his head as smooth as shark skin, and I'm thrown back into my corner. The memory of his words punch me in the face and kick me in the stomach. *Cunt. Bitch. Fucking slut. Little whore. You're dead.*

"Can everyone please take your seats? We'll start," I blurt with little finesse. Everyone makes their way to their seats as I dim the lights. The Canopy Studios leopard appears on the movie screen, roaring beneath the canopy of the jungle tree, as the orchestrated theme music blasts. I push open the door knowing that light is streaming in and everyone's attention has turned to me, Charity Trickett, that girl who lost the movie. I have to endure one last torturous moment before making my escape.

I walk through the bullpen, past all the bulls ignoring me, and then down that fucking staircase, passing all the Oscars and my dead dreams. The elevator stops at six different floors, packing people in like sardines and taking its sweet time before depositing me into the lobby. My shoes click too loudly on the marble floor, drawing far too much attention to the fact that I am both speed walking and almost crying. I know this sounds insane, but I'm certain that the larger-than-life oil painting of Dick Canopy is looking at me with disapproval. When I finally get outside, the stairs that run the length of the building are scattered with people. Where do I go to break down in private?

I turn left and cross Century Park West, heading toward a long hedge of cedars that borders a residential area. I wedge myself into the trees, hiding from the passing cars, and I cry. I cry so hard that pressure builds in my sinuses, and I have to gulp air between sobs. I let myself break down knowing that I'm hidden, knowing that traffic will dull the sound of my sobs. I cry the kind of cry where your chest heaves so much you feel the strain on your ribs. I don't know how long I cry for, but now my phone is ringing.

I reach into my back pocket and see that it's a Canopy number. "Hello. Charity here," I manage to say.

"Charity," the curt voice on the other end says. "It's Judith, the lawyer who came to your office the other day."

"Hello." A truck barrels by.

"You have a meeting today with the FBI," she says.

"Pardon me?" I could not have heard that right. The FBI wants to meet with me? Like, an interrogation?

"You have a meeting with the FBI today at one thirty," Judith says.

"In an hour?" I ask.

"Yes. That won't be a problem, will it?"

"No."

"Good. You are to meet Agent Brad Walker at the Coffee Bean on North Beverly and Santa Monica. Know the one?"

"The Coffee Bean? Like, the coffee shop?" I ask.

"Yes. The one in Beverly Hills on North Beverly. You know it?"

"Yeah. I know it."

"Good. One thirty." The line goes dead.

Three red brick steps, laid in herringbone style, lead down to the garden patio. Raised beds of flowers and black bamboo enclose a scattering of tables. Red umbrellas float above, casting a warm hue and blocking out the afternoon sun. He calls my name and walks toward me wearing a conservative smile. He motions toward the garden. "Please," he says kindly. I follow him.

We weave through a handful of people who are enjoying the afternoon before reaching a koi pond. The water makes a peaceful trickling sound. I look at the man I follow. Under his polo shirt, he has quarterback shoulders. His ass sits high in his khaki pants like two small helium balloons that could float up to the sky were it not for his leather belt.

"This okay?" he says, nodding toward a wall of bougainvillea in front of which sits a wrought iron pedestal table and two delicate chairs. He pulls my chair out for me, and I sit. "I'm going to grab a coffee. What would you like?" he asks casually, like he's not the FBI and I'm not shitting my pants.

"I'm fine," I say.

"Really? Come on. Tea?" He drops his briefcase onto the ground and tosses some papers on the table.

"Okay. Green, please."

I watch as he goes, thinking that if I saw him on the street, I would definitely look at him twice before realizing he's way too straight for me. He'd be perfectly cast for a Dockers ad in a military magazine. So far, this feels way more like a blind date than an FBI interrogation. A cute guy pulled my chair out for me, and he's even paying. But instead of ending in romance, this coffee could end with me being incarcerated.

On the table in front of me, among some loose papers, rests a file with my name on it. I can only assume that this is my case file, and I wonder if Agent Walker knows I'm a tea drinker from something written in that file by a man who went through my trash. Why would an FBI investigator leave the suspect of a federal crime alone with her case file moments before being questioned? Is this a test? Is that couple sipping coffees actually a couple, or are they undercover FBI investigators who are assessing my every move? I imagine what they're thinking. *If Charity doesn't look at the file, it means she's a good person. She follows the rules and probably didn't do it. Why would she look? Only a guilty person would look.*

Then again, why wouldn't you look? Only a stupid person wouldn't look. One should always come prepared to an FBI interrogation. He wouldn't have left the file here if I wasn't allowed to look at it. He's the FBI, so I assume he's not a careless guy.

I continue this game of pros and cons until I decide that I've wasted too much time debating. If I want to look, I have to do it now, or I'll miss my opportunity. I pull the file toward me and open it. First I see an official-looking piece of paper, like a passport application, with all my personal information. I slide it aside and find a picture of a man who is probably in his early fifties. His hair is unwashed and disheveled. He wears a five-o'clock shadow and a light blue golf shirt.

"What are you doing?"

I practically jump out of my seat. I look up to see Agent Walker looking pissed. "I was—I just . . ."

"You're not supposed to look at that," he says.

"Then why would you leave it here?" I ask.

"I didn't think you'd look at it."

"It has my name on it."

He takes a deep breath, places my green tea on the table, and sits down across from me. He takes the file back and seems annoyed as he reaches into his back pocket. He pulls out a wallet from which he produces a gold badge and an FBI ID card with his picture on it.

"I'm Agent Brad Walker," he says. His all-American smile and demeanor have disappeared. "I am a Federal Bureau Investigator for the United States of America. This is my identification."

I lean back in my chair and cross my arms. Something doesn't seem right.

"Is there a problem?" Agent Walker asks.

"Well, I wouldn't have a clue what a real FBI badge looks like. I do know that I work for Canopy Studios and I've seen a lot of different kinds of badges on prop trucks, so."

"Are you doubting my identification?" he says.

"I just would never know if this is real or not," I say, lifting his badge off the table. It's heavier than I expected.

"If you think that I am impersonating a federal agent or if you are at all uncomfortable, then we can get into our cars right now and you can follow me to the bureau. I assumed you'd be more comfortable here." He's absolutely right. This Coffee Bean is quite pleasant. If I had to sit in an FBI interrogation room, I'd probably pee my pants.

But there's a part of me that thinks this whole scenario is weirdly written. The location is all wrong. This Agent Walker is perfectly cast, but dum-dum left the file on the table. Did Canopy set this up? If I did say that I'd like to be taken to the bureau, where would Agent Walker take me? Back to Canopy Studios where I'd be yelled at again or to an actual FBI interrogation room? Both options lack appeal. It's best to play along. If this is what Canopy wants, fine. If this is what the FBI wants, fine. I just want this to be over.

"I'm fine," I say politely.

"Are you willing to be questioned?" Agent Walker asks.

"Yes."

He sits back and takes a sip from his paper cup, then pulls a tape recorder from his briefcase on the ground. "May I record this interview?"

"Yes," I say. Agent Walker presses a button on the small device.

"Wait. Do I need a lawyer?" I ask.

"Why would you need a lawyer?"

"Well, can this be used against me in a court of law?" I say, feeling foolish, like an ill-prepared actor playing a cop on TV.

"Against you . . ." Agent Walker simply sits there, letting his non-statement rest in the air for an uncomfortable amount of time. The void he makes is so unsettling that I feel an overwhelming need to fill it.

I tell him my story and include every detail I can remember, starting with the moment Casper asked me to get him a copy of the film and Dave's reluctance to give it to me. I tell him about standing with the executives after the screening, sure that the DVD was under my arm, to searching trash cans and coming up empty. I describe my fall from grace, being treated like a pariah, having my job being handed off to Saffron. I describe everything in heartbreaking detail. When I finish, Agent Walker opens his file and reads for a minute. "Why did you take the DVD to the theater? Why wouldn't you pick it up from Canopy Studios after the screening and then deliver it to Casper's home?" he asks.

"That's not what I was asked to do," I say. "Casper asked me to bring it to the screening."

"Casper told you to bring a copy of the film *Diffuser* to the test screening in El Segundo?"

"Yes," I say.

Agent Walker opens his file and produces the picture of the disheveled man. He slides it across the table and leaves it in front of me. "Who is this?" he asks.

"I don't know," I answer.

"You don't know this man?"

The man in the picture looks like a criminal, a predator who sits in a dark room all day and whose personal hygiene is an afterthought. I pronounce every syllable as if each is needed to save my life: "I do not know that man."

"What if I told you that he knows you?" Agent Walker says.

"I know, like, three people in this city other than Canopy employees. And he is not one of them."

"That's not what he says. He says that he knows you well." I look at Agent Walker and wonder if he's enjoying terrorizing a young woman who is drowning in this sick city with its stories and fabrications.

"I was doing my job," I say. Suddenly I feel all the emotion, all the fatigue and frustration. I feel my dreams die. "I have lived here for two seconds," I say, letting my tears fall. "I have three friends in LA. I have, like, no savings. My car is ready to die, and my job ends soon. Canopy isn't going to hire me again. Bellotti says he's going to ruin me. Casper wants nothing to do with me. I have no leads on a new job. Everybody knows that I'm under FBI investigation for piracy. News travels fast in this city. I became a lesbian overnight." I'm hysterical now. I've really worked myself into a tizzy. I'm bawling crying, short of breath, and have snot trickling out of my nose.

Agent Walker hands me a paper napkin.

"Thank you," I say, taking time to calm myself down. "Why aren't you questioning Casper? Why not Dave? Why me? I'm the assistant. I'm the lowest of the low on the food chain. People tell me what to do, and I do it. If I don't do it, they will find someone who will. And I was this close to moving up. Close to doing something where my voice is heard, where people care about my vision. I was close to getting there." My head is down and I sense his hand moving toward me. A business card comes into view. Through my tears, I look up at Agent Brad Walker.

"You call me if you need anything," he says. He gets up from the table, and I watch him leave, my thoughts spiraling out of control.

Scenario Number One: Fall Girl. Casper and Dave are saying they didn't know I brought the DVD to the test screening. Canopy believes that I am part of a pirating ring and stole their movie. Now the FBI is looking for my boss, thus the interrogation. My problem with scenario number one is that if I were Canopy Studios and someone had stolen a multimillion-dollar commodity from me, I would want the suspect interrogated in an unmarked building or someplace where they have to be driven to blindfolded. Scare the shit out of that little thief. A Coffee Bean in Beverly Hills is an odd choice for an FBI interrogation. Also, I'm sure that if the real FBI tapped away at their computers for a couple of minutes, they would discover that I am not designed for a life of crime. I am designed for ski weekends and games of charades. I'm sure they can easily figure out that I studied theater at university and spent most of my classes sitting crisscross-applesauce in a circle.

Which leads me to Scenario Number Two. Sure, maybe there is an FBI investigation, but I'm not a suspect. Yet Canopy still needs to decide whose head should roll. Who is going to be punished for costing the studio so much? Who should they make an example of? Casper and Dave still have a job to do. It would be foolish to fire them and bring in someone else to finish the edit when they're so close to being done. I'm dispensable. I'm just a perk for the director; I make his life easier so he can work effectively. Ruining my career costs Canopy nothing while sending a strong message to its employees: *Don't fuck with the studio.* So, was the FBI agent real?

I flip his business card around in my hand and a scene plays in my mind:

INT. CANOPY STUDIOS BOARDROOM — DAY —
A group of very serious men in suits gather around a boardroom table. Some stand, some sit. All are intense.

                        Suit #1
    I suppose HR should go talk to her. Get
    to the bottom of this.

                        Suit #2
    No. Let's send Legal. Send her a strong
    message.

                        Suit #3
    You really want to send her a message,
    send in the FBI.

                        Suit #2
    Huh. You're onto something there.

                        Suit #3
    I could set the whole thing up. Hire

some unknown actor, get a badge made up.
Maybe it will expedite this thing, get
some answers.

Heads nod in agreement.

                    Suit #2
Good thinking. So, we're all in agreement? You're going to handle everything?

                    Suit #3
Yeah. Leave it to me. It'll happen
tomorrow.

                    Suit #1
Great. So, we should know by tomorrow
whose head should roll.

They exit the room while approvingly slapping
each other on the back. Murmurs of golf games
and Cuban cigars in the BG.

CHAPTER 22
GOLDEN GIRLS

After my tea/FBI interrogation at the Coffee Bean, I drive back to Canopy Studios, but instead of stopping, I keep driving west along Pico Boulevard. My phone rings, and I turn it off without looking at it. I turn the music up loud, so I can't hear the awful sound my car is making, and drive until I hit the ocean. There's barely anyone on the beach, and I'm thankful. I take my shoes and socks off and walk into the ocean. The cool water hits my feet, sending a surge up my body that I can't contain. "*Fuck Casper!*" I yell. "*Fuuuuuuuuuuuuuuuck him!*"

While I was getting interrogated by the FBI, he was at a post-screening lunch with Blake Anthony and all the Canopy Studios bigwigs in a private dining room at the Beverly Hills Golf Club. Why isn't Casper getting interrogated by the FBI? What did he tell Canopy? Why has he not said anything to defend or even just support me? I can't exactly be surprised about this. In retrospect, he warned me. When he wouldn't fight for Vivy that day on his patio, he also said he wouldn't fight for anyone. He's only taking care of himself.

I'm furious at my stupidity, and I blame it on being an assistant. Ever since I got into this world, all I ever say is yes. That's an assistant's job. And yes, sometimes we get asked to operate outside the lines. We've all done it, from organizing nights out at a strip club to scoring drugs. But what I did for Casper goes beyond telling my boss which hotel bars have call girls. This is serious.

I plunk myself onto the dry sand and watch the seagulls dive into the ocean. What are my options? Quit working for Casper and find another job. No, other way around, dingbat—I can't afford to be out of work. Find another job, then quit Casper. I pull out my notebook and a pen and make a list of all my past bosses. The list is impressive but short, and I worry that Bellotti will make good on his promise that I will never work in film again.

Before I know it, the sky has turned pink with the sun hovering below the clouds. Instinctively, I reach for my phone to check the time, but it's off. I can't bring myself to turn it on. I know that there will be a message from Casper or Saffron asking where I've been all day. Reality will have to wait. I'm going to pick up El Pollo Loco and a box of wine, then head home to watch *Beaches*.

I slowly climb the stairs to my apartment, my sadness making my body tired.

"Here she is."

My heart skips a beat at the sound of this familiar voice. There, leaning against my door, is my favorite person in the world, Pup. You would think I'd bounce up those last few stairs to get to her, but instead I break down and cry, relieved that for the first time since losing the movie, I have someone who will console me. Pup comes to me, puts her arms around me, and walks me up the stairs.

"Eating and drinking our feelings tonight, I see," she says, helping me carry my load. I allow a little huff of laughter and wipe my tears. "Let me guess. You were going to watch *Moonstruck*?"

I shake my head.

Pup takes my keys from my hands and opens my apartment door. "*Beaches*?"

"Yes," I say.

"I came at the perfect time, then," she says, guiding me into my apartment.

The four of us are lined up in competition. I've never been naturally athletic, but carnival games are my jam, so Pup organized this night at the Santa Monica Pier with Daniel. When Albana texted me this morning, I thought back to how much fun she had playing Ping-Pong, so I asked her to join. Best decision ever. She is so entertaining that, miraculously, I am laughing.

Pup and I are side by side, paying more attention to Daniel and Albana than to the ring toss game we're supposed to be playing. Albana eyes Daniel as he lines up his ring toss with so much concentration that I wonder if he thinks that he can actually win at a carnival game. Just before he tosses the ring, Albana gives him a little hip nudge and his ring ricochets off the glass bottle. "Hey! No fair. Give me one of yours!" He reaches over Albana and snatches a ring from her cup. She giggles, and I get the feeling that, at heart, Albana is a wild child.

Pup grabs my arms in quiet hysteria. "Oh my God," she whispers. "She's going to do it again."

Albana smiles with all the joy in the world as Daniel lines up his shot again, and man, is he focused. Just before he releases his ring, she nudges him again with her hip. Daniel turns and looks at her incredulously.

"Are you fucking serious?" he says to Albana, who is clapping her hands and laughing. He reaches over her again and snatches another one of her rings. She lets him, and it's plain to see that Daniel is playing ring toss while Albana is playing Daniel.

Later, we sit in a circle in a bucket high in the sky as we go around the Ferris wheel. The lights dance playfully off the ocean below us. "So, let's talk business," Albana says, and I think, *Yes. For Albana, a Ferris wheel is the perfect office.* She says, "*This Family Thing.* I would like to direct it."

I look at her and think, *Did she just . . . ?*

Pup kicks my leg.

"Sorry," I say. "You said? What did you say?"

"Would you let me direct your movie?" Albana says.

I look at Daniel. "Did you know about this?" I ask him.

"No," he says.

I look at Pup's broad smile. "Of course, Albana," I say.

"Good. I can finally get rid of this!" Albana pulls a bottle of champagne from her purse along with four Solo cups. We hoot and holler as she pops the cork, champagne bubbling down the sides of the bottle and all over Albana's hands. She holds the overflowing bottle outside our little bucket, letting the champagne fall into the night sky and sprinkle on the people in the bucket below us. "Hey!" they cry.

Albana leans over the wall of the bucket, looking down on her victims. "Cheers!" she says, raising the bottle over her head, which makes us all giggle. We finish the champagne while high in the sky, which is good because our cups and empty bottle are confiscated once we step off the ride and we are asked to leave the Santa Monica Pier.

The rest of the night is full of making plans and talking movies. Over drinks in a dive bar close to Venice Beach, Albana talks about her investors, a group she has worked with in the past. She's confident they'll like the script. Once they jump on board, it's easy to get lines of credit and bank loans to make up the rest of the budget. She is asking for the biggest budget she's ever worked with.

Pup says they should shoot in Vancouver for the tax credits, which sends her and Albana into a nuts-and-bolts conversation about film financing. My girl Pup is good with numbers and knows production inside and out. Albana is impressed.

Daniel talks cast—he knows everyone. Albana talks director of photography and production designers. Her independent-film friends are award winners and beautiful artists. My friends talk with certainty and enthusiasm, and I let them, because what else can I do? Can I say,

So, guys . . . minor buzzkill, but there's a chance I could be convicted of a crime that could have me banned from Hollywood for the rest of my life? No way!

Instead, we take shots of tequila, share appies, and clink our drinks together. Cheers to us.

"It's not gonna happen," I say, letting my eyes fall shut. I can feel Pup in the bed beside me, turning over so we're face-to-face. I don't have the energy to open my eyes.

"Albana sounds pretty confident that it will," she says.

"Once she finds out, it'll be all over."

"What? The FBI thing?"

"The FBI thing?" I can't help but laugh. "Yes. The FBI thing."

"Are you drunk joking or drunk serious?" Pup asks.

"Bellotti's never gonna let it happen," I say.

"You're drunk depressed."

"I was interrogated by the FBI yesterday!"

"Yeah, but at least it was in a Coffee Bean in Beverly Hills. That's a positive," she says.

I scoff.

"And didn't you say the agent was kinda hot? That's cool," Pup says.

"Agent Brad Dum-Dum."

"And we're drunk, after celebrating with Albana Rugova, who wants to direct your script."

"Depressed drunk."

"Fuck Canopy, Charity. It was never your dream to be the world's best assistant, to work in a fucking high-rise with a bunch of power-hungry people in business suits. You're a screenwriter—soon to be a produced screenwriter."

"Don't you get it, Pup? Sure, maybe I don't go to jail. Maybe they see that I lost the film. I dropped it. It's gone. Whatever. But I will never work in this town again. Quote, Bellotti."

"He didn't say that," Pup says, looking at me skeptically.

"He said it. He said so many horrible things, and that one was the worst because it's true. Even if he doesn't intimidate someone into not hiring me, word's gonna get out, Pup. Albana will take off, Daniel will take off. Nobody is gonna want to work with Charity Trickett."

"What if you get in front of it? Daniel will understand. He's your friend," Pup says.

I open my eyes. "I have no friends here."

"Now you're drunkenly dramatic," Pup jokes.

But this is no joke. "If someone does have *Diffuser* and they put it on the black market, Canopy will make less money. Blake has a back-end deal. The more money the studio loses, the more money Blake loses. I could have cost Blake Anthony millions of dollars. So you see? Some friend I am."

I close my eyes even though my mind is racing and I won't be able to sleep.

CHAPTER 23
ALL I REALLY WANT

Days turn over, and I become completely stripped of any responsibilities associated with *Diffuser*. It's to be expected. What kills me is that Casper has completely shut me out; he doesn't even make a phone call through me anymore. Saffron has taken over my job entirely. Yet again, bravo, Saffron. If she stole the movie from me, she got the outcome she wanted.

I get the sense that Casper has let everyone know I'm on my way out. When I do pick up the office phone, there are no more pleasantries on the other end of the line. Some people even sound shocked when they hear my voice. To compensate for my lack of real work, Casper has me handle the annoying yet time-consuming tasks of everyday life. I fill out his passport-renewal application, I look for cheap flights to Europe, and I write him a CliffsNotes version of *Eat Right for Your Blood Type*. My guess is that he's planning for his honeymoon. I research toxin-free pesticides and home survival kits. I search the Yellow Pages for bars in Hollywood so I can find which one he left his credit card at. The worst, though, is that Casper struggles to act normal around me. Sometimes I wonder if he can stand me.

Multiple times a day, I wonder, *What am I still doing here?* The answer remains the same: I'm stuck. If I apply to be an assistant for some executive at a new studio, will they do a criminal record check, and will it say that I'm under FBI investigation? I'm not taking any chances. I'll go on the job hunt when this thing is over. That is, if Bellotti hasn't told all of Hollywood that I'm a "filthy bitch who should be run out of the industry." His words, not mine.

Saffron is interesting. She's gone from being the most brutal person I've ever worked with to being nice. Twice she has arrived at work and handed me a chai tea from my favorite tea store in Beverly Hills. She asks me how I'm doing and seems sincere about wanting to hear my answer. But her biggest act of kindness is ignoring me. She no longer asks me a hundred pointless questions a day, nor does she micromanage me. Not that there's much to micromanage.

Around the Canopy Studios building, I diligently avoid any human contact, maneuvering around the building like a spy in enemy territory. I walk quickly and quietly. I take corners with caution, ensuring that the coast is clear before heading down long hallways. I hide while I wait for the elevator, making sure it's empty before chancing a ride. I prepare every lunch at home and eat at my desk. I come in early and leave late all to avoid pedestrian traffic around the building.

The only thing that brings me joy is working on *This Family Thing*. I have worked on the written pitch for potential investors, and I believe that I have it crafted to perfection. Albana and Pup have made a budget together, breaking down each scene and the cost to film it. The pitch package is ready, and Albana should be meeting with her regular investors within a week. I try to keep my hopes in check, but *This Family Thing* is the one and only bright light in my dark world. Sometimes I even find myself sitting at my desk at Canopy lost in a vision of myself on stage at the Shrine Auditorium with an Oscar clutched in my hands, a delicate tear tracing the arch of my cheek, thanking Albana and Daniel for believing in me while Bellotti watches from the audience.

Casper comes into the office dragging his rolling cart. It's fixed with two Tupperware bins and a desktop computer.

"What's all this?" I ask.

"CDs. It's my collection." He opens one of the Tupperwares, and there are hundreds of CDs organized alphabetically. Saffron comes out of her office and leans against the doorframe.

"Wow. How many are there?" I ask.

"Over five hundred here. More at home," he says, parking his rolling cart in front of my desk. "I need you to download all of these CDs onto my computer and store them as MP3s. I got one of those portable MP3 players."

"Oh, wow. Okay."

"With each song, you'll have to name the album first, then the track number, then the song title," he instructs.

"Got it." I lug one Tupperware off the rolling cart, and it cuts into my hands. I let it drop onto the floor behind my desk.

"Oh, hey," Casper says. "The submission spreadsheet for *Break Room*. Email the list to Saffron."

I'm stunned. I'm crestfallen.

Casper continues. "Saffy, did Rick say anything about the contract?"

She walks into Casper's office with a pad of paper, and just like that, they dive into the kind of conversation I'm not invited to anymore.

I look down at the CDs. This should have me chained to my desk for a while. Five hundred CDs at about ten minutes a download is five thousand minutes. That's, like, two months of work if I dedicate all day every day to downloading CDs. And there are more CDs at home? It looks like Casper found me a project that has absolutely nothing to do with his current film or his next film and could take up the rest of my time at Canopy Studios.

The lunchroom in Jack's office is kind of depressing. It's gray and institutional, but I'm more comfortable here than anywhere else in the building, other than my desk, and I need a change of scenery. His accountant colleagues are nice, and none of them think of me as a giant fuck-up. Jack picked up burrito bowls for us, and now he's dousing his last bites with hot sauce. "Let's take a lap around the building after this," Jack says.

"Can't," I say.

"Okay, what's going on? This is the third lunch we've had in the depressing break room of Henderson, Victor, and Kline. You're pale. Like, do you go outside anymore? And you never have anything fun to say."

"Hey," I say.

"You're not miserable company, but if I wanted to be bored out of my mind, I'd have lunch with the accounting dudes."

"I'm sorry I'm not some cheery California girl for you," I say, tossing the rest of my burrito bowl into the garbage.

"Hey. I'm sorry. I'm trying to ask you if you're okay. I can't help sounding like a dick sometimes."

Is he apologizing? Am I supposed to say something here?

He says, "Are you okay?"

"I'm fine."

"Are you embarrassed to be seen with me?" he asks.

"No!" I say.

"Because I dated this girl for, like, three months, and I was like, why doesn't she introduce me to her friends? I think she was embarrassed to be seen with me but liked the nice restaurants I took her to, so."

"I'm sorry, Jack," I say, my heart breaking a little for him. "My work is stressful and busy right now. It's nice to come here and decompress, you know?" I open the cupboard in search of the fancy chocolate the accountants stash in little wooden boxes.

"I think you come here for the chocolate," Jack says.

I turn and face him, wondering if he's insecure. His shoulders are slumped, and I get the feeling he's had a rough go of it when it comes to the ladies. "I come here to track your progress."

He looks up from his burrito bowl with a confused look.

"Your de-douching," I explain. "I think you're doing a great job at becoming a decent dude."

Jack tries to hide a smile.

"The chocolate is a bonus." I open another cupboard, looking for it.

"You ate them all," Jack says.

"As if," I say. I haven't really eaten all the chocolate, have I?

"Sure have, Tubbo," Jack says.

"Jack!" I gasp, and he flashes me a cheeky smile.

The door flies open, and Casper comes in looking angry. "Trickett, where you at with the DMV?" he says. Shit.

I walk into his office and brace myself for the inevitable. Casper has to renew his driver's license, and he doesn't want to go to the DMV to do so. Last week, I told him I couldn't find an alternative to going to the DMV and he was adamant that there was a person who makes house calls. I haven't been able to find that person and Casper's license expires in days, so here I am breaking the bad news to him again.

"I checked into it some more, and the DMV doesn't make house calls," I say.

"They can't come to me?" Casper says.

"Afraid not."

In exasperation, Casper rubs his face with both hands.

"I went to the DMV and spoke to the manager," I say. "He told me they have to take your picture and they need the computer to process everything."

Casper stares at his computer screen, obviously annoyed with me.

"I talked to Blake, and he said that he goes to the DMV."

With this Casper finally looks me in the eyes. It's been weeks since he's looked me in the eyes, and now I see it. It's disdain. I'm thrown. I have never been met with such a look.

"Has he ever thought not to go to the DMV?" Casper questions.

"Nobody at the studio has any idea on how to avoid the DMV. I asked everybody," I say.

"Are you telling me that Bill Gates has to go to the DMV and wait in motherfucking line?" he bites.

"I'll do some more digging," I say while backing out of his office. What I want to say is this: *Casper, what you are asking for does not exist for you. Perhaps it exists for Bill Gates because he is one of the most respected minds of our time and world leaders turn to him for guidance. So yes, you are probably correct in assuming that Bill Gates doesn't have to wait in motherfucking line at the DMV, but you do.*

This can't be how my career in film is going to end after years of grunt work, years of paying dues, years of working long hours for little money. I'm a failure? No. There has to be a way to turn this around. I grab my key card and leave the office. Kai might have some advice.

When I enter the bullpen, the look on Jessica's face conveys utter shock. "Charity!" she exclaims.

"Charity!" A man's voice booms so loudly and so angrily that I am stunned into motionlessness. Coming out of the men's room is Bellotti. "You're fucking Charity?" he screams. A vein threatens to explode from the side of his neck, his face as red as his hair, and he is coming straight for me.

Why the fuck did I come up to the executive floor? Stupid, stupid Charity Trickett. Bellotti grabs me by the arm. He pulls me down a hall and through a set of thick wooden doors and practically throws me into a corner. I hold on to the wall to steady myself. When I turn around, I find that I'm in a room full of men in power suits. It looks like every Canopy Studios executive and board member is present, filling every space available, blocking the sunlight that should be streaming through the floor-to-ceiling windows, taking up precious real estate with their broad shoulders and egos.

Seated in the middle of the activity is FBI agent Brad Walker. He regards me quickly, then returns to the men in the room. "Does anybody else have any information that they'd like to share?" he says. A few cold and severe eyes look at me expectantly. Then I see Saul. His shoulders are slumped and he looks tired. I can't help but feel responsible. A lump so large I can barely swallow forms in my throat.

"The good thing is that the suspect is attempting to extort such an exorbitant amount from the studio that it's challenging for him to receive the funds, which makes it easier for us to catch him," Agent Walker says. Canopy Studios is being extorted? How much does he want? Millions? Heat rises into my cheeks. Bellotti stares at me with such intensity that I look away, and when I do, I'm met with a room filled with powerful men, all of whom blame me and want me to know it.

Don't cry, Charity. Hold it together. Don't be that girl who cries. Not in this room full of men, working in a company that is completely controlled by men. Don't give them any ammunition to say that women cry under pressure. Don't give them one reason to deny any woman any job because they think that women can't handle it. I can handle it. I take a deep breath, willing my heart rate to slow.

I see a figure quickly move toward me. He places a hand on my shoulder. "Charity," he says. It's Steve. His voice is soft and his hand is steady. He is guiding me out of the room.

"Steve!" Bellotti shouts.

"Fuck you, Bellotti!" Steve says, trying to usher me out of the room.

"Wait," I say. "I'd like to . . ." Steve shushes me.

"I'd like to hear what that little bitch has to say," Bellotti says.

Steve looks me in the eyes. Is he willing me to leave the room? Is he willing me to be strong enough to face a group of men powerful enough to ruin my career? I straighten my back and face them. I take my time, looking at each face in turn, acknowledging every bit of their anger and disdain. I have their full attention. I only hope that when I open my mouth, the words come out clearly and with strength.

"I'd like to apologize to you all. I am very sorry."

All I have is the sincerity of my remorse, and delivering this apology has me feeling strong and powerful in my own right—proud of my resolve for not allowing intimidation to chase me out of the room and proud of taking ownership for my part in a disastrous situation. I know these Hollywood men will never acknowledge the part they played by breeding an environment where assistants are expected to do anything and everything that is asked of them. If they acknowledge that assistants get fired for saying no, gone are the secret perks that come with having an assistant. They risk losing the ability to make assistants do all the inappropriate things some of them depend on. Gone are the hotel bookings we make for their mistresses with our personal credit cards so the wives don't find out. Gone are the drugs they ask us to purchase for them. Gone are the lies we're expected to tell to protect them. Gone are the late-night phone calls requiring a quick response—always *yes*.

I push on the heavy doors and leave the boardroom knowing that I can handle the big boys. In the hallway, waiting for me, is Kai.

"Come on," he says. He wraps an arm around me and pulls me into him.

"I'm okay," I say.

"You sure? Bellotti dragged you down the hall like you were a rag doll."

"He won't touch me again. I'll make sure of it," I say. "Hey. What do you know about *Break Room*?"

"Is Casper upset?"

"He's unusually unhinged."

Kai nods toward the boardroom I just came out of. "Right before this meeting, Steve told Casper he didn't get it."

"Because of me," I say.

"No, Charity. Because of Casper."

CHAPTER 24
FINALLY

Vivy walks into the garden wearing what looks like a hazmat suit. "Put this on," she says, handing me an identical one.

"We're going to be twins?" I say, unfolding the garment.

"Cute, right?"

"What is this?"

"It's a beekeeping suit." Oh, God, I wanted this Saturday to be a haven from my life, not stressful like every day has been since I lost the movie.

"I'm not, like, very comfortable with bees," I say.

"You, my friend, have not seemed comfortable since you got here," Vivy says.

"What do you mean?" I ask.

Vivy takes the mesh covering off her head and places it on the grass. As she walks toward me, she takes her gloves off and lets them drop. She stops about a foot away from me, raises her hands so that her palms face my chest, and breathes deeply with her eyes closed. We stand like this for about fifteen uncomfortable seconds before she opens her eyes and looks at me with deep concern.

"What's wrong?" she asks.

I know I can trust her; I just don't know if she trusts me. If I tell her about the investigation, will I spook her?

"Your chakras are off," she says, moving behind me. She runs her hands from the bottom of my skull down my back. "The root chakra is in the base of the spine. It represents our foundation. It's our feeling of being grounded." Her hands continue down my legs and land at my feet. "It's important to feel grounded and connected with the earth."

Okay. My root chakra probably needs some work. "Well, my apartment is pretty sad," I say. "I would never want to be rooted there. And working with Saffron and Casper isn't what I thought it would be."

She puts a hand high on my stomach, where my diaphragm sits, and her other hand presses on my back. "The sacral chakra is in the abdomen. It's our connection to the sense of abundance, well-being, pleasure, and sexuality."

"I mean, you try working with Kai every day and not touch him," I partly joke.

"Yeah. You should go for it. Who cares what Canopy thinks? They're assholes."

I laugh. If it were only that easy, Vivy. I would love to sleep with Kai, but I don't want him to get in trouble when he's moments away from his big promotion.

She places a hand on my heart. "The heart chakra is connected with the ability to love," Vivy says.

"Hey, now, I'm a lover," I say in my defense.

"You totally are, Charity. You just need to express it," she says. "The throat chakra is the ability to communicate." Vivy wears a smug smile and brushes her hand up my neck as if she's sweeping words out of me. "Your solar-plexus chakra is out of whack." She wraps her arms around my shoulders and pulls them back, causing me to straighten. "This is connected to confidence and control in your life."

"Huh," I say, knowing she's right. I have no control over what will happen to me with this investigation. I am confident that nobody will come to my defense, and I have confidence in Bellotti's ability to ruin my career.

"Most important is your third-eye chakra," Vivy says. "It's the ability to see the big picture."

"If we knew the big picture, there would be world peace," I say.

Vivy gently places her thumb between my eyes and says, "Your truth. Your picture. You have no control over others, but you do have control over you. What is your big picture?"

This Family Thing. That's my big picture, I guess. I need to stop focusing on Canopy and work on the big picture. But that's so hard to do when you have something so terrible hanging over you. "Have I made things worse for you?" Vivy asks.

"No," I say truthfully.

"Good. Why don't you put that beekeeping suit on and we'll check on the bees?" I step into the suit, not because I want to see the hundreds of tiny creatures who can cause significant amounts of pain but because I trust Vivy.

The CD drive opens, announcing the completion of the 98th CD to be uploaded to Casper's computer, and I sigh as I plop another one into the drive. Hopefully Casper or Saffron will send me on one of their random errands that take hours to accomplish. This has become more and more common these days. I embrace the errands because they take me away from the stress of being in the Canopy building. I drive my little car with my windows down, soak up the fresh air and sunshine, and enjoy a moment of freedom and a simple song on the radio. I don't care that I am no longer Charity Trickett, the assistant everyone wants. I am complacent in my new role as errand girl and find little pockets of happiness where I can.

While picking up camera lenses for Casper's Leica, I discover an amazing shop that sells organic iced teas. I pick up Casper's dry cleaning from a place next to a playground and take a couple of minutes to watch the children play. While waiting for Casper's car to get cleaned, I sit in the sunshine with my script in hand and make scribbles in the margins for when I get home. I wait at Casper's house for the plumber and sit on his deck enjoying the view of the Hollywood sign in the distance.

I know I have lost the motivation that made me a good assistant. I also know it's affecting my productivity—that and the fact that I never really know where I'm going when I drive around LA, and reading a map is not a skill of mine. Every route I take is jammed with traffic. I don't know where the good organic grocer is or the Thai place with those really good prawns. I don't know where to park when I'm sent to Tower Records, and I have yet to find a shortcut between Brentwood and the Pacific Palisades. As much as I am embracing my role as errand girl, it's not my forte. I take too long, so I rush and make careless mistakes. I know it's pissing Casper off, so I hurry more and make more careless mistakes. To compensate, I am annoyingly polite. I am a suck-up. I hear myself speak and I cringe. I'm moody. I'm distracted by my writing and often daydream. I'm annoyed when Casper and Saffron interrupt my thoughts. I'm unhappy. I try to mask it. Some days I can't. I say *Yes* and *Happy to* when I really want to say *Fuck you*.

Just as I load another CD into the drive, Saffron comes out of her office fuming. "What the fuck, Charity?" she says, making a beeline to my desk. I stiffen. What now?

"What's wrong?" I ask, trying to sound concerned.

"There's a meeting today with Casper and all the producers on *Diffuser* except me," she says, turning red in the face. I look down at the printed schedule on my desk, and sure enough, Saffron is right. "Why is every single producer involved in this meeting except me?" She towers over my desk, and for the first time since moving to LA, I can't care to be intimidated by her.

"I don't know. Steve called the meeting. Want me to call Jessica to find out?" I ask. She gives me a horrified look, which I guess means I shouldn't call Jessica. "I'm sure it was a mistake. Just show up."

"Just show up to something that I wasn't invited to? I'm not crashing a frat party. This is Canopy fucking Studios."

I have had it. I don't care anymore.

"If you don't want me to call Jessica there's not much I can do," I say, hoping to put an end to her crazy.

"You should have known that there was a meeting, Charity. And you should have made sure that the attendee list was correct before the meeting was announced." Saffron is crazy.

"Okay," I scoff. "From now on, I will call every executive assistant first thing in the morning and ask them if there are any meetings that Saffron can join," I say, not kindly.

Saffron turns on her heels and heads out of the office. *Good. Leave me alone.*

Albana is taking *This Family Thing* to her investors tomorrow, and I need to focus on what's important. I've been waiting to call Pup all day to get her advice.

"Hey, kitten," she says, answering her phone in a seductive voice.

"Hi, doll. Where'd I catch you?" I ask.

"We're shooting in Stanley Park. Just broke for lunch. Good timing."

"Good. I have something to float by you," I say.

"Shoot."

"I should tell Daniel, right?" I say into the phone.

"Tell Daniel what?" Pup says.

"Me losing the movie, the investigation, everything."

"Oh."

"What if word about me is out there and we don't get funding for *This Family Thing*? What if Daniel and Albana find out about me from some investor? I think you're right—I think I should get ahead of this," I say.

"You're right. Tell him," she says curtly.

"But what if Daniel tells Blake? I wonder how Casper will feel about that?"

"Who the fuck cares how Casper feels about it?" Pup says forcefully.

"It would be so awkward."

"Yeah. Maybe. Don't tell him."

"Daniel and Blake may never find out," I say.

"That's right," Pup says. She sounds distracted.

"How do I figure out how widespread this is? I mean, Hollywood is pretty small. Everybody seems to know everybody, and Bellotti did say he was going to ruin me."

"Maybe you should call up random studios and production companies and say, 'Hey, have you guys heard of this Charity Trickett lady?'"

"Come on."

"No, I'm serious. We'll make an alphabetized list. Start with ABC, then CBS, Fox—"

"You're tired of me talking about this," I say.

"Yes. No. I'm sorry. I'm not tired of talking about your investigation and the end of your career and what a bitch Saffron is and people bugging your phones and invasion of privacy." Pup sounds super annoyed.

"Okay. I get it," I say.

"How about you ask me how I'm doing every once in a while?"

"I'm sorry, Pup. How are you?"

"I'm fine. Thank you for asking."

"I appreciate you," I say.

"I know. You're going through things."

"Thanks for talking me through it all."

"You're welcome. I'm going to go line up at the lunch truck. Later, you little criminal."

"Love you, Puppy."

There's a knock on the door, and a twist of anxiety knots my stomach as it does with every knock on the office door. When is security going to escort me out of the building? When is the FBI going to take me away in handcuffs? But when I open the door, there stands Kai. The anxiety melts away instantly.

"Hey," he says, walking into my office. He sits himself down on the couch and drapes an arm over the backrest, making himself at home.

Sigh. Looking at this stud makes me mourn the days when we would shamelessly flirt. "What's up?" I say, standing in front of my desk. I expect to see serious Kai, the one who looks out for me with his serious thoughts and serious face. This Kai, the one who sits on the couch in my office, looks amused.

"This came across my desk." He tosses a script onto the coffee table, and there's something about the way the letters fit on the page that makes it instantly recognizable. It's mine.

I walk toward Kai. "Oh. God. I'm sorry. Did Saul ask you to read it for him? You don't have to. He asked for it."

"I found your script on my desk with this Post-it on it." Kai holds up a yellow Post-it note, and I move toward it.

I feel his eyes on me as I take the note from him and read it: *Pass on script but make sure this writer has an open-door policy with the studio.* I'm dumbfounded. I plunk myself onto the couch next to Kai, reading and rereading the note on the little yellow square. The handwriting is cursive and familiar. The note is from Saul.

"An open-door policy? Does that mean that Canopy Studios will read whatever I submit to them?" I ask.

"Yes, by our ever-disgruntled team of submission readers," Kai says.

"Saul knows that everyone at the studio wants me fired, right?"

"Yeah. He doesn't think it's fair. And he thinks you're a good writer. This is his way of pushing back against the bullies a little."

I shake my head in disbelief. I was convinced that no good would come to me in this building. "So Saul . . ." I can't finish my thought, and I don't have to.

"I don't think anyone at Canopy believes you're the mastermind behind a multimillion-dollar attempt at extortion," Kai says.

"Attempt. So, it's over?" I ask.

"I haven't heard anything in days. But let's get to the important stuff. Your script—I like it. A lot," Kai says, drawing me in with those eyes again.

I can't help myself. I move closer to him on the couch. "Really?" I say.

"You were right, Charity. That morning on our walk. You're a very good writer, and I'm sorry," he says.

Umm. What? Kai is *sorry*? I found my boyfriend in bed with another woman, but he never said sorry. Yet Kai is apologizing for being pompous for about five seconds months ago? I fucking love this man.

"I've been working with Albana on it. She's pretty amazing."

"Really? That's great. I want to hear all about it. Tonight."

I shake my head, coming back to reality. "Kai," I say.

"Do you have any other scripts? You know, something with explosions and CGI. You know, something marketable."

"Uh . . ."

"I'm joking," Kai says.

The door flies open, and Casper comes in with Saffron in tow. I practically jump off the couch while Kai remains seated, and I wish he didn't look so comfortable. Casper and Saffron stop dead in their tracks when they see Kai.

"Kai," Casper says.

Kai rises to his feet and casually extends a hand toward Casper. They slap palms and smile.

"Hey, man," Kai says. "How are you, Saffron?"

"I'm good, Kai," she says, looking at me sideways.

"What's up, man?" Casper asks.

"Oh, I was just here to talk to Charity. Saul—"

"Saul wanted to borrow this Shirley Temple VHS I have for his granddaughter. It's in my car. We were just going to grab it. Is that okay?"

Before Casper can answer, I snatch my script off the coffee table and pull Kai out of the office.

Once we're in the hall, I walk quickly to the elevator, Kai lagging behind me a little.

"Charity, slow down," he calls out, laughing. "Charity." He grabs my arm and forces me to stop. "What's going on?"

"It's just easier with Saffron if she thinks that my life is complete shit," I say.

"What?"

"When things go my way, she's awful. Right now, things are going so badly for me that she's a nonissue."

"That's messed up."

"Well, that's how it is."

"Alright. So, what do you want to do now? Go make out in your car for a few minutes, or save it for tonight?"

"Kai, the company you work for hates me."

"I don't care," he says, moving closer to me.

"I'm under FBI investigation," I whisper.

"Why are you whispering? Are they listening right now, do you think?" He wraps his arms around me.

I slap my script against his chest lightly. "Seriously. I got interrogated!"

"I know!" Kai says with a laugh. "At a Coffee Bean!"

"It was intense!"

"I want to hear all about it." He snatches the script out of my hands and slaps it against my bottom before he walks away. "I'll pick you up at seven."

What is he doing? Why is Kai sitting across the table from me acting . . . professional? I know I've pushed him away many times, but it's unlike him not to persist. We flirt, I draw a line, he tries to cross it. That's what we do. Where's the Kai who asks me every five minutes if I want to make out? Why isn't he cuddled up close to me, cupping the inside of my thigh and eating my food? Why doesn't he put his mitts on me? Instead, he's munching on his mixed greens and asking me questions about my script. This feels more like a meeting than a date. "The relationship between Samantha and her mother," he says. "Is that because they're so similar or because they're different?"

"I think Samantha sees aspects of her mother in herself that she's not comfortable with."

"Yeah, I can see that," he says, taking a sip of red wine. I lean back and study him. Did I say no so many times that Kai thinks that I'm not interested in him? I take my fork and poke around his salad, hoping this familiar act will make the meal feel less like a business meeting. He goes on about this and that, and I'm getting annoyed. It's wonderful that Kai is taking such an interest in my work, but is this what we are now? Colleagues?

We are halfway through the main course when the waitress pours Kai a second glass of wine. He raises his glass to me. "Well, cheers. That was a good meeting," he says.

I clink my glass against his. "That was a meeting?" I say.

"Yes. Now the meeting is over." He gets up with his dinner plate in hand and places it on the table next to mine. I scoot over on the banquette, and Kai slides in next to me. He slips a hand between my crossed legs, just above my knee, and leans in to take a bite of my food. This is better. I inhale the sweet smell of Kai. This is the best.

"So, the meeting's over?" I say, leaning back and watching him eat my food with delight.

"I got the impression that you wanted to keep distance between work us and *us* us, so I'm making a very clear distinction between the two."

"That's a good idea."

"I'm full of them." Kai smiles. He places his fork down on his plate and looks at me. "I also get to write this dinner off."

"You're the smartest man I know," I say, leaning into him. I breathe

Kai in. All the problems of my small world disappear. There is nothing else but this man, and he is perfect.

Kai brushes his body against mine, his breath hot on my cheek, and I am one hundred percent certain that waiting this long to kiss this man has been wasted time. I place my hand on the back of his head and draw him into me. We kiss. It's the kind of kiss that could never be too long. The kind of kiss you miss the moment it's over.

Albana and I are on the street corner while a chivalrous Daniel tries to hail a cab for us. Dinner was boozy and disappointing. Albana's investors don't want to back *This Family Thing*. And I can't help but feel responsible. Albana said she's still interested in working with us—we just need to work harder. We went through our list of other potential investors and put a plan together. But throughout dinner, I thought, *What's the point? Bellotti is warning all of Hollywood to stay away from Charity Trickett.*

"Guys," I holler. Daniel turns to us. "I have something to tell you."

"What?" Daniel says, walking toward Albana and me. I take a deep breath and try to look at my friends, but this is so embarrassing.

"It's my fault your investors backed out, Albana," I say.

"What are you talking about?" she asks.

"Charity," Daniel says, placing his hand on my arm.

"Let me get this out. It's bad," I start.

"Is it ever! Pup told me everything," Daniel says.

"She didn't," I say, shocked. But then not shocked. Damn Pup and her mouth.

"Told you what?" Albana asks.

"Charity is part of a pirating ring," Daniel tells Albana. "She's under FBI investigation." He turns to me and slaps my shoulder. "They tapped your fucking phone! Flowers by Irene outside your apartment!" Daniel is enjoying this far too much.

I turn to Albana, who looks confused. "I lost a copy of *Diffuser*.

The FBI is investigating me. Canopy is pissed. Bellotti told me that I'd never work in Hollywood again. I think he found out about us and got to your investors."

"How did you lose a copy of the movie?" she asks.

"Casper asked me to bring it to a test screening in El Segundo. I had it in my hand one minute, and the next it was gone."

Albana's brow furrows as she looks at me.

"I was stupid. I shouldn't have done it. Bottom line is that I'm done in film. Bellotti's going to make sure of it. Your investors don't want to make *my* movie because of him." It takes everything I have not to cry.

Daniel opens his arms, making an inviting space for me to lay my head. I can hear his heart beating steadily against my cheek. "It's okay," he says. He holds me for a while. Then he says, "Albana, I can't believe you haven't heard all this yet. It's all over town."

I pull away from Daniel so I can look him in his eyes. Is he serious?

"And your name. Charity Trickett. It's sticking in people's heads." He taps his finger against my temple. "All of Hollywood is talking about the girl who lost Blake Anthony's biggest movie ever, Charity Trickett."

I'm shocked. Words won't form in my mouth. It's all over Hollywood! Everyone knows my name! I'm done. My career is over.

"I'm fucking with you," Daniel says. "Pup also told me how self-involved you're being. Nobody's talking about you, Charity. Besides, the people who know you and know what happened, they know that it's not your fault. Come here." He hugs me once more.

"I want a hug, too," Albana says, squeezing in.

CHAPTER 25
DON'T LET THE SUN GO DOWN ON ME

I woke up this morning to a text from Kai that read *Morning, beautiful,* and it started my day off perfectly. Well, almost perfectly. I would have preferred to have woken up in Kai's bed and have him say "Morning, beautiful" as he kissed my neck, but we're not there yet. Right now, I'm enjoying the anticipation of Kai's bed, the pent-up desire, and the foreplay. It fuels me with fantasies and dirty thoughts.

I cruise up the Hollywood Hills to Casper's house with the top down on my little Volkswagen, appreciating the beauty of the day and noting that I've missed this feeling of simple happiness. Sunlight shimmers through the canopy of trees above me, and I imagine these hills as they were in the 1960s when the homes were hidden oases for artists, hippies, and partiers.

Suddenly my car clunks. I look at the gauge on my dashboard, knowing it's going to overheat. Then I hear a louder clunk and my car starts to rattle and shake. Something is seriously wrong. I turn around and put her in neutral. My plan is to coast down the hill, cross Sunset Boulevard, and pull into the parking lot at Bristol Farms where there is a pay phone with a Yellow Pages. Hopefully I can find a mechanic that is close so I don't have to pay for a tow.

The old man in coveralls looks doubtful before I even hand him the keys. Thirty minutes later, he gives me his diagnosis. "You need a new transmission," he says.

"Well, how much is that?" I ask.

"Five thousand," he says, shaking his head. I look at the grease on his capable hands and bite my lip.

"That's a lot," I say.

"Yes. And maybe not a good choice. The car is probably worth about that much. You might be better off getting a new car."

"How much is a reliable used car?"

"More than five thousand dollars," he says.

"Well, I replaced the brakes last year, so we might as well go for it," I say, depleted. "How long will it take?"

"About a week," the mechanic says.

I sit on the curb to think. The majority of my work with Casper has been running his errands lately, so if I don't have a car, I'm obsolete. Will I have to rent a car? How much is that? I pull my bankbook out of my purse and start the depressing task of assessing my finances.

I'm not the best with financial management, and I think it's finally caught up with me. Work in the film industry is fickle. When I started out, I relied heavily on my credit card, with its 22.9 percent interest rate, to compensate for the intermittent work. I know it's a crazy interest rate, but I didn't know any better back then. It was my first credit card, the one I got at university when someone from MBNA stopped me on campus and offered it to me. I was thrilled, especially since I had no steady employment and my greatest academic accomplishment was a haiku. Now I'm on a hamster wheel of debt. I keep thinking I'll make more money, I'll have steady work, I'll move up from being an assistant and get a pay raise, or I'll sell a script, but none of that has happened.

This new transmission puts me dangerously close to my breaking point. I decide to put three thousand dollars on the card so I have enough money in the bank to cover the minimum payment and pay my rent. It's more important now than ever that I find a new job and fast, but with Bellotti's threats and the FBI investigation, I'm not confident that anyone will hire me. Albana and Daniel are trying to find new investors for *This Family Thing*, but even if they are successful within the next few weeks (the odds of which are slim), getting paid for the script could take some time.

I wonder if I can get a line of credit. You hear ads about consolidating debt all the time on the radio. Maybe I can get, like, five percent interest and pay off my credit card. My phone dings, and I hope it's Kai with another one of his flirty texts. I look at the screen. No such luck. It's Casper asking me to pick up his dry cleaning and bring it to his house. Ugh. Where's the closest car rental?

I've been waiting almost ten minutes for Karl, the wonder-boy financial advisor at City Bank, to return to his office so he can offer me a line of credit at a good rate and I can start down the path of financial responsibility. I have given him all my details, listed my assets (a car worth five thousand dollars—once the five-thousand-dollar transmission gets installed, that is, but Karl doesn't need to know that), provided Canopy Studios paystubs proving my employment, and included my address, social security number, and zodiac sign. (Not necessary, but everyone likes a Pisces, right?) My bank card isn't working, though. In an attempt to figure out the problem, Karl had tapped at his computer for five silent minutes while sporting a look of confusion. Finally, he took my card and left. It's been five solid minutes since I last saw him.

"Sorry about this," Karl says, returning to his office. "Yeah. It seems like your account here is frozen."

"Frozen?" I say.

"Yeah. Looks like it," Karl says.

"Why?"

"Um. Yeah. I've never seen this code before. So I've asked my manager to come take a look."

A slightly older, slightly more boring-looking man who I can only assume is the manager, comes into the office. "What do we have here?" He looks at Karl's computer screen. "So, your account is frozen."

"Yes, but why?" I ask, trying not to sound irritated.

"There's a code here." He squints at the screen.

"Yeah. I've never seen this code before," Karl notes unhelpfully.

"Neither have I," says the boring one. He leaves the office without a word.

Karl looks at me mutely, and I give him a pleasant smile as though taking eons to rectify whatever technical snafu they're having isn't holding up my day. I want to be perceived as amicable so they share their piles of money with me. Then the boring one comes back in the office carrying a small City Bank handbook. He flips through the thin pages and runs his finger down a row of alphanumeric lines. "Here we go. It looks as though the government has frozen your account."

"Oh" is all I can say. I'm guessing a line of credit is now very much out of the question. "Does it say when my account will unfreeze?" I ask.

The manager examines the computer screen once more and presses a seemingly random selection of buttons on the keyboard. "No," he concludes.

I stare at Karl and the boring bank manager, who don't seem to know how to proceed. "So, I can't get my money?"

"I'm afraid not," the manager says.

"Can I leave?" I ask. The manager seems unsure of how to answer. He looks in the little book of codes, and I hold my breath as he seems to read every word of small print in front of him. Finally, he nods and looks up at me with relief.

"Yes. You can leave," he says.

I burst out of the bank and onto the street. Cars speed by me. I want to call my parents, but I don't want to use my cell because the long-distance charges are crazy expensive. I walk up the block and into a 7-Eleven where I purchase a calling card for five dollars. Right outside the 7-Eleven, I use the pay phone to call my parents. My mom picks up. I don't want to cry, but goddamn it.

"Mom," I say with a croak.

"Charity. Charity." The line is bad, and the traffic makes it difficult to hear.

"Mom," I say, louder this time, making me sound panicked.

"What's wrong?" my mother asks.

"They froze my bank account."

"What?"

"The government froze my account. My car needs a new transmission, and I can't pay for it because I can't get at any of the money in my account."

"Are you calling for money?" My mom is annoyed.

"I need my car for work." I can't help but cry. I'm in an awful situation and need to find a way out.

"Charity, don't cry. Honestly, if you call us one more time crying, I don't know what I'm going to do," she says.

"I'll pay you back as soon as my bank account is up and running."

"Only you, Charity. Only you can get yourself in this kind of mess."

"This kind of mess? Mom! I've never been in trouble with the law."

"Well, you're going to have to figure it out," my mom says.

"Okay," I say, feeling as though she kicked me in the gut.

"Good luck," she says before I hang the phone up without saying goodbye.

This is madness. I know my mom is a hard-ass and wants me to be able to take care of myself and everything, but fuck. I need a little support. If you're not going to give me a loan, you can at least help me figure something out. I am livid. I'm livid at my mom, livid at Casper, livid at the FBI.

I dig through my wallet and take out dum-dum FBI Agent Brad

Walker's business card. I'm going to give him an earful. I pull out my cell phone for this one. I want him to hear me loud and clear.

His dumb militant voice comes through my phone. "Brad Walker."

"You froze my bank account." I am one decibel below screaming.

"Charity?"

"Yes. It's Charity. Doesn't the FBI have caller ID? You froze my bank account!"

"I'm aware," Brad says in a calm and controlled voice that makes me want to dive through the phone and scratch his eyes out.

"You could have told me," I say.

"Sorry. I should have, yes. The interview was . . . well . . . unconventional."

"Oh, really? Interviewing a suspect of a hundred-seventy-million-dollar theft in a Coffee Bean is unconventional?"

"Yes, that part, too," he says.

"I need five thousand dollars to purchase a new transmission for my car." I hear him tapping away at his computer.

"For your Volkswagen Cabriolet?"

"Yes."

"I wouldn't recommend a new transmission. You see, that car is probably not worth five thousand dollars."

"Yeah, I'm aware that it's not the best move. But if you take a look-see at my financial records there, you'll see that I can't exactly afford a whole new car. I didn't call for advice, Brad. I called to tell you that I need my money. Without my car, I can't work—and I can't afford not to be paid." There is silence from Brad that only infuriates me more. "There's less than four thousand dollars in there," I say. "What do you think I'm going to do with four thousand dollars? Can I escape the United States and set up a new life with a new identity on four thousand dollars?"

"It's too late to do anything about it today. But you will have access to all the funds in your account tomorrow."

"Am I really in so much trouble that I'm a flight risk?"

"No, you're not in any trouble," Brad says.

"Then what the fuck?"

"Your account shouldn't still be frozen. There's a process to unfreezing, lots of paperwork. It's easier to freeze than unfreeze."

"So, the investigation . . ."

"It's over. You were pickpocketed. By a pro, too. He's known to us."

"What happened? Did you arrest him?"

"He's in custody, yes," Brad says proudly.

"For real?"

"Yes. For real."

"How did you get him?" I ask.

"I can't tell you that."

"Does Canopy Studios know that you got him? Does Casper? Do they know that I had nothing to do with this?"

"The company knows. Once we had the suspect in custody, the legal department was notified. As for your boss, we have not been in contact with him."

"But how long has Canopy known?" I ask.

"The person in question was taken into custody last Tuesday, and that was when Canopy Studios was notified."

Relief fills my body, but so does the crushing realization that nobody cared to tell me. Canopy has known for a week, and nobody thought to inform me that this hell that I've been going through is over?

CHAPTER 26
GOODFELLA

Daniel and I walk along Melrose Avenue window shopping, people watching, and licking our wounds. Earlier, Albana had joined us in a meeting with a producing duo that we thought would be a perfect fit to invest in *This Family Thing*, but they were not interested. Time is ticking like a bomb. I sent out fifteen resumes last week and only got called in for one interview. I have never interviewed for a job and not gotten it, so I was shocked when they told me they were hiring someone else. I'm used to being a big fish in a small pond, but here in LA, I'm an amoeba. Good thing my car is fixed because I will most likely have to drive it back to Vancouver, where I will move in with my parents as a complete loser.

"How bad is it?" Daniel says.

"I have no savings. I've never really worked enough to save. I worked enough to live, and then I would take time off to write." I cringe as I say this.

"I get it," Daniel says, placing his arm around me.

"Last week I had to get a new transmission for my car. I put almost all of it on my credit card. I'm almost maxed out. I can make the minimum payment if I'm working, but my gig with Casper ends in a couple of weeks. I'm looking for a new job, but no luck yet."

"I can ask around and see if anyone needs an assistant," Daniel says.

"Daniel, I know you don't think that Bellotti has the kind of reach he says he does. But Beth told me that when his last assistant quit, he ruined her. The job she had lined up fell through and she never worked in film again. This was his assistant. She never messed up— she was just moving on with her career and he didn't want her to. I royally fucked up. I could have cost Canopy hundreds of millions of dollars, and Bellotti could have lost his job because of me. I think we should consider that *This Family Thing* may never get made."

Daniel deflates. His head tilts to the side sympathetically. "How much debt are you in?" he asks.

"A lot," I say.

"Aside from *This Family Thing*, got any other low-budget scripts?"

"Not really. You know how they tell you to write a variety of scripts to show that you can adapt to any genre? I have a dystopia movie, an action, a period piece, a thriller/horror. *This Family Thing* is my little indie," I say.

Daniel lets out a sigh. "Okay. There's this producer. Henry something-or-other. I've known him for a few years. He does low-budget. His turnaround is insane. He always has three projects on the go—one in development, another being shot, and another in post. Movie of the week, straight to DVD, that kind of thing. He's always looking for material. I'll send him *This Family Thing*," Daniel says.

"What about Albana?"

"I'll send him the original. None of Albana's work will be in it."

"This is heartbreaking," I say.

"I'm not saying we stop working with Albana. It would be a fucking dream to have her direct this. In fact, I'm ramping it up. I will neglect my duties with Blake Anthony and move down my list of potential investors at double speed."

I give Daniel a doubtful look.

"I know a shit ton of rich people, Trickett. Someone ought to secure a line of credit. I'm not giving up on working with Albana, but as your manager, I'm telling you that you need a backup plan."

★ ★ ★

These days, I am impressed with my little car when I drive through the many canyons and steep hills of Los Angeles. With the new transmission, I no longer drive with my fingers crossed, listening to the terrifying rattles and shakes. I effortlessly get up the hill to Vivy's Malibu ranch house, and I complete Casper's errands with ease. But life has become a financial balancing act: Deposit paycheck in the bank; pay rent in cash; transfer the amount of my minimum payment to my credit card; pilfer honey, tea, and milk from the Canopy Studios break room to subsidize grocery shopping; pay for whatever essentials I need with my credit card and hold my breath until the little screen reads *Approved*.

My life is running at a 22.9 percent deficit, and it has to stop. Everything goes on my credit card. Spending $20.00 on gas actually costs me $31.45. Groceries that are $44.08 at the store accumulate to $54.17 after the monthly interest. If I get another job as an assistant, I'll be able to make the minimum monthly payment, but trickle-in finances won't get me out of the hole.

As a result, I'm driving up and over the hill to Burbank so I can meet Henry, the low-budget movie producer. He's willing to pay me $40,000 for *This Family Thing*. I push on the gas and cruise up the last steep hill before driving down into Burbank, using five dollars' worth of gas (sorry—$6.15).

Although I need to sell the script to Henry, I don't want to—so as I drive, I'm bouncing an idea off of Daniel that I think is golden. Daniel doesn't agree.

"Daniel, Henry could want to invest in *us*," I say. "Think about it. We're looking for investors, and here's this Henry guy. If he hires Albana to direct, we can make our movie."

"Henry has his own—" His voice cuts out. Ugh. Cell reception is awful in the canyon.

"Sorry, Daniel. We're cutting out," I say.

"These people work on all his films," Daniel continues, not realizing we have a poor connection. "He has a formula on how to make money, and his team—"

"Oh, you cut out again," I say.

"This is a take-the-money-and-run scenario," I finally hear Daniel say.

"But when he sees how much better the film is with Albana's ideas . . ." I say.

Daniel cuts me off. "Charity, Henry and Albana make very different films. It's not a good fit. You are taking the meeting for one purpose: to sell the script," Daniel says. "Now, look. Really quick. Henry's kind of an odd guy."

"Odd like how?" I ask.

"If you took fifty percent Joe Pesci from *Goodfellas* and fifty percent Joe Pesci from *My Cousin Vinny* and peppered in a hippie way past his prime, you would make Henry," Daniel says.

"Is he . . . Daniel? Daniel?" The line is dead, and I'm left with my orders. Sell the script.

Henry sits across the table and looks past me. "She should not wear that," he says.

I lean toward him to make sure I heard correctly. "Pardon me?" I say. Henry points his gray-haired chin in the direction of a young waitress. I follow his eyes to her ass. She wears a short skirt. Henry looks like he's a man who would appreciate the miniskirt, having been witness to its inception and all, but he looks unimpressed.

"I mean," he says, shaking his head like that's a sufficient explanation.

I get who Henry is. Henry is the kind of guy who values a girl for her eating disorder. If an actress doesn't contribute to a certain Hollywood aesthetic, she's worthless. I want to say something, but this meeting isn't going well, and confronting his misogyny could end in disaster. Take the money and run. I have bills to pay.

Feeling shameful, I'm struck with the overwhelming desire to get this over with. We've been scribbling on my script, Henry in red ink and me in pencil. It started innocently enough. He asked if he could change a character's age and if we could do without the family dog—little stuff that didn't have much impact. "Change that car driving scene, will ya? Have 'em standing on a quiet street or in a park instead."

I'm not here to discuss the script. This is not a brainstorming session with Albana. I'm here to administer the changes Henry wants based on his budgetary restraints and personal comfort. When I asked why he wanted to change a night scene to a day scene, it all became clear. "Shooting at night, Charity. I mean, it's more money. A lot more. And fitting it into the schedule is a pain in the ass. We're talking pushing call times; we're talking overtime for the crew. And who wants to shoot at night anyway? Nobody wants to stay at work until two o'clock in the morning. You know?"

I turn the page in my script. We are a third of the way through.

"The mom," Henry says. "What do you think about changing her art form?" I think this is interesting. In fact, Albana and I have discussed this a bit, too. Albana wants the mother to be an artistic innovator who is in high demand for both her art and mind. The kind of woman who would lecture at colleges and be an international name. Now here's Henry wanting to change the mom's medium as well. Maybe I really missed something by making her a sculptor.

"What would you like her to be?" I ask.

"A painter. On canvas. Acrylics."

"Oh. Why?"

"Sculpture . . . I mean, it's hard and flat," Henry says simply.

"Hard and flat?"

"Hard to shoot. Flat on the screen. Hard: Got to show all the sides of a piece of sculpture. Got to see the whole thing. More shooting, more setups. That's time and money. And flat: Like a piece of stone or cement? Just a colorless blob on the screen. Canvas, there's color. You can make it pop on camera. And you only have to shoot one angle."

Color popping on screen. Okay, I get it. A stone sculpture could look like a lifeless blob.

"What kind of paintings?" I ask.

Henry lights up. He reaches into his well-worn satchel and pulls out an envelope of four-by-six photographs.

"I found this artist. He's really something. This kid is really talented. You'll be blown away." He pushes a picture of a painting toward me. The acrylic painting is colorful and it certainly pops, but not in a good way. The quality is of the kind that can be found in a small-town coffee shop that sells the owner's paintings because his hobby takes up too much space in his home. "It's something, huh? He's an undiscovered genius. And he's agreed to supply the film for free."

"How did you find him?" I ask, pretending to take a greater interest in the painting than I actually have.

"He goes to school with my son. Can you believe he is in eleventh grade? He's going to be famous one day." I can't tell if Henry believes what he's saying or if he's selling me hard because he found some free paintings.

"Yeah, that mother character. There's an idea there," I say. "I was thinking about making her famous. Like, really famous. Then the family things that they're going through are really rooted in the mothering. The kids may feel neglected or resentful. Now we see those childhood insecurities fester in adulthood." Henry looks startled, so I continue to talk in the hope that he may feel compelled to contribute. "Makes those issues they already have more complex."

Henry lets out a little laugh. "Charity. I think you're reading too much into this," he says.

"Well, I wrote it," I say, confused. "Shouldn't a writer think about these things?"

"The intentions of the character?" Henry shakes his head, smiling to himself as if I'm being quaint.

"The point is that the work the mother produces, whether it's a painting or a piece of sculpture, should be extraordinary given her level of fame."

"Okay, Charity." He flips his script, searching for the next note, and I'm left to wonder about how that discussion ended.

Discussing script notes with Henry is a soul-crushing experience. I am changing my beautiful script based on the considerations of someone with no artistic consideration. But I'm tired. LA has slapped me around, and I want out of the ring. Selling the script to Henry would allow me time to catch my breath. I would be able to pay off my credit card. I could take all the good bits that Albana and I worked on together and make a completely new script. A better script. This is what I tell myself so I don't feel so guilty about ditching Albana. This is what I tell myself to prevent the heartbreak of sacrificing my work for money.

When the meeting ends, we walk out of the restaurant. I turn to Henry and ask, "Do you have a director in mind?"

"Yeah. Me," Henry says. No. He can't direct *This Family Thing*. Throughout the meeting, I held on to the hope that the director would surely be someone with imagination and an artist's sensibilities. With Henry directing, my script will be ruined.

"I have other scripts, too," I say, reaching for one last attempt to save my script. "I bet you'd really like this psychological thriller I wrote. It's basically a two-hander. Would be really cheap to film. You remember *The River Wild* with Meryl Streep and Kevin Bacon? It's kind of like that . . ."

"Shooting in the wilderness? No," Henry says decisively.

"I have a big, goofy, off-the-wall comedy," I say.

"I'm no Mike Myers. Look, let's get this one in the can, then I'll look at your other stuff. 'Kay, kiddo?" Henry says while patting my arm.

A part of me dies as I climb into my car and tell him I'll send my changes by early next week.

CHAPTER 27
"THERE'S MY FLAIR!"

Casper has a cold, so he asked that I go to this old deli in Westwood that's rumored to have a matzo ball soup that cures all ailments. I take a sharp right up Wonderland Avenue and place a hand on the precious cargo that sits in my passenger seat, the incline of the street threatening to spill the soup.

I knock on the front door of Casper's house and hear a muffled "What's up?" from inside, so I let myself in. A little black puppy who will one day be a big black dog barrels toward me, slipping on the hardwood. He jumps up on me, and I clutch the soup protectively while trying to pet this cute ball of energy. "Hello?" I call out.

"You're here," calls Casper. "Could you heat that soup up for me?"

"Sure," I holler. "You got a dog!"

"Rex," Casper yells. The puppy follows me excitedly toward the kitchen, bouncing off my legs and slapping me with his tail. I place the soup on the kitchen counter and bend down to the little guy to rub him behind his ears.

"Nice to meet you, Rex," I say, pressing my head to his. The puppy scurries to the sliding door and scrapes at it with his front paws, sliding and slipping down the glass. "Can I let the puppy out?" I yell out to Casper, wherever he is.

"Yeah. Thanks," he yells back. I pull on the heavy slider, and the puppy hurries out and pees on the deck. I cringe, thinking I should hose the urine off the deck, but cleaning up my boss's dog's pee would be yet another crushing example of how far I've fallen from grace, and I just can't bring myself to do it.

I let Rex back in, and he happily follows me as I place the bowl of soup on the kitchen table along with a spoon and napkin.

"It's ready," I call out.

"Can you bring it in here?"

I pick up the soup and walk toward the direction of Casper's voice. "Casper?" I say, moving down the hall.

"Yeah. Come on in." I push on the door at the end of the hallway, and there's Casper lying in bed. Not seductively. Sickly. He's sick in bed, and I'm bringing him soup. This isn't like me bringing him soup while he's working late in the editing suite. This is a very personal soup delivery, one that should be made by his fiancée or mom.

"Careful—it's hot," I say, handing him the soup.

"Thanks." He takes a slurp. "This is good."

"'Kay, well. Do you need anything else?"

"Yeah. I'm supposed to take Rex to the vet. Can you take him?"

"Sure," I say. I start to walk out of the room, then stop. I turn to Casper. "Hey, did you know that the FBI investigation is over?"

"Thank Christ," he says.

"You knew?"

"Yeah. You got pickpocketed," Casper says.

"When did you find out?"

"Uh . . . last Wednesday."

"Over a week ago," I say quietly. Casper looks up at me from his bowl of soup, the duvet curled around his waist. "Casper, I . . ." I want to say, *I quit.* But instead, I say, "Why didn't you tell me?"

"Nobody told you?"

"No. Funny story. I found out about it a couple days ago when I was at the bank."

Casper gives me a blank look. "The FBI froze my bank account." Casper looks surprised but still doesn't say anything. "So, I called the FBI agent who interrogated me, and he told me."

Here you go, Casper. I've opened the door for you. Time to apologize. He shakes his head, so it must be sinking in.

"They froze your bank account!" He laughs like he can't believe it—like this is entertaining.

Well, believe it, Casper, I think. *I got interrogated, I got called every horrible name imaginable, I got threatened, I probably got spied on, my bank account was frozen, and I couldn't go home to be comforted by my family. I was alone in a new city with nobody I could confide in, and I was scared. Meanwhile, what happened to you?* I want to say all of this so badly. I want Casper to know that while he was editing his blockbuster film that's going to make him one of the biggest directors in Hollywood, my career and happiness have been dying a slow death. And it's all because I was doing a job he asked me to do. But I don't have the luxury to say any of this. I need a paycheck. So I walk out of my boss's bedroom holding my tongue and cursing myself for misjudging Casper.

Rex pulls me into the vet's office with the surprising strength of a monster puppy. "Who do we have here?" sings the lady at the front desk.

"This is Rex," I say.

"Rex. Come here. Good boy." I let the leash drop and smile as the goofy black puppy bounds over to the nurse. "Okay. Come on back after four. He'll be groggy from the sedation, but that's normal."

"Sedation?"

"He's scheduled for a neutering, correct?"

"Oh. Really? I didn't know that. I'm the owner's assistant." I bend down and Rex jumps on my knees, wagging his tail. My heart sinks for this unsuspecting puppy. I rub his back and belly. His wet little nose rubs against my cheek. "Okay, Rex. Sorry to do this to you, buddy," I say, kissing his little head. Then I watch as the nurse takes him away.

While I wait for CDs to upload onto Casper's computer, I work on Henry's notes. When I become too heartbroken and discouraged from the process of butchering my own work, I craft pitches for Albana to suit individual investors. It feels like I'm in a race against myself, and I don't know which option I'm cheering for. On one hand, selling my script to Henry would give me a lot of financial freedom. On the other hand, working with Albana and Daniel has been the most rewarding time of my life as a writer and I don't want it to end.

When the phone rings, I'm not overly surprised to hear Casper on the other end asking me to pick up his puppy from the vet.

In the parking lot of the veterinary clinic, I look down at Rex sitting on the warm cement, his peripheries completely shielded by a plastic cone. I have to call his name a few times before he can find me. I look into his eyes, which are glazed over from medication. This puppy is stoned.

I bend down to Rex and look deeply into his eyes. "You are in good hands, my friend," I say to him softly. I remove the plastic cone, thinking that he's far too sedated to lick his stitches.

I gently lift the puppy into the back seat of my car and roll the windows down so the little guy gets plenty of fresh air. I keep the music off and drive as if any movement could make the dog feel nauseous. Want to be more fucked up than you already are? Just lie down in the back seat of a moving vehicle with your eyes closed—you'll vomit for sure.

My phone rings, and I press the speaker button to answer.

"Where you at?" Casper says.

"I have Rex. We're on the way to your house," I say.

"Can you swing by the office and grab those scripts off my desk?"

"Okay," I say. What I really want to say is, *You couldn't have asked me this an hour ago when you called me at the office?* Now I'm going to have to drive that steep corkscrew ramp all the way up to the top of the parking lot, where my spot is. That won't sit well with poor Rex. Plus, I can't leave him in my car on the rooftop—it's too hot outside.

I'm on Olympic Boulevard when my phone rings. I put it on speakerphone and hear Daniel's sweet voice.

"Trickett, my little star," he says.

"You're in a good mood."

"I am. Just spoke to Henry, and he's eager to get the revisions. Any idea on when you'll get him the script?"

"Ugh. They're almost done. But Daniel, are we really going to sell it to him? Where are you and Albana at?"

"We're no further along than before your meeting with Henry. Sorry."

"Look, I have a few more weeks at Canopy, so I have money coming in. Let's stall him."

"Stall him? You know he has a crew lined up."

"He has months before he shoots. There's time."

I hear Rex retching in the back seat. I look behind me. His little head hangs over the seat. He's going to vomit. "Shit. Daniel, I've got to go."

I pull over and run around the car to open the door. "Come on," I call to the puppy, but the poor guy is so stoned and consumed with nausea that he can barely lift his head. Maybe I have something that can catch the puke. I ransack the car, and the best I can find is a Snapple bottle. I toss its contents and place it under the puppy's mouth, but the opening of the glass bottle is tiny compared to Rex's snout. I'll get vomit all over myself.

I look down at the puppy and say "Sorry" as I wrap my arms around him, then gently lift. I've managed to get his front paws out of the door when he retches again, this time vomiting. It lands on my legs and in my shoes, on the upholstery and floor mats. I look at Rex, not believing my luck. He looks at me with sadness and misery in his eyes. He moans and lays his head in the vomit that is splattered on the back seat. "It's okay, Rex."

We are fifteen minutes from Canopy Studios and at least forty-five minutes from my apartment. Showering and cleaning this mess up before going to Canopy to get Casper's scripts would mean subjecting Rex to two and a half hours of driving. Not showering, going to Canopy, picking up the scripts, and then going straight to Casper's house would be only forty-five minutes of driving. I'm sticking to my plan and going to Canopy first.

I hate to play the whole damsel-in-distress bit, but I'm covered in puppy puke and the thought of walking through the Canopy building like this, subjecting myself to more humiliation, is unbearable. Besides, my hero is pretty darn cute. I watch Kai stride toward the parking garage with Casper's scripts tucked under his sturdy arm and a sexy smile on his face. He approaches but stops before getting too close. "Do you smell puke?" he asks, searching the ground for the offending smell.

"It's puppy puke," I say, motioning to Rex in the back seat.

"You got a puppy?" Kai says with excitement. He pokes his head through the car window.

"No. It's Casper's."

"Did Casper's dog puke on you?"

"A little bit. He's heavily sedated and nauseous," I say.

"Is he okay?" Kai asks.

"He's fine. He just got neutered."

"You took Casper's dog to get neutered?" Kai is obviously shocked.

There's a lump in my throat, and I'm embarrassed by how far I've fallen in my career. I manage to look at Kai when I say, "Yes. I took Casper's dog to get neutered."

"Charity, you don't have to do things you don't want to do. You can tell Casper to take his dog to the vet himself."

"He's sick," I say.

"Yeah, that is sick. It's his puppy. You would think that he'd want to take the little guy to the vet himself."

"No, Casper is ill. I had to bring him soup this morning, at which point he asked me to take his dog to the vet."

"You brought soup to Casper's home?" Kai asks.

"I delivered it to him in bed," I say, coming completely clean. Kai looks so disappointed that I'm compelled to explain myself. "I know. I want to quit, but I'm broke. I can't afford not to work, Kai, and I don't have a new job lined up. Trust me, I'm looking. I would have loved to go home and shower before seeing you, but then this guy"—I motion to the passed-out puppy—"would have to be in a car driving around for, like, two hours. That's not fair to him."

Kai digs into his pocket and pulls out a key. "Go to my place. Shower there," he says.

"It's okay," I say. "I'll be home soon."

"Charity, you shouldn't have to go about your day covered in vomit because of Casper. He's done enough." Oh. Serious Kai is here. Serious Kai is intense and sexy as hell. He pulls out his phone and types away. "I'm texting you Canopy's account number for a car wash on Pico. Use it to get your car cleaned. You can probably clean this guy off there, too." He reaches into the car and runs his hand down the sleeping puppy's back. "I'll be home in a couple hours."

"Thank you," I say.

He moves closer to me. "You are welcome." He bends toward me and I think he's going to kiss me, but he stops.

"I'm so gross right now," I say.

"It's really bad. Get out of here," he says as he brushes a hair away from my eyes.

There's something sexy about being in Kai's apartment without him here. Taking my clothes off in his bathroom, warming my body in his shower. I use more soap than usual because it smells like him, dousing the sponge, making the suds thicker, and covering my body with lather. I'm consumed with him. I wrap myself in his towel. I use his lotions and creams; I run his toothpaste on my finger and slide it along my teeth. I cover myself head to toe in Kai.

I toss my clothes into the washer and wonder what I should wear. I don't want to wander around Kai's apartment in a wet towel for the next hour. In his closet, I run my hand down the stack of neatly folded T-shirts. There's a row of sneakers on the floor and a handful of hoodies up high. Collared shirts and suit jackets. Baseball hats and jeans. I slip on one of his white V-neck T-shirts. The neckline plunges down my chest, and the material is just thin enough to give Kai a hint of what I'm not wearing underneath. I run my fingers through my wet hair and wrap it into a bun while I scan the shelves for bottoms. I pull on a pair of navy track pants. I have to roll them three times at the waist and feet or they fall off. Not a cute look. I open a drawer and find boxer shorts. A smile spreads across my face at the thought of Kai coming home to me wearing his underwear. It seems I have no other option.

Rex is still passed out on the couch. I sit down beside him and lift his little head onto my lap. His tail wags lethargically. I stretch my feet onto the coffee table, proud of how strong my legs look under my runner's tan. The front door opens, and my stomach flutters when I see Kai.

"You look comfortable," he says.

"I hope you don't mind," I say, knowing he doesn't mind. He shuts the door quietly behind him.

"Are you kidding? I could come home to this every night." He straddles my legs and pats the puppy on his head. His face is inches from mine. I look up at him, and we lock eyes for a moment before he kisses me. "Now, how important is it for Casper to get these scripts? Because I can get a courier over here and we can drop the puppy off later. I'll order us some dinner." Kai lifts the puppy's head off my lap and gently places it on the couch. He takes my hands and pulls me up to him, then folds me in his arms. "We can take our time."

"I'll call Casper."

I'm thinking the phone will go to voicemail when Casper answers. "Hey," he says. There's noise in the background, and it's not the television.

"Hey. Where are you?" I ask.

"Your soup did the trick. I'm out. What's up?"

"Well, Rex got a little sick in the car so I'm cleaning everything off, then I'll get him to you. He's fine. He's sleeping on the couch," I say.

"Cool. I left the key under the doormat. Don't know when I'll be home."

"If you're out for the night, I can keep Rex with me. The vet said that he shouldn't be alone. He's pretty out of it."

"Really? Thanks," Casper says.

"Want the scripts tonight or in the morning?"

"Tomorrow's cool." Kai must be able to hear Casper because a smile spreads across his face. He leaves the room as I finish the conversation. I hear the fridge open and close, followed by the rattling of cutlery in a drawer. I hang up, and Kai appears with a chilled bottle of white wine and a wicked smile on his face.

"That was very well done," he says.

"Thank you. Years of practice."

"Now, this puppy looks sick. Far too sick to move. You two should spend the night."

"I'd hate to impose," I tease, knowing full well that we both under-stood I wasn't going anywhere tonight.

Kai places the bottle of wine on the coffee table and reaches his cold hand up the back of my T-shirt—or, more accurately, his T-shirt. I arch my back at the chill and press my body against him. I tilt my head up, expecting him to kiss me. Instead, he runs his mouth down my neck. God, he smells good. It's intoxicating. I lick my lips in anticipation of a kiss. Kai gets down onto his knees and lifts my T-shirt, running his tongue along my stomach and pulling me into him. I hold on to his strong shoulders as he reaches up and cups my breast, gently nibbling the crest of my waist. Delight surges through me.

I need to taste him. I get down onto my knees and cup his face with my hands. I kiss his sweet lips, devouring him, breathing him in. His hands move to the waistband of the boxer shorts that are practically falling off me. We drape ourselves on the floor together, limbs intertwined, lips finding their rhythm together until the world falls away and we are all there is.

Casper opens the front door, and Rex pulls me with such strength that I let the leash drop from my hands. The powerful puppy runs full tilt through the house, his plastic cone scraping the floor and bouncing off the walls.

"Glad you're here," Casper says. He's wearing a bathrobe. This again? I don't want to see my boss in his bathrobe or in his bed or even in his bare feet. I just want a normal working relationship.

"He's not supposed to run because of the stitches," I say.

Casper lets me in and calls for his fiancée, Charlotte, who appears from the hallway, her silk bathrobe swaying behind her. Do these two think I'm a masseuse on a house call?

"Charity. My God, am I happy to see you!" she says. "There's so much to do!"

I follow Casper and Charlotte out to the balcony where about fifty folding chairs are stacked high and folding tables lean against the house. Crates of dishes, stemware, and linen are lined up, waiting to be assembled for what I assume is going to be a large dinner party.

The sun sits above the canyon, casting a warm glow on the forest below. "Couldn't get more perfect weather than this," Casper says.

"It's perfect," Charlotte says. "So, Charity, we need to set the tables and chairs up. I was thinking on a diagonal so that most people can enjoy the view. The caterers will be here at five thirty."

If I were an event planner or caterer, I might *ooh* and *aah* over the flower arrangements and twinkle lights piled in the corner. I would be thrilled to design the perfect party for a Hollywood director and his famous friends. But I'm not a party planner. I'm a screenwriter. A lump forms in my throat, and Charlotte's voice becomes a distant hum. I can't do this anymore.

I look at Casper. My boss. The man who believed in me so much that he brought me to Hollywood. The boss who I was invested in, who I worked hard for, and who I cared about. I am overwhelmed with disappointment. I'm disappointed in Casper, and I'm disappointed with myself for being spineless. As his fiancée goes through my to-do list, Casper looks out at the view, oblivious that I'm looking at him. "We're going for California chic with a touch of glamour," Charlotte says.

"This isn't what I do," I say. Casper and Charlotte look at me, confused. "Casper, I appreciate you bringing me down here. The move would have been a lot harder without the job. I know you're trying to keep me busy, and I appreciate the paycheck, but I don't want to see my boss in his bathrobe. This isn't what I do. This"—I motion toward the deck and the party waiting to be set up—"is what a party planner does. I don't bring you soup in bed; I don't take your dog to the vet. I'm an assistant in film, not in your domestic life."

Casper looks down at his bare feet.

"We both know it was about to end anyway, right? I'm just beating you to the punch."

"I got a TV pilot I'm moving on to. So yeah," he says.

I shake my head. Casper is predictably disappointing. "And you've probably known about that for a while. Like how you knew the investigation was over and you didn't tell me," I say.

"Charity, don't be like that."

"Be like what? When you came to Vancouver and we hung, that wasn't part of my job. That was me being nice, making a friend. I liked you. And I know that with you becoming my boss, the relationship had to change, but when I moved here, you disappeared. Then you threw me under the bus."

"Hold up."

"You didn't?" I wait for an answer that never comes. "I did what any assistant would have done in my position. I did what my boss told me to do, and you've never even said to me, 'I fucked up,' or better yet, 'I'm sorry.'"

"Hey, guys. Where are you?" Saffron calls from the front door. We all stand silent. She comes out to the back deck and plops her sunglasses on top of her head. "Here you are. Casper, I wanted you to take a look at this guy's demo reel for *Snow*. Thought we could watch it quick before the party." Saffy looks to Casper, who looks at his bare feet. Then she turns to me and Charlotte. "What's going on?" she asks.

"I'm quitting, Saffron. Doesn't that make your day? Now you can add me to your list of assistants that you have seen come and go."

"Hey!" Saffron says like I hurt her feelings.

"Don't, Saffron. Just don't." I turn to Casper and say, "This one's not doing you any favors. But you already knew that, didn't you?"

"Oh, please," Saffron moans.

"Oh, please. Let's talk about how you took every opportunity to sabotage me. You were ruthless and backhanded. You tried to ruin the reshoot, and I know you erased all my *Break Room* files. You were so horrible that at one point, I thought that you stole the DVD from me."

At this, Saffron scoffs.

"I mean, what's a more plausible scenario? I get pickpocketed by an expert whose plan was to extort millions from Canopy Studios, or you were sabotaging me? Given all the shit you put me through, it's not a crazy assumption. Isn't it amazing that after all that effort you put into ruining my career, you didn't have to do any of it? Casper did it for you."

I walk away feeling like I've finally stood up for myself. It's odd, though. I thought quitting this job would make me feel strong and liberated. I thought I'd want to go out and celebrate. Right now, I just want to sleep.

CHAPTER 28
TORN

Saul hands me a dirty dish, and I rinse it before placing it in the dishwasher. He and Elaine invited me over for dinner followed by a screening of Hitchcock's *Lifeboat*. I couldn't be happier. "Seeing as the both of you are now unemployed, I will leave the cleaning of the kitchen to you," Elaine says, pouring herself another glass of chardonnay.

"With pleasure. That meal was delicious, Elaine. Thank you," I say.

"Anytime," she and Saul say in unison.

"You two sure are good medicine for homesickness," I say.

"I hear that you may be working with that lady who directed *Penny*," Elaine says. "I love that movie."

"Yeah. Maybe. We haven't found investors yet. But we're working on it. There's this other producer who wants to buy the script, but he wants to cut a bunch of stuff and the script is taking a hit because of it."

"Why would you sell your work to someone who wouldn't make a good movie out of it?" Elaine asks.

"Money," I say simply.

"Are you an Edgar Allan Poe or an Oscar Wilde?" Elaine asks, amused.

I have to laugh. Comparing myself to artistic geniuses like Poe and Wilde is definitely out there. "I've certainly skirted the burden of full-time employment to write and I like nice things. It's not the best combination for financial success."

"You're young," says Saul. "You have plenty of time for financial success."

"But to work so hard on your art then see it all go to waste for a paycheck . . . Artists make the world beautiful. They make the music, provide the ambience, bring heart to the heartless. You can't change your art into something awful for the sake of money," Elaine says.

"This one is full of ideas. Don't listen to her," Saul says, scrubbing a pan.

"Saul, please. You agree, don't you?" Elaine says.

"My wife's latest idea is to join our twenty-eight-year-old son on a trip to South America to try ayahuasca," Saul says.

"That sounds amazing," I say.

"She could break a hip in the middle of the Amazon. Have to take a two-hour canoe ride down the river, then get in a jeep to drive God knows how long to a hospital," says Saul.

"Apparently it opens your mind. You know who could use a little mind-opening?" Elaine points to her husband.

"You only eat organic because you don't want to poison your body. Now you're going to fill it with drugs in South America," Saul says, throwing a dishtowel at her.

She catches it easily and giggles. "I am a silly old lady. But I'm true to who I am. And you should be true to who you are, Charity. And ayahuasca is organic. It's a plant in the jungle."

"You're going to be the old lady who shits her Tommy Bahama muumuu," Saul says.

"I'll be so high I won't care," Elaine says. We all have a good laugh.

Yoga. Ugh. I hate yoga. So why am I in a yoga class? Vivy Parker. Apparently my energy has never been so off. She's right. I'm exhausted.

I am unemployed, with no job prospects, and I can't stall Henry for much longer. If Daniel and Albana don't get funding for *This Family Thing* within a couple of days, I'll have to sell Henry the shitty version of my script. I'm heartbroken, so here I am pretending I can sort out my problems with yoga, but really, I'm so awful at it that it's only adding to my stress. I can't balance in tree pose or glide gracefully into warrior, and my hamstrings are so tight from running that my downward dog looks more like dog pooping.

I look at Vivy beside me, fully blissed out, doing cobra with a gentle smile on her face. Every so often, she lets out a gentle sigh, and I'm sure angels in heaven make that exact same content sound. I don't know how Vivy is so relaxed. Every person in this studio knows who she is, and they keep stealing peeks at her. Doesn't she feel it? Mind your business, people—my girl's trying to relax. We move into warrior two, and as I look over my fingertips, I notice two girls in the corner. They whisper to each other, then steal a glance in my direction. Busted. It's been a while since I've been Vivy Parker's girlfriend, but here we are again, I guess.

We flip over to downward dog, and I close my eyes in an attempt at relaxation. I push into the floor with my hands, sway my head around, and let my breath out, sinking into the stretch. The instructor tells us to roll up to a standing position. I take a deep breath, finally allowing my mind to settle. With my eyes closed, I feel every little muscle stretch as I roll myself up slowly. But then, out of the blue, I lose my balance and fall over sideways, right into Vivy. She shrieks, and we tumble over, me landing on top of her on her yoga mat. Vivy bursts into a fit of laughter. Every head turns in our direction, and I know that by tomorrow, there will be an article about Vivy Parker, her girlfriend, and their lack of yoga skills.

We're walking up the hill toward Vivy's house, where we will cut fresh lettuce and spinach out of her garden and pick a lemon from her tree so we can make salads. The midday heat feels heavier than normal, and it's draining my energy.

"You okay?" Vivy asks.

"Yeah. Just dehydrated, I think. I'm okay," I say.

"I can call my security guy to pick us up," she says.

"No, I'm good. Let's keep walking." I sip my water bottle, shaking off a dizzy spell. "Any new projects you're interested in?"

"No. Same old scripts. Same old role," Vivy says. She looks dejected. "You know, I've gotten a couple of scripts with potential. But they haven't hit me. Not like *Break Room* did."

"I'm sorry about that."

"Not your fault at all. Charity, please. You brought me an amazing script. You had my back," Vivy says. Is this my opening? Should I pitch Vivy *This Family Thing*? My mind is cloudy. What is wrong with me? I can't think straight. I'm so tired. If I'm going to pitch Vivy Parker, I need to put serious time into crafting the perfect pitch. I can't do it here, walking up a hill, me feeling depleted and her feeling dejected.

"Something will come along," I say.

I can luxuriate in a shower for ages, hot water pounding into my muscles, steam filling my lungs. I stay in there until my internal heat can carry me through the day. It's a habit born from the cold, damp Vancouver climate. Today, though, I rush. I rush because Kai is in my bed and I want to climb back onto his body before he wakes up to start his busy day as a studio executive. I want him under the covers and pressed against my damp body. I want him before his phone starts ringing, before he puts his tie on, before he can think about his new desk in Saul's old office where his responsibilities have multiplied.

I wrap a towel around myself, and goose bumps of anticipation perk my arms. Last night, after dinner, Kai said I looked tired and told me to take it easy while he washed the dishes. I brushed my teeth, washed my face, and fell asleep immediately. This morning, I'm going to make up for the wasted night. I open the bathroom door, and there he is, standing with his back to me, still wearing the white boxers he slept in. I walk toward him and let my towel drop to the floor. I wrap my arms around him and press my chest into his back. He turns to me, and we kiss deeply. Half of me wants to melt and half of me wants to push him onto the bed.

"You've been writing," he says.

"Not really," I say, a little disappointed. Because for the first time in my life, I haven't been writing. Instead of being creative when I sit in front of my computer, I tick off items from Henry's chore list with a sour taste in my mouth. I don't write, I un-write.

"What's this?" Kai says, holding up the script with Henry's changes. I sigh. Our moment is lost. We are back to the realities of life. I grab Kai's rumpled T-shirt off the bed and pull it on.

"The guy who's interested in buying *This Family Thing* wants me to make some changes," I say, plopping myself on the bed.

"I've only flipped through it, but Charity . . . all the stuff you and Albana worked on?"

"Well, he doesn't want Albana involved, so I'm working off the original."

"Right, but what about . . ." Kai sits next to me on the bed and opens the script to page seventy-one. I know what he's going to say.

"I know," I say.

"That was the best scene in the movie, and it's gone."

"I know."

"I loved that scene."

"Yeah, but the producer didn't want to spend the money on it, so."

"Then write it cheaper."

"He didn't want that. This is what he wants."

"So you're a crap writer for hire now?" I lean away from Kai. Did he just call me a crap writer? He puts his hand on my knee in an immediate attempt at apologizing. "I didn't mean it like that. What happened to Albana?"

"Nothing. We just haven't had any luck with financing. This guy is ready to pay me for it—now."

"So you're just going to sell it to some guy?" Kai looks disappointed.

"I didn't say that."

"Then why make the changes?" Kai is letting his frustration get the best of him.

"To figure things out," I say.

"How much money is this guy giving you to turn your script into this?" Kai says, holding the script in the air like it's a piece of garbage.

"Jesus, Kai. You're being mean."

"I'm being truthful. You should stick it out with Albana."

Okay. I'm trying to tell Kai my mind isn't made up yet. I'm trying to tell him I've been going back and forth in my head for days, but this Kai is a self-righteous know-it-all. He is trying to tell me what to do before I give him the full picture. Besides, I never asked for his advice.

"That isn't your decision to make," I say.

Kai doesn't let me start my next sentence. "You have an extremely talented up-and-coming director interested in working with you. That's the path to take," he says.

"Her financers don't want to make the movie."

"Then get different financers."

"We're trying. It's not happening fast enough."

"Then try harder."

"I don't have the time—"

Kai cuts me off again. "Of course you do. Don't be stupid."

"Stupid and a crap writer. Tell me what you really think, Kai."

"I think you're being rash. I don't think you're being logical."

That's it. Now I'm frustrated. Not only is Kai refusing to listen, he's also judging me. If I continue this conversation, I'm going to say something that I regret. I need a time-out, so I get off the bed and return to the solitude of my bathroom.

By the time I put my makeup on and blow-dry my hair, Kai is gone. He left without saying goodbye, without leaving a note. He just left.

CHAPTER 29
POINT BREAK

hang like a rag doll, letting the patterns on the Afghan rug, inches from my face, blur. A dull pain has been building in my back, and I've attributed it to the old wooden chair I've been using while editing *This Family Thing*. I let my head dangle loosely from my spine and feel a stretch through the back of my ribs. Albana, Daniel, and I just read through Henry's version of the script, and it was torture. Seeing their reactions to the changes makes me regret how I treated Kai this morning. The script is awful. Kai was being honest; he was being a producer, and I took offense.

"How bad is it? Your finances," Albana says, tossing the script into the garbage. "Sorry. Did you need that?"

"Nope," I say, happy to see the script land in its rightful place. "I've had some bad luck since I've been here, and my credit card is almost maxed. I could try to up my limit, but I shouldn't bury myself in more debt. It's already at the point of scary."

"Why didn't you tell me you were so broke?" she asks sympathetically.

"I thought I could make it work. I'm telling you now."

"I would float you if I could," Albana says, and I know that she's genuine.

A lot of people assume that everyone in Hollywood is rich. The actor who was in that breakout role from that little indie film that won an Oscar must be rich. The movie was so popular. The film grossed so well. Well, that's not necessarily the case. Most of the time that breakout actress in that indie film got paid a normal salary for her job because she wasn't a star *yet*. It's how movies make money in Hollywood. Pair that rising-star actress who is still cheap with a script so good it doesn't need the bells and whistles of a blockbuster rollout. If you can do that, your margins could be up there with the biggest films of the year. Albana is a rising star, but she's a director. She'll never be the ambassador for Gucci or the face of L'Oreal. She relies on her directing income alone. It took Albana two years to make her last film, and she made just enough money to cover the cost of her work/live bungalow in Venice. Albana won't be paid again until her next job, and she doesn't have anything lined up.

Daniel gets up from the couch like a man of action. "So, here's what we're thinking, Albana. We have one week to find investors or change your investors' minds," he says.

"A challenge," Albana says with a smile, and I can already tell that she's game.

"If we're not successful, Charity sells *This Family Thing* to Henry. But there's an upside to selling to Henry—not only will Charity be able to afford to stay in LA, but we can take all those beautiful scenes that Henry cut out of the script and make it into something new and exciting. What do you think?"

"Okay," she says. I can't help but wonder if her enthusiasm is a mask for her disappointment. "What about this Henry fellow?"

"We gave him the script with all the changes, and he likes it. But I told him that *This Family Thing* was just optioned in its original form. The producers have seven days to secure financing," Daniel says.

"You've been working for Henry without a contract?" Albana asks.

"I didn't want to commit to him," I say.

"And he didn't push you into signing anything?" Albana asks.

"No," I say.

"There's no guarantee he's going to buy the movie," Albana says. My heart jumps into my throat as the reality of this gamble hits me. How realistic is it for us to secure two million dollars in a week? What if we don't get funding and Henry loses interest?

"I can still work on it from Vancouver," I say, trying to be positive.

"You don't want to move back to Vancouver," Daniel says. "We can do this. Let's get to work."

We rework the lists: investors to reach out to, bankers to call, actors for all roles. We talk about getting a bigger name for a smaller role. We can use the name for financing and publicity without paying the star the leading role rate.

"What about Vivy? Can we revisit that, please?" Daniel says.

"Let me think about it," I say, my body feeling too heavy to make any decisions.

As Albana and Daniel brainstorm other actors to pitch, my mind wanders to Kai. It's almost six, and I still haven't heard from him. I'll call him later.

Pizza arrives. Daniel opens the box, and Albana's living room fills with the smell of green pepper and feta. My stomach turns. My throat tightens and saliva builds in my mouth. I feel like I might vomit. I tell them I feel sick and go home.

There is something oppressive about the California sunshine. It doesn't let you sloth. The clear blue sky and perfect temperature are like giant hands pushing you out the door, scolding you for your laziness. It reminds me of my dad when I was a kid telling me to just "get outside and enjoy yourself, goddamn it." Under my duvet, I try to ignore the sunshine and the guilt I feel for wasting it. I try to ignore the guilt I feel about Kai. I shouldn't have walked away from him when he was trying to help me. I'll call him after my nap.

I wish I had a heating pad to put on my aching back.

If I could get a Popsicle, then I would feel so much better, I think with my head in the toilet. I stumble back to bed. When I wake up, I'll have the energy to drive to the store.

My sheets are wet with sweat. My stomach feels empty, but I want to throw up again. I walk unsteadily to the bathroom, holding the wall for support. I plunge my head into the toilet bowl and dry heave. I grip the sides of the seat as my back and stomach heave without control. I lie on the cool tile. It feels good against my cheek but cold against my feet. I push myself off the ground and slide against the wall to the kitchen. I open the fridge. Nothing. No ginger ale, no juice, no iced tea, nothing. There's some eggs, moldy bread, butter, and olives. I need sugar. I need a sugary drink.

I fall into bed. I reach for my water and feel my cracked lips absorb a drop from the rim of the glass. My head hits the pillow hard.

Where's my phone? I should text Kai and ask him to bring over a Gatorade.

My arm drapes off the bed, and it feels heavy. I should move it back onto the bed. But it's so heavy. I'll move it when I wake up.

I turn on the bathroom light, and the brightness stings my eyes. I retch again. Nothing comes up. There has to be more. If I can throw up, I'll feel better. I jam my fingers down my throat. Useless. I pull them out of my mouth, fingers covered in stringy saliva. I can't be bothered to use soap. I run them under water. I'll shower when I wake up in the morning.

"Charity. Charity." I open my eyes to a pounding sound. "Charity!" It's the door. Someone is pounding on the door.

I slump out of bed and onto the floor. I can't stand up. I crawl to the door slowly. I reach up for the doorknob and try to hoist myself up, but my arms are too weak. I push myself off the floor, but my legs won't get under me. They're not working. From the ground, I turn the knob, and the door creeps open. It's Daniel. He looks shocked. I need to lay my head down, it's so heavy. Daniel bends over me, and I feel him move my head. *Leave my head alone.*

It's loud here. Frenzied voices float aimlessly around me. I open my eyes and realize the voices are not talking to me. They're on the other side of the yellow curtains that surround me. There's a weight on my lap, and I look down to see a man's hand in mine. I'm now aware of the cool sensation floating up my arm. What an odd feeling. I turn my head slowly and see Daniel sitting in a chair beside me, staring at our intertwined fingers.

"Hi," I say with a groggy voice.

"Charity," he says.

"I'm fine."

"You're not fine," he says, dropping my hand and turning to me. What did he say? I'm not fine? I sit up slowly, with greater effort than anticipated, but I manage to sit.

"I'm not fine?" I say in a panic.

"Oh, you will be fine. You will be fine. You have a fucking kidney infection that almost went septic."

"Oh."

"They gave you something for the pain, and you have antibiotics in this bag thing." He points to the IV that I'm attached to.

"Oh, good." I lean my head back with relief. I'm exhausted. "I'm thirsty," I say.

Daniel rushes through the yellow curtains and returns with a nurse carrying a cup. As I suck on ice chips, the nurse delivers information that I can't absorb. I look at Daniel and know that he's taking mental notes. I lay my head on my pillow and let my eyes close.

Daniel paces the small space at the foot of my hospital bed. "How can you let yourself get this sick?" he says.

"I thought I had the flu or something," I say.

"When you left Albana's, you didn't look good, so I called the next day and you didn't answer. You never called back. I assumed you were hanging out with Kai. But it's not like you to not call back. So, I called the next day, and nothing again. It's really not like you to disappear. I mean, the amount of times in Vancouver when I was, you know, getting along with a lady and I wished that you would disappear, you never would. So you disappearing for a couple days, it's not like you. Because, you know, you can be a little annoying. And I didn't like the feeling it gave me. I don't like not knowing where you are. It's fucked up because you are so not sexually attractive, but I didn't like not knowing where you were. So I came to your apartment this morning, and Charity, you could barely move." I close my eyes, trying to put a timeline together.

"To you," I say.

"What?"

"I'm not sexually attractive to you," I say.

"Trickett, you should see yourself. You're not sexually attractive to anyone right now."

"Wait. Albana's was three days ago?"

"Yeah." Daniel turns his back to me and buries his head in his hands. His shoulders shudder in a sob.

"Daniel. It's okay," I say.

"It's so fucking sad. You could have died. You're like a lonely cat lady. But worse because you don't even have cats."

I can't help but laugh.

"It's serious. I need to check in on you more. What if you fucking died?"

"Daniel, you saved my life." It must be the pain meds; Daniel managed to call me an annoying, lonely, un-sexy cat lady while labeling himself a hero, yet I've never loved him more. "You saved my life, and now it's up to you and you alone to keep me alive. Are you up for it?"

"Is it bad that I was thinking about how good the press would be for *This Family Thing* if you did die? Work in perpetuity sells."

"That's awful." I laugh, and Daniel plops himself on the side of my bed. I move over so he can lie down next to me. "You're happy I'm alive," I say as Daniel places his head next to mine.

"Oh my God, you stink."

"Shut up."

"No, seriously. Your breath, your body—ugh, your hair. I can't lie here. You really stink." I laugh as he buries his face in his shirt to get my smell out of his nose.

That evening, I'm discharged. I have a list of instructions from the doctor and a prescription for antibiotics. I wanted to wear my gown home, but Daniel said that was way too *One Flew Over the Cuckoo's Nest* for him, so I'm back in the clothes that I assume I have been wearing for the last three days. Daniel rolls my wheelchair up to the discharge desk. I give the nurse all my personal information: address, date of birth, the whole drill.

Then she hands me an envelope. "What's this?" I ask.

"Your bill. You don't have insurance, right?"

"No, I don't." Daniel squeezes my shoulder. I open the envelope: $6,749.19. There's a lump in my throat. This has to be a mistake. This can't be. "I wonder if there's been a mistake," I ask the discharge nurse. She looks unimpressed but takes the bill from me nonetheless. She flips to the second page.

"Here's the itemized list. Two bags of fluid, the medication, the doctor's consult, the hourly rate for an ER bed. Yes, this looks right."

"Come on, Charity," Daniel whispers into my ear. As he guides me toward the exit, I repeat that figure in my mind: $6,749.19. I'm done.

We cruise steadily on the number ten highway. I turned Daniel's music off—it was far too happy for my current mood. My head rests against the window. It feels heavy and my chest is tight. Tears blur my vision. I blink and feel a wet line trace my cheek. Daniel reaches over the center console and holds my hand. I let more tears fall. This is the end for me. This is where I pack my little car with everything I own and move back to Vancouver. This is failure.

"Okay. Should I call Henry and give him the script, or . . ." Daniel says.

"There's no time for *or* anymore. There was barely time for *or* before I went into the hospital. I was kidding myself."

Daniel presses a button on his cell phone, and I can hear it ring through the speaker. Oh, Henry. Henry, the giver of terrible notes. Henry, the misogynist. Henry, the least imaginative person to ever work in a creative industry. Henry, the one person who can get me out of this mess.

"Yeah. Hello," I hear him say. I cross my arms over my body, holding myself.

"Henry. Daniel here," Daniel says into the phone.

"Daniel, what can I do for you?"

"Well, the other party has passed because of financials. The script is all yours." Relief fills me. Sweet Daniel. In an hour, Daniel can have me out of this mess. In an hour, I can sign a contract with Henry and have a check for forty thousand dollars in my hand. In an hour, I can fall asleep in my bed without worry. In an hour, I will have peace of mind.

"I've moved on," Henry says.

"I'm sorry?" Daniel says calmly.

"Yeah. Couldn't wait. You know, I got the crew all booked, so I bought another script."

"I understand. Sorry to give you the runaround, Henry. If you want to tie it up for a future project, we would consider optioning it," Daniel says. Good thinking, Daniel. I'll take whatever money I can get. I can't leave LA like this. I can't go home a failure.

"No thanks," Henry says.

"Alright, Henry. The rewrites—we're going to shop the script around, and if any of the rewrites you suggested to Charity should end up in somebody else's finished product . . ."

"Yeah, yeah, yeah. Look, Daniel, if I want the script in the future, I'll let you know. Until then, do what you want with it. No skin off my nose."

"Okay, Henry. Thanks. I'll be in touch if I find anything else for you," Daniel says.

I close my eyes, knowing that as soon as I'm on my feet, I'll pack up my apartment and move back to Vancouver.

CHAPTER 30
IT AIN'T OVER
'TIL IT'S OVER

A large arm reaches around me to lift the mattress that's protruding from the back seat of my Volkswagen. "Thanks, Ben," Vivy says to her security guard. "Can you please put it in the basement?"

"Let me help you?" I say.

Vivy places her hand on my shoulder. "You'll only be in his way," she says.

"Thanks for letting me store this with you," I say.

"I've got the room. So how long are you going home for?"

"Just until I get on my feet. I'm pretty wiped from this infection, and I need to save some money," I say.

Vivy looks at her feet and kicks the dust on her driveway. "I didn't know you were having money trouble. Why didn't you tell me?"

"Vivy. There's a lot I didn't tell you."

"Why? Don't you trust me?" she says.

I look at the delicate young actress in front of me, her eyes full of sympathy, but there's something tentative about her body language. She makes patterns in the dirt with her feet, averting her eyes, and I get it. When you have money and fame, a lot of people ask for a lot of favors. So I'll be vague, not wanting to put any pressure on Vivy, but I also know that not sharing my life with her has put a wedge in our friendship.

"This Hollywood thing has been a ride." I tell Vivy about how I lost a copy of *Diffuser*. I tell her about the FBI investigation and all the horrible names Bellotti yelled at me. I tell her about my transmission dying and the government freezing my bank account. I even tell her about Casper's dog puking in my car. I tell her that nobody at Canopy, not even Casper, thought to tell me that the investigation was over. I tell her that all is not lost. That Daniel and I have been working together to produce one of my scripts.

"We have this great director interested in it," I say. "Just a little snag with the funding. Once that's all settled, I'll be back."

"Who's the director?" Vivy asks.

"Albana Rugova," I say.

"Oh my God. *Penny*! I love that movie."

"Me too!"

"Charity Trickett. You cannot leave LA. Albana Rugova wants to make your movie."

"I can work remotely. Besides, money's more Daniel's thing than mine."

"You can stay with me until you're on your feet."

"That's really kind, Viv, but no. I wouldn't feel right about it. I literally have no money. I can raid my parents' fridge, but it would feel weird to be completely dependent on a friend," I say.

Vivy sighs with exasperation. "Well, at least let me read your script."

"I'd love you to. Any notes you have would be amazing." I reach into the back seat of my car to fish out a script and feel optimistic for the first time in days. "There's this one part near the end that I'm still playing with. Well, you'll see." Vivy takes the script from me and my emotions take me by surprise. "Thank you," I say, holding back the impulse to cry.

"Of course. I'm kind of insulted you wouldn't have wanted my notes sooner. I am a movie star, you know." Although Vivy means to be lighthearted, we both know that there's some truth behind her words.

"Vivy, I was in so much trouble, and I thought—part of me still thinks—Bellotti is going to ruin my career. Daniel says I'm being crazy, but I worry that we keep getting turned down by investors because of me. And if you came on board, I'd be obligated to tell you everything, and I didn't want you to know that I'm a gigantic fuck-up. I'm embarrassed. But now that I'm leaving, it feels like the right thing to do." I can't hold back the tears any longer, and I let them fall.

"Charity, you're my girl. I already know that you're a gigantic fuck-up."

I guffaw with such force that I need to cover my nose for fear that snot may fly out.

Vivy smiles at me with tenderness and opens her arms, folding me into her. "What does Kai say about all of this?" she asks.

"We had a fight," I say. "Then I got sick and went into the hospital. He called me five times, but I was out of it for days. I had no idea. I called him back a couple of times, but he's not picking up."

Vivy holds me at arm's length, studying me. "Wait. Kai doesn't know that you're leaving?"

"No."

"What did he say in his messages?" Vivy asks.

"He didn't leave one. I just saw the missed calls."

"What did you say in your message to him?"

"I didn't leave one. I thought he would see that I called and would call me back."

"You see! The throat chakra! The ability to communicate!" Vivy slaps me. "You are the worst. After your first fight, he called you five times and then he had to wait for days before you called him back. He's mad because he doesn't know the whole story. You need to call him and tell him what happened. Leave a message, you idiot." She stands there, looking at me expectantly.

"Now?" I ask.

"Yes, now!"

I pull my phone out of my back pocket and dial Kai. I take a few steps away from Vivy for privacy, and she turns around to look at her ocean view instead of at me. Predictably, Kai's phone goes to voicemail. The sound of his voice forces more tears, and I swallow back my sadness so I can talk. "Hi. It's me. I'm sorry about the fight. I know that you were looking out for me. I'm also sorry I didn't call you back. It wasn't intentional. I got sick that night. Really sick. I was out of it for days and didn't know that you were calling. Not to sound dramatic or anything, but Daniel found me and took me to the hospital. I'm fine now. I have a kidney infection. I'm on antibiotics. But the hospital bill broke the bank, and I have to move back to Vancouver. I'm pretty much packed up. I'm leaving today, actually. I'll be back, though. I'd really like to see you or at least talk to you. So . . ."

There's so much I want to say. I want to say *I love you*. I want to say that my heart is broken. I want to ask him to come back to me. I want to tell him I'm worried that I ruined us forever.

"So, look. If I don't see you, thank you. Kai, you are a thoughtful and wonderful man. I—I—you're in my heart."

Across the street is Grauman's Chinese Theatre. The Hollywoodized temple is dwarfed by Blake's image floating high above it on the largest billboard that Hollywood Boulevard has to offer. Men place giant searchlights under the tall red columns that flank the theater entrance. It's the perfect venue for the *Diffuser* premiere, iconic enough for the biggest star in Hollywood and steeped in history for Saul's farewell picture. I lean against my little car, which is packed to the gills with all my belongings, and watch the red carpet being rolled out. I can't help but sigh in disappointment. This isn't how I envisioned my Hollywood ending.

"Tell me why you aren't coming to this thing again?"

I jump, startled to find Kai a foot away from me. "What are you doing here?" I say. The look on his face tells me he has something weighing on him, like I do.

"They're giving a presentation and gift to Saul at the premiere tonight. I'm making sure everything's in order."

"That's nice," I say.

"I didn't listen to your voicemail from this morning. I ignored it. Well, I tried to ignore it. I've been thinking about it all day. I didn't want to listen to it. I didn't want to erase it. Then I'm walking down the street, doing my job, and here you are, so while you were looking at this, I was looking at you, listening to your message." Kai takes my hand, and it's as though a hundred butterflies come alive inside me. "I'm sorry. When you didn't return my calls, I thought you were one of those girls who likes to play head games, you know?"

"I would never," I say.

"I know. I know. But I kept calling and you didn't answer, and I thought back to all the times you said no and I kept persisting, and I thought, oh, she's a game player. I read her all wrong." He looks broken. He looks ashamed.

"Kai." I move closer to him.

"You're packed up," he says, looking in my car.

"Yeah." I shrug my shoulders pathetically. "I'm going to move back in with my parents." I look across the street to Grauman's Theatre, the *Diffuser* premiere, and the life that isn't meant for me. "I was just saying goodbye to Canopy and was going to hit the road," I say.

"Move in with me," Kai says.

"Kai. I can't even afford to feed myself. I barely have enough money for gas to make it home."

"I don't care that you don't have any money."

"I do. I don't want to have to depend on a man. In a few years, after I make a small fortune, fine. I'll put my feet up and let you do all the work." Kai wraps his arms around me, and I inhale him. "But I need to bring something to the table."

"You bring plenty to the table," Kai says, moving his hand lower until it rests inside the back pocket of my jeans.

"I'll be back. Just need to get myself sorted."

"Stay the night with me, then," Kai says. "Come on. Come to the premiere. We'll make a short appearance. You can congratulate Saul. One last night together before you leave. Not that this is goodbye. I've always wanted to check out Vancouver."

"I can't go to the premiere. Bellotti, Casper, Saffron . . . I mean, it's a room full of people who hate me."

"Charity, it's a huge party with hundreds of people. You can avoid whoever you want to avoid. I'll help you," Kai says. The thought of being at a Canopy Studios event is scary. At the same time, the thought of not celebrating something I worked really hard on is tough to swallow. This movie has been a big part of my life for the last year. *Diffuser* is important to me.

Kai turns me around to face Grauman's Theatre. Security guards are walking through the thin crowd that has started to gather. "Have you ever walked a red carpet?" he asks. Kai pulls my hand, and we jog across the street. At the curb, we stop and look up at the Chinese Theatre towering in front of us, the shrine of Hollywood. "You have to imagine. Your limousine pulls up here, and through the tinted windows, you see lights flashing and a haze of people. The car door opens for you, and a hand appears to help you out of the car." He offers his hand to me as though helping me to step out of a limousine. "Right here. Right here is where they place the most exuberant fans and some paparazzi, so get out like a lady. I know how you like to wow the paparazzi, Trickett, but we don't need any panty shots."

I slap him lightly on the chest.

"As soon as you step out of the car, you wave and sign autographs. You're smiling, signing, signing, and smiling. Wave to the crowd." Kai reaches to unclip the velvet rope barricading the red carpet. When a security guard approaches, Kai explains who he is, giving us carte blanche to do whatever we want. Once we're alone again, he presents his hand to me in an elegant gesture. "Now, the red carpet," he says.

I look down, watching my white Converse hover over the ruby red below me. My first red carpet. I look up at Kai.

He flashes me a brilliant smile, and I step onto the runway with him. He says, "Once you're on the red carpet, there's more fans. You have to remember that these are the real fans, the ones who line up for hours hoping to meet you. You ask them their names and take pictures with them. The press is down there a bit. See?" He points to a set of bleachers roped off for photographers. "From there, they get good shots of the celebs on the red carpet with the fans, the kind *Vanity Fair* eats up." He wraps my arm through his, and we move along the red carpet like those Hollywood couples on a date. "Wave, wave, wave. Pose. I'll say something into your ear, something nobody else can hear. It will, of course, be filthy—dirty—and you'll give me one of your sexy looks that says you can't wait to strip out of your clothes and climb on top of me. The look will be captured by the paparazzi, and our image will be plastered all over *Us Weekly* tomorrow morning. You know what that's like."

After a pause, he continues. "We see an actor friend. We shake his hand or give her a kiss." We stop in front of the photographers' bleachers. There's a peppering of *Diffuser* and the Canopy Studios leopard logo behind us on a banner that runs along the red carpet for about thirty feet. "Flash, flash, flash," Kai says. "So many lights. It's blinding, but you smile like it's nothing. What's that?" Kai cups his ear, acting like he can't hear something an imaginary photographer said. "You want one of Charity alone?" He smiles graciously and moves aside, leaving me to stand awkwardly on the red carpet. "You would pose some more, say thank you to the press." He joins me again, escorting me closer to the theater. "Here is where the interviews take place. *Entertainment Tonight, Extra, E! News.* Questions are asked and answered. Thank the interviewer, wave to the fans one more time, and that's the red carpet."

Kai pulls me into him. His hand cups the back of my head and his fingers thread through my hair. He kisses me. He kisses me, and I thank God that he's holding me tight, because in this moment of sheer bliss, I may just melt.

"Charity, I love you," he whispers into my ear. I look into Kai's eyes, certain I'll spend the night with him. I'm certain that he will be mine when I'm in Vancouver, and I'm certain I will be his when I come back to LA. This is not the end of us.

Julie is so intensely close that I can smell the gin and tonic on her breath. She's wound up, and I'm grateful that she's at least stage-whispering. "Another fucking classic example of how women are treated in this industry. Casper. Fucking Canopy. Boys' club. When Steve told me about the—" She looks around to make sure nobody can overhear, and my eyes follow hers. The *Diffuser* premiere party is filled with beautiful people, low lights, and loud music. Everyone is on a high after watching what will surely be this year's biggest blockbuster. Julie turns back to me and mouths *FBI*. She says, "I was speechless."

Steve approaches us and casually slides an arm around his wife's waist. "You ladies having fun?" he asks, taking a sip of his red wine.

"That cheap shit's going to give you a headache," Julie warns.

"No, it won't. It's that Barolo you like. I stashed a couple bottles behind the bar."

"Oooooo. Smart hubby. We're just talking about Charity and the—" Again, she mouths the word *FBI*.

Steve takes a big breath. "You made it through, Charity. You know, this is Hollywood, where the line between fucking up and being fucked over is thin." He says this matter-of-factly. Julie solemnly nods in agreement. "And look," Steve says. "You're still standing. Cheers." He holds up his Barolo, and we clink glasses.

Conversations flow in and out as they do at parties, moving from one person or group to another with sloppy transitions. Daniel and I stand side by side watching Kai, who is having an animated conversation. Daniel pinches me right above my elbow and bends down to whisper in my ear. "Kai is fiiiiine," he says, spreading out the last word in admiration. "I mean, Charity." He fans himself with his hand, and I nudge him to stop.

But looking at Kai, I want to fan myself, too. He runs his hand through his hair, and I can't help but blush because that hand was up my skirt about an hour ago. He pulled me into a dark corner of the party, pressed me against a wall, and kissed me so tenderly that I teetered on my stilettos. When I felt his hand move up my leg and pass the hem of my miniskirt, I reluctantly pushed him away.

When I feel an arm drape over my shoulder, I instantly know it's Blake. "What are we looking at?" he says.

"Charity's boyfriend," Daniel says.

"Charity has a new boyfriend? Which one is he?" Blake asks.

"It's the stud over there," Daniel says, pointing his vodka soda in Kai's direction. "He's talking with—who's Kai talking with? Is that . . . ?"

I look closer at the woman who has her back to us: waif-thin; long, thick hair; mannerisms almost ballerina-like.

"Is that my friend Vivy Parker?" I say, suddenly filled with love.

"Sure looks like it," Daniel says.

We walk toward my new love and my new friend, who are chatting easily with each other, and I am overwhelmingly happy.

"What are you doing here?" I say to Vivy.

"You know what's crazy? I'm Vivy Parker. I can show up at literally any party, and people just let me in."

"Me, too," says Blake, overjoyed by this connection.

"Blake Anthony. I have asked Daniel to introduce us, like, five times. Thanks a lot, Daniel," Vivy says.

"Don't mention it, doll," Daniel says. I am finding this interaction very enjoyable. Daniel, on the other hand, isn't. I thread my arm through his in solidarity.

"Vivy. It's a pleasure," Blake says. For an awkward moment, I think he's going to kiss Vivy's hand, but he restrains himself and instead shakes it delicately.

"First person I see when I get here: Casper. He comes up to me, and I'm like, no, I'm not talking to you," Vivy says.

"Why?" Blake asks.

"You have a lot of catching up to do," I say to Blake. "I'll tell you later."

"Then I see Daniel, who introduces me to Kai." Vivy puts her hand on Kai's forearm and says to him, "I was more excited to meet you tonight than Blake Anthony."

Blake takes a step back and grabs his chest dramatically. "Oh, that hurts!" he says.

"Burn!" Daniel laughs.

Then Vivy turns to me with a pissed-off look on her face. "So what the hell, Charity? Why would you hold out on me?"

"W-W-What do you mean?" I stammer.

"The role of the daughter . . . it's kind of perfect for me. Don't you think?" Vivy says. I'm stunned.

"Charity's script!" Blake says, happy that he's finally keeping up with the conversation.

"As soon as I finished reading the script, I called Daniel," Vivy continues. "Charity, I'd love the role if you guys would also consider taking me on as an executive producer."

"I already said yes," Daniel jumps in. "I was like, sure! You'll be the third executive producer with no executive-producing experience. It's perfect!" Daniel says.

"Aren't you sneaky, Vivy Parker," I say.

"I have to be. Your throat chakra isn't working," Vivy says sternly.

"So I guess this means that we'll get funding," I say.

"Oh, we'll get funding," Daniel says.

"Now that Vivy's involved," Blake says, "I'll guarantee a line of credit."

"I suppose you want a producing credit, too," Daniel says, rolling his eyes at Blake.

"No way. Producing looks like a headache," Blake says.

"Are you serious, Blake? Because I will personally escort you to the bank tomorrow to get this shit done," Daniel says.

"Let's do it," Blake says.

"Does this mean I'll get paid?" I say, not believing my luck.

"All we need to do is get contracts signed and secure the line of credit. After that, finding an investor to make up the rest of the budget should be pretty easy. You could be paid and out of debt in less than a month," Daniel says.

I'm thrilled. I look to Kai, Vivy, Daniel, and Blake—my support, my LA family—and I'm washed over with delight. This isn't the end. I'll go home, wait for my money, and then come back to LA to start work on producing my first feature film.

"I'll be back in a month!" I say.

"Wait a second," Daniel says. "You can't leave town. You need to be in the pitch meetings for new investors. You need to sell yourself. Plus, we need to cast the other roles. You may need to do some rewrites."

Vivy jumps excitedly in place, clapping her hands like a little girl. "We can be roomies!" she exclaims.

"Hold on," Kai says. "If she's moving in with anyone, it's me."

"Kai, we can't move in together," I say.

"It's only for a month," he says.

"Nobody moves in with their boyfriend and then moves out unless the relationship is over," I say. "I love you, but I'm not rushing us. I'm not messing this up."

"I win!" Vivy says with a smile.

"What the fuck, assholes!" When I turn around, there's Jack with Elaine's arm wrapped through his and Saul by his side. I honestly didn't think the night could get any better, but then this happens.

"Did you sneak in here?" I throw my arms around him.

"Almost," Elaine says. "I was keeping an eye out for him."

"I brought him in with me," Saul says, impressed with himself.

I don't think I've ever felt so light, and I think that it's from relief. We drink, we laugh, and we make ourselves full with fun. We dance. Everyone is on the floor. The actors, the camera crew, Steve and Julie, Blake, the publicist who was puking on set in Vancouver, Daniel, Vivy, and Kai. My Kai. And about a hundred people I don't recognize. I spin myself around in a freeing twirl. When I stop I see Casper and Saffron hunched together.

Vivy sees them, too. "We should go say hi. Tell them we're doing a movie together," she says.

"What's the point?" I say. The thought of standing in front of Saffron and Casper to say *look at me* feels wrong. Soon the damage they've done will fade away and I'll be walking tall. I move again to the music, and Vivy moves with me. Kai appears and drops a glass of water in my hand.

"Time for your antibiotics. And no more bubbles," he says, kissing my cheek. He's been doting on me all night, and I hope this continues for my entire lifetime.

I dig in my clutch for my pills. I pop one into my mouth and take a sip of water to wash it down. Then I find myself pointed straight at Bellotti. He stands on the periphery of the dance floor. We lock eyes. I freeze. *Bitch, slut, cunt* fills my head. Bellotti holds my gaze with his cold expression, and a chill hits me with such strength that I'm breathless.

Then sweet Vivy grabs my hand, oblivious to the fact that I was just pulled back to the worst moment of my career. She sings along with the song's refrain, swaying to the music. Kai and Daniel are just behind her, heads bent toward each other in conversation. In their faces, I see everything that I should celebrate. The future.

I turn back to Bellotti, his slick red hair shining in the party lights, and feel the weight of him and everything he represents lift from me. I dance, leading Vivy deeper into the crowd, not to escape Bellotti and Canopy Studios but to leave all of that behind.

THE 411 ON THE CHAPTER TITLES

Each chapter title is a pop culture reference from the '90s. Do you recognize them?

Chapter 1 — Clueless (1995)
When someone calls *Clueless* a classic film, they are one of my people.

Chapter 2 — My So-Called Life (1994)
Claire Danes and Jared Leto give us the ultimate view of teen life in 1994.

Chapter 3 — Pump Up the Volume (1990)
When Christian Slater was *everything*. I had the soundtrack on cassette tape, and I wore it out.

Chapter 4 — Welcome to the Jungle (1987—but timeless)
I hung a Guns N' Roses poster on the ceiling over my bed, and I named my dog Axl. LA may just bring Charity to her *Shan-n-n-n-n-n-n knees.*

Chapter 5 — Meet-Cute
A meet-cute, in film terms, is when boy meets girl in a cute, romantic way.

Chapter 6 — Girl Interrupted (1999)
Angelina before Brad and so rad.

Chapter 7 — Reality Bites (1994)
When smoking was cool, Winona Ryder and Johnny Depp were together, and not washing your hair was a look.

Chapter 8 — Fight Club (1999)
"The first rule of Fight Club is you do not talk about Fight Club."

Chapter 9 — Impulsive (1990)
Wilson Phillips.

> *I don't wanna think about it, don't wanna think clear,*
> *Don't analyze what I'm doing here.*
> *Wanna be impulsive, reckless, and lose myself in your kiss.*

Chapter 10 — She's All That (1999)
Come on! We are all jealous when we watch those movies where the people at a high school dance or nightclub, spontaneously bust into a perfectly choreographed routine. That's why people line dance, in search of that moment.

Chapter 11 — O.P.P. (1991)
Naughty By Nature song: Other People's . . .

Chapter 12 — Cruel Intentions (1999)
A movie about manipulation, power, control, revenge, deceit, and the importance of appearances.

Chapter 13 — Poetic Justice (1993)
Janet Jackson and Tupac Shakur.

Chapter 14 — Bravo
There's nothing to hide and nothing to be ashamed of. We all watch Bravo TV. And those who say they don't are lying. Trust me.

Chapter 15 — True Romance (1993)
A story about a girl and a boy who love each other, but people seem to get in their way.

Chapter 16 — Just a Girl (1995)
There is No Doubt that I wanted to *be* Gwen Stefani.

Chapter 17 — Still Not a Player (1998)
Big Pun makes me laugh so hard. His lyric *I'm not a player, I just fuck a lot* brings a smile to my face.

> *Ayo, I'm still not a player, but you still a hater*
> *Elevator to the top, hah, see you later*
> *I'm gone, penthouse suite, Penthouse freaks*
> *In-house beach, a, 10 thou' piece*

Chapter 18 — I Left My Wallet in El Segundo (1990)
A Tribe Called Quest. Like Charity, I really did lose a copy of a blockbuster film at a test screening in El Segundo.

Chapter 19 — Scream (1996)
This chapter is Charity's horror movie. Plus, I'm a fan of anything Drew Barrymore.

Chapter 20 — "Your spy car is a Mini?" (1999)
Quote: *Austin Powers: The Spy Who Shagged Me.*

Chapter 21 — Misery (1990)
Coincidence that *Misery* is an MGM film?

Chapter 22 — Golden Girls (1985–1992)

> *Thank you for being a friend*
> *Traveled down the road and back again*
> *Your heart is true, you're a pal and a confidant*

Chapter 23 — All I Really Want (1995)
Alanis Morissette.

> *All I really want is some peace man*
> *A place to find some common ground*
> *And all I really want is a wavelength, ah*
> *And all I really want is some comfort*
> *A way to get my hands untied*
> *And all I really want is some justice, ah*

Chapter 24 — Finally (1992)
"Finally" by CeCe Peniston. This song cheers for love!

> *Finally, it's happened to me, right in front of my face*
> *And I just cannot hide it.*
> *Meeting Mr. Right, the man of my dreams*
> *The one who shows me true love*

Chapter 25 — Don't Let the Sun Go Down on Me (1992)

George Michael and Elton John's version. If you don't have an emotional reaction while listening to this song, you may be dead.

Don't let the sun go down on me
Although I search myself, it's always someone else I see
I'd just allow a fragment of your life to wander free, yeah
But losing everything is like the sun going down on me

Chapter 26 — Goodfella (Goodfellas) (1990)

If you took Joe Pesci from *My Cousin Vinny* and Joe Pesci from *Goodfellas* and mixed in a hippie with a chip on his shoulder, you would make a torturous character I used to work with.

Chapter 27 — "There's my flair!" (1999)

The most enjoyable quitting scene in a movie ever: *Office Space*.

Chapter 28 — Torn (1997)

The best Australian export, other than Tim Tams, is Natalie Imbruglia. Her song "Torn" sums up Charity's emotions.

I'm all out of faith
This is how I feel, I'm cold and I am shamed
Lying naked on the floor
Illusion never changed
Into something real
I'm wide awake and I can see the perfect sky is torn
You're a little late
I'm already torn

Chapter 29 — Point Break (1991)

"Little hand says it's time to rock and roll." —Bodhi

Chapter 30 — It Ain't Over 'til It's Over (1991)

A Lenny Kravitz song about love, but don't get the message twisted. Charity loves Hollywood just as much as she loves Kai.

So many tears I've cried
So much pain inside
But baby, it ain't over 'til it's over

ACKNOWLEDGMENTS

Thank you to all the bosses, the producers, directors, crew members, actors, other assistants, and executives who educated me in an art form and an industry that I have always loved. Thanks to the Ludwigs, who helped me get my first gig. Thanks to my pal Val who, after reading the first one hundred pages of this book, urged me to keep writing. Thank you, Richard Curtis, who signed me as a client during the uncertainty of early 2020 when nobody knew what the pandemic's impact would be on the book industry. You were gracious with your time and thoughtful with your notes. Thanks to my early readers, a group of women who are truly the best: ZouZou; Sara; Kristi, the original Pup; Stephanie; Kathleen; Natascha; and Denise—your notes were just as solid as your friendships. Love yous! Thank you to Kendra Harpster at Kevin Anderson and Associates. You are a fantastic editor who helped me tell Charity's story in a more powerful and dynamic way. Thank you to SparkPress for your guidance and expertise. Thank you to Crystal Patriarche, Hanna, and Taylor at SparkPoint for taking me on and getting Charity Trickett out there. Big thanks to my Canadian PR team, ZG Stories. You ladies are an absolute pleasure. Thanks to my parents who took me back into their home when I returned from LA broken and depressed. Thanks to my little wonders, Lola and Farrah. You fill me with so much joy; I feel like my heart is made of sunshine. And the biggest, sexiest thank-you goes to my husband, Sam. Your support never wanes, your strength—unyielding. I love you endlessly.

ABOUT THE AUTHOR

photo credit: Sarah Jane Photography

Christine Stringer is a former MGM assistant who was investigated by the FBI for piracy of a film starring The Rock. So yeah, she does find herself in little snafus from time to time. She has a BFA from the University of Victoria where she studied theatre and English. As a screenwriter and novelist, she strives to brighten people's days, writing stories based on her film career, love life, and general mishaps. She lives in beautiful Vancouver, BC, with her husband and two young children who bring her joy every day, even though they have banned her from singing in the car.

Copyright Credits

Looking for your next great read?

We can help!

Visit www.gosparkpress.com/next-read
or scan the QR code below for a list
of our recommended titles.

SparkPress is an independent boutique publisher
delivering high-quality, entertaining, and engaging
content that enhances readers' lives, with a special
focus on commercial and genre fiction.